Wives v. Girlfriends

KATIE AGNEW

First published in Great Britain in 2009 by Orion Books,
an imprint of The Orion Publishing Group Ltd
Orion House, 5 Upper Saint Martin's Lane
London WC2H 9EA

An Hachette UK Company

1 3 5 7 9 10 8 6 4 2

Copyright © Katie Agnew 2009

A CIP catalogue record for this book is
available from the British Library.

ISBN (Hardback) 978 0 7528 9866 7
ISBN (Trade Paperback) 978 0 7528 9867 4

Typeset by Deltatype Ltd, Birkenhead, Merseyside

Printed and bound in the UK by CPI Mackays, Chatham ME5 8TD

The Orion Publishing Group's policy is to use papers that are natural,
renewable and recyclable products and made from wood grown in
sustainable forests. The logging and manufacturing processes are expected
to conform to the environmental regulations of the country of origin.

www.orionbooks.co.uk

For my girlfriends

OK, so I get the glory, but it takes a lot of people to write a book. I'd like to thank my amazing agent, Lizzy Kremer at David Higham Associates, for her unflinching support, advice and friendship over the years. Thanks to the lovely Genevieve Pegg, and all the staff at Orion, for believing in me and for doing such a fabulous job. Thanks to my family, especially John and the kids, for being so patient and understanding when I disappeared behind the computer for weeks on end. And thanks to Bronwyn and Steve Obourne for the use of their idyllic Cornish cottage when I needed a writer's retreat. And finally, thanks to all my friends for their input, advice, inspiration and willingness to share a bottle of bubbly (or five) when I finally finished the damn thing! This one's for you, 'girlfriends'. You know who you are ...

Chapter One

The girl hugs her bare knees to her chest, her back against the wall, and buries her tear-stained face into her bruised and bleeding flesh. She shivers in her thin summer dress. The room is almost pitch black but earlier, as her eyes had become accustomed to the darkness, she'd made out the shapes of vicious-looking metal implements – knives, axes, some kind of sharp-toothed trap – lurking in the corners. And then she'd sensed the hulking form of the man, bearing down on her, the whites of his eyes flashing in the darkness, his hot, rancid breath smelling of whiskey and tobacco.

She has no idea where she is. He blindfolded her as soon as he bundled her into the car. But she knows the building is cold – much colder than the summer day she left outside – and she came down some steep stairs, tripping as he pushed her, banging her head on what must have been a stone wall. The walls were rough and damp. Her captor's hands were rough too. Like sandpaper on her smooth skin.

She's alone now. Her captor has left her but she knows he'll be back. He promised he'd be back. When he slammed the heavy metal door behind him she'd heard the clunk, clunk of a lock, and then another lock. There are no windows in the room, just a tiny chink of light around the frame of the door.

She pulls herself into the smallest, tightest ball she can manage and rocks backwards and forwards, sobbing with what little energy she has left. 'I want Charlie,' she finds herself crying. 'Where are you, Charlie? Help me!'

Chapter Two

'You need to be in Marbella in thirty minutes.'

'What?' Grace Melrose mumbled into her phone, scrambling off her sun lounger and dropping her sunglasses and her iPod as she groped around for her watch.

Ouch. The sunlight hurt her eyes as she tried to focus. It was eleven thirty a.m. in Andalusia and Grace had enjoyed exactly one hour of her holiday – her first proper, non-working holiday in three years.

'I said be in Marbella by midday,' barked the voice. 'You sound half-asleep, woman.'

Christ! She had been asleep. She'd left her mews in Highgate at five o'clock this morning to catch her flight from Gatwick and she'd been at work until midnight last night. She'd only been at this pretty farmhouse in the mountains long enough to dump her suitcase, rummage for her bikini and collapse on a sun lounger by the pool, where she'd promptly fallen asleep. And now bloody Miles was on the phone. Already. She'd half-expected a call from her boss at some point during the week, but not yet. This was ridiculous. Grace sat back down and took a deep breath.

'Right, Miles. What exactly is it you need me to do?' Of course, whatever it was she would do it. There was no point in arguing. Arguing with Miles Blackwood was just a waste of breath.

Miles sounded mildly exasperated. 'I repeat, you need to be in Marbella ASAP. Some tasteless mansion in Puerto Banus I imagine. I'll email the address and your brief.'

There was no please. No thank you. There never was. Miles had the social skills of a five-year-old with ADHD. It didn't seem to matter how many awards she won, her best was never enough. Grace veered from loathing her employer with a passion to being in awe of his talent. Right now, as she gazed longingly at the turquoise pool and the breathtaking mountains beyond, she definitely hated him.

'I'm an hour away from Marbella,' she pointed out.

Miles tutted as if Grace was the one being unreasonable. 'I'll stall them. You've got forty-five minutes. Tops. Call me when the job's done.'

He was about to hang up when Grace interjected. 'Miles, just one question.'

'What?' he barked.

'Who am I doing this time?'

'Oh, yes, that. It's Jimmy Jones and Jasmine Watts.'

Damn! Grace had hoped that if her holiday had to be so rudely interrupted it would at least be for something worthwhile. She didn't mind doing celebrity interviews, as such. She knew that it was her knack of getting famous people to spill the beans that had propelled her career from local rag reporter to broadsheet heavyweight. And now she was the darling of the tabloids. But Jimmy Jones, footballer, and Jasmine Watts, glamour girl? Jimmy Jones was famously obtuse with the press and his fiancée Jasmine Watts was the 'It girl' for the chav generation. At least Jimmy had a talent, Grace supposed grudgingly, but Jasmine Watts was nothing but a walking, talking, blow-up doll. The girl had breasts like cantaloupe melons, legs up to her armpits, a footballer in her bed and vacuous nonsense in her oh-so-pretty head. It was hardly worth losing a day of tanning for that, was it? Not that Grace had met her before. But these girls were all the same. Flavours of the month, created for and by the public's ever-increasing appetite for new celebrities. They had no specific talent. They weren't good at anything much – other than shopping and, presumably, sex. Girls like Jasmine Watts made a mockery of journalism. Jasmine would have nothing interesting to say; Grace had been in her job long enough to know that.

She didn't automatically dismiss all celebrities. Grace had met countless intriguing, enigmatic and intelligent stars over the years, but glamour girls and footballers? She'd worked for the broadsheets. She'd interviewed prime ministers, presidents and terrorists. Just because she'd been lured by the money and profile of the tabloids, didn't mean her brain had evaporated. Grace made a mental note to talk to Miles when she got back about exactly how lowbrow she was prepared to go. Not that he would listen.

Grace stared at the contents of her Mulberry suitcase and sighed despondently. She was usually groomed to within an inch of her life, but she had no time to iron anything. Her white Ghost sundress was the least crumpled item and would have to do. Teamed with gold Jimmy Choo sandals and her new De Beers diamond necklace (a guilt present from her boyfriend McKenzie) it didn't look too bad. She brushed her sleek, short, blonde bob, dabbed on some lip gloss and she was ready for the off.

She checked her BlackBerry for instructions from Miles. Casa Amoura. Yep, sounded about right. At least it wouldn't take long to interrogate Mr

Jones and his WAG. There couldn't be much going on in their heads. Grace doubted they had a GCSE between them. If she was lucky, she would be back by the pool in time to soak up the last rays of the afternoon sun. She jumped in her hire car, Gucci shades firmly in place, the White Stripes blaring from the stereo, air-con blasting, and set off back down the winding mountain road towards Marbella.

Jasmine Watts was about to step into the shower when the bathroom door opened and her fiancé appeared.

'I thought you were still asleep, babes,' she smiled.

He looked half-asleep, with his blonde hair all mussed up and falling into those sexy greeny-blue eyes. But he shook his head.

'I'm awake and I need you to come back to bed,' he grinned.

He was naked. Bronzed, toned, honed and smooth like a statue of Adonis. Jasmine could see that at least one part of his anatomy was awake and raring to go. He grabbed her hand and pulled her back from the shower towards the door, but she held her ground.

'Jimmy,' she giggled. 'It's late and we've got loads to do today. We'd better get ready.'

He shook his head mischievously and tugged her arm.

'Jimmy,' laughed Jasmine. 'Stop it.'

But she didn't want him to stop it, really. He was so damn sexy. Just the touch of his hand on her arm was enough.

'Come here, gorgeous,' he said, pulling her towards him.

He kissed her neck just below her ear and she shivered with delight. His hands stroked her back and caressed her buttocks. Then he placed his hands round her waist and lifted her effortlessly on to the marble top by the sink.

'We really don't have time for this,' she protested, but he kissed her quiet. It was the kind of kiss that sent tingles right down to her toes.

When it came to Jimmy Jones, Jasmine was a pushover. She found herself melting under his touch as his kiss drifted down over her collar bone, round each erect nipple, her navel and – ahhh, bliss! – towards her pussy. She groaned in ecstatic anticipation of what was to come. Jimmy made love like he played football – instinctively, beautifully, perfectly. He pushed her thighs apart and started caressing the soft skin there with his tongue, coming close, but never quite touching the parts that really ached for him. She gasped.

'Oh God, Jimmy,' she begged. 'Kiss me there. Oh, yes, baby, just there.'

Her back arched involuntarily as he found her clitoris and her hands reached for the back of his head, stroking his hair and pushing his tongue deeper into her.

'That's it,' she panted. 'That's it. Oh! My! God!'

She threw her hands out and a bottle of perfume crashed on to the tiled floor, smashing into a million pieces. The air filled with the scent of vanilla and roses as Jasmine reached a crashing climax.

Jimmy looked up at her and laughed. 'Don't worry, darling. I'll buy you a new one.'

'I don't give a toss about the perfume,' she gasped. 'I just need you inside me now!'

And then he lifted her up and carried her to the bedroom, threw her on to the four-poster bed and pushed himself gently inside her. He stroked her breasts with his soft hands and stared right into her eyes as he slid deeper and deeper into her. She wrapped her thighs around his back, offering herself to him completely, swimming in his gaze, overwhelmed with love and desire. And then they moved as one, faster, harder, more desperately. Their mouths searched hungrily for each other. Jasmine felt as if her body was melting into his.

And then she was riding a wave, a delicious crashing wave and she was coming again, oh my God, and it was so perfect and she heard herself moan, too loudly, and she dug her nails into his back and squeezed her thighs and then she could feel Jimmy coming too, so deep, deep, deep inside her very core and oh ...

It was when they made love that Jasmine knew she was doing the right thing in marrying Jimmy. The chemistry between them was unbelievable. She had never felt that way about any man before and as Jimmy gazed at her now, so obviously full of love, she felt certain that together they would conquer the world.

Afterwards, Jasmine gazed adoringly at the beautiful sleeping boy beside her. Jimmy always fell asleep after sex. Jasmine felt wide awake. Wide awake and tingling with the sheer joy of being alive and young and in love. In love with Jimmy Jones. And, what's more, he was in love with her. How lucky was that? Just silly little Jasmine Watts from Dagenham and here she was engaged to the most gorgeous and talented footballer of his generation. And it wasn't just Jasmine who thought that. She'd read it somewhere too. Yes, definitely, it was in the *Sun*, or maybe it was the *Mirror*. 'The most talented footballer of his generation,' it had said 'George Best reincarnated for the new millennium.'

Sometimes Jasmine wanted to pinch herself to make sure she wasn't dreaming. Sometimes she wanted to pinch *him* just to check he was real. But he probably wouldn't like that. Jimmy wasn't very good with pain. She remembered the fuss he'd made when he'd bruised his metatarsal last season. Bless him! But then he was only a baby, just twenty-one, three years younger than she was. So instead Jasmine busied herself with gently stroking his smooth brown chest and carried on gazing, patiently, until her fingers got restless and travelled south. That roused him and then he was on her and in her again …

'Fucking hell, babe,' said Jimmy when it was over. He was dripping with sweat even though the air-con was on full blast. 'You work me harder than the governor does.'

He had such a sexy voice. Even though he'd been scouted and moved south at thirteen, Jimmy hadn't lost his Glaswegian accent. Compliments sounded so much better coming from Jimmy's full lips than they ever had from the Essex boys she'd grown up with. And he was always complimenting her. She was so lucky to have a fiancé who respected her like that. Jasmine knew only too well that not all men knew how to treat their women with respect.

Jasmine smiled and smoothed his damp blonde hair off his face. He'd been growing it long all year and it suited him. Made him look a bit rock and roll. The advertisers loved Jimmy's new look too. In fact it had been a three-million-pound deal for a designer sunglasses campaign that had paid for this new place in Puerto Banus.

'I'm just making sure you keep your stamina up for next season, darling'.

Jasmine gave him one last squeeze before reluctantly peeling her bare legs off his. She didn't want their lie-in to be over, but there was work to be done. She got up, stretched and headed towards the ensuite. Her long hair felt damp and tangled and she was worried there wouldn't be enough time to wash it and get it dried. It was kind of her trademark – her mane – but it was so high maintenance. It was longer than ever now and Jasmine could feel it brushing her bare bottom as she walked.

'Where are you going?' demanded Jimmy.

'For a shower, remember? We've got that journalist lady coming in a minute and I can't exactly meet her like this!'

Jimmy's face fell. 'Oh, do we have to?' he whined.

'Yes we do. It's work, Jimmy.'

You could say what you liked about Jasmine Watts – and people often did – but she was proud of the fact that she worked her socks off. Jasmine never forgot where she came from and how fortunate she was to be where she was today. When she remembered pole dancing in that dodgy Dagenham club she couldn't believe only three years had passed. Now she was gracing men's magazine covers and being interviewed by award-winning journalists for national newspapers.

There was a knock on the door and Blaine, their manager, called, 'Ten minutes, guys.'

'Be ready in five,' promised Jasmine. And she was.

Jasmine had just secured her ample bosom into a tiny zebra print string bikini when she heard a car pull up on the gravel drive outside. Jimmy, who'd only just dragged himself out of bed, half stepped on to the balcony and strained to have a look at the newcomer without being spotted.

'What does she look like?' asked Jasmine, who was terrified of journalists, especially the female ones. They could be so bitchy!

'Quite fit actually,' replied Jimmy. 'Old, like. Thirty-ish. Mind you, can't tell these days, can you? She might be even older. But, yeah, she's quite a sexy bird, I'd say.'

'I meant, does she look *nice*?' said Jasmine.

Jimmy wandered back inside and shrugged. 'Yeah. A little blonde thing. Not in your league, obviously, honey. I mean her tits are nonexistent ...' He put his arms around Jasmine from behind and playfully squeezed her famous breasts. Then he added cheekily, 'Nothing a decent boob job wouldn't fix, though.'

Jasmine hit him gently over the head with her towel. She wasn't the jealous type and she didn't mind Jimmy looking at attractive women. She'd been around enough men in her time to know that they all did it. But he hadn't answered her question.

'Does she look like a nice person?'

Jimmy looked perplexed. 'I don't know. You can't tell whether someone's nice just by looking at them.'

'Course you can,' said Jasmine, slipping on four-inch mules. 'It's written all over their face.'

Chapter Three

Charlie 'The Char' Palmer smiled at his reflection in the mirror as he patted his freshly shaved cheeks with aftershave. He'd fared pretty well over the years and at forty-two he was still a handsome bugger, even if he did say so himself. Olive-skinned with a square jaw and an aquiline nose, his pale-blue eyes twinkled mischievously back at him. It was a nice face. A friendly face. A fair face. Hadn't his old mum always told him so, even when others had doubted it? And she'd always been right, God rest her soul. His dark hair was receding ever so slightly, but he'd shaved it all off yesterday and it looked much better now. Charlie Palmer could pass for thirty-five, easy. Yeah, he still had it. He was still a player, of that he was sure.

He chose a dark-grey Armani suit from his walk-in wardrobe, a crisp white T-shirt and black Prada loafers. He had one last bit of business to take care of before his flight and Charlie always felt better – more powerful – when he was dressed the part.

The beautiful girl lying in his bed stirred as he picked up his leather holdall and his briefcase.

'Where you going, dahling?' she murmured sleepily.

'Work, sweetheart,' he replied, kissing her soft blonde hair and breathing in her musky smell one last time. It wasn't a lie.

He would miss Nadia. She was a little cutie. Gave the best blow job he'd ever experienced *and* she mixed a mean martini. Loaded, too – the daughter of a Russian oligarch. She had her own penthouse in Mayfair, but she'd been a permanent fixture in his Butler's Wharf apartment since the spring. But Charlie believed in travelling light and, lovely as she was, Nadia amounted to too much baggage. Besides, her father had had a 'quiet word' with Charlie the other night and it turned out Mr Dimitrov wasn't best pleased with his daughter's sleeping arrangements. And Mr Dimitrov could be a very persuasive man.

Nadia snuggled back down under the duvet. 'I see you later, dahling,' she purred.

'Yeah, babes,' replied Charlie. 'Later.'

And without a backward glance at the place he'd called home for the past five years, or the girl he'd called babe for the last three months, Charlie Palmer shut the door behind him and took the lift down to the cobbled street outside. London was hot. Too hot. The Thames smelled stagnant. The sky was more grey than blue and the atmosphere was close and airless. A storm was brewing. It was as good a day as any to get out.

Gary was waiting for him in the black Range Rover as arranged.

'All right, boss?'

Gary was the son of a pub landlord Charlie knew from the old days in Chingford. He was seventeen and he'd been in a bit of trouble with the filth so his old man thought Charlie might be the bloke to straighten him out. He had that sort of reputation back home and he liked it. It made him feel proud because he'd been in trouble with the filth himself at Gary's age and no one had thought he'd amount to much. But look at him now, eh? Forty-two and about to retire a very wealthy man.

Charlie had had his doubts about Gary at first. The boy looked like a complete plonker with his baggy jeans pulled down and belted way below his boxer shorts and his baseball cap perched on the top of his head at a drunken angle. He was a skinny redhead with freckles who'd been brought up in a nice house in Chigwell, but he obviously thought he was some cool black dude from the Bronx. But, much to Charlie's surprise, the kid had worked out pretty well. He was keen and respectful and did as he was told, no questions asked. Charlie liked Gary. Perhaps he could find a job for him in the new place. He would have to wait and see how things turned out.

'Heathrow is it, boss?' asked Gary.

Charlie nodded. 'But I need to stop off in Hammersmith on the way.'

'No worries, boss.'

Nadia Dimitrova watched her lover leave from the third-floor window and sighed a little sadly. As the Range Rover rolled out of view she pulled Charlie's fluffy white bathrobe around her slim frame and breathed in the musky scent of his aftershave. She would miss Charlie. She really would. Silly boy. He thought she didn't know he was leaving, but she wasn't stupid. Why did men always think she was oblivious to what was going on? Her father was just the same. But Nadia knew more than either man could imagine. She was not the innocent little girl they took her for.

She wiped a stray tear from her cheek and turned from the window. Never mind. It had been a delicious love affair, a real treat while it lasted, and Charlie was such a handsome man…but he was not the only handsome man in London. Nadia threw herself on the bed and picked up her phone. She scrolled down her contacts until she came to a name that interested her. Ah, yes! This could be fun. Not something her father would approve of, of course, but then that was the biggest part of the attraction. She pressed the 'call' button with a naughty grin on her face.

Charlie and Gary sat in silence as the Range Rover crawled through the mid-morning London traffic. Fridays were always the worst. Charlie wouldn't miss the crowds. Not one bit. He contemplated the job ahead. He'd been through it a hundred times in his head and he knew what had to be done.

Gary pulled into a quiet dead-end road and parked.

'Five minutes,' said Charlie, picking up his briefcase.

Gary nodded and flicked on the radio. He would sit and listen to music on XFM and wait. Five minutes or five hours, the kid would wait. No questions asked. Yeah, he definitely deserved a job in the new place.

The building site was round the corner. Luxury riverside apartments had been going up at a staggering rate on the site of an old tyre factory as part of some regeneration project or other. But rumour had it that the property developer was in trouble, the latest victim of the collapsing housing market, and work was grinding to a halt.

The site was eerily deserted, much to Charlie's relief. McGregor had promised it would be, but you never knew. There was something of the Marie Celeste about the place – tools had been downed mid-job and a half-drunk mug of tea still sat waiting in vain for its owner to return on a half-built wall. It looked as if everyone had left in a bit of a hurry.

Charlie could see Donohue by the water's edge, chatting into his mobile, shades firmly in place despite the black clouds that were gathering ominously overhead. He was wearing a bad suit, a cheap approximation of Charlie's. That was part of Donohue's problem. He thought he was one of them – a player – but he was just a cheap, spineless little shit. A tiny fish in a huge pond full of sharks. And he'd got in way over his head.

'Chaz, my man!' Donohue snapped his mobile shut and slipped it into his jacket pocket.

Charlie flinched. No one called him Chaz. Who did this little fucker think he was?

'Good to see you, mate. McGregor said you'd got something for me.'

Charlie forced his features into a smile and shook Donohue's small hand just firmly enough to show him who was boss. Donohue's palm was clammy and Charlie wondered whether the small man was nervous or just too hot in his nylon suit.

DC Dave Donohue was thirty-seven years old, short, slight and balding.

'Take off the shades,' said Charlie.

'Why?'

'Cos I like doing business eye to eye.'

Charlie's facial muscles ached from holding the false smile.

Donohue placed his sunglasses on top of his head. His grey eyes were small and shifty, forever darting around, looking for some action. Now he was looking everywhere but into Charlie's face. Was that shame? Too much coke? Or just lack of respect? Charlie wasn't sure, but the man made him want to throw up. He was everything Charlie despised – a vice cop who lorded it over the pimps and dealers he arrested while snorting their cocaine and shagging their girls as some sort of perk. Charlie didn't do drugs, never had, and he didn't pay for sex either. He had too much respect for himself *and* the opposite sex to do that. Of course Donohue wasn't the only one in the vice squad who abused his power, but lately he'd gone way too far and now McGregor had had enough.

'Yeah, I've got something for you.'

Charlie squatted down and placed his briefcase carefully in the dust. He opened it slowly, oh so slowly, and then stood up. The handgun felt heavy and cold in his hand, but it was as comfortable to him as a hammer was to a carpenter. The gun was just a tool of his trade. It was such a familiar feeling – cool metal against warm flesh – and Charlie found himself wondering, for a moment, if he would miss it.

Charlie was almost a foot taller than Donohue and so, when he finally drew the gun, it was exactly in line with the shorter man's eyes.

'Oh, Jesus fucking Christ! Charlie, what are you doing, man?'

Donohue's shifty eyes widened. He leapt backwards but then realised that the river was only inches away and that there was nowhere to escape to. His mouth gaped open and shut, open and shut, but no more words came out, just gurgled, garbled noises. The confusion in his eyes turned to shock and then sheer, unadulterated terror as the seriousness of the situation seeped into his drug-addled little brain.

Charlie continued to smile but said nothing. The longer he remained silent the more Donohue would have to think about why he was here.

'What … what … what's this about, Charlie?' he stammered. 'I've done nothing wrong. I don't understand.'

Charlie continued to stare at Donohue, trying to bore into his very soul, if he had such a thing, willing him to redeem himself in some way. Just tell the truth, man, he thought. Just say the thing out loud. But Donohue was the type who needed a bit of persuasion. And still, he wouldn't meet Charlie's eye.

'I, I, I really don't have a fucking clue why you're so … so … so …' Dave glanced at the gun and then quickly looked away again. 'So pissed off with me, Charlie. I don't.' He shook his head manically. 'I don't. I really don't. I've done nothing. Nothing wrong at all.'

At last Charlie spoke. 'What do you think this might be about, Donohue?' he asked calmly. 'What dirty little secrets of yours might have come to my attention?'

Donohue shrugged almost petulantly and looked at his feet. Charlie dug the gun into the smaller man's forehead, forcing his head up, and took a step closer. He could see the sweat trickle down Donohue's face and smell the fear on his breath.

'I'll give you a clue,' continued Charlie. 'Her name was Clara.'

'Oh, fuck. Oh, shit,' stammered Donohue. 'The ... the ... that.' He seemed to shrink then, to deflate, as if the very worst case scenario had been confirmed. Which, of course, it had.

'What did you do to her?' demanded Charlie.

'We had a kind of ... a sort of ... an altercation, of sorts ...' Donohue rambled.

'Oh, an altercation? Is that what you call it? You and Clara had an altercation and somehow she ended up dead.'

Donohue raised his hands in front of him with his palms open towards Charlie.

'I didn't mean to kill her,' he said. 'I swear. Things got out of control.'

Charlie thrust the gun harder into Donohue's forehead. He couldn't hold the false smile anymore and when he demanded, 'Tell me exactly what happened, you fucking little shit,' he more or less spat the words into Donohue's face.

Donohue closed his eyes. He was shaking.

'She tried to run. She'd nicked my ID, for fuck's sake. I just hit her to stop her going; I didn't think I'd done it that hard. I didn't mean her to die. Jesus, Mr Palmer, you'd have done the same.'

Charlie couldn't believe what he was hearing. How dare this piece of shit suggest that Charlie would have killed some poor young girl? Charlie had never laid a finger on a female in his life, let alone a child.

He twisted the gun so that the barrel dug deep into Donohue's forehead. Blood trickled and merged with the sweat that ran down the man's face and dripped on to his cheap suit.

'How old was Clara?' demanded Charlie.

'I don't know. Young.'

'Thirteen,' said Charlie angrily. 'She was thirteen, Donohue. She'd run away from home. Her poor mother was waiting for her to come home. You should have been protecting her, you fucker. You should have been the one taking her home.'

'Shit, I didn't know she was thirteen,' mumbled Donohue. 'I honestly didn't know she was thirteen.'

'And what were you doing with Clara?' Charlie continued. 'What were you doing alone with Clara, up some Dalston alleyway, Donohue? Explain that.'

'I was … I was arresting her for soliciting.'

'Try again,' shouted Charlie. He was getting impatient now. He knew the truth, but he needed to hear Donohue admit it. 'What were you doing with Clara?'

'We were having sex,' Donohue whispered so quietly that Charlie could barely make out the words.

'Speak up, Dave. I didn't quite catch that.'

'We were having sex,' Donohue repeated, more clearly this time.

'No, you weren't,' spat Charlie. 'You were raping her. Sex is consensual.'

At last Donohue met Charlie's stare and his eyes were full of desperation.

'Please, Charlie, don't do this. It was an accident. I didn't mean to hurt her.' He was pleading now. 'What about my wife? What about my girls?'

'Your wife will be better off without you. And your girls? Your girls are only a couple of years younger than that kid you killed.'

'She was just another little whore. They're ten a penny out there. You know that.'

'She was a kid. Someone else's kid. And you know what that makes you, mate,' Charlie spat with disgust. 'That makes you a nonce. And we all know what happens to nonces, don't we?'

Charlie could smell urine as a large wet patch appeared on Donohue's trousers. Disgusting little maggot. He unleashed the safety catch with a loud snap.

'Please, Mr Palmer, I'm begging you. Don't do this. I'm a cop. You can't go around shooting cops and getting away with it. What about McGregor? He'll never let you get away with this.'

That was just like Donohue, to hide behind his badge for protection. Charlie remembered what McGregor had told him and he lowered the gun slowly.

'You're right, Donohue. I do have to think about McGregor.'

Donohue sobbed in relief and fell to his knees. He looked up at Charlie with sheer gratitude. 'Oh fucking hell, you really had me there, mate. I honest to God thought I was a goner. Look I'm really sorry about that girl. It's not going to happen again. McGregor doesn't know—'

Charlie interrupted. 'McGregor does know. Why do you think I'm here?'

13

Donohue looked confused and then the terror filled his eyes again. Charlie lifted the gun a fraction and calmly shot DC Dave Donohue in the groin. Blood and flesh splattered on to the dusty ground. Donohue collapsed to one side. His grey eyes stared uncomprehendingly at Charlie. Charlie watched without emotion as the small man's face contorted in pain for a few moments and then, keen to get the day's business over and done with, he lifted the gun to Donohue's head and finished the job. The odious little shit was no more.

Charlie dropped the gun into his briefcase and snapped it shut. Without looking back he walked towards the building site and tossed the briefcase and its contents into the damp concrete foundations. He watched as the evidence was swallowed up for ever. Very neat. Very tidy. Just how he liked it. And anyway, it wasn't as if he'd need a gun where he was going. Then he called McGregor.

'DCI McGregor,' said the gruff voice.

'The job's done.'

'Good. I owe you. That little bonus we talked about should be cleared with the accounts department early next week.'

'Thanks, guv.'

'You off now?'

Charlie checked his watch. 'Plane's at one.'

'Well, have a good trip. Oh, and Char ... The wife and I are coming out your way in August if you fancy a round of golf.'

'Look forward to it.'

And that was that. The business was done. McGregor would send some plain clothes off to 'find' the body and DC Dave Donohue would die a hero, having been shot in the line of duty. His wife would be duly compensated and Donohue would receive a posthumous award for bravery. The murder would be pinned on some lowlife scum the filth had been trying to get rid of and the job would be a good'un all round. No one would ever know that his death had been arranged by his own chief inspector to save the force a scandal. No one, that is, but Charlie. And Charlie, being Charlie, would take that piece of information to the grave.

It had been a while since he'd had to get his hands dirty. He'd paid his dues in the early days of his career and that had stood him in good stead. He was well-respected in the business and most people knew not to cross him. If you're nice to Charlie Palmer, then Charlie Palmer will be nice to you. As the years passed he'd found that his reputation alone was enough to trade on. A threat from Charlie was usually enough to get the job done without resorting to anything too heavy. And he liked it like that. Charlie didn't enjoy killing people. It was a messy business. But some lowlifes needed to be sorted good and proper and, unfortunately, Donohue had been one of those. And now, because of that little maggot, Charlie had to scarper.

'That was quick,' said Gary as Charlie slid back into the passenger seat of the Range Rover.

'Yeah, wasn't anything important.'

'Straight to Heathrow, then?'

'Straight to Heathrow,' confirmed Charlie.

Yeah, London was too hot for Charlie now. It was time to get out.

Chapter Four

'Right, I can do this,' Maxine de la Fallaise told herself out loud, squinting at the cookery book propped open on the granite work surface. She swept her curly blonde hair out of her eyes and wiped her hands on her apron. Then she read through the list of ingredients again.

12-18 slices prosciutto – check.

3 cloves of garlic, peeled – check.

1 good handful of dried porcini – eh?

'Isabel!' called Maxine. 'Isabel! What's a porcini? I don't have a porcini!'

Maxine's maid sauntered into the kitchen from the terrace outside. She was wearing a high-cut black one-piece and carrying a copy of *Hola!* in her hand. She leaned against the central island with her head on one side and an 'I told you so' look on her face. Maxine had given Isabel a couple of hours' break while she prepared a special lunch for Carlos. Isabel had been grateful for the time off but sceptical about Maxine's abilities in the kitchen.

'Have you ever actually cooked a meal before, Miss Maxine?' she'd asked in her alarmingly good English.

'Of course I have,' Maxine had scoffed, remembering a disastrous episode with a roast chicken during a domestic science lesson at boarding school. The local fire brigade had been a little bit peeved, but the other girls were delighted with their afternoon off lessons. 'I'm just a bit rusty, that's all.'

Could it be so difficult to become a domestic goddess? Her household certainly seemed to think so. Her long-term lover Carlos had laughed his head off when she'd offered to cook for him.

'Chica! Chica!' he'd cried, between great guffaws. 'You have many, many special talents but you are no, what do you call her? Nigelica.'

'Nigella,' Maxine had corrected him. 'I'm no Nigella.'

'My dahling, there is a reason why this town is full of top-class restaurants. It is because glamorous women like you are too busy being beautiful to worry about cooking, no? Anyway, we have Isabel. Isabel is a wonderful cook. She is from Seville. Women from Seville are all wonderful cooks.'

Sometimes, Maxine felt that Carlos and the staff ganged up on her for being the only non-Spaniard in the place. OK, so she was born in New York, raised in LA, educated in Britain, and London remained her 'official' home, but she'd spent the best part of the last two years here and she loved it. Couldn't they see she was an honorary *señorita*? Sometimes she felt they ganged up on her, full stop. They were always laughing at her. Oh, they did it affectionately, she knew that. But it did bother her sometimes. Why did no one take her seriously? She wasn't a kid anymore. She was a mature woman who'd been round the block a few times. OK, so she didn't know how to switch on the extractor fan, but so what? She could learn. She was determined to prove to Carlos that she was proper 'wife' material.

It had been during one of their many discussions about his wife, Esther, that she'd had the idea to cook for him. Carlos and Esther had been married for almost thirty years but had spent the last fifteen of them leading entirely separate lives. While Esther was ensconced in her Beverley Hills mansion, Carlos was here, on the Costa del Sol, with Maxine. The Russos were married on paper only. It was just a technicality. Esther point-blank refused to grant Carlos a divorce on the grounds that she was a devout Catholic and he didn't see any reason to push the subject. But Maxine did. She'd been with Carlos for ages now and she loved him passionately. She wanted to be Mrs Russo.

'Dahling, you are not really the wifely type,' Carlos had smiled patiently when Maxine had brought up the subject again.

'Yes I am,' Maxine had insisted crossly. 'I've already been married three times!'

At that Carlos had laughed out loud. 'And exactly how long have these marriages lasted?'

'Almost a year, one of them,' Maxine had replied earnestly.

'Exactly, chica!' Carlos had said, still laughing. 'You are not the wifely type!'

'So what is the wifely type?' Maxine had snapped. She did so want to be that woman.

Carlos had shrugged. 'A woman who can cook. A woman who can bear getting fat long enough to become a mother. A woman who can leave the house without spending three hours preparing herself.'

Leaving the house without her make-up on? Well, that was never going to happen. And pregnancy? That still scared the living daylights out of her (although lately she had been warming to the idea). But cooking? Perhaps she could master cooking. And so Maxine was going to surprise him today with a … she glanced at the cookbook again. With a roasted fillet of beef rolled in herbs and porcini and wrapped in prosciutto. But he would be back from the golf course in an hour and the beef wasn't even in the oven yet. More to the point – what was bloody porcini when it was at home?

'Miss Maxine,' said Isabel patiently. 'I told you already. I bought all the ingredients for you yesterday.' She pulled open the larder unit and handed Maxine a bag of dried porcini.

'Oh, mushrooms,' said Maxine with relief. 'Well, why the hell don't they say that in the book?'

Isabel grinned. 'You want me to help you?' she asked.

'No, no, no,' insisted Maxine, shooing Isabel back out on to the terrace. 'I'll be fine. I need to do this on my own.'

Maxine did as Jamie Oliver told her to. She soaked the porcini in water, then fried it with garlic. She wasn't exactly sure what reducing meant, but she carried on regardless. The mixture stuck to the pan and ended up looking a bit gritty, but never mind. She spooned the lumpy grey mixture on to the prosciutto. It didn't look very appetising at the moment but it would be OK once it had been in the oven, she was sure. She covered the beef Isabel had bought at the farmer's market with herbs and then attempted to roll the ham and mushroom mixture around the fillets. Disaster. However hard she tried it wouldn't even begin to look anything like the neat little packages of meat in the picture. Oh, bugger it. Maxine searched furiously through the unfamiliar kitchen drawers until she found some string. That would do. She tied the string around the beef fillets and then threw them into the range oven. The clock on the oven said twelve thirty. Oh shit! Carlos would be home in half an hour and it said the beef would take forty minutes to cook. She turned the knob from two hundred degrees to three hundred. There, it would cook quicker that way. Ta da! All done. This cooking business wasn't as difficult as it looked.

Maxine glanced in the mirror. There were mirrors everywhere in the house. And not because Maxine was vain, either. It was exactly because she wasn't vain that she needed the mirrors. Maxine knew she looked totally rubbish in her natural state and used the mirrors to check that her hair and make-up were always just so, lest the 'real' Maxine de la Fallaise should ever rear her ugly head. Jesus! How did those TV chefs manage to look so appealing in the kitchen? Maxine was beetroot in the face, sweaty in the armpits and mascara-smudged in the eyes. Eurgh! Her trademark tumbling curls had turned into a frizzy mess. And, oh my God, were those mouse-coloured roots showing beneath the peroxide? She made a mental note to get to the hair salon that very afternoon for an emergency appointment. She ran to the nearest bathroom to fix herself up, took off her apron (she was wearing nothing but a gold string bikini underneath) and joined Isabel on the terrace with twenty minutes to spare.

'Is everything OK?' asked Isabel, doubtfully.

'Everything's fine!' announced Maxine confidently, picking up a copy of *OK!* in search of pictures of herself and her many celebrity friends. The spreads from Cannes should be in this issue. Oh, yes! There she was next to Liz Hurley. Hmm, those white jeans were doing nothing for her thighs. She made a mental note not to wear them again.

It wasn't until fifteen minutes later that Isabel noticed the burning smell.

'Oh my God!' Maxine exclaimed, peering through the smoke into the oven. 'Are they supposed to be black?'

'No, Miss Maxine, I don't think so,' said Isabel patiently. 'I will make *Señor* Carlos something else.'

'Crap!' announced Maxine. 'You see, Isabel? There's something else I'm useless at.'

Isabel smiled warmly at her mistress. 'You are too hard on yourself, Miss Maxine,' she said, gently. 'You're not useless. You're a successful businesswoman. Now you own a nightclub, remember? *And* you're the nicest employer I ever had.'

By the time Carlos returned from the golf club, Isabel had made him a lovely frittata and Maxine's Shih Tzu, Britney, was enthusiastically tucking into some charred beef. Maxine was perched innocently on a bar stool, filing her nails and flicking through her magazine.

'Hi, handsome,' she said cheerfully, slipping off the stool and planting a juicy kiss on her lover's cheek.

And wasn't he handsome? Six foot two, suave, broad-shouldered and raven-haired (with a little help from his hairdresser), Carlos was a dead ringer for Cary Grant. His pale-blue golf shirt set off his tan and his chocolate-brown eyes perfectly. She'd fancied Carlos Russo when his melodic ballads had topped the charts in the eighties. And she still fancied Carlos Russo now. Except these days she got to live with him. Yes, Maxine was a lucky girl.

'What's that burning smell?' asked Carlos, sniffing the air cautiously. 'Have we had a fire?'

'Don't be silly, *señor*,' scoffed Isabel. 'I just burned the frittata a little.'

'You did?' asked Carlos, suspiciously.

'I did,' lied Isabel.

Maxine shot her a grateful look.

'Oh my goodness,' shouted Carlos suddenly. 'What's wrong with Britney?'

Everybody turned to look at the tiny creature, who was heaving and choking dramatically in the corner.

'Do something!' squealed Maxine, watching her little 'baby' convulse in agony. 'Carlos, save her!' She dissolved into floods of tears and covered her eyes with her hands. 'I can't look!' she wailed.

Ever the hero, Carlos grabbed the little dog, forced open her jaws and fished around for the cause of the problem.

'What on earth is this?' he asked, baffled, pulling a burnt piece of string from the dog's throat.

Maxine picked up her treasured dog, who was shaking uncontrollably after her ordeal, cuddled her into her chest and kissed her fluffy head passionately. 'Poor little Britney! I almost killed you,' she said to the dog.

'You?' asked Carlos, bemused.

'I tried to cook for you,' explained Maxine sheepishly. 'It went wrong. Britney was eating the evidence.'

Carlos's handsome face broke into an amused smile. 'Oh well, no harm done, Maxi.' He laughed heartily, patted Maxine playfully on the bottom, and sat down to eat his frittata.

Maxine flinched. She hated it when Carlos patronised her like that and treated her like a silly little girl. Hmph! She was highly competitive. Always had been. Just because she'd failed in the kitchen department, it did not mean she was a failure. She might have lost this battle, but she would never lose the war. From now on she would leave the domestic goddessery to Isabel. But she would find another way to convince Carlos of her marital virtues. When she set her mind on something she was like a dog with a bone. Or, perhaps, a dog with an incinerated piece of beef. Like Britney, she wouldn't let go without a scene. It was time to come up with a Plan B.

As Gary crawled through the West London traffic, Charlie undressed. He slipped off his suit, T-shirt and loafers and shoved them into an empty sports bag. Gary didn't bat an eyelid as his boss stripped down to his Calvins. He'd seen it all before. A couple of posh birds in an open top Audi TT noticed Charlie's buff naked body though and they beeped and whooped on their way past on the M4 slip road. Charlie winked at them. Then he took his neatly folded navy linen shorts and a white linen shirt from his holdall and struggled into them. He held up his new brown leather Mui Mui sandals that he'd bought up west with Nadia the day before.

'Are these a bit gay?' he asked Gary.

'No, boss. They're class. Like something Beckham would wear, innit?'

Charlie nodded, satisfied, and slipped them on. He threw the sports bag on to the back seat.

'Get rid of that once you've dropped me.'

Gary nodded. He would burn it once it got dark.

As Charlie got out of the Range Rover at the airport he tossed Gary a set of keys. 'For my flat,' he said. 'Make yourself at home. I'm going to be away for a while.'

'Eh?' Gary looked perplexed.

'And keep the motor ticking over for me. Stay out of trouble, keep your nose clean and I'll be in touch.'

Gary scratched his head, forcing his baseball cap up into an even more peculiar position than usual.

'And don't call me unless it's a real fucking emergency, OK?'

'Right, boss,' he said uncertainly.

'Send Nadia home to her dad,' Charlie continued. 'Oh, and tell her I'm sorry about running out. Nothing personal and all that. Grab her some flowers on the way back. Classy ones. Not from the garage, OK? Here.'

Charlie tossed a huge bundle of fifty-pound notes on to the passenger seat. 'That ought to cover it. Keep the change. Thanks, Gary. You're a good kid. I'll see you around.'

Gary was still staring open-mouthed at the enormous wad of cash as Charlie disappeared through the revolving doors towards departures.

Chapter Five

'What do you mean, you're not coming? You're supposed to be on the bloody plane! They're holding the flight for you!'

Lila Rose realised, too late, that she was shouting. She could see the smirks and nudges of the assembled group, her so-called loyal staff, out of the corner of her eye. They were vultures. They pretended to like her but they were paid to do that. She knew they were all just waiting for their pound of her flesh. And when they got it they would sell it to the tabloids … or on eBay for fifty quid. She turned her back, lowered her voice and continued.

'I don't understand, Brett. You *have* to come. You promised.'

Her husband's voice crackled from across the Atlantic.

'I know, sweetheart, but it's beyond my control. It's a really important meeting about a big, *big* part. The director starts shooting in Montreal on Monday so it's this weekend or not at all.'

Lila sighed and raked her hand through her glossy brown hair. Brett was lying of course. Brett spent his whole life lying. He'd been an actor for so long that he'd completely lost the knack of telling the truth. Three Oscar nominations said that her husband was one of the greatest movie stars of his generation, but his wife could still see right through him. The fact was that any director would move heaven and earth to secure Brett Rose as their leading man. This meeting – if there was any meeting – would easily have waited until Brett returned from Europe.

'You're a shit, Brett. A complete fucking first-class shit. What am I supposed to tell my parents? How do I explain this to the children? They've all been looking forward to this weekend for months.'

And so have I! Lila could feel her cheeks getting hot and tears welling up in her eyes.

'Oh, come on, honey. Don't be mad. I'm disappointed too, but you know how it is out here. Things move fast. Your folks will understand and I'll make it up to the kids. Hey, I'm still coming; the trip's just on hold for a few days, that's all.'

'My dad's birthday is on Sunday,' Lila reminded him, coldly.

'Huh? It's a bad line, honey.'

It was indeed a bad line but Lila could tell that Brett was somewhere noisy. There was music playing in the background and voices – excited, high-pitched voices. It was four a.m. in LA and, as usual, her husband was partying like the young bachelor he'd been before they'd met.

'Anyway, sweetheart, I'd better go. I'm sorry, yeah? I'll call you tomorrow and let you know my plans. Right now, I gotta get to bed.'

Lila hung up without saying goodbye. The poor baby needed to go to bed. The question was, with whom? Lindsay Lohan? Paris Hilton? Somebody nubile and a fraction of Lila's age, no doubt.

She excused herself and headed for the ladies' where she locked herself in a cubicle and dissolved into tears. Why was she surprised? He was always letting her down. But she'd desperately hoped that this would be the week to get their marriage back on track. It was her father's sixty-fifth birthday party and the whole family was going to be there. Lila had been so excited at the prospect of having everyone she loved in one place – her parents, her children and, most importantly, her husband. After years of feeling alone, the thought of being surrounded by her entire family had been too delicious for words.

She took a deep breath and unlocked the door, then stared in horror at her reflection in the mirror. Even heartbreak had looked hauntingly beautiful in her youth – it had suited her huge, watery blue eyes and quivering full lips – but now all Lila saw in the mirror was a pathetic, broken woman sliding inelegantly towards middle age. Desperation sure as hell felt the same as it had at eighteen, but it certainly looked worse at thirty-six. Lila noted how her mascara had run into the laughter lines around her eyes. Mother Nature was a bitch – it wasn't as if she'd had much to laugh about recently. With her face flushed with tears the broken veins in her cheeks were clearly visible. Maybe it was time for a chemical peel. Or something more radical, perhaps. Lila had always been appalled by plastic surgery, and she'd said so publicly many times, but that was before the wrinkles set in. The irony was that women's magazines continued to hail her a great British beauty. If only they could see her now! Talented make-up artists and great photographers were all that stood between Lila Rose's adoring public and the grim truth. And the truth was, in Lila's mind at least, that her famous good looks were nothing but a fading memory. All washed up, just like her acting career. Lila longed to get back into work now the children were getting older, but who would cast her? She was too old for the 'love interest' roles and too young to be considered a 'character' actress. Plus she didn't have an ounce of self-confidence left. She was nothing. A big fat nothing.

There was a gentle knock on the door.

'Are you all right, hun?'

It was Peter, Lila's PA and the only man, other than her father, whom she could truly trust. He was not one of the vultures. He was gay, of course. Peter was too sensitive and compassionate to be straight. Not to mention well-groomed, witty, insightful and tactile. He was everything her husband was not. Brett called Peter her 'designer handfag' but he was so much more than a beautiful accessory. For the past decade Peter had been Lila's rock – her PA, her style advisor, her confidant, her shoulder to cry on, her son's godfather and more than anything her best friend. He took one look at Lila's crumpled face and smudged mascara and threw his arms around her. She buried her face in his cashmere sweater and sobbed. Peter rocked her like a tiny child and didn't seem to care a bit that Lila's mascara was running all over his pale-blue top.

'Brett the Bastard strikes again, then?' he muttered, more to himself than to Lila.

Lila nodded but was too upset to speak. Peter stroked her dark hair gently and kissed the top of her head. Then, once the tears had subsided, he carefully reapplied her make-up.

'There,' he said when he'd finished. 'Stunning.'

Lila looked in the mirror. Even she had to admit that with enough make-up on she still scrubbed up pretty well. But it was just a mask: illuminating foundation to make her skin all dewy, shimmering eyeshadow to brighten her eyes, lip-plumping lipstick to swell her pout and rose-pink blusher to fake a nice youthful bloom to her cheeks. None of it was real.

'Just one thing missing,' said Peter.

'What?'

'A smile.'

Lila nodded, took a deep breath and switched on her famous winning smile. The mask was complete. She was ready to face her public. It always amazed Lila how everybody fell for the pretence and bought into the idea of the Roses' perfect celebrity marriage. Peter knew the truth, of course. And her mother, Eve. Eve saw through the false smile and immaculate make-up to the broken little girl inside. But only one other person had seen through the mask; a journalist called Grace Melrose who'd interviewed her last month.

What was it she'd written? *'The Rose fairytale romance is the stuff of Hollywood fantasy. Ten years of blissful togetherness is practically unheard of in the quickie divorce culture of La La Land. But, alas, I suspect that's all it is – a fantasy. All is clearly not well in the House of Rose. Indeed Lila wears her pain etched into every line on her beautiful face.'*

Brett's PR people had gone completely mental when the story was printed. They'd threatened to sue and vowed never to give the paper access to the Roses again. And, yes, part of Lila hated Grace Melrose too – partly for stripping her soul bare, but mostly for noticing she had lines! It wasn't easy on the ego, being married to a Hollywood megastar. Brett was the same age as Lila, but while mid-thirties is still youthful in a man, it's practically geriatric in a woman, in Hollywood at least. And yet, despite Grace Melrose's harsh words, a bit of Lila respected the woman for looking beyond the mask and into her eyes. It was the first time in such a long while that anyone had bothered to see her as a living, breathing, feeling human being and not just some wife of a movie star. Lila suspected that if she were allowed to live in the real world a woman like Grace Melrose would make a very good friend. But friends were a luxury Lila couldn't afford. She'd learned from bitter experience that members of her own sex were the first to stab her in the back. And straight men were no better. And so she had Peter.

'What time is it?' she whispered to Peter as they strutted back into the VIP departures lounge, side by side.

'Nearly two.'

'God! The plane was supposed to leave an hour ago.'

'Oh, don't worry about that,' Peter scoffed. 'They've held it for you.'

'I know, but the other passengers will think I'm such a diva.'

'Oh, don't be silly. They'll be over the moon. Having Lila Rose on their flight will make their holiday.'

Lila sighed. Having Brett Rose on the flight was the only thing that would have made her holiday.

Charlie was getting nervous. The plane had been sitting on the runway for far too long. He wasn't a big drinker but he'd already had two glasses of complimentary Jack Daniels in the comfort of his leather window seat. Charlie usually loved flying, especially now that he could afford the best seats; it gave him such a buzz to think that he, Charlie Palmer, could afford to lord it over the 'ordinary' people crammed in to economy like battery chickens. When the curtain was drawn between him and the masses behind it was like a line being drawn over his past. No bickering families and screaming kids on his journey, thank you very much. Mind you, those kids were lucky to be going abroad at all; he'd never got further than Margate at that age.

It was pissing down outside now. Maybe the weather was holding them up. But why did that trolley dolly keep going to the phone and having hushed snatches of conversation? And why hadn't they closed the doors yet? Charlie was an expert people-watcher. He'd had to be in his line of work. The cabin crew kept giving each other meaningful glances and he could tell they were all excited about something. The plane felt charged with an atmosphere of anticipation. Something big was about to happen and Charlie was concerned that it might have something to do with him. He eyed the open cabin door, half-expecting an armed police raid. Could McGregor be trusted? He'd thought so. He'd been sure. But the longer Charlie sat there, the less convinced he became.

And then it happened. Flanked on all sides by an entourage of designer-clad minions, Lila Rose swept on to the plane and into the empty seat directly in front of Charlie. He was so close he could smell her perfume. Charlie grinned to himself with relief. And then he grinned again because he couldn't believe his luck. Lila Rose: now there was a classy bird. Beautiful, talented and smart, she was pretty much Charlie's ideal woman. She was tiny, or at least tiny by Charlie's standards, but then Charlie was six foot four. But she was curvier than most actresses these days. Charlie liked his women like that, with a bit of flesh on their bones. Not fat. Just the way nature intended, rather than starved half to death. Her hair was dark and glossy, like something out of a shampoo ad and her face ... well, Charlie had always thought it was the face of an angel.

He'd always thought she was a really amazing actress, too. He'd actually cried when her character died during childbirth in that silly soap opera she'd been in. Not that he'd ever admit that to anybody, of course. Oh yeah, and then there was that time he'd gone to see her in that chick flick. His girlfriend at the time had twisted his arm. The film wasn't his thing at all – no sex, no violence! In fact it had been some weepy period drama. But gazing at Lila Rose on the big screen, her lily-white cleavage heaving in a tight corset, her huge blue eyes weeping over some unrequited love and her full lips trembling and moist ... that had been pure cinematic Viagra. Oh yeah, she was some woman. He couldn't for the life of him remember which girlfriend he'd been on that date with, but he hadn't forgotten those images of Lila Rose. And here she was, right in front of him. If he reached out he could touch that perfect dark hair.

Charlie sighed. Pity she was married to the most handsome man on the planet. Charlie knew his good points, but he also knew his place in life and sitting behind Lila Rose for two hours was as close as he was ever going to get to Hollywood royalty.

Within minutes the cabin doors were shut, the engines started and the plane was taxiing down the runway. Once they were airborne the captain's voice came over the tannoy, welcoming the passengers to the flight.

'The temperature in Malaga is a very pleasant twenty-eight degrees, the skies over Spain are clear and we don't expect any further delays, so just sit back and enjoy the flight.'

Oh, I will, thought Charlie, staring at the back of Lila Rose's head, I will.

Chapter Six

Grace speedily read Miles' email on her BlackBerry as she waited for Jimmy Jones and Jasmine Watts under the shade of a gazebo overlooking the pool. She couldn't help giggling at his notes. *Jimmy Jones, good at football but IQ of an amoeba. Wedding next week – Scoop! magazine have exclusive but see what you can get. Details of meringue? WAG bridesmaids? Beckhamesque thrones? Is she up the duff? Jasmine background (classy stuff) – hails from Dagenham, used to be a pole dancer at Exotica, family are pond life, mother's an ex pro, brothers in and out of jail, younger sister had baby at fifteen. Father's deceased. Jasmine claims she's adopted (I would too). Most important: are her tits her own? Must admit they're magnificent.*

'Something funny, Grace?'

Grace looked up and squinted into the sunlight at the approaching hulking figure in the canary-yellow Hawaiian shirt. And then she laughed again, but this time in resignation. Blaine Edwards. She might have known he'd be behind this.

'Blaine, you tart, I should have known you'd be sniffing around somewhere.'

'Sniffing around?' Blaine pretended to be insulted. 'I'll have you know that the JimJazz brand is the latest addition to the Edwards dynasty. The only reason you're here is because *I* said it was OK.'

Grace groaned inwardly. This was the last person on earth she wanted to bump into on her holiday. Blaine Edwards, PR guru, was an overweight, overbearing Australian, who dressed like something out of Miami Vice and acted like a slobbering St Bernard on heat. Somehow, over the past five years, he'd managed to claw his way from paparazzo photographer to celebrity fixer extraordinaire. Now Edwards controlled half the cheesy pop bands, glamour girls and reality TV stars in Britain and every tabloid journalist knew that he was a man to be kept sweet.

He was vile, of course: full of puffed-up self importance and prone to outrageous hissy fits. He was much more of a diva than any of the girls on his books. It was quite evident, to Grace at least, that he was only in it for the sex. A man as unattractive as Blaine wouldn't stand a chance with the opposite sex in the real world but, with the promise of fame at his finger-tips, he always managed to have some eighteen-year-old wannabe by his side on the red carpet. He made Grace's stomach turn, but she pretended to find him charming for the sake of her career.

Grace stood up and allowed Blaine to kiss her on both cheeks. Eurgh! As always he held her too close, for too long, and planted his damp lips too close to her mouth. He was sweating and smelled of Hawaiian Tropic and cigarettes.

'You're looking radiant as always, Grace.'

Blaine threw himself onto a wooden lounger beside her, folded his chubby arms behind his head and grinned at her. The lounger creaked under his weight.

'You're looking, erm, different,' ventured Grace.

'Ah, the hair? Do you like it?' He didn't let her answer. 'Great, isn't it? You know me, always one step ahead of the fashion pack.'

Blaine's hair had been dyed blue and sculpted into a Mohican. Needless to say, he looked ridiculous.

'Anyway, more to the point, what are *you* doing here? I was a bit surprised when Miles said you were in the neighbourhood. Didn't think Marbella was exactly your scene. I had you down as more of a culture vulture. I mean, you're far too posh for Spain, aren't you?'

'Actually, Blaine, I love Spain but you're right, Marbella is not my scene. I've rented a farmhouse in one of the white villages up in the mountains. I'm supposed to be on holiday. Not that Miles seems to have grasped that concept. I had planned to get away from the celebrity circus and spend a bit of time unwinding.'

'Ah, got some bloke tucked away up there, have you?'

Ouch! Grace flinched. Blaine had hit the nail on the head.

'No. I'm on my own. I like it that way.'

'On your own! I can't think of anything more tragic than having to spend seven days in my own company.'

I can't think of anything more tragic than spending seven days in your company, either, Blaine. But Grace bit her tongue and shrugged noncha-lantly. 'We can't all be party animals like you.'

The truth was Grace was supposed to be on holiday with McKenzie – as in McKenzie Munroe, MD of Global Media Incorporated. McKenzie owned not only Grace's newspaper but half the newspapers, magazines and TV channels in the Western World. She'd been having an affair with him for two years now and not a soul knew. Especially not McKenzie's wife. And yet, somehow the woman had telepathic powers. Every time Grace and McKenzie planned something Mrs McKenzie would suffer some kind of crisis. Usually it was a migraine when they were due to have dinner. This time it was more dramatic. McKenzie had called her at the office yesterday afternoon.

'We've got a problem,' he'd said, ominously.

'What is it this time?' Grace had demanded. 'Jean again?'

'Uh, yes; she's been in a car accident.'

'Oh God! That's dreadful. Is she OK?'

'Yes, yes, she's fine. She's got a broken collarbone and a mild concussion. It's nothing life-threatening but obviously I'll have to cancel our trip ...'

'Obviously,' Grace had replied, tartly.

An hour later the De Beers necklace had arrived by courier with a note saying, 'Sorry darling. Next time xxx'. It was in his assistant's handwriting. And so Grace was to spend the week alone in the mountains while McKenzie played the dutiful husband at the hospital bedside.

Blaine was still talking. 'Anyway, Grace, I can't wait for you to meet Jasmine. You. Are. Gonna. Love her!'

Grace raised a sceptical eyebrow. The last starlet that Blaine had promised she would love had turned out to be a monosyllabic airhead.

'Ah, come on Grace, give her a chance. She really is a lovely girl. And be gentle with her. She's a puppy and you're a fully grown Rottweiler. I've warned Miles already – none of your poison pen nonsense, OK?'

'I write as I find, that's all.' Grace smiled sweetly.

'Yeah, I saw that piece you did on Lila Rose.' Blaine sucked in his breath. 'Bet that didn't go down too well with her people.'

Grace shrugged. 'I just do my job to the best of my ability. If people don't want column inches they shouldn't hog the spotlight.'

'I agree,' Blaine nodded enthusiastically. 'If it wasn't for those column inches we'd both be out of a job, eh?' He snapped his fat fingers in the direction of the maid. '*Señorita*! Drinks! Pina Colada for me and ...' He turned to Grace.

'A sparkling mineral water, please.'

Blaine curled his top lip in disgust and mimicked Grace's cut-glass accent. '"A sparkling mineral water, please." Fucking hell, girl. You do need to unwind. We're in the Costa del Sol. Let your hair down.'

'Maybe later,' replied Grace. 'When I've finished work.'

Grace was just dreaming of the ice-cold glass of rosé she'd have the minute she filed her copy when she spotted the girl. She was walking, ever so carefully, down the wide marble steps from the house in a barely-there bikini and ridiculously high heels, carrying what appeared to be a tiny puppy. She was tall, Amazonian even, and far more athletic than the skinny little wretches Grace usually had to interview. Her long, long hair was almost black and tumbled in damp ringlets over her toned brown shoulders and down to her tiny waist. Even from a distance Jasmine Watts was seriously beautiful. Grace had spent a lot of time in the company of the beautiful (and the damned) and she knew beauty when she saw it. It struck Grace that Jasmine didn't look British. She was too tanned and too comfortable in her bikini. She was one of those perfect creatures you see on the beach, the ones who make you want to keep your kaftan on all holiday.

Grace was pretty adept at reading people on sight, but this girl was confusing. Her brown, almond-shaped eyes looked tentative, almost scared, like a wild deer eyeing a hunter's gun, and yet she'd had the nerve to come out and meet a perfect stranger in nothing but the skimpiest of bikinis. Surely most women, even the gorgeous ones, feel at their most vulnerable when they're naked. Grace's mind was working overtime as Jasmine approached. She was trying to figure out her prey. *Her good looks are her armour and her amazing body is her weapon, but she's not confident of her mind. She's trying to intimidate me with her perfect flesh before I intimidate her with my questions. And it's working. I can't think of one opening line because I'm transfixed by her beauty and beside myself with envy. What a genetic lottery that girl won. Why the hell don't I look like that?*

Blaine's grin was straining his cheeks and his eyes were open so wide that he was forgetting to blink. What a letch, thought Grace.

'Jesus fucking Christ, is she something else, or what?!' he said without taking his eyes off Jasmine for an instant.

For once, Grace had to agree with Blaine.

'Hiya,' gushed Jasmine. 'You must be Grace. I'm so very pleased to meet you.'

Jasmine's looks were pure Hollywood but her voice was still Dagenham through and through and she had an air of someone who knew her station in life – a working-class girl with respect for her elders and betters. When Grace stood up and shook her hand she could have sworn Jasmine almost curtseyed. She was really reminding Grace of someone, but she couldn't quite put her finger on whom.

'I've read all your stuff and I think you're brilliant,' Jasmine enthused. 'You must have met so many interesting people and Blaine says you're writing a book, too. That's amazing. I could never do that. All those words! Do you need a drink or anything? Are you hungry?'

Grace was taken aback. She wasn't used to celebrities treating her like a guest. She shook her head and indicated the water the maid had just handed her.

'I'm a bit peckish myself. Maria, do you think I could have a cup of tea and a biscuit or something, please? Oh, and a beer for Jimmy, thanks.'

The maid hurried off towards the house.

'Where is Jimmy?' asked Blaine impatiently, glancing back at the house. 'Miss Melrose here wants to speak to both of you, remember.'

Grace could see Jasmine blush. 'I'm really sorry, Miss Melrose. Jimmy's just coming, I promise.'

Grace shrugged. 'It's fine; I'm not in a hurry. Oh, and call me Grace, please. Miss Melrose makes me feel like a teacher.'

Grace watched closely as Jasmine smiled shyly, and then shifted uncomfortably in her seat. Every now and then the puppy – a scruffy little tan-coloured mongrel – would kiss its mistress adoringly on the lips.

'And who's this?' asked Grace, reaching out and stroking the puppy.

Jasmine's face broke into a wide smile. 'Oh, this is Annie – orphan Annie. I found her in the old town. She was a stray. We were having dinner in a restaurant and the waiters kept kicking her away. I just had to save her.'

'Jasmine would open a dog sanctuary here if Jimmy would let her,' said Blaine, rolling his eyes. 'She's a sucker for waifs and strays, aren't you, Jazz?'

Jasmine nodded. 'Don't you think animals are just *so* much nicer than people?' she asked Grace, nodding her head ever so slightly in Blaine's direction and smiling cheekily.

Grace had to stifle a laugh. 'Yes,' she agreed. 'I've met many people I'd like to have put down, but no dogs. In fact I always had dogs when I was growing up. Black Labradors. Lovely beasts.'

'I love your accent,' said Jasmine and then she blushed again. 'I mean, you talk really refined. It's lovely. Isn't it, Blaine? Her voice, it's lovely.'

'Oh yeah,' deadpanned Blaine. 'Her voice is delightful; it's her writing that's vicious.'

Grace narrowed her eyes at Blaine. 'Ignore him,' she told Jasmine. 'I'm harmless.'

'Do you have a place in Marbella?' asked Jasmine, putting Annie down on the ground.

Grace laughed. 'No, unfortunately. I just happened to be on holiday in the mountains.'

'Ooh lovely,' cooed Jasmine. 'I made Jimmy drive me up to Ronda last week.'

'Did you?' Grace couldn't keep the shock out of her voice. Imagine Jasmine Watts fancying a daytrip in the Andalusian mountains.

'It's gorgeous when you get away from the built up bit, isn't it?' Jasmine was continuing. 'I love Spain. It's funny, but I feel really at home here.

Even when the weather's bad. It rained last week and everybody else was complaining but I still love Spain. Even in the rain.'

And that was when it hit Grace. When she said 'Spain' and 'rain' with those East End vowels – the rain in Spain falls mainly on the plain – Jasmine sounded just like Audrey Hepburn in *My Fair Lady* before she learned how to talk 'proper'. Audrey Hepburn with breasts. Now there was an angle for her story.

'Oh, at last. Here's Jimmy,' said Jasmine.

They all turned to look. Jimmy Jones was male-model handsome with a chiselled jaw, high cheekbones and striking turquoise eyes. He was wearing a lightweight white shirt completely unbuttoned, khaki combat shorts and green Havaiana flip flops. His smooth, tanned skin glistened with suntan oil and his six-pack rippled as he strode towards them. Grace noticed he looked just as good in the flesh as he did on the billboards she'd seen on the Underground back in London. A little shorter than she'd expected maybe, but pretty nearly a perfect specimen. All that was missing from the ad campaign image was the megawatt smile. But Jimmy wasn't smiling now. In fact he was kind of pouting at them from beneath his floppy blonde fringe. The boy obviously took himself very seriously indeed and Grace had to stifle a giggle as he approached.

Lila Rose and her entourage were whisked off the plane before everyone else, much to Charlie's disappointment. He had been hoping for one last lingering look, perhaps even eye contact, before she walked away. But it wasn't to be. Never mind. Charlie still had plenty to be excited about. Today was the first day of the rest of his life. And from now on things were going to be a lot less eventful. Or at least, that's what he hoped.

As he stepped off the plane he could feel the strength of the Mediterranean sun on his skin and smell the sea in the air. He strode purposefully through customs, out into the departures lounge and towards his new life. In London he was known as The Char because he cleaned up everybody's mess. But here, in Spain, things were going to be different. The Char had retired. And Charlie Palmer wouldn't be cleaning up after anybody.

He knew people over here, of course. The Costa del Sol had become Essex-on-Sea over the years and now half of Chingford had second homes within spitting distance of Malaga airport. Most of them were in Marbella. That's where he would head. But where should he go first? His goddaughter was in town and he couldn't wait to see the little darling, but that should probably wait until he'd found himself somewhere to stay. He didn't want to crash at her pad tonight, much as he loved her. Charlie needed his own space.

And he'd have to pay old Frank a visit pretty pronto. He hadn't seen Frankie in years but he'd know Charlie was coming – Frank made it his business to know everybody's movements – and he'd be expecting a courtesy call at least. He'd be insulted otherwise. And you couldn't go putting Frankie's nose out of joint.

But not yet. Charlie jumped in a taxi and told the driver to take him to the Marbella Club Hotel. First he'd have a long shower, a cold drink and a walk on the beach. Yeah, a walk on the beach would clear his head.

Chapter Seven

She's been waiting in the darkness for ages. Waiting for something to happen. But when she hears his footsteps and the clunk of the lock she yearns for the silence again. As the door opens, the light blinds her, and he's nothing but a black shadow looming towards her.

'Hello darling,' he says.

His voice is so familiar and yet eerily unreal. Now she knows why she's never liked him, always been wary of him. Understands why she felt uncomfortable when he stood too close, and sickened when he kissed her hello. Warning bells had chimed. In hindsight. But this? Even in her darkest nightmares, how could she have imagined this?

The light is flooding in; his shadow is shifting, becoming a man, but there's no colour. Everything is black and white. She refuses to look at his face; she can't meet his eye. And now he's stroking her cheek, and her bare arm, and her body through her thin summer dress. Her eyes are clenched shut, hot tears are streaming down her face and still he paws her. Make him go away, Charlie! Make him go away.

Chapter Eight

Lila spotted the photographers outside her parents' drive from halfway along the street.

'What the hell are they doing here?' she exclaimed in disgust. 'How did they know I was coming? And how do they even know my parents live here? Oh God, Peter, this is awful. My poor mum and dad.'

Peter shrugged his shoulders at Lila, obviously as perplexed as she was. Lila was used to having her publicity tightly controlled by her team. The Roses were powerful people and they could afford the very best PR machine. Lila was used to it working like clockwork. She was only photographed when she needed to be – at film premiers or award ceremonies. She was not the kind of downmarket star who was 'papped' popping out for a pint of milk without her make-up. And anyway, even her staff didn't know the address. She'd sent all of them, except Peter and the driver, to a boutique hotel in the old town.

Peter hurriedly rang ahead to the house so that the gates swung open as they approached. The windows of the Mercedes were blacked out, but Lila bent forward and shielded her head just in case.

'That is so weird,' said Peter as the car flew round the corner and came to an abrupt halt.

'What?' Lila sat up.

'They didn't even look at the car,' explained Peter. 'They seemed to be watching the house next door.'

'Oh,' said Lila. 'How very strange.'

But Lila didn't have time to dwell on the matter. The minute she opened the car door, two tiny people rushed at her shouting, 'Mummy! Mummy!' And then her body was entwined with their little limbs and her face was wet from their kisses and a feeling of sheer, blissful love overwhelmed her.

Sebastian, aged seven, and Louisa, just five, had been staying with their grandparents since school broke up last week and Lila had missed them terribly. They looked tanned and healthy and Sebby's blonde hair had turned almost white in the sun. Then the children turned their attention to their darling Peter and Lila embraced her parents.

'Hello petal,' said her dad, hugging her tightly. 'How was your flight?'

'Fine, fine,' she answered. 'We were held up but we got here in one piece. Hi, Mum.'

Lila kissed her mum warmly and squeezed her hand. 'You look so well,' she said and meant it. They'd both shed years since retiring to Spain last year. At first Lila had been horrified at their insistence on moving to Marbella. She'd thought, *Marbella of all places. How terribly nouveau riche!* She'd offered to buy them a place anywhere in the world. Literally anywhere. And they'd chosen here. Eurgh! But the fact was that half of their friends from their Cheshire golf club had retired to southern Spain and the other half seemed to have time shares in the area so Lila had accepted, grudgingly, that it made sense. There was Dad's arthritis to think of and the climate did seem to suit him here. He was back playing golf every day now and her mum was having something of a second youth, shopping enthusiastically in the town's designer boutiques and booking herself in for manicures and pedicures at every opportunity. She was proud to announce that she and 'the girls' (over sixty, each and every one) were now 'ladies who lunch'.

And the villa itself was gorgeous – Lila had made sure of that, having picked it out herself. It was architect designed, on one of the most exclusive avenues in town, and it had its own private beach. Lila was delighted to see her parents enjoying their new life of leisure. God knows they'd worked hard enough over the years, her dad as an accountant and her mum a nurse. They deserved this. And what was even better was the fact that they weren't Lila Rose's parents here. Not like they had been at home, where everybody had watched Lila's rise to fame from British soap star to Hollywood wife. In Marbella, they were just plain Eve and Brian Brown from Knutsford and that's how they liked it. Lila would keep a low profile during her visit. She didn't want to blow her parents' cover.

Eve strained her neck at the Mercedes as if waiting for someone else to get out.

'Brett's not coming, Mum,' explained Lila calmly. 'Not yet, anyway. He got held up.'

'Where's Daddy?' demanded Louisa. 'You said Daddy was coming, Mummy.'

Sebby frowned. 'Daddy's not coming, Lulu.'

'But he promised!' Louisa burst into tears. 'He said!'

'What difference does that make?' replied Sebastian a little too knowingly for a seven-year-old.

'Never mind, never mind,' said their grandpa a little too chirpily. 'Let's go inside and let your mummy and Peter relax, shall we? Then we can fill them in on all our news.'

As the children disappeared into the house, Eve squeezed her daughter's hand and gave her a sad little smile. Their eyes met for a moment and Lila knew that her mother knew that her heart had been broken – again.

'Shall we tell them our biggest news now?' asked Brian, pausing by the front door with a glint in his eye.

'Go on,' said Lila, expecting some report of a mixed doubles victory at the club.

'We've got new neighbours.' He nodded his head in the direction of the twelve-foot hedge behind the house.

'Have you?' asked Lila, trying to sound suitably excited. 'What happened to the German guy? I thought you got on well with him.'

'Oh we did,' enthused Eve. 'Dieter was a lovely chap.'

'But he's defected,' Brian elaborated.

'Defected?' asked Peter.

'To the Algarve,' explained Brian. 'He says the climate's better – less hot in August – and that there is a better class of people there.'

'But anyway,' continued Eve, excitedly. 'That's not the news. The news is *who* bought Dieter's place.'

'You'll never guess,' teased Brian.

Eve and Brian grinned at each other and shared an excited little knowing look. Lila swore that her mother was almost bouncing with excitement.

'Who?' asked Peter, clapping his hands together and warming to the game.

'Oh come on, Mum,' said Lila. 'You're going to burst if you don't spit it out.'

'Jimmy Jones and Jasmine Watts!' exclaimed Eve. 'Isn't that amazing?'

Lila was dumbfounded. Her parents had met some of the best actors in the world. Their son-in-law was an Oscar winner, and yet here they were getting their knickers in a twist about some footballer moving in next door with his glamour-girl girlfriend. She looked at Pete, hoping to share an exasperated look of, *What are my parents like?* and was horrified to see that her best friend was also in raptures.

'No! Bloody! Way!' he screeched. 'How utterly chavtastic! That's better than living next door to the Beckhams.'

Oh well, thought Lila, at least that explained the paparazzi outside. As long as she kept her head down there would be no need to blow her parents' privacy.

Jasmine had relaxed into the interview and was talking, twenty to the dozen now, about how the couple had met (at Exotica, the 'upmarket' Leicester Square club where she'd danced), their first date (a WAG wedding at a

French chateau), the proposal (champagne, diamonds and fireworks on a private beach in the Maldives) and their first home (a sixteen-bedroom mansion in Hertfordshire with a moat).

Grace thanked heaven she wasn't relying on her shorthand to catch it all and prayed that the batteries didn't run out on her Dictaphone. It was pretty good stuff and Jasmine didn't sound as if she was stopping any time soon. Jimmy, meanwhile, barely said a word. He gazed out to space most of the time, seemingly uninterested in either Grace's questions or Jasmine's animated answers. Occasionally, when prompted by his fiancée, he would mumble a, 'Yeah, that's right, Jazz.' Or a 'Don't remember, babe.' He did reluctantly answer a few specific footballing questions with mono-syllabic yeses and nos, but, generally, he was mute. Mute, that is, until Grace broached the subject of Jasmine's career.

'So, where do you see your career heading?' asked Grace.

Jasmine opened her mouth to speak, but before she could answer Jimmy jumped in.

'She's not going to be getting her kit off any more once she's Mrs Jones,' he announced, patting Jasmine's bare thigh protectively.

Jasmine looked a bit surprised. 'Well, I'll still be modelling,' she said.

'No bare boobs, though,' said Jimmy adamantly.

'Right, well, we haven't really talked about it much, have we, babes?' Jasmine seemed a bit thrown.

'What's there to talk about?' asked Jimmy, removing his hand from her leg and crossing his arms. 'A married woman shouldn't be getting her tits out. It's just not right, is it? I'm not having the guys in the changing room ogling my missus, never mind the fans!'

Grace noticed Blaine shoot the 'JimJazz brand' a warning look and smiled to herself. Things were getting interesting. There was tension in the camp.

'It's what I do though, Jimmy. Isn't it? I'm a glamour model. What will I do if I don't do that?'

Jimmy shrugged. 'What do the others do?'

By others, Grace assumed he meant the other WAGs.

'They go shopping and have lunch and have their nails done,' replied Jasmine. 'I'd get bored. I'm used to working.' Jasmine was smiling sweetly at her fiancé but her tone was defiant. The girl was no walkover.

Grace watched the exchange with the zeal of a Wimbledon spectator on Centre Court.

'So write a book, design some clothes, do what Colleen does,' suggested Jimmy. 'But you're not getting your tits out anymore, OK?'

'Come on guys,' Blaine laughed nervously, trying to pretend the exchange had all been in jest. 'Let's move the conversation on, eh?'

But Grace was not about to let Blaine ruin the best bit for her. She hadn't earned her reputation as one of the most ferocious interviewers on Fleet Street by avoiding the difficult questions. She levelled her eyes at Jimmy.

'Isn't it up to Jasmine? It's her career, surely. Shouldn't she decide what she does and doesn't feel comfortable doing?'

Jimmy's eyes flashed with fury. 'I think it's none of your business,' he snapped. 'I think it's between me and my future wife.'

Grace shrugged and then turned to Jasmine. Jasmine gave her a hint of a smile and then said, 'We'll talk about it later, Jim.' But when she met Grace's gaze, it was clear that she'd been grateful for the support.

'Och, I've had enough, anyway,' said Jimmy, suddenly getting up out of his seat. 'I'm too hot. I need to cool down. I'm going for a swim.'

'Good idea!' shouted Blaine as Jimmy stripped off to his Speedos, ran towards the swimming pool and disappeared under the turquoise water with a sleek racing dive.

'Sorry,' said Jasmine quietly. 'He's just shy. He doesn't mean to be so …'

'Defensive?' suggested Grace.

Blaine shot Grace a warning look. She smiled back at him with faux innocence.

'He's not defensive.' Jasmine replied. 'He's just not very good with words, that's all.'

'Move on, Grace,' warned Blaine. Grace knew Blaine well enough to know that he would stop the interview if he saw fit so she changed the subject back to Jasmine's upbringing.

Chapter Nine

Frank Angelis lived on the most exclusive *alameda* in the most upmarket part of Puerto Banus. As Charlie drove slowly along the palm-lined avenue, he felt as if he were travelling into a postcard. The sky was a perfect, cloudless blue, and the high walls on either side of the road were pure bright white, with shocking pink bougainvillea tumbling down them. As he peered up the driveways, he noted that each villa was more elaborate than the next. Every house was different and each one seemed to have a theme – there was a Moroccan palace, a Mexican hacienda, an art nouveau house in the shape of an ocean liner, a Chinese-style pagoda and even a pyramid, for crying out loud! At the end of the drive, Charlie found 'The Gables', an enormous monstrosity of an English faux-Georgian mansion with a sweeping drive, rolling green lawn, topiary hedges and a grand fountain out front. It looked like a dolls' house on steroids. This was where Frankie lived.

Once he was buzzed through the security gate, Charlie made his way up the drive towards the house and parked at the bottom of a grand stairway. At the top of the stairs, standing on the stone terrace, in front of his porch and flanked by gigantic pillars, was Frankie Angelis. He was wearing a dark-red silk dressing gown and black leather slippers. His shock of white hair was blowing gently in the sea breeze, revealing a large bald patch. As always, Frankie puffed self-importantly on an oversized cigar. The elderly man was towered over on either side by a couple of curvy blonde bombshells in bikinis. The girls held on to an elbow each and simpered over their master in a ridiculously subservient manner. Charlie had to stifle a laugh as he got out of the jeep. He'd heard that Frankie had turned into Marbella's answer to Hugh Hefner, but seeing it with his own eyes was something else.

'Charlie, my boy!' called Frankie from his elevated position as king of the castle. 'You've aged.'

Charlie grinned. 'Yeah, Frank, happens to us all, I'm afraid. You look well, though.'

Charlie ran up the steps two at a time and offered Frankie an outstretched hand. But Frankie shook the girls off his arms and gave Charlie a bear hug instead. The old man felt stronger than he looked. He'd shrunk a little over the years, but he was still built like a brick shithouse under the silk robe. An iron fist in a velvet glove, remembered Charlie. That's how his old man had described Frank Angelis all those years ago when he'd warned Charlie never to cross him.

Frank Angelis – or 'The Angel' as he was known in the business – was an old-school gangster. He'd built up a huge empire in London during the sixties, owning and controlling nightclubs, bars and brothels, and when Charlie was growing up in the East End it had seemed that everyone he knew worked for him in some way or another – his old man included. 'The Angel' was known to be a fair boss if you did as you were told and he rewarded loyalty generously.

His dad had been unflinchingly loyal to 'The Angel' – even doing time for him once. He'd heard his mum and dad arguing about it. His mum didn't understand why his dad had to take the flack for Frankie. But his dad had just said that that was the way it was. Charlie could still see his old man now, dressed in his best suit, off to the Old Bailey for his trial. His mum had worn her favourite pink hat. Angelis had sent a taxi and when they'd climbed in, in all their glory, it had looked to Charlie as if his parents were off to a garden party at Buckingham Palace. It was the last time Charlie saw his dad in three years.

Charlie still remembered the shame of having a father in prison. The pitying looks from his teachers and the way the 'nice' kids' parents wouldn't let him play with their boys. His mum would get the bus to Wormwood Scrubs every Tuesday. She said Charlie was too young to go. When his dad finally got out, there was a new house waiting for the Palmers in the leafy Essex suburbs. It had three bedrooms, a shiny new kitchen and a lovely little garden. It was a thank you from 'The Angel'. It certainly beat their stinking little flat in Bethnal Green. 'See?' his dad had said to his mum. 'Frankie always looks after his own.'

'Hmph,' his mum had replied. She'd never been a fan of Frank Angelis.

Then, when he left school at sixteen, Charlie had found himself working for Frankie too. It was 1982 and although the City of London was booming, with yuppies flashing their cash, the rest of London – the real London – was in recession. Unemployment was at an all-time high. There were no jobs for the likes of Charlie. But Frankie Angelis offered him work as a gofer. Charlie drove Frank around, stood guard on the doors of his clubs, warned troublemakers to stay away. Charlie found he was good at his job. He had grown into a big man and people were scared of him. Frank gave him more responsibility and paid him well. Soon Charlie had nice clothes, a nippy little Golf GTI and a flat in Docklands. But these things came at a price. The first time Charlie killed a man, his hands were shaking so much that he could barely pull the trigger. The victim – a Chinese guy who'd stolen money from Frankie – was tiny and it seemed an unfair match to Charlie. But Frankie had been standing behind him, ordering him to do it, so he'd had no choice. Afterwards, Charlie had thrown up violently. He didn't sleep for days. But, after that first time, it got easier.

In time Charlie had branched out on his own, buying shares in his own clubs and restaurants, and even owning a couple of greyhounds down at Walthamstow. But until Angelis 'retired' to Spain about ten years ago (straight after the mysterious death of a young marquis in one of his clubs), Charlie had still worked for him, on and off. He'd always found it hard to say no to 'The Angel'.

Rumour had it that Frankie still controlled a couple of small brothels in Soho, but these days he had nothing like the power he'd had in his prime. Everybody knew that Frankie Angelis could never step foot on British soil again and so there was a limit to what he could do. He was an old man now. A dying breed. But Charlie still had to come and pay his respects. For old times' sake if nothing else.

Of course, Charlie knew there was very little that was angelic about Angelis. He'd been a friend of the Krays in his youth and he shared their work ethic. His only angelic quality was that, if you did him wrong, his was likely to be the last face you saw before going to meet your maker. But the Palmers had never wronged Frankie and so Charlie was greeted like a long-lost son. Frankie held Charlie at arm's length and looked him up and down.

'You're built like your father but you look just like your mother, my boy. And that's a fortunate state of affairs, let me tell you, because your old man was never much of a looker.' Frankie laughed and wheezed at the same time, blowing cigar smoke in Charlie's face as he did so. 'How he ever landed your mother continues to baffle me to this day. Such a beautiful girl, your ma; I was devastated to hear about her passing. Devastated. I'd have come over for the funeral but you know how it is, boy. I'm in exile here.' He let go of Charlie's arms and swept his hand dramatically around in the air. A huge gold sovereign ring glinted in the sunlight. 'This, my boy, is my prison and it will be my final resting place. It breaks my heart to know that I'll never see England's green pastures again.'

'Well, it certainly beats Wormwood Scrubs,' chuckled Charlie, grinning up at Frankie's mansion.

'That it does, young Charlie. That it does. Now come on through. We've got a lot of catching up to do.'

43

Charlie followed Frank and his wenches through a vast marble-floored hall with ancient swords, antique pistols and even a magnificent gold machete hung on the walls. They passed a sweeping *Gone with the Wind*-style staircase and went into an opulent lounge complete with heavy mahogany furniture, oriental rugs and an enormous, ornate fireplace. Above the fireplace was a life-sized portrait of Frankie himself dressed in full fox-hunting gear. Charlie stared at the painting in disbelief. Frank Angelis had never been fox hunting in his life!

French doors led on to another vast stone terrace with glorious views over the treetops to the sea below. Beneath the terrace was a beautiful eternity pool, designed to look like a pond. The water lapped over the edges of the wooden deck and there were several wooden platforms jutting out in the middle of the water. Everywhere Charlie looked, curvy blonde babes were sunbathing, chatting or swimming on their backs with their naked breasts thrust into the air.

'Wow! That's some pool,' said Charlie, not quite sure how to react to the sight before him.

'Yes, I wanted it to look like the men's pond on Hampstead Heath. I spent many a happy day there in my youth before the bleeding poofters took it over.'

'And so many ... um, girls!' said Charlie. He couldn't exactly ignore the fact that at least a dozen young ladies were littering the garden, but wasn't quite sure how to refer to them.

Frankie did his wheezing laugh again and grinned maniacally. 'Yes, they're lovely, aren't they? Who said money can't buy you happiness? Bloody idiot whoever he was. These gorgeous creatures are my staff. They cook, clean, bathe and comfort me. The bright ones even do my accounts. They don't speak much English – Eastern European, you see. Much less lippy than English girls, I find. And cheaper too! My friends are all dead or dying but I need young blood around me. I'm still eighteen in here.'

Frankie patted his heart and then clapped his hands loudly. All the girls turned round to look at their master.

'Say hello to my friend Charlie, girls,' he instructed.

'Hello Charlie!' they greeted him enthusiastically with thick accents.

Charlie couldn't quite believe his eyes. Every girl was practically a carbon copy of the next – blonde, long hair, blue eyes, tanned, leggy with large naked breasts. Not one looked a day over twenty-five. And a couple of them didn't look a day over fifteen. One girl was perched on the edge of the pool, slowly rubbing sun cream into her naked breasts. She stared at Charlie as she did so, with her full mouth open and her tongue licking her front teeth. Charlie felt himself blush and looked away, only to be confronted by a completely naked babe, pulling her dripping body out of the water in front of him. 'Oops,' she giggled, bending forward and giving Charlie a close-up view of her bare bum. She retrieved a tiny pair of bikini bottoms from the pool and stepped slowly back into them.

It was clear that they were here as Frankie's sex slaves – his harem – and yet they looked giddily happy with their situation. Charlie suspected that these must be the lucky ones. He knew that Frankie's involvement with brothels back home meant that he must have some control over the import of girls from Eastern Europe. Charlie looked at the beautiful creatures in front of him with their perfect figures and fine Slavic bone structure and guessed that these girls had been creamed off for the boss. Their less beautiful friends and sisters were probably imprisoned in some grotty hellhole of a brothel back in London.

The thought made Charlie's stomach churn. Oh, he'd seen it all in his time – murder, torture, blackmail – but the one thing he'd never been able to stomach was the sex trade. Young girls being bought and sold for sex? Nah, it just wasn't right.

Behind the pool was a large wooden summerhouse, painted white with a dovecote on the roof. Frankie led Charlie round the pool and into this little house. Inside was a fully stocked bar and some old-fashioned wicker garden furniture.

'Drinks please, Yana,' ordered Frankie. 'We'll have Pimm's, I think.'

Charlie was gobsmacked by Frankie's set up here in the Costa del Sol. It was like some Florida theme park styled to look like England. But not the England Charlie knew. Hell no. Or the England Frank had belonged to. They were urban men, brought up to be quick-witted and good with their fists, not to play cricket on the village green. They'd travelled by bus and Tube and black cab, not on horseback through green fields. They knew every back alleyway from Camden Town to Camberwell, but neither of them had ever stepped foot in a real stately home. This little bit of England was something straight out of Frankie's imagination. He had obviously built his own station in life, having felt that he'd missed it somewhere back home.

'And so, Charlie,' said Frankie, as Yana handed the men their drinks and another girl, Ekaterina, relit Frankie's cigar with a gold Zippo lighter. 'What exactly brings you to Marbella?'

Charlie shrugged. 'London's changed, Frank,' he explained. 'As I'm sure you know. Armed police patrolling the Tube. Russians buying Belgravia by the streetload. Kids carrying guns to school. Yardies have taken over south of the river and it's all about drugs these days. I've never been interested in drugs, Frank; you know that. London doesn't feel like home anymore. There are no real Londoners left.'

'What about Essex? Your mother and father worked hard to get you there,' Frankie reminded him.

Charlie knew that the old man was looking for gratitude and was careful not to offend him.

'I know, Frank. And I appreciate your help there. Mum and Dad were much happier once they got out of the East End. But it's not for me. Maybe if I had a wife and kids I could imagine settling down. Buckhurst Hill, maybe. Wanstead, perhaps. But I haven't got anyone but myself to look out for and, anyway, the last job I did was a bit, erm, tricky. Thought it might be best to get out altogether if you know what I mean.'

Frankie nodded solemnly and puffed on his cigar. 'So what now, my boy?'

Charlie shrugged, raised his glass of Pimm's and said, 'Sun, sea and a bit of the other if I'm lucky!'

He looked out to sea and imagined waking up to a view like that every morning. He couldn't wait to find himself a place. The bright-blue Med beat the stinking grey Thames any day of the week.

'You're not thinking of retiring, are you?' asked Frankie. It sounded more like a warning than a question and, despite the searing heat, Charlie felt a shiver go down his spine.

'You're too young to retire, Charlie. You need to keep your hand in. A man's nothing without a purpose in life.'

Charlie looked at the old man, flanked by his upmarket prostitutes, and wondered what Frankie's purpose in life was these days. He had no family. No wife to share his mansion with, no children to pass on his fortune to and no grandkids to spoil. And he had no real career left, either. He wasn't considered a big player anymore. No one back home thought of him as anything but a dinosaur. OK, so he still had his fingers in a few pies, but that was only because the real power players allowed him to do so out of some sort of respect for his age and his standing in the old days. He was something of a laughing stock, if the truth be known. Frankie Angelis and his ilk were exactly the reason why Charlie wanted out. He didn't want to spend his old age like this. He wanted a clean break. He wanted to meet a nice girl, settle down, have kids, maybe even try a proper job for once. But Charlie knew that Frankie wouldn't understand.

'I don't know what will happen in the future, Frankie,' said Charlie thoughtfully. 'But for now, I just need a break.'

Frankie pulled hard on his cigar so that the tanned skin above his thin top lip puckered like old leather. His left hand stroked his neck where

46

Charlie noticed a large port wine stain in the shape of a heart. Frankie stared at Charlie with watery grey eyes and said sternly, 'That's a shame. I had a favour to ask you.'

Oh no, thought Charlie, his heart sinking. *Here it comes.* Frankie was about to offer him a job. And he knew what that meant. Charlie had always lived by his instincts and his instincts now were telling him to run. But, of course, he couldn't.

'I'm not working, Frankie,' said Charlie, trying to remain respectful to the old man but sticking to his guns nonetheless.

'Oh, it's just a small job, Charlie, my boy,' insisted Frankie. 'Wouldn't take you long. I'd make it worth your while. I could set you up with a nice pad round here if you like.'

Charlie was blown away. A place round here cost a few million; this was not going to be a small job. But even the lure of a luxury villa wasn't going to change his mind. He had his own money. He'd buy himself a nice apartment.

'No, honestly Frankie. I'm not up for any jobs, even small ones.'

'Come on, Charlie. You wouldn't want to offend me, now, would you? What would your poor dead father say about that?'

He'd say, 'Be careful, boy. Iron fist in a velvet glove, remember.' Charlie cursed himself for even coming here. What did he expect would happen?

'No, really, Frank. I'm sorry. But I'm not interested.'

Frankie's eyes remained steadily set on Charlie for a few moments longer. Charlie shifted uncomfortably and took a sip of his drink. And then, at last, Frankie seemed to relax.

'Oh well, never mind,' he said chirpily. 'I've got plenty of time to work on you. You'll get bored soon enough.'

And then he laughed his wheezing laugh, slapped Charlie on the back and grinned. A gold tooth glistened in a shaft of sunlight breaking through the windows of the summerhouse. Charlie felt slightly relieved, but he knew that the matter hadn't been dropped altogether. This problem would rear its ugly head again soon and Charlie would have to be prepared next time.

'So, what are your immediate plans then, Charlie?' asked Frankie.

'Well, first I'm going to see my goddaughter ...'

'Ah, yes. Doing rather well for herself, I see,' said Frankie with a glint in his eye. 'Lovely-looking girl, isn't she?'

Charlie nodded, but he felt uncomfortable at the thought of Angelis admiring his goddaughter.

'She never liked me, mind you,' Frank continued. 'Her father poisoned her mind against me at a young age.'

Charlie smiled, thinking about his best mate and his elevated moral standards. 'Yeah well, Kenny always was a good boy, Frankie. Didn't approve of us lawbreakers.'

'I never understood why you wasted your time with him, Charlie. A talented boy like you hanging out with that lily-livered ponce.'

'He was the closest thing I ever had to a big brother,' explained Charlie. 'He started looking out for me when I was still in nappies.'

'Still, shame about what happened to him, eh?' continued Frankie, not looking at all remorseful. 'Cancer, wasn't it?'

Charlie nodded, reluctant to elaborate on his poor dead best friend with the likes of Frankie Angelis. It still hurt to think about it, even now.

'And what the hell happened to that sister of his?' demanded Frankie, becoming animated. 'She was a right little cracker, I remember, and then she lost her bleeding marbles, didn't she?'

Charlie shrugged. 'She's doing all right,' he said gently. 'Anyway, Frank ...' Charlie stood up and drained his glass. 'I must be off.'

'So soon?' asked Frankie. He looked genuinely disappointed and Charlie found himself wondering if he had many guests, other than his girls, of course.

As Charlie drove away from the Angelis madhouse he glanced back in his rear-view mirror. Frankie Angelis stood on his steps, waving regally with Yana and Ekaterina on either side. It was a sight Charlie never wanted to see again.

Chapter Ten

Jasmine was in full swing now. She'd seemed grateful for Grace's support earlier, when Jimmy had got annoyed about her stripping. Since then, with Jimmy gone, Jasmine had been more than willing to answer Grace's probing questions. Even better, Blaine had rushed off to take a 'very important business call' and had left the women to it.

'Probably about *Big Brother*,' explained Jasmine, rolling her eyes. 'He's trying to get control of the contestants as they come out of the house. It'll be a big money spinner if it comes off.'

I bet it will, mused Grace. Then she turned her attention back to the glamour model. 'So Jasmine, is it true your mum was a prostitute?'

Jasmine nodded a little sheepishly and blushed beneath her tan. 'Well, it's no secret, is it?' she replied quietly. 'It's been all over the papers that my mum was on the game.'

'And she had problems with drugs?'

Jasmine chewed her bottom lip and stared above Grace's head. Her jaw was set firmly but her eyes were watery and Grace could tell that the subject upset the girl. 'Yes, she did have a bit of a drug problem for a while. Heroin and crack. But that really wasn't her fault – the pimps get their girls hooked so they can control them. Anyway, she's clean now. We sent her to the Priory,' said Jasmine, levelling her eyes at Grace. 'Jimmy paid for it. He's good like that. A family man.'

'It must have been pretty tough for you, growing up under those circumstances,' Grace suggested.

'Well yeah …' agreed Jasmine uncertainly. 'We didn't have any money and I suppose we were the lowliest family in the flats, you know? The kids at school used to say I smelled. And I probably did, because my mum never used to bath us or anything. It wasn't until I was older – twelve maybe – that I started to get really paranoid about it.' She leaned forward and whispered in true confessional style, 'I'm really not proud of this but I used to shoplift Impulse from the chemist on the high street so that I smelled nice. I still like smelling nice now.' Jasmine held her delicate wrist under Grace's nose. 'Do you like that?' she asked earnestly.

Grace nodded. Funnily enough, Jasmine smelled of jasmine.

'I didn't steal that, by the way,' she grinned. 'I can buy my own now.'

'So how did you get out of that situation? It can't have been easy,' continued Grace.

'Well, the only thing I had going for me – and I'm not being big-headed or anything – but the only thing I had was my looks. Men always liked me, you know? So what were my choices? There was no way I was going on the game like my mum, so when my stepdad suggested stripping I thought, why not?'

'Your stepfather?' Grace interjected in dismay. Her own father had been sorely disappointed when she'd decided against studying law. He'd thought tabloid journalism was sleazy, never mind stripping!

Jasmine nodded. 'Yeah … well, no. He's not actually my stepdad 'cos he's never got round to marrying Mum, but they've been together for years and he always lived with us. Not that Mum let the social know that, of course. If they'd known Terry was living with us we'd have lost the flat.'

Grace had done her research and knew this was a new angle. Jasmine hadn't talked about her family's involvement in her career before. Nor had she mentioned this Terry. Who was this boyfriend who'd pushed a schoolgirl into stripping? It was time to go fishing.

'Didn't you think that was a bit odd?' asked Grace, gently. 'Most fathers try to discourage their daughters from taking their clothes off.'

Jasmine was distracted. The puppy had jumped on to her lap and was licking her face enthusiastically. 'Get off, Annie!' she half-squealed, half-laughed. 'Your paws are sharp! Sorry, Grace, what were you saying?'

'Your mum's boyfriend,' Grace continued. 'Terry. He sounds quite an unconventional father figure.'

'Annie!' spluttered Jasmine, between canine kisses. 'I'm trying to talk to Grace. Sorry Grace, um, yeah, Terry. Not exactly conventional, no. There's nothing conventional about Terry Hillma—'

Suddenly Jasmine was quiet. Her wide eyes became wider still and she bit her bottom lip hard. It was obvious to Grace that she'd said too much. The word hung heavily in the air. Hillman. That's what she'd been about to say. Terry Hillman. Grace could feel her heart pounding in her chest. This was priceless. Jasmine's 'stepdad' was Terry bloody Hillman!

'Terry Hillman, as in Sean and Terry Hillman?' asked Grace, trying to hide her excitement. 'As in the Hillman brothers?'

Jasmine placed the puppy back on the ground and stared at her feet. 'Yeah, not exactly something I'm proud of,' she muttered.

Oh. My. God! thought Grace. The notorious Hillman brothers had been well known in the local press as bully-boy Essex gangsters when Grace was a fledgling reporter on a London newspaper. They'd been pretty big news – especially when Sean turned up murdered about ten years ago. Even the nationals covered that. Grace tried to remember the details – the body was dumped in Epping Forest, single bullet wound to the chest; no one was ever charged over the incident. Since then, Terry Hillman had been much quieter. This was a huge story. Why had no one picked up the link between Jasmine Watts and the Hillmans? Grace could see her front-page splash already – what a scoop!

'I'd rather you didn't print anything about that, actually,' said Jasmine, looking up at Grace. Her eyes were pleading.

Grace nodded, but her heart was still racing. This was such a great angle. She wouldn't be able to let it slide.

'Terry's not a very nice man really,' Jasmine added, quietly. 'He's treated my mum really badly and he's never wanted me around.'

'Because you're not his biological daughter?' asked Grace.

Jasmine shrugged. 'Maybe. But then I'm not actually related to any of them. I'm adopted. My mum and dad couldn't have kids of their own and my dad loved kids, so he was desperate for a baby. My mum says she wasn't really bothered, but that the council always gave the best flats to families with children, so that's where I came in. Then, when I was still really little, my mum started seeing Terry and she kicked my poor dad out.'

'How old were you?' asked Grace gently.

Jasmine shrugged, 'About two, I think. I don't really remember. Then my mum and Terry started having their own kids. There's Bradley – he's twenty-one; Jason's nineteen and Alisha's sixteen. But Alisha isn't Terry's because Alisha's black. I think her dad might be Junior, Mum's old pimp, but Mum's not entirely clear on that point. Like I said, my mum and Terry have a very on/off relationship. Terry's got loads of other kids by different women.' She took a sip of her tea and looked Grace in the eye. 'I bet your family's a bit neater than mine, eh?' she teased.

Grace grinned, 'Yup, Mum and Dad, me, my big brother, the dogs and the ponies. Life's tough on the mean streets of Godalming! Embarrassingly middle class, I'm afraid.'

Jasmine's gorgeous face broke into a grin. 'No, that's good. That's what I'd want for my kids. I mean, look at my little sister. Alisha's only just got her braces off and she's already got a baby of her own. A little girl called Ebony. She's a lovely little thing, but it's not right, is it? What chance has she got?'

'Maybe your success will give Alisha a boost,' suggested Grace.

'Maybe,' said Jasmine. 'I mean, I've bought my mum a house away from the estate. But all Alisha's mates are there so she just keeps going back.

Now she says she wants to be a glamour model too, but I'm not sure she's got the right look.' Jasmine sighed. 'Anyway, we're a bit of a mixed bag.'

Grace nodded. She thought again of her own smugly affluent upbringing – boarding school, skiing holidays and ponies – and felt suddenly guilty. 'And you said it was Terry Hillman who encouraged you to start, erm, stripping?' Grace asked.

'Yeah, he did me a favour, I suppose. When I was sixteen I got a job at a club that belonged to his boss. It was pretty seedy, looking back, but everyone's got to start somewhere.'

'And then your career really took off?'

'Uh huh, I got spotted by an agent from Exotica, which is really up-market; only the best girls work there and loads of celebrities come in.'

'Ooo, which ones, tell me ...' begged Grace.

Jasmine giggled naughtily. 'Well, all the footballers, obviously; that's how I met Jimmy. But Hollywood actors too – I once did a private dance for Brett Rose, no kidding!'

'Really? Can I print that?' asked Grace, wondering what Lila Rose would think of this piece of gossip.

'I guess so,' said Jasmine. 'It's no big deal, is it? It's only a man appreciating a woman. They all do it.'

'Do they?' asked Grace, thinking about McKenzie and trying to imagine him in a strip joint. Surely not!

'Well, they might not all go to places like Exotica, but men ogle women all day every day. Watch them next time you're on the beach. If a hot girl in a tiny bikini walks past all the men will have to turn over and lie on their fronts. It's human nature.'

'So, don't you believe in true love?' asked Grace. 'I always thought that you should marry a man who's only got eyes for you.'

'Oh please,' scoffed Jasmine. 'True love, yes, but no man is going to stop *lusting* after other women.'

Grace laughed. Jasmine was pretty insightful, really. Not the bimbo she'd expected at all

'Even Jimmy?' asked Grace, intrigued.

'Even Jimmy. He was eyeing you up when you arrived.'

'He was?' Grace felt her cheeks burning, but she couldn't help feeling quite pleased. Jimmy was an idiot – but a very good-looking idiot all the same. She tried to regain her composure. 'But you're famously lusted after by practically every man in the country. That must give you a certain confidence that every woman Jimmy looks at is going to pale in comparison to you.'

Jasmine blushed and shrugged her shoulders. 'I don't know. There are loads of pretty girls out there. I'm not that special. And anyway, good looks aren't all they're cracked up to be. They can get you into trouble too. Attract the wrong type of men, you know? Of course you know; you're not exactly ugly, are you?'

Grace thought of McKenzie. Yes, she was perfectly capable of attracting the wrong type of men – married men.

'So, are you married?' Jasmine suddenly asked Grace, as if she were a mind reader.

Grace shook her head.

'Never met the right man?'

Grace grinned. 'Oh, it's not that. I've met the right man a couple of times. It's just he's always been married to someone else.'

That made Jasmine laugh. 'Sorry, I shouldn't laugh, should I?' she said. 'It must be horrible always being the girlfriend, never the bride.'

'No!' said Grace, looking at Jasmine incredulously. 'Sometimes being the girlfriend is good. I get the best bits – the romantic dinners, the weekends in Paris, the great sex. The wife gets the dirty socks, the tax returns and the bad moods. And anyway, if he's just a boyfriend you can change your mind. Once you're married, it's a real headache to get rid of a man.'

'I'll never want to get rid of my Jimmy,' insisted Jasmine.

'How do you know? How can you be so sure he's "the one"?'

Jasmine wrinkled her nose. 'I just do. He's everything I ever dreamed of. Anyway, if I don't marry Jimmy some other girl will snap him up. If I've learned one thing in life it's this – you've got to get that ring on your finger. Nobody takes a girlfriend seriously, but a wife? A wife's got power.'

'You really believe that?' asked Grace. 'But you've got money and a career in your own right. Doesn't that give you power?'

Jasmine shrugged. 'A bit, I suppose. But it's all thanks to Jimmy. I only got famous because I was Jimmy Jones's girlfriend. I'd still be stripping at Exotica if I hadn't met him. I'd be nothing without him.'

'I don't think that's true,' said Grace. 'I think you're selling yourself short.'

'You do?' Jasmine looked surprised.

'Yes, I do. And I mean this as a compliment from one professional woman to another, but you're a really warm-hearted, interesting and, well, for want of a better word, nice young woman,' said Grace. 'I'm sure you'd do well in any career you set your mind to, no matter who your boyfriend is. You don't *need* a man. A nice guy should just be a bonus in life.'

Jasmine smiled and blushed at the same time. 'Thanks, Grace,' she said. 'Nobody's ever said anything like that to me before.' And then she laughed again and added, 'But I'm still marrying Jimmy.'

'Well, he is pretty cute,' conceded Grace.

'And even though you say it's not what you want, I really hope you meet your perfect man one day. Your perfect unmarried man. Every girl deserves to be a bride.'

Grace grinned. 'I'll bear that in mind,' she said, not meaning it one bit, and then she continued with the interview.

Blaine returned, looking even more puffed up and pleased with himself than usual and sat back down with the women.

'So, Jasmine, what do you think you'd have done if you hadn't become a glamour model?' asked Grace, genuinely interested now.

'Oh, I was never going to amount to much with my background,' she scoffed. 'I did all right at school but my mum made me leave as soon as they'd let me so that I could start earning money. We needed food on the table and, let's face it, I was never going to go to Oxford bleeding University, was I?'

She laughed at the thought. But Grace had gone to Oxford, and she'd met lots of girls there who were a lot less savvy than Jasmine Watts.

Jasmine started laughing at a fond memory. 'When I was little my dad used to say I should be on the stage. But I don't think he meant with a pole between my legs! Bless him. He'd have been horrified if he'd seen how I'd turned out.'

'I bet he wouldn't,' said Grace. 'I bet he'd have been very proud of you.'

Jasmine's lovely face broke into a smile. 'I suppose so. My dad was an absolute star, you know. A real gentleman. Nothing like most blokes you meet. One in a million. Always the way, isn't it? The good die young and all that. I was just lucky to have him, even if it didn't last long.'

Grace felt bad for scoffing at Jasmine earlier. She'd never met anyone with such a troubled upbringing before and yet the girl seemed cheerful, warm-hearted, optimistic even. 'How did he die?' she asked.

'Cancer. Mercifully quick, really. He was diagnosed in the summer and dead by Christmas. I guess it's just one of those things. I was thirteen. That was the worst Christmas of my life.'

'It must have been,' said Grace, softly. 'You said already that you're not very close to your mum so it must have been really difficult for you when you lost your dad.'

'Oh, I was gutted. We all were. Especially my Auntie Juju. She's my dad's sister. Her name's Julie, but we call her Juju. She's a bit ...' Jasmine made a face.

'A bit what?' probed Grace, sensing a story.

'Oh, nothing. She just suffers from her nerves, that's all. My dad used to look after her so after he died she was lost, you know? He was her big brother. She says she was lucky to have him. Even says he still looks after her now. She has conversations with him and everything.' Jasmine laughed but her eyes looked sad.

'Are you close to your siblings?' asked Grace.

'My brothers are a pain in the butt. They're always in trouble but I suppose I do love them,' Jasmine continued. 'And my sister – she's a right one! Alisha gets her kit off more than I do and she's not even paid for it! I'm really worried about how my family will behave at the wedding. I mean, Victoria and David are meant to be coming and I can't have Bradley and Jason chatting up Posh, can I?' She rolled her eyes and grinned mischievously. 'I did think about not inviting them, but can you imagine what my mum would say when she saw the pictures in the newspapers?'

Jasmine laughed and then added quickly. 'But don't print that. I don't want to hurt their feelings. And anyway, they'd beat the living daylights out of me!'

Grace didn't doubt it for a second.

'Who's walking you down the aisle?' asked Grace. 'Terry?'

'God no!' scoffed Jasmine. 'I haven't even invited him. No, Charlie's doing it. My godfather. He was my dad's best friend and he's really looked out for me since my dad died. He's a really successful businessman too. And dead handsome. He'll do me proud at the wedding.'

'So, what *are* your plans for the wedding?' Grace started digging.

'Well, I can't really say anything about that because of the exclusive we've signed, but I can promise you this: it will be bigger and better and glitzier and sparklier than any wedding that's ever gone before. A proper fairytale do.' Then Jasmine smiled warmly at Grace. 'You should come!' she announced. 'To the wedding.'

'Me?' replied Grace, completely taken aback.

'Her?' spluttered Blaine, choking on his cocktail.

Grace ignored him. 'But I thought the magazine had the exclusive.'

'No, I don't mean as a journalist,' said Jasmine. 'I mean as a guest. You can leave the Dictaphone at home.'

'Damn right she can,' muttered Blaine.

Right on cue Prince Charming reappeared, dripping with pool water. 'Are we finished?'

It was more of a statement than a question. And when Blaine nodded Grace knew her time was up. She turned off her Dictaphone. It was fine; she'd got plenty from Jasmine and although Jimmy hadn't said much, his behaviour had given Grace more ammunition than he'd ever realise.

'Think I might have a swim too,' said Blaine. 'Excuse me, ladies.' He waddled towards the house and Jimmy dived back into the pool.

Grace watched the boy in the pool. It seemed evident to her that he still had a great deal of growing up to do.

'Are you going to have children straight away?' she asked Jasmine after a while.

Jasmine opened her mouth to answer but was interrupted by a loud whooping noise and the thwack of bare feet running on wet tiles. With that, Blaine Edwards careered back into view, resplendent in a fluorescent pink thong, hairy beer belly wobbling as he dive-bombed into the pool, splashing the girls as he did so.

'Oi, what the fuck are you doing, fatso?' yelled Jimmy, jumping on Blaine's head and dunking him under the water.

'Sorry, what did you say?' asked Jasmine.

'Children. Are you going to have children yet?'

Jasmine stared at the grown men fighting in the pool and shook her head. 'No. Not for ages. I think I've got enough kids to deal with at the moment.'

As she was gathering her things to leave Jasmine said quietly to Grace, 'There is one thing I'd like to do.'

'Oh, what's that?'

'I sing,' whispered Jasmine. 'I'd like to be a world-famous singer one day. But I don't want Blaine to know. I like singing classy stuff. Billie Holliday. Eva Cassidy. That sort of thing. Not the kind of poppy nonsense he likes. But don't print that. Please. For now, the singing's just for me. I'll do it in my own time and my own way. I just wanted you to know that there's more to me than a pair of boobs.'

'I can see that,' said Grace and as she leaned forward to kiss the crown princess of Marbella goodbye she found herself hoping that all Jasmine's dreams would come true.

'I'll see you at the wedding!' called Jasmine as Grace climbed into her car.

Wow. So Jasmine had meant it. Grace was going to the wedding of the year! She couldn't help feeling more than a little excited by the prospect. As she waited for the electric gates to release her from Jimmy Jones's villa, she noticed a small group of paparazzi on the pavement opposite. Tipped off by Blaine, no doubt. She felt a wave of sympathy for Jasmine. How awful to live your life in a goldfish bowl, having to reveal your secrets to journalists and being photographed endlessly. Grace made her living revealing other people's secrets, but she kept her own very close to her chest.

As she left Villa Amoura she spotted a black jeep waiting to be let in. The top was down and the driver – a man who looked to be in his late thirties – was clearly visible. He had very short dark hair, was well built, broad-shouldered and handsome, ever so handsome, in an old-fashioned Charlton Heston kind of way. He wasn't Grace's usual type at all. She normally found herself involved with charismatic media men who tended to be skinny and cerebral rather than conventionally handsome (not to mention married). No, this guy was pure beefcake. But Grace found she couldn't stop staring and when the gates eventually opened she drove away rather reluctantly.

Chapter Eleven

Frank Angelis sat at his desk, staring at the figures on the papers before him. However hard he looked, they just didn't add up. He needed money and he needed it now. The Russian wouldn't wait any longer. Yana entered the study with the whiskey he'd ordered. She placed the crystal tumbler down on the desk and began rubbing Frankie's shoulders with her long, nimble fingers. He shrugged her off.

'Fuck off, Yana,' he grunted. 'I'm not in the mood. Now, piss off and leave me alone.'

Yana pouted, like a little girl who'd been told off by her beloved grandpa, and slunk out of the room, closing the door behind her.

Frankie was alone with his problem. And it was a big fucking problem. If Charlie wouldn't do the job for him, he was stuffed. He'd have to work on Charlie. He was sure he could convince him. The Palmers had always been walkovers. Far too nice to be in this game, that was their problem.

And if Charlie wouldn't do it? Well, there were always ways of making money quickly. Frankie had never been beaten before. And he wouldn't give up this time without a fight.

'There's a Mr Palmer at the gate,' said Maria uncertainly. 'He says he's family.'

'No way! That's brilliant! It's Charlie!' Jasmine screamed and charged towards the drive at full speed. If there was one person in the world Jasmine was always, *always* delighted to see it was her godfather.

He'd barely had time to get out of the jeep before she'd thrown her arms around his neck and planted a soggy kiss on his smooth cheek. His body felt as strong and warm and comforting as it had done when she was a little girl.

'What a brilliant surprise. I can't believe you're here. God, it is so bloody good to see you, Char.'

Jasmine looked around excitedly for Jimmy. He was sitting on the side of the pool.

'Jimmy! Jimmy! Look who's here! It's Charlie. Isn't that amazing?'

'Amazing,' said Jimmy, but he didn't look particularly amazed. Jasmine frowned. Jimmy was in a funny mood today. First he'd been stroppy with her during the interview and now he was being offish with Charlie. What was up with him? He wandered with no great urgency towards them. Jasmine gave Charlie another hug. She always felt so safe when he was around.

'Calm down, Jazz,' warned Jimmy. 'Give the man some air.'

'All right, Jimboy?' asked Charlie cheerfully, holding his big hand out. If he'd noticed Jimmy's standoffishness he wasn't letting on.

'Never better,' said Jimmy. 'What are you doing out of London?'

'Thinking about retiring out here, actually.'

'Really?' Jimmy looked surprised.

'Really?' asked Jasmine. 'Wow. That's brilliant. We can see you whenever we're here and we're going to be here all summer ... apart from the wedding and the honeymoon obviously and ... God, this is great. Are you staying with us?' asked Jasmine, hoping he'd say yes.

'No, darling, I've booked myself into the Marbella Club for now,' explained Charlie. 'Thought you two lovebirds might need some space before the big day. I'll probably start looking for somewhere to rent tomorrow. Just thought I'd drop by and see how my favourite girl's doing.'

'I'm great,' grinned Jasmine. 'Come on. Let me show you around. Jimmy, can you get Charlie a drink please?'

'Martini please, Jim,' said Charlie.

Jasmine heard Jimmy muttering, 'Who does he think he fucking is? James Bond?' as he went and hoped Charlie hadn't heard it too. She would have to have a word with Jimmy in private later. Something was obviously bothering him today.

'Lovely pad,' enthused Charlie. 'You've done so well, darling. I'm really proud of you.'

Jasmine felt a warm glow inside. It meant a lot to her to know that Charlie was proud of her. He'd been like a second father over the years. Her dad, Kenny, had been the most loving and kind man in the world and when he'd died Charlie had stepped right into his shoes, always looking after Jasmine when times got rough. He could handle anything.

'Come and meet Blaine. He's our new manager.' Jasmine led Charlie by the hand towards the mahogany deck that stretched across the back of the villa. Blaine was lounging on a steamer chair with a cocktail glass resting on his hairy, fat tummy.

The two men shook hands amicably and agreed with each other that the view was truly magnificent. Jasmine gazed across the sloping terraces towards the glistening blue sea beyond and grinned to herself. Sometimes she just couldn't believe her own luck.

'Thanks baby,' said Jasmine, when Jimmy reappeared with the drinks. 'You OK?'

'Me?' replied Jimmy a little coldly. 'There's nothing wrong with me.'

But clearly there was. What had happened to change his mood? Had he had another one of those phone calls? Lately he'd been having secret little conversations on his mobile. It was always the same: he'd take himself off somewhere and she'd just hear hushed little snatches of conversations. Afterwards, Jimmy was always jumpy and distant, but when Jasmine asked who he'd been speaking to he just said, 'It's business,' and walked off. But what business could Jimmy be doing? His contract wasn't up for another two seasons.

'So, Jasmine, tell me,' Charlie was saying. 'Who was that I just saw leaving?'

Jasmine dragged herself back into the moment. 'Ooh, that was Grace Melrose. She's a journalist.'

'She's a right fucking wee madam,' retorted Jimmy.

'Oh, she was nice enough,' said Jasmine. 'You just don't like journalists.'

Jimmy scowled.

'I don't like journalists, either,' announced Charlie. 'Far too keen to get to the bottom of things. They don't understand the art of keeping secrets.'

'So Char,' said Jasmine, swiftly changing the subject. 'Are you up for a party?'

Charlie shrugged. 'What's on offer?'

'We've got some friends coming over and then we're going to the opening of a new club. It's on a ship in the marina. Maxine de la Fallaise is hosting it!'

'Oh really?' Charlie looked interested. 'I've seen her in the papers. Do you know her?'

Jasmine nodded proudly. 'I've met her a few times at parties and stuff. She's a brilliant laugh. It'll be a fab night.'

'Well, why not, eh? I could do with letting my hair down.'

Jasmine looked at Charlie's newly shaved head and grinned.

'You haven't got any hair left to let down!'

Just then Charlie's mobile rang. He frowned at the number and then said, 'Excuse me, I'd better get this.' He walked away.

Jasmine watched him standing by the pool and she could tell it was bad news. She had a horrible feeling that Charlie wouldn't be coming out with them that night after all.

'Has something come up?' she asked as he returned.

He nodded. 'Sorry, sweetheart, but I've got some calls to make. Just some unfinished business back in London. I'd better get back to the hotel and sort it. I'll give you a call in the morning. Maybe I could take you out for lunch.'

'That would be lovely,' said Jasmine, trying not to show her disappointment that he was leaving so soon. It had always been like that. He'd arrive, cheer her up and then some crisis or other would take him away from her again. Once he'd disappeared for two whole years. He'd told her he'd been doing business in America but in hindsight, she guessed he'd probably been banged up. She'd never actually known what it was exactly Charlie did for a living, but she suspected it wasn't entirely kosher. Not that it mattered. Jasmine knew Charlie didn't have a bad bone in his body, whatever the law said.

Shit! Shit! Shit! Charlie's head was in an awful mess. His first few hours in Spain were not going entirely to plan. First Frankie Angelis had propositioned him and now Gary had been on the blower saying that Nadia was missing. Missing? How the hell could she go missing since lunchtime? That's what he'd demanded of Gary.

'I, I, I dunno, boss,' Gary had stammered, obviously shaken by the afternoon's events. 'When I got back to the flat she was going out. I didn't even get a chance to tell her you'd left the fucking country! She just shouted "Ciao!" and jumped in a black cab.'

And that's when Charlie had got really nervous. Nadia didn't take black cabs. She had her own limo and driver. Her father insisted.

'Was anybody with her?' Charlie had asked Gary, desperately.

'There was some bloke in the taxi already. I couldn't see his face. Just the back of his head. He had dark hair. That's all I noticed.'

'Did she seem upset?' Charlie had persevered, trying to find something that would make sense of Nadia's disappearance.

'No, boss. She was quite chirpy and all dressed up to the nines like usual. I didn't really think nothing of it but then, a couple of hours later, I'm about to get in the motor when two massive Russian geezers jump me,' Gary had continued. 'They beat the fucking shit out of me, Char. I was bricking myself. They kept asking where Nadia was and where you were and what we'd done with her. They said she's not answering her phone. They said that Mr Dimitrov is not a happy man. I'm scared, Char. I'm really fucking scared. Those Russians are heavy duty, boss. They think we've hurt Nadia. We shouldn't be messing with them.'

'We're not, Gary,' Charlie had tried to reassure the boy. 'There's just been some sort of mix up. I'll sort it out.'

Charlie had sent Gary back to his mum's house. He was only a kid and this wasn't his mess. Mind you, it wasn't exactly Charlie's mess, either. Nadia hadn't even known he was leaving the country. But her father would know that by now and how would it look? His daughter goes missing and Charlie jumps on a plane to Spain. How the fuck did this happen?

Charlie stood on his balcony and listened to the sound of the waves below. The wind had picked up and the sea was choppier than it had been before. It was almost dark now and the beach was all but deserted. He thought of Nadia's cheeky little smile and trusting wide-set eyes and hoped to God that nothing bad had happened to her. But Mr Dimitrov was a very wealthy man and his daughter had a high price on her head. Charlie would never have done anything to hurt her, but there were plenty of others that would.

His brain raced. How could he fix this? How could he keep Gary safe? How could he let Dimitrov know that this had nothing to do with him? How could he help find Nadia?

Shit! Be banged his fist hard on to the balcony rail. Why was life so fucking complicated? Charlie stared into the half-light of dusk. The waves were crashing on to the beach, swallowing up the day's sandcastles. Charlie watched for a while, in awe of the sea's power. He would fix this mess. Somehow. He wasn't quite sure how, but somehow he'd straighten it all out. It was his job, after all.

He took a deep breath and called McGregor. It was not something he wanted to do; he didn't like asking anybody for help, but McGregor always knew what was going on in London. Perhaps he'd heard something about Nadia.

'McGregor,' said Charlie when the DCI answered the phone. 'It's Char.'

'Oh, oh, right,' said McGregor. He sounded wary.

'Listen, I could do with your help with something. Somebody's gone missing and—'

Before he could get the words out, McGregor jumped in.

'It's not a good time,' he replied brusquely. 'I can't talk to you right now.'

And then the phone went dead. Just like that. Charlie stared at his phone in disbelief. This was a man he'd just killed for. 'Tosser,' he muttered to himself. It wasn't the first time he'd learned that when the shit hit the fan he was on his own.

And so the beautiful Princess Jasmine sits in her shimmering palace above the Mediterranean waiting to be crowned Queen of the WAGs. And this really is a true fairytale, complete with a real wicked stepfather. For the first time we can exclusively reveal that Jasmine Watts's mother, Cynthia Watts, is the common-law wife of Terry Hillman, the notorious Essex gangster ...

Grace was sitting on the terrace of her mountaintop villa, enjoying a generous glass of rosé in the fading afternoon sun and tampering with her copy before she emailed it to Miles. She read over what she'd written one last time.

Grace stared at the words and remembered what she'd promised Jasmine. Usually she'd have no qualms about printing anything a celebrity said, so why did she feel so guilty? Her finger hovered over the 'send' button but she couldn't quite bring herself to press it.

'Oh, bugger it,' she said to herself and then she highlighted and deleted the paragraph about Terry Hillman. What did it matter if she didn't print that bit? No one would know she'd ignored one of the best scoops of her career. She was just keeping a promise to a young girl with a dream. A girl who'd been kind enough to invite her to her wedding. And she did so want to go to that wedding. There was no way a gold-embossed invitation would pop through her door if she printed the stuff about Hillman. Anyway, the wedding would be a good networking opportunity. She was just thinking about her job. It wasn't as if she was losing her touch. Grace Melrose was not going soft.

Chapter Twelve

Lila had always been a strong swimmer. As a child her parents had called her their 'little mermaid' because she practically lived at the local swimming baths. She'd even swum for the county as a teenager. Of course she had a private pool now in London, and she used it every day, but there was nothing Lila loved more than swimming in the sea. It was the thing she missed most about the Malibu beach house – its proximity to the ocean. And so, as soon as she'd unpacked, she'd walked down the steep steps to her parents' private beach and thrown herself into the glittering, turquoise sea. The cold water had taken her breath away at first, but quickly the waves had begun to soothe her.

Lila didn't look around at the view, or bask lazily on her back. Instead she threw herself into a powerful front crawl. As she swam she began to feel invigorated, strong, alive. Her heart pounded as her arms forced their way through the water and her head buzzed with thoughts of her husband. The more she swam, the more optimistic she felt. Maybe he was telling the truth. Perhaps there was an important meeting. Lila knew it wasn't easy being Brett Rose, megastar. Everybody wanted a piece of him and it was hard to keep them all happy. OK, so maybe he took her for granted and it did sometimes feel as though he was putting her last. But what was that saying? You can please some people some of the time but you can't please all the people all the time? Something had to give. Brett knew Lila and the kids would always be there for him because they loved him. And so he made them wait. Directors and producers only loved him while the box office takings were up and so he had to keep them sweet and make sure he landed the next big role. There was no shortage of hot, young actors snapping at his heels.

And it was difficult for him to get away from LA. They say a week's a long time in politics, but it's a lifetime in Hollywood. Perhaps expecting Brett to drop everything and come to Spain for her father's birthday had been too much to ask. And it wasn't actually his fault that they saw so little of each other. She was the one who had insisted on leaving LA, who'd thought the children should grow up 'ordinary' and 'British' and as far away from the insanity of Hollywood as possible. It was Lila's fault that she spent most of her time alone in London, not Brett's. And it wasn't as if he was cruel to her. He still said the sweetest things on the phone. Only the other day he'd said that Lila was his rock – always there for him, standing strong in the background, while the world rushed by. Lila would forgive him this time. Just like she always did. By the time she stopped for a break and looked back at the beach, her parents' villa seemed an awfully long way away.

After a long bath and a delicious cuddle on her bed with the children, Lila felt rested and happy. She joined her family on the patio. The table was spread with bread and olives and a carafe of red wine and her mum had just appeared from the kitchen with an enormous pot of steaming paella.

'I've gone native,' Eve announced proudly. 'Now, where's Peter?'

Lila looked round and spotted Peter sprawled on a hammock, under a palm tree in the garden. He was chatting animatedly on his mobile and smoking a cigarette. She did wish he'd give up that nasty habit, especially in front of the children. Lila waved at him and pointed to the food on the table, and he ambled over.

'Guess who's heard you're in town?' he said as he sat down beside Lila.

'Who?'

'Maxi,' he said with an excited grin. 'She's hosting a party in the harbour tonight and she would absolutely love it if you could come. You've to call her back.'

Lila sighed. 'Oh Peter, you know I hate parties.'

He pouted. 'Oh come on,' he begged. 'Please, Lila. It'll be fun.'

'But I don't want anybody to know I'm here,' said Lila, aware of the whine in her voice.

'But Maxine's your oldest friend, isn't she, love?' asked Eve. 'It might be nice to see her.'

Lila shrugged. Maxi was an old friend. Sort of. At least, she was the nearest thing Lila had to an old friend. She was kind and she'd always been loyal to Lila. They'd met at a magazine photo shoot in the nineties when Lila was still a soap-opera actress and Maxi was married to … Lila had to think about it. Who had it been that time? Oh yes, Riley O'Grady, the Indie singer. Or perhaps she'd just been dating him at the time. Yes, that was it. Maxi had only been there as 'the girlfriend' and yet somehow she'd wangled her way into the photograph. Maxi always managed to make herself the centre of attention, even when the focus was supposed to be on someone else. Lila smiled as she remembered her first impression of Maxi – big hair, big boobs, big smile, big personality, big heart.

Lila had been fairly new to the whole fashion magazine scene and had found the shoot pretty intimidating, but Maxi had taken Lila under her wing and made it fun. She'd even gone out of her way to help her get into the ridiculously small dress the stylist had insisted she wear. And even though Riley had been horrible to Maxi that day (he'd spent the entire time fawning over a supermodel) Maxi had remained cheerful and friendly.

Of course, Riley O'Grady had turned out to be a complete prat. But then Maxi had a habit of picking useless men. Her three exes made Brett look like the perfect husband. And what was she doing now? Living with a married man who was old enough to be her father!

Lila and Maxine had been close for a while. Very close. And Lila had spent the wildest part of her youth in Maxine's company. Maxine had been a very bad influence on her. But a fun one. Lila suddenly remembered Glastonbury 1997. She and Maxi had been drinking beer all day (something Lila never did) and then, when Maxi offered her a joint, it had seemed like a good idea (something else she never did!). Lila had ended up so out of her head that she'd crawled on to the nearest bus in the VIP area, curled up, and gone to sleep. When she woke up in the morning she found herself sharing a tour bus with the boys from Oasis. They were very good-natured about it and if she remembered correctly Noel Gallagher had even made her a cup of coffee. She giggled to herself.

'What?' asked Peter.

'Nothing,' replied Lila. And it was nothing. A brief moment of madness in her youth. That was all.

When Lila moved to LA and met Brett, everything changed. At first it had been utterly mindblowing. Brett had swept her off her feet, lavished her with diamonds and introduced her to Hollywood legends. If she wanted something – anything – she could have it. All she had to do was ask. A new car? No problem. Would an Austen Martin convertible do? A house on the beach? Sure thing. Will Malibu suit? But then, as the relationship progressed, Brett's publicity machine had clamped shut around her. Suddenly she had an army of 'people' to do things for her. There was a girl who did her make-up and a stylist to choose her clothes and PR managers to say whom she could and couldn't hang out with. Maxine de la Fallaise had been deemed far too D-list for the future Mrs Rose. Maxi was quite well-known in Britain but she was a nobody in LA. Lila remembered drawing up a list for her birthday party (it must have been her twenty-sixth) and having an almighty row with the party planner when he'd refused point blank to include Maxi. Lila had tried to explain that Maxi was her friend, but the party planner had just said, 'Girl, this is

LA. You gotta get yourself some new friends, pronto.' Much to her shame, Lila had done so, and she'd barely seen Maxine since.

Oh, the women had kept in contact sporadically over the years. Maxi phoned and emailed regularly but mostly Lila kept her at arms' length. She had come to their New Year's Eve party in LA last year with Carlos (now she was living with Carlos Russo she had risen to the B-list and scraped in on her lover's coat tails). But Maxine had drunk far too much champagne and had trodden on Salma Hayek's bare foot with her spiky heels. Salma had been very good about the incident, but Lila had been mortified. Maxi was a good-time girl who was always in the papers, wearing some ridiculously short skirt, falling drunkenly out of some nightclub or other. It was great that Maxi had set up her own nightclub now. She was a smart cookie and Lila was sure the place would be a success. But Lila couldn't be seen in company like that. Or at least, not very often. And not tonight.

'I'm not sure I can be bothered with getting all dolled up and socialising,' she explained to Peter and her family. 'Anyway, I'm here to spend time with you guys.'

'You've got all week to see us,' said Brian. 'And the kids are going to bed soon, aren't you, champs?'

Sebastian nodded and Louisa shook her head.

'Oh come on, Lila,' coaxed Peter. 'We're on holiday. If Brett was here he'd be up for it.'

That was true. Brett was always up for a party. And in fact, Brett adored Maxi. He thought she was hilarious and called Lila 'uptight' when she got embarrassed by Maxi's brazen behaviour. But Brett wasn't here, was he?

'Oh, I don't know,' said Lila.

'You could wear that gorgeous dress that Chanel sent you,' Peter coaxed. 'And those Louboutin shoes. The gold ones.'

Lila thought of the white shift dress still in its box. It was lovely and she hadn't had a chance to wear it yet. Maybe they could go for an hour.

'Well, I think it will do you good to get out,' added Eve.

'I'd like to go to a party,' said Louisa, hopefully.

'We're having a party for Grandpa on Sunday, sweetheart,' explained Eve. 'This party is for grown-ups. Mummy will enjoy it.'

'OK, OK,' Lila conceded. 'We'll go for a little while. But we're coming home the minute I've had enough, Peter. That's the deal, all right?'

'Deal,' grinned Peter, handing Lila the phone. 'Now ring Maxi before you change your mind.'

As soon as Lila heard Maxi's voice she realised she'd made the right decision.

'Oh my God, Lila!' squealed Maxi. 'It's so good to hear your voice. It's been *way* too long, babes. Now, listen, you are coming tonight, aren't you? I mean, I won't take no for an answer.'

Lila tried to say yes, she was coming, but she couldn't get a word in edgeways. Talking to Maxi on the phone had always been a somewhat one-sided affair.

Maxi continued, 'Tonight is my biggest night ever because Carlos has bought me this club and it's the launch evening. All the press will be there, and the footballers, and the Marbella Belles, and the Spanish glitterati and ... God, I am beside myself with excitement and nerves and it will be so, so, sooooo much better with you by my side. And anyway, the press will wet themselves when you turn up, so I need you there for the photo ops if nothing else ...'

Maxi cackled to show she was joking and then she said more gently, 'I mean, I have really missed you, hun. I thought you didn't want to be my friend anymore.'

'Don't be silly, Maxi,' Lila reassured her. 'I'll see you later. We'll catch up properly then.'

After dinner, Lila bathed the children and put them to bed.

'Will you come and show us when you're ready to go out?' asked Sebastian. 'We like seeing you all dressed up. We haven't seen you like that for ages.'

'Oh yes please, Mummy,' said Louisa. 'I want to see you dressed up like the queen.'

Lila couldn't help smiling. She liked herself best when she saw herself reflected in her children's eyes.

Looking at herself naked in the full-length bedroom mirror was a different story, though. She stared at the stranger gazing back at her. Her alabaster skin had seemed luminous in London but here, in the Spanish light, it just appeared pale and unhealthy. She drew her fingers across the stretchmarks on her hips and then stroked the bicycle tyre of excess flesh around her middle. Having children had changed her body permanently. She had made two perfect creatures but she had sacrificed her own perfection in the process. She turned sideways and sighed at what had once been a pert bottom. It was flat now and wider than it had been. Lila's was a mother's body now. Her breasts looked empty too. She had breastfed both children for a year and when the pregnancy weight was gone she'd been left with droopy, flat bags of flesh. Her nipples were red and permanently erect, like a couple of overripe raspberries. Lila's hands cupped her tired breasts and circled her suckled nipples.

She sighed with a longing to be caressed. It was not a perfect body anymore, but it was still a body that yearned to be touched. Was that so wrong? The desire to be desired had not faded with time. She wished Brett was here to hold her and touch her and make her feel like a beautiful woman again. But she was alone, as usual, and there was no one to satisfy her needs.

At least the Chanel dress was to die for and Lila felt almost attractive once she had it on. When she glanced at herself in the mirror she thought she caught a faint glimmer of the girl she'd once been – the beautiful girl with her whole life before her who'd left Cheshire for London and its bright lights. Lila had been keeping the dress to wear for Brett. It was quite short for her – mid-thigh – and he'd always had a thing for her legs. She hadn't worn a short skirt for years, preferring floor-length gowns for red carpet events and smart designer jeans when she was off duty, so she knew he would like it. He was always encouraging her to dress more adventurously. But Brett wasn't here and Lila felt almost guilty for baring her legs in his absence.

The kids were almost asleep when she popped her head in to say good-night.

'You look beautiful, Mummy,' enthused Louisa. 'Like a teenager!'

This was praise indeed from her daughter. Louisa was five going on fifteen.

'You're the most beautiful mummy in the world,' confirmed Sebastian. 'Daddy would love to see you like that.'

Oh, they were biased of course, but Lila took their compliments to heart and walked out of the house with a bounce she'd lost over recent months.

Peter was leaning against the car bonnet, cigarette in hand. He looked incredibly dashing all in black.

'Wow, baby, a guy could swing for you!' he announced, eyeing up Lila. 'Very foxy. Come on. Let's go!'

'I'm just going to call Brett,' said Lila, fishing for her mobile in her clutch. 'I hung up on him earlier and I need to make my peace. I think I might have been a bit harsh on him.'

Peter rolled his eyes. 'Well, if you must,' he said. 'But make sure you tell him you're going to a party. Tell him it's a party full of eligible young men who'll be trying to get into your knickers. Actually, tell him you're not wearing any knickers! Make him sweat for a change.'

Lila laughed. What would she do without Peter to cheer her up?

Shanna Lloyd smiled smugly to herself as she stretched her bare legs under the cool Egyptian cotton sheets. Her thighs felt strong, like they did after a workout at the gym, but this time they'd just finished gripping the naked hips of Brett Rose. Fan-fucking-tastic! That had been more satisfying than any session with her personal trainer. Brett Rose was officially the sexiest man on the planet – *Cosmopolitan* readers had crowned him with the title again only last month. He was older than most of the guys Shanna had been with but he had the most buff body and gorgeous green eyes she'd ever seen. Plus he was the man that every jobbing actress in LA most wanted to bed and Shanna was the one who'd gotten him.

Shanna loved to win. And this battle had been in the planning stages for months. She'd had a pretty small part in the movie and only a couple of scenes with Brett, but she'd always made sure she was at the next table in the catering tent, or the next barstool in the hotel bar. Before filming had started she'd had her tits done in anticipation and an extra bit of lipo on those thighs. What was it Brett had just said? Oh yes, those *glorious* thighs! Glorious ... now there was a compliment. She must tell her surgeon that next time she saw him.

Her hair had never been longer or blonder (God, she loved whoever the hell it was who'd invented hair extensions) and, at last, she'd managed to squeeze into those size two designer jeans (zero, here we come!). All in all, Shanna had never felt hotter. And she'd always been a hottie. She was only twenty-one and she had good Californian genes on her side, but everybody needed a little extra help in this town. The natural look was for losers and Shanna was no freakin' loser. No way. She'd known she would get him eventually. OK, so it took several bottles of Cristal and a couple of grams of coke at the wrap party to finally do it but here she was, at last, victorious in Brett Rose's bed!

She stared at the photograph of Lila Rose on the bedside table. Snooty English bitch. What the hell was Brett still doing with that one? She'd been pretty enough when she was young, Shanna supposed grudgingly. Pretty enough if you like that classy, brunette, English rose kind of thing. But now? Eurgh! She looked, like, forty or something! Shanna thought for a moment and did some math – never her strong point at school – and gradually realised that Lila Rose probably *was* pushing forty. Oh well, she didn't look how forty-year-olds look in LA, not with all the procedures available. Lila Rose looked like forty-year-olds used to look in the olden days. Before Botox. Really, there was no excuse. No wonder Brett craved, wait a minute, what had he said? Oh yeah, 'luscious young flesh'. Hear that, Lila Rose. Hear that and weep, loser.

When Brett reappeared from the kitchen with a couple of glasses of fresh pomegranate juice, he was talking on his cell phone.

'What am I doing?' He spoke into the phone but his eyes were all over

Shanna's naked tits. 'I'm just having me some juice and a shower and then I'll be on the phone sorting out my flight to you, baby.'

He put the juice down and, with the phone still lodged between his ear and his shoulder, he straddled Shanna and began stroking her nipples. The white towel around his hips was loose and the tip of his erect penis poked out, gently tickling her bare navel. She gasped involuntarily as he pushed his penis down towards her clit. God, she wanted him; she wanted him back inside her right now, but he was teasing her. He put one finger on her lips – *shush* – and with the other hand circled his penis around her damp pussy. He was still talking to his wife.

'Yes, honey,' he was saying, calmly. 'I've got presents for the kids.'

God, he was a good actor. He was as stiff as a board but his voice was totally neutral. Shanna could barely take the teasing anymore. He was rubbing harder and harder against her now and she was so close to losing it, she couldn't hang on. She wanted him inside her, needed him inside her, but it was almost too late. She bit his finger to stop herself from screaming, arched her back and started to come, over and over again in delicious waves of ecstasy.

'Just a second, babe; there's someone at the door,' Brett was saying to Lila.

He put the phone under a pillow, opened Shanna's legs and thrust himself deep inside her, never taking his eyes off her tits. He banged her hard and fast for less than a minute before he climaxed, so deep inside her that it kinda hurt. Then he rolled off, took a glug of his juice, fished the phone out from its hiding place and continued the conversation he'd been having with his wife.

It took a while for Shanna to get her breath back. She lay there panting and getting her head together. Brett had his back to her now and he was deep in conversation.

'Wow, babe. That's hotter than here. I'd better pack my sunscreen,' he was saying.

Shanna pulled the covers back up over her naked body, feeling suddenly vulnerable and alone and maybe even a little bit silly.

'You're going out, honey? That's great. Send my love to Maxi. Have a good time but not *too* good a time, OK?'

He laughed at some unheard comment from the other side of the world.

'You're wearing what? Jeez, I am aching to see you, to get my hands on you, you sexy little minx,' Brett purred down the phone. 'I love you, baby, you know I do. You're my gal. Always my number one gal.'

It was slowly dawning on Shanna that she might have been used. She glanced once again at the photograph of Brett's wife. She noticed a slight smirk playing on Lila's lips that she hadn't spotted earlier. Suddenly Shanna didn't feel like such a winner anymore.

Chapter Thirteen

'Do not touch your nails!' ordered Sandrine, the French beautician as she finished putting a topcoat on Maxine's toenails. 'They are perfect. If you smudge them I will kill you. There, all done. Pretty toes!'

'Lovely,' said Maxine, admiring them. They now matched her scarlet talons. 'Thanks.'

'What are you wearing, then?' demanded Sandrine.

Sandrine was a formidable woman in her late forties, with peroxide-blonde hair and an enormous bosom that looked way too heavy for her tiny frame. She always wore her hair scraped back in a tight bun, red lipstick, stilettos and a tight white lab coat over her pencil skirt. She took her job very seriously ('Beauty is a science, Maxine!') and, after eight years of experience, Maxine had learned to treat her with respect.

'I was thinking Dolce and Gabbana,' mused Maxine. 'My leopard-print mini-dress, I think.'

Sandrine curled her top lip. 'It's a little obvious, I think, Maxine. Why not something French? A classic Chanel dress is so sophisticated on a woman.'

Maxine laughed. 'I agree, Sandrine. But I'm not a sophisticated kind of girl, am I?'

Maxine looked up at her beautician from beneath her heavy false eyelashes. Sandrine was eyeing her critically, sprawled as she was on her shocking-pink velvet chaise longue wearing nothing but a black lacy thong and a matching balcony bra.

'No, darling. You are not that sort of girl.'

Maxine wasn't insulted. She knew her strengths and, like cookery, sophistication was not one of them. Maxi had built an entire life around being a glamourpuss and her revealing dresses were as much of a trade-mark as her big blonde hair and thirty-six-inch legs.

'I expect Lila will wear Chanel,' mused Sandrine, as she packed up her lotions and potions. 'Such an elegant woman. So poised ...'

'Lila *always* wears Chanel,' Maxi reminded her.

God, she couldn't wait to see Lila. She hadn't seen her friend in months, not since the Roses' New Year's Eve party in LA. They'd known each other for years and Maxine adored Lila, even though the two women were like chalk and cheese. Even their backgrounds were polar opposites: Lila had had a nice middle-class upbringing in Cheshire while Maxine had had a crazy, fucked-up, jet-set childhood surrounded by spaced-out rock stars and drug-fuelled parties. Lila's dad was an accountant – you couldn't get much more respectable than that – while Maxi's was a French Formula One racing driver with a penchant for fast women as well as fast cars. Lila's mum was a nurse. Maxi's was an American heiress.

While a teenage Lila was studying hard for her A-Levels, Maxi was getting kicked out of boarding schools for bringing local boys back to her dorm. Roedean, Cheltenham Ladies' College and Benenden had all had enough of her by the time she was sixteen. By the time Lila had secured a place at RADA, Maxi had been labelled a 'wild child' by the tabloids and was usually found either dancing topless on a table in Annabel's nightclub, or slumped drunkenly beneath one.

At eighteen Maxine de la Fallaise married twenty-year-old pop star Davie Donovan, who'd turned out to have no balls. The marriage lasted three months and ended with Maxine breaking a deckchair over his head at a polo match. She was only trying to wake him up after he'd collapsed drunk and unconscious in the Veuve Cliquot tent, but he'd taken it all very personally. He'd dropped the assault charges eventually, but filed for divorce on the grounds of her unreasonable behaviour.

Husband number two had fared only slightly better. Alberto was a minor European royal who had married to stop the constant press speculation that he was gay. Unfortunately, six months into their marriage, Maxine had caught him in bed with his (male) tennis coach, and had had to admit that she was never going to be the love of Alberto's life. 'I am sorry, Maxine,' he'd shouted after her as she'd fled from the chateau. 'If you were a man you would be my perfect woman!'

It was while she was dating husband number three, Indie rock god Riley O'Grady, that she'd met Lila at a *Vogue* photo shoot. It was 1997 and the magazine was celebrating Cool Britannia. Both Riley and Lila had been chosen to appear. Lila had just left a very successful soap opera and was about to embark on a career in Hollywood. Maxi was just there as a hanger-on. 'I'm with the band,' she'd probably said, as she often did in those days. If she remembered correctly, Riley had been particularly obnoxious that day, spending most of his time chatting up the supermodel Amy Dury.

Anyway, Lila had been a lot curvier in those pre-Hollywood days, and the sample size dress the stylist had chosen for her to wear wouldn't do up at the back. Maxine had offered to crouch down behind her and hold the dress together while the shoot took place. And so she'd spent four hours on her knees, hiding behind Lila's back so that the starlet's boobs didn't fall out. Lila had been completely mortified by the incident and kept whispering, 'Thank you so much,' to Maxine. At one point Lila had lost her balance and toppled on top of Maxi. As the two women stood up they were clinging to each other with Maxi still holding Lila's dress. They were helpless with laughter, their heads thrown back in mutual mirth, hair tossed in the air, eyes shining, a vision of youthful exuberance. The moment was not wasted on the quick-witted photographer. It was this photograph that had been used in the magazine. Maxi had not been expecting to appear in the shoot, but the coverage had cemented her reputation as a 'somebody' on the party scene and modelling jobs and little bits of TV presenting had soon followed.

Lila was so sweet and well-mannered that Maxine fell in love with her there and then. She'd just known Lila was going to be a huge star. Everyone had very high hopes for her that summer, just as they'd had for Kate Winslet and Catherine Zeta Jones. It was such a shame that it hadn't worked out for Lila like that. She'd been such a good actress; it seemed madness that she hadn't actually been in a film this millennium. Mind you, she hadn't exactly done badly for herself, had she? Bagging Brett Rose was worth a zillion Academy Award nominations.

The girls' friendship had blossomed from that day on. A few months later, Lila was a bridesmaid at Maxine and Riley's wedding and she'd been there for Maxi again, a year after that, when Riley got Amy Dury pregnant. Apparently they'd been seeing each other since the day of the Cool Britannia shoot. Maxi still couldn't quite believe that Riley and Amy now lived on a farm in Gloucestershire with their four children and a herd of organic dairy cattle.

Maxine had been the one with the hard-partying reputation, but she soon learned that Lila wasn't quite as innocent as she looked. Yes, she was always perfectly presented, but she was quite capable of letting her hair down and having a really good, girlie laugh. The two were inseparable for a year or two – forever appearing together in magazine spreads, arms linked, eyes flashing, strutting in high heels from one celebrity bash to another. Lila always made the 'best dressed' articles, but Maxine was more likely to appear in the 'worst dressed' category. It didn't bother her. Maxine wasn't a proud woman. Something about Lila's 'otherness' filled a void in Maxine. Lila was yin to Maxi's yang.

Maxi didn't know what she would have done without Lila in those days. God, the scrapes she'd got into that Lila had saved her from! There was the time on the yacht in Cannes, during the film festival, when Maxi had been in bed with a very well-known actor. Lila had been the one who'd spotted his equally famous wife when she'd arrived unexpectedly by speedboat from the mainland. Lila had knocked on the door, ordered Maxi to hide and then rushed back on deck just in time to explain to the wife that the film star had come down with a sudden stomach bug and that he was resting. It had been a bit uncomfortable under the bed for the next three hours, but better than being caught by the wife!

And in darker times too, it had been Lila who had helped Maxine out. Maxi had dabbled with 'soft' drugs for years, but she had once briefly become hooked on cocaine. Lila had pulled her back from the brink before the problem got too out of hand. Lila was the one who'd bundled her out of a club at four a.m. and driven her to rehab. Most of her other so-called friends had dealt with her growing addiction by offering her more drugs, but Lila sat with her as she went through cold turkey and afterwards, when she was beginning to feel stronger, Lila had taken her to Italy. They went shopping in Rome, went to the art galleries in Florence and then spent a blissful week sleeping, reading and sunbathing in the rolling hills of Tuscany. Yes, Lila had always been a good influence.

But then Lila had married Brett and everything changed. Lila had been swiftly propelled into the upper echelons of Hollywood society. Brett had his own friends and they were *really* famous. It was as if a door slammed between the two girls and as the years passed their lives moved apart again. Lila became a mother and, Maxine guessed, a proper grown-up. But Maxi's relationships kept falling apart so she just kept on partying. She had no responsibilities, no babies of her own, and no other real purpose in life, and so while Lila Rose evolved into the sophisticated Hollywood wife, Maxi remained a London party girl. Silly, maybe, frivolous, definitely, but always loads of fun. And now she was here in Spain with Carlos. Still just the girlfriend, thanks to Esther. Not married. Not a mother. And not a wedding in sight. Hmph!

It hurt that Lila didn't keep in touch very often these days, but Maxine was used to being abandoned. Her parents had done it constantly, even leaving her with a nanny when she was a week old so that they could make Monte Carlo. She was always so grateful when they did remember her that she forgot to be angry and forgave them instantly. She felt the same as an adult – eternally grateful for the smallest morsel of attention thrown her way. Perhaps that was why she surrounded herself with crowds the whole time. As a little girl, friends had been as easily lost as they had been made. There was the constant moving around and switching schools and then, when she was older and wilder, there were the friends whose parents banned their daughters from seeing her.

Maxine had always been branded a bad influence, but she knew she wasn't a bad person. Her heart was in the right place. She wasn't a bitch and she was loyal to her friends. If only Lila would let her back in, she'd show her what a good friend she could be. Even getting Lila to come to the party was a breakthrough. And the very fact that they were both in Marbella at the same time was a minor miracle. Tonight would be like the old days. She started singing an old Carly Simon song to herself: 'Two hot girls on a hot summer night, looking for love …'

'Darling, your voice is not your strong point,' scolded Sandrine. 'Please be quiet. You give me a headache!'

Just then Carlos swept into the room. 'Chica, you must get dressed.' He seemed alarmed by Maxi's nakedness. 'The guests will be arriving in …' He checked his Rolex. ' … half an hour. You are the hostess. You cannot possibly be late.'

'Hey, chill out, Daddy Bear,' soothed Maxine. 'I'll be ready in two ticks.'

Carlos liked to play the father figure with her. He was fifty-seven, after all, and much closer in age to her dad than he was to her. But unlike her absentee father, Carlos was loving, responsible and a constant ally. In fact, if it wasn't for his bloody wife, he'd be completely perfect.

It made Maxine laugh when she remembered having Carlos's poster on her wall in her dorm at boarding school. She must have been about twelve, and while the other girls had pictures of ponies, Maxi used to kiss Carlos every night before bed and swear that, 'One day I'm going to marry him.' OK, so she didn't have that ring on her finger yet, but she was working on it.

Carlos had been such a superstar in the eighties – this gorgeous, dark, Spanish hunk of a singer, with just a hint of an accent when he sang his heart-melting love songs. OK, so it was all a bit cheesy in hindsight, but it was the eighties, for God's sake – the decade that taste forgot. Carlos could still fill a stadium now. Mostly with middle-aged women, granted, but he still got knickers thrown at him on stage (and not all of them support girdles either).

In theory, Carlos and Esther were based in LA, while Maxine still called London home. But Carlos missed his native Spain and recently they'd been spending more and more time together here as a couple, in their secluded beach house on the coast, several kilometres east of Marbella. Now Carlos had bought Maxine a boat in the marina and had it converted into a nightclub.

'You are so good at playing the hostess, chica,' he'd explained. 'I thought you might like a nightclub of your own.'

Maxine checked her appearance in the mirror one more time, added another layer of scarlet lipstick and then reached for her contraceptive pills. She was about to pop one into her mouth when Plan B suddenly popped into her brain. 'That's it!' Without a second thought (Maxine had always been impulsive) she dropped the pill into the sink, turned on the tap and watched it swirl down the plughole. She winked at herself in the mirror. 'Bye bye Esther Russo, hello Maxine Russo!' she said to herself with a cheeky grin.

'Ta da!' said Maxine, as she appeared from her dressing room in her itsy bitsy animal-print dress and four-inch diamond-encrusted heels.

'Magnificent, chica!' announced Carlos proudly.

'Tsk, tsk,' muttered Sandrine. 'How many times do I have to tell you that bare legs and a bare décolletage are vulgar, Maxine.'

'Sandrine,' scolded Carlos. 'My Maxi is never vulgar. She is a perfect specimen of womanhood. She is Venus herself!'

Sandrine raised a perfectly plucked eyebrow at Maxine and whispered in her ear, 'I trust he has still never seen you without your make-up on.'

Chapter Fourteen

When she first opens her eyes the girl has no idea where she is. She's lying on her back on a hard, flat surface and above her head a bright, neon striplight is flickering and buzzing. Bluebottles and moths are throwing themselves at the light, committing suicide. She watches them die. Gradually, as she comes to, the pain sears through her body and the nightmare of what has happened replays in her head. And then he's there again. Grinning down at her.

She's never liked him, always been wary of him. But this? No, she didn't see this coming.

'Hello, darling,' he leers. 'Feeling better after your rest? You looked like Sleeping Beauty.'

She musters all the energy she can find and starts pummelling his chest with her fists.

'Let me go!' she screams. 'Let me go!'

He laughs. He grabs her thin wrists and places her arms gently back by her side.

'Don't be silly,' he says, sounding amused. 'We haven't finished having fun yet, have we?'

The girl has no idea how much time has passed. Hours? Days? And where the hell is she? It isn't the same room she was locked in earlier. She raises her head a little. It's difficult to move. Her entire body aches. She appears to be in some sort of empty factory or warehouse. The floor is concrete and filthy. The walls are covered with those old-fashioned brick-shaped tiles that you see in public toilets. They must have been white once, but now they're grey and stained with ... what is that? It looks like blood.

The vast room is almost empty other than a few metal racks with enormous hooks hanging off them. The girl is lying on some sort of table with a thick wooden top. And there are more of those gruesome-looking tools lying around, like the ones she saw in the smaller room earlier. On closer inspection they look more like weapons than tools. The room stinks of something stale and vile and stomach-churning but she can't quite put her finger on what the stench is.

'Place is an old meat market,' grins the man. 'This was the abattoir.'

Ah, the girl realises with a horrified shudder, the smell is blood and raw flesh. The stench of death. How appropriate. Is she going to die here too? No! She won't die. She's too young. She has too much to live for.

'I've cleaned you up all nice,' says the man. 'We're going to have a party.'

'Wh-what?' The girl lifts her hand to her face and feels thick make-up on her skin that wasn't there earlier. She realises her lips are sticky with lipstick and her hair, which had been loose, is now in a ponytail. What has he been doing while she was unconscious? Playing with her like a doll? The bile rises in her throat. She realises she's dressed in different clothes. For some hideous reason she's wearing a schoolgirl's uniform. The skirt is ridiculously short and the white blouse is undone to well below her cleavage. He's forced her breasts into a nasty red push-up bra which is several sizes too small. As she struggles to sit up she can feel the underwiring dig into her broken rib. Suddenly she retches and throws up on the filthy floor.

'Don't mess up your nice new clothes,' scolds the man.

She manages to slide off the table – obviously a butcher's block – and stand up on wobbly feet. The room swims and her head throbs.

'Let me go,' she demands again, looking desperately for an escape route. There is none. The only door is locked.

'What? So you can go straight to the filth? I don't think so, darling,' laughs the man.

'Let me go now and I'll tell no one,' she promises in a shaky voice. 'I'm begging you. Let me go.'

'Don't be silly,' he says. 'I told you. We're about to have a party.'

The picture is blurring, the man's face distorting, but somewhere in her mind she sees a gun being waved in front of her face. And then she's sliding down, down, down, and her head is crashing on to the ground but she feels nothing except the cold floor against her tear-soaked cheek. Then everything is quiet.

Chapter Fifteen

Over the years, Charlie had grown eyes on the back of his head. He was rarely – hell, never! – taken by surprise by anyone. But out here, on an empty beach, a thousand miles from home, he'd let his mind wander. It was stupid. He'd let his guard down. And only now, too late, did he realise what a mistake that had been.

After a lonely dinner in his room watching golf on Sky Sports, Charlie had decided that a walk on the beach might help him make sense of the day's events. He'd strolled out towards the water's edge and sat down, just beyond where the waves lapped. He'd taken off his new sandals and felt the cold, damp sand beneath his toes.

It was a clear night. He'd looked over at the marina, a kilometre or so to the west, and noticed a ship docked there. The vessel was entirely covered in fairy lights and it twinkled in the harbour like a million stars. He'd guessed that was where the party was happening tonight. But Charlie was no longer in the mood for partying. Gary's phone call had unsettled him. In fact, Charlie had been so lost in his thoughts of Nadia and what on earth could have happened to her that he didn't realise he had company until the sand crunched right behind him.

'Nice night for it,' said a familiar deep, wheezing voice.

Charlie took a deep breath and composed himself. What the fuck was he doing here?

'Evening Frank,' said Charlie. His voice was calm but his heart was pounding and his mind raced. 'How did you know I'd be here?'

Frank slumped his old body down on to the sand beside Charlie and patted him on the back.

'You said you were staying at the club, your motor's in the car park and I guessed you wouldn't be very far away. Then I saw some sad Billy No Mates on the beach and thought, "There we go. That's Charlie."'

Charlie laughed half-heartedly but he felt anything but happy. The fact that Frankie Angelis had ventured out of his Playboy mansion could only mean one thing: business.

'I felt we ended our conversation a little prematurely this afternoon,

Char,' said Frank. His tone was friendly enough, but the very fact that he'd leaned right into Charlie's ear, close enough for Charlie to feel his hot cigar-breath on his skin, was enough to make it clear that this was not a social call.

'Did you, Frank?' said Charlie, staring out at the sea.

'I'm not sure I made myself entirely clear about that job I mentioned,' Frank continued.

Charlie closed his eyes for a moment. His mouth had gone dry and when he replied, 'I'm not interested, Frankie. No offence. It's just not the right time,' his voice sounded croaky and weak. Hell, he felt weak. Frank Angelis could make Charlie feel like that sixteen-year-old gofer again in an instant.

Frankie sat back and leaned on his hands. 'Charlie, Charlie, Charlie,' he scolded. 'I've never asked you for a favour before but this time I really need you to help me out. I had hoped that, what with everything I've done for you and your family over the years, you'd understand. I think you owe me.'

It was a thinly veiled threat and Charlie knew it. Perhaps if it was just a small job it would be worth doing just to get the old man off his back.

'What's the job?' Charlie asked despondently.

'I need someone taken care of. Someone who's been stepping on my toes,' said Frank.

'Where?'

'London.'

Charlie shook his head. 'No, Frank. I'm not going back there yet. I just got out. It's not safe for me in London just now.'

'Oh, Charlie, you know me better than that. If you're worried about the Donohue incident—'

'Jesus fucking Christ!' said Charlie, pounding the sand with his fist. 'Do you know everything?'

He could see the old man's teeth glinting in the moonlight as he grinned. 'Course I do, my boy, and don't you forget it. McGregor, Donohue, that little Clara bird – I make it my business to know what's going on. Anyway, don't worry about that now. I can get you in and out of the Smoke in no time. No one will know you're there. I've got a mate flying in to City in a couple of days. Private plane. No questions asked. You'll be there for a few hours, tops.'

Charlie picked up a handful of cool sand and let it slip slowly between his fingers. Frankie could make trouble for him if he knew about Donohue.

'Why does it have to be me?' asked Charlie. 'You must have half a dozen blokes back home who could help you out.'

Frank sucked in his breath. 'It's complicated. Business has been a bit ...'

The old man narrowed his eyes and looked thoughtful. 'Let's just say I'm not sure who I can trust anymore. That's why I need you to do this job for me. We've got history, Charlie. I know you won't let me down.'

Charlie's head was beginning to pound. He didn't want to do any job. Not for Frankie. Not for anybody. He just wanted a bit of peace.

'Who is it?'

'No names,' muttered Frank, looking around him, checking the beach was still deserted.

Charlie sighed. 'I need a name, Frankie. I need a name before I agree to anything.'

Maybe it would be a simple hit. Some lowlife scum that Charlie wouldn't mind eradicating from the world. If it was easy, maybe it would be worth doing, just to get Frankie off his back. Maybe ...

'So you'll do it?' said Frankie. It wasn't really a question.

'I might if you tell me who it is.'

'All right, all right; it's a Russian bloke. Name's Dimitrov.'

Charlie felt the blood drain from his face and despite the balmy evening, he shivered in his thin shirt. Was it his imagination or was the world shrinking at an alarming rate?

'I can't do it,' he said adamantly. 'No fucking way.'

'Why not?' Frankie shouted and then looked around the beach again. He lowered his voice and repeated, 'Why the hell not?'

'Because Dimitrov is big time, Frankie. He's not just some little thug; he's a frigging billionaire with legitimate businesses. He's got powerful friends. And he's a fucking Russian. I don't want to die of bleeding radiation poisoning, thank you very much. Besides, I have other reasons.'

'What other reasons?' demanded Frank, clearly angry.

'Well, mainly the fact I've been shagging his daughter all year. It's too personal. I can't touch Dimitrov. No fucking way.'

'And that's your final word on the subject, is it?' demanded Frankie. He was shouting now and didn't seem to care whether anybody was listening anymore.

'Yes,' said Charlie defiantly. 'That is definitely my final word on the subject. I ain't touching Dimitrov. End of.'

Frank struggled breathlessly to his feet. 'That ain't the end of anything, my son,' he warned Charlie. 'You know too much now. You're a fucking liability to me.'

'Frank, Frank!' Charlie jumped up and tried to place a soothing hand on the old man's forearm. But Frankie snatched his arm away. 'Listen Frank,' Charlie continued as calmly as he could. 'You can trust me, OK? I won't say a word to no one about this, you have my word.'

'Oh, I have your word, do I, Charlie?' spat Frankie. 'And what the fuck is your word worth, eh? After everything I've done for you, my boy, this is how you repay me!'

'I ain't being disrespectful,' Charlie insisted. 'I just can't do this job.'

'Won't, more like,' grunted Frankie, stepping away. 'Well, you mark my words, boy. No one refuses Frankie Angelis, all right? No one.'

Charlie listened to the old man's footsteps getting fainter and fainter in the sand until there was nothing left but the sound of the waves. He sat for a while, cursing his fucked-up existence, wishing fate had led him down a different path. He let his mind wander to a dream place, with a quiet life and a beautiful wife and sweet, innocent children who never had to see the things he'd seen. It was a life he felt sure he'd never have. Then he dragged himself back into reality, stood up and wandered slowly back down towards the water's edge, searching for his sandals. Eventually he found them, floating gently on the incoming tide. 'Fuck it!' he said to the deserted beach. 'They cost me three hundred quid!' But the sodden designer sandals were the least of Charlie's troubles.

He was walking back towards the hotel, his head spinning, when his mobile rang. The screen told him it was an 'unavailable number'. What the fuck now? He was tempted to leave it, but what if it was Gary, needing his help? Or Nadia, even? He answered it reluctantly.

'Hello?'

'Ah, Charlie Palmer,' said a deep, heavily accented voice. 'Is Vladimir Dimitrov here. You are not easy man to track down.'

Charlie could feel his heart beating in his throat and wondered if Dimitrov could hear it too.

'Mr Dimitrov,' he said, as calmly as he could. 'I hear Nadia is missing. I hope you're calling me to tell me you've found her.'

'Ha, ha, ha.' It was the least mirthful laugh Charlie had ever heard. 'Ees good, Mr Palmer. Ees very good. You know I not find my Nadia. You have my Nadia. What you want? My money?'

'Mr Dimitrov, I don't have Nadia,' said Charlie as firmly as he could. 'I haven't seen her since this morning. She was fine when I left. You've got to believe me.'

'Why?' barked Dimitrov. 'Why I must believe you? Nadia live with you. She love you. She do whatever you tell her. Now you go. You not in London. What you do with her, eh?'

Dimitrov sounded eerily calm. There was no sense of panic in his deep, heavily accented voice. He spoke clearly. Definitely. And every word dripped with menace.

Charlie tried to squeeze every ounce of sincerity into his voice.

84

'Mr Dimitrov,' he said, 'I swear on my mother's grave that I have no idea where Nadia is. I haven't laid a finger on her and I don't want your money. I do, however, want to help you to find her, so if there's anything I can do ...'

'You do enough, Charlie Palmer,' spat Dimitrov. 'You do enough already.'

And then the phone went dead.

'FUCK!' screamed Charlie across the deserted beach.

He dropped to his knees and bent his head into his hands. There were no answers. Just questions. So many fucking questions. He'd left London to get away from his troubles but they seemed to have followed him and multiplied during the journey.

Chapter Sixteen

Casa Amoura was lit up with fairy lights and Jasmine's favourite salsa music was blaring from the sound system. She was wearing her new silver, sequinned Prada dress – a present from Jimmy – and sipping her first mojito of the evening as she watched for her friends' arrival. The villa looked gorgeous, magical even, and she couldn't wait for them all to see it. Tonight was their first public unveiling of the place and Jasmine was bouncing up and down with excitement.

'Calm down, love,' said Jimmy, kissing her bare shoulder. 'We're just having a few mates round before the party.'

'I know, 'said Jasmine. 'But I'm really proud of this villa. And I'm really proud of you for earning it!'

She threw her arms around his neck and kissed him fully on the lips. 'And I'm sorry if I annoyed you earlier. During the interview.'

Jimmy shrugged her off. 'You didn't annoy me,' he said. 'I just hate all that media bollocks. I'm a footballer. Why do they need to know what my favourite colour is, or what I ate for fucking breakfast? It does my head in, that's all.'

'I know, babes,' soothed Jasmine. 'But it comes with the territory, doesn't it? They're the opposition. You just need to know how to play them to your advantage, that's all. Just like on the pitch.'

'Hark at you, Alex Ferguson,' laughed Jimmy.

Jasmine grinned. 'So, we're good, yeah?'

Jimmy nodded. 'We're good, darling,' he said, and he squeezed her hand. 'And Jasmine?'

'Yes?'

'I love you. You know that, don't you?'

She nodded gratefully. She did know it. And she also knew she was one lucky girl.

'Oh my God, here they come!' she shouted.

She could always tell when someone was arriving at the house before they got to the gates because the lenses on the cameras across the street would suddenly start flashing. The paparazzi had obviously worked themselves into a frenzy tonight because the street was lit up like a fireworks display. The press knew that half the Premiership and their glamorous 'other halves' were in town this week. The football season had just finished and a lot of the big players had houses in Marbella. Perhaps the paps had guessed that the other players would be checking out Jimmy and Jasmine's new pad this evening. Or perhaps Blaine had tipped them off.

The gates opened slowly and a black Mercedes pulled into the drive, followed by a red BMW 4x4 and a silver Porsche. Jasmine could hear the press shouting out her friends' names from across the road. They spent so much time following the footballers around that they recognised their cars.

'It's so good to see you all!' squealed Jasmine as her friends spilled out of their cars.

Crystal (real name Christine) was Jasmine's best mate in the whole world and the pair hugged passionately and kissed each other properly with lip-glossed 'mwah's to both cheeks.

'You look amazing, Chrissie!' enthused Jasmine, taking in her friend's multi-coloured Pucci maxi-dress. 'That dress is gorgeous on you.'

'I know,' giggled Crystal, spinning around. 'I've got myself a stylist. She's bloody brilliant. Should have got one years ago. This is vintage. Original seventies. It's older than me!'

'Wow,' said Jasmine. 'That's so cool and it looks fab with your tan and your hair. And, oh my word, your new boobs! They're wonderful!'

Crystal had recently gone blonde and had a thick, swishy fringe cut over her sparkly blue eyes. She'd lost weight again too. But the biggest change were the 34D boobs that Calvin had bought her for her birthday. They sat just below her collar bone, and were as perfectly round as Seville oranges, and they were enjoying their first public outing this evening. *Yup,* thought Jasmine, *she really looks the part these days.*

At twenty-one, Crystal was the youngest girl in the group of footballers' wives and girlfriends but she'd been on the scene since she was a teenager. She and Calvin Brown had been together since school and had taken the rough ride from obscurity to tabloid stardom together. The papers had been pretty cruel to Crystal over the years, poking fun at her ginger hair and forever commenting on her fluctuating weight. She always laughed it off in public, but Jasmine had been there to mop up the tears when the columnists stuck the knife in. 'I never pretended to be a blooming supermodel,' she'd sobbed. 'I'm just Calvin's girlfriend. What gives them the right to pick me to bits just because my bloke can kick a ball into the back of a net?'

Jasmine found them the most down-to-earth couple in the group – yes, they dressed glamorously, they drove flashy cars and lived in a huge house, but Crystal and Calvin somehow stayed true to their roots. There were no airs and graces with those two. Jasmine found that she could just as easily slob around in a Juicy tracksuit, eating popcorn and watching a movie with Chrissie as she could waft around Harvey Nics spending Jimmy's and Calvin's fortunes. She'd asked Crystal to be her bridesmaid at the wedding next week and she knew that no one would calm her nerves more as she got ready to walk up the aisle. She gazed at her friend's reincarnation as an uber-babe and smiled proudly. What would the press say when they saw her tonight? And then a worrying thought crossed her mind.

'Chrissie, love?'

'Yeah, Jazz?'

'How many cup sizes have you gone up?'

'Three,' she stated proudly. 'I was flat as a bloody billiard table before.'

'It's just I think we're going to have to alter your bridesmaid's dress,' giggled Jasmine. 'Big time.'

'Holy fuck, I never thought of that!' squealed Crystal. 'I'm so sorry, Jazz.'

'No probs, babe. We'll get the designer to fly it out to you on Monday.'

'Um, Jasmine,' said Cookie McClean, Jasmine's second best friend. 'I think we might have to alter my dress too.'

'Why?' asked Jasmine. Cookie had had her boobs done long before the dress fittings.

Cookie stood back and smoothed her Gucci smock dress down over her stomach. Cookie was a tiny slip of a thing, barely five foot tall and stick thin. But, as she revealed her silhouette beneath the billowing dress, a definite round mound of tummy appeared.

'Oh my God, you're not, are you?' asked Jasmine in shock.

'She is,' nodded her husband, Paul, proudly. 'Four months gone. Can you believe it? We're going to have a baby!'

'Well, that's it, mate,' laughed Jimmy. 'You'll have to trade the Porsche in for a people carrier!'

And then everybody was whooping with delight, hugging the parents-to-be, congratulating them and calling for champagne to celebrate. Jasmine was pleased for Cookie, she really was. Cookie had never made a secret of her love for babies, and in fact she'd been a nursery nurse until she'd met and married Paul. Cookie would be a brilliant mum. But would Paul be such a great dad? Jasmine remembered how he'd been a regular at Exotica – always the horniest of the footballers, shoving fifty-pound notes into the girls' thongs and requesting private lap dances. He'd paid more for 'extras' too. Something that was against the rules but that happened regularly in upmarket hotels once the club closed its doors. It wouldn't be such a problem if he'd changed his ways. But Jasmine knew from her friend, Roxy, who still worked at the club, that Paul remained a regular at Exotica and that he'd formed a 'special friendship' with one of the new girls, Pamela. She'd been wondering what to do with the information for weeks now. Should she tell Cookie? Should she discuss it with Crystal? So far, she hadn't told a soul. Not even Jimmy. Although she suspected Jimmy probably knew about Perky Pammy already. Boys did tend to boast about these things to their mates. Jasmine watched Paul as he patted Cookie's tummy protectively. Cookie looked totally blissed out. Well, she couldn't say anything now, could she? Not tonight.

Jasmine felt a shadow cross her heart briefly as she watched her blissfully pregnant friend. Would that baby grow up with both Mummy and Daddy around? Or would Daddy's affairs end up splashed across the front pages? Would that child's family be ripped apart before he or she was even out of nappies? Jasmine sometimes thought that people had babies without thinking of the consequences. Why had her real mum even bothered giving birth to her when she'd had no intention of raising her? Jasmine had been passed from pillar to post and never really felt she belonged anywhere. She would never do that to her own children. That was why she wasn't ready for babies yet. She would wait until she was properly settled in one place and until Jimmy had grown up a bit and then she would have children. And she would give them everything that she'd never had – love, security, money. Oh yes, when the time came, Jasmine would try to be the best mother that ever lived; the kind of mother she'd never had herself.

Suddenly a hush fell on the crowd and everybody turned towards the drive. Jasmine spun round and saw Madeleine and Luke Parks walking, arm in arm, on to the terrace. The Parks were the undisputed king and queen of British football. Luke smiled smugly and nodded his head in an 'I know, I know, you're really lucky that we've graced you with our presence' kind of way. Urgh! Jasmine thought he was vile. She'd never met such a smarmy, egocentric prick in her life – and that was saying something, considering some of the men she'd met. OK, he was the best footballer in the country, bar none (although there were those who predicted that Jimmy would be stealing his crown in a season or two) and he was handsome in a clean-cut, catalogue-model kind of way. He was the captain, the top dog, the oldest and most respected guy on the team. The blokes thought he was a demigod, but Jasmine had never seen the attraction. The truth was, Luke Parks had the charisma of a tree. Jasmine had tried many times to strike up a conversation with Luke, but all he did was talk about how brilliant he was. He'd never once asked her anything about herself. He bent down and kissed Jasmine on each cheek as if he were doing her a favour.

But it was Madeleine Parks who really freaked Jasmine out. The woman was just plain scary. She was the oldest, tallest, skinniest, most expensively dressed and frequently photographed of the girls. Madeleine was Head WAG, that was for sure, and none of the other girls dared mess with her. She never smiled, never laughed and never made a fool of herself. She was the Ice Queen – indisputably beautiful with white-blonde hair, flawless, alabaster skin, sparkling ice-blue eyes and a permanent sneer of superiority. Jasmine was terrified of her. Madeleine was a 'proper' model, not a glamour model like Jasmine, and she had made it perfectly clear in the press that she disapproved of the likes of Jordan, Jodie and Jasmine. What was it she'd called them? Oh yes, that was it: 'cheap tarts'. Madeleine thought Jasmine was a cheap tart. Which was why, when Jasmine saw what Madeleine was wearing, she wanted the ground to swallow her up. She and Madeleine were wearing exactly the same sequinned Prada dress.

'Oh God, Madeleine, I'm so sorry,' apologised Jasmine as she kissed the air somewhere in the proximity of Madeleine's razor-sharp cheekbones. 'I had no idea you had this dress.'

Madeleine looked Jasmine up and down slowly, but her face showed no expression. It never did. 'Too much Botox,' Crystal had explained. 'Her muscles are permanently paralysed now.'

Eventually Madeleine spoke. 'I didn't recognise it as the same piece, to be honest,' she sniffed. 'It looks so different in a large size. Anyway, no harm done. You can change. It doesn't really do anything for you anyway.'

'It doesn't?' Jasmine couldn't have been more hurt if Madeleine had slapped her across the face. She'd thought she looked pretty good in the sparkly dress. Jimmy had chosen it himself. She loved it.

'It doesn't,' confirmed Madeleine. 'It's designed for a much smaller frame than yours. And the colour's not right on you. This is a blonde's dress. I would definitely change if I were you.'

Jasmine swallowed the lump in her throat, blinked back the tears, and tried to regain her composure. 'Of course, Madeleine, I will. I'll just get you a drink first.'

Jasmine forced herself to smile sweetly at Madeleine, as if grateful for the fashion advice, but she felt like scratching her eyes out. She moved off towards the bar on the terrace but Madeleine blocked her way with a stiletto-clad foot.

'No, Jasmine,' she said coldly. 'Change now. Before anyone notices.'

Madeleine was not smiling, but her eyes twinkled with mischief and the corners of her mouth were twitching as if they wanted to smirk. She was enjoying herself.

Jasmine glanced towards Crystal for support, but Chrissie was giggling with Calvin, Blaine and Jimmy and was oblivious to what had just gone on.

Jasmine wanted to shout, 'Piss off, you stuck-up old cow! I'll change when I'm good and ready!' but of course she didn't.

'OK, Madeleine,' she said politely. 'I'll be back in a minute. Maria will get you a drink and there are canapés on the terrace.'

As Jasmine turned to go Madeleine added, 'And Jasmine ...'

'Yes?' Jasmine turned back to look at the older woman. Madeleine stared at her with thinly disguised contempt as she tossed her shiny, platinum hair over her bony shoulders.

'Here's a quick tip for you. Don't make the mistake of thinking a designer label will make you look classy. Class isn't something you can buy. It's something you're born with.'

Jasmine felt the tears begin to trickle down her cheeks as she turned on her heel and ran towards the villa and the sanctuary of her bedroom. She'd spent her entire life trying to climb out of the social mire, but one conversation with Madeleine Parks was enough to throw her right back to the bottom of the heap. Here she was in her three-million-pound Marbella dream home, still feeling like the girl who stole deodorant to mask the smell of poverty.

Jasmine splashed cold water on her face and then touched up her make-up. She tried hard not to look tarty. She didn't wear much make-up – just a bit of mascara and lip gloss. She threw the Prada dress on the bed and rifled through her wardrobe in search of something sophisticated.

'Och, here you are, Jazz,' said Jimmy, bursting into the room. 'Everyone's wondering where you've gone.' He gazed quizzically at her naked body and asked, 'What are you doing, babe?'

'I've got to change,' she explained. 'I was wearing the same dress as Madeleine.'

'So?' Jimmy didn't seem to understand the problem. 'I'm wearing the same jeans as Paul but we're not bothered. What's the big deal? Have you been crying about it? Jesus, I'll never understand women!'

'I'm fine, Jim, I just can't be photographed in the same dress as Madeleine, that's all,' explained Jasmine, unwilling to let her fiancé see how upset she was.

'Well hurry up,' he said. And then he looked at her strangely. 'You have been crying, Jazz. I'm not stupid. What's up?'

Jasmine shook her head. 'It's nothing, really. Madeleine was just a bit mean to me, that's all. She said the dress didn't suit me.'

'Och, she's just jealous of you,' scoffed Jimmy. 'Take no notice. You'd look fucking amazing in a black bin-liner and she knows that. She's just a stick with tits – and fake ones at that. The woman needs a good fry-up. There, wear that pink one. You look great in that.'

Jasmine took Jimmy's advice and slipped on her trusty hot-pink Matthew Williamson number. 'Can you do me up, please?' she asked.

'Och, do I have to?' he replied, slipping his hand under the fabric and fumbling for her breasts. 'Like I said. You look great in that dress, but you look better without it.'

Jasmine laughed politely and removed his hand. 'Come on, Jim, just do me up, yeah?'

He slid the spaghetti straps off her shoulders and shoved his hand back down her dress, groping her roughly. 'Ah, come on baby. Just a quickie, eh? You were gagging for it earlier.'

'Jimmy,' said Jasmine, slightly exasperated. 'All our friends are out there waiting for us. Let's just get on with the evening, yeah?'

'What?' Jimmy looked surprised. 'Are you getting frigid on me?'

'Oh shut up,' said Jasmine, feeling her cheeks burn with indignation. 'You know I hate it when you talk like that.'

'Oh, but I know you want me, baby. You're always gagging for it.'

'That's not true,' warned Jasmine, getting angry with him now.

'Och, you love it, Jazz. You fucking love it. Just give me a quick blow job and I'll stop bothering you.'

'Piss off,' she responded, struggling to do the zip up herself.

'What?' Jimmy looked put out. 'God, you're really pissed off, aren't you?'

'Yes,' replied Jasmine. 'You make me feel cheap when you say stuff like that and I'm not, OK?'

'All right, love,' he said in an exasperated tone. 'Keep your hair on. I don't know why you're getting upset; it's not like you're Mother Fucking Teresa. All I'm saying is that you're a right horny wee madam, eh? It's not an insult.'

'OK,' conceded Jasmine. 'Let's just leave it and get back out to our mates, all right?'

But then, as they walked out of the bedroom, Jimmy blew it. He muttered, 'You are pretty easy though, eh?'

That was it. He always had to have the last word and he always went too far. Jasmine felt the sting of those tears again. How dare Jimmy make her feel like this! She wasn't cheap and she wasn't easy. Yes, she enjoyed making love to the man she adored, but sex was a big thing for her. She'd only had two boyfriends before Jimmy and she'd always been totally monogamous. Just because she took her clothes off for a living it didn't mean she gave her body away for free. She was not a piece of meat to be groped and pawed over. Her body belonged to her, and her alone. It was up to Jasmine to decide if and when she felt like sharing it, not Jimmy's right to take it whenever he fancied. If only Jimmy knew the things she'd seen. Then he wouldn't be so quick to joke about her being easy.

'Jimmy,' she said as calmly as she could. 'I think you should go and have a cold shower and think about what you just said to me, OK? Imagine how you'd feel if someone said that to your sister.'

'But—' he started.

'No buts, Jim,' she said sternly. 'Just leave me alone for a bit, OK? I'm really pissed off with you right now.'

Jimmy didn't go for a cold shower. He joined his mates for a beer instead and as Jasmine glanced over at him, laughing and joking on the terrace, he seemed totally unaffected by what she'd said. He didn't understand. How could he?

'You all set for next weekend, then?' asked Cookie. 'You are going to be the most beautiful bride ever. It all sounds so perfect.'

Jasmine pulled herself back into the moment and thought about her impending wedding. Yes, it would be perfect. She'd been waiting her whole life for this day and nothing was going to ruin it. Certainly not Jimmy.

She chatted to Cookie and Crystal for a while about who should sit where.

'Who's going to have the bad luck to be sitting next to the Wicked Witch of the West?' asked Chrissie, nodding towards Madeleine.

'I'll pay you fifty grand to sit me on the opposite side of the room,' offered Cookie with a shudder.

'I was thinking about putting one of my brothers on each side of her,' giggled Jasmine. 'They can keep her entertained with their stories about prison!'

'Ooh, yes, do,' enthused Crystal. 'She'll be even more sour-faced than usual if you do that.'

Just then a figure appeared on the steps leading up from the sea. Theirs was a private stretch of beach and no one should have been able to access their garden from down there.

'Who's that?' wondered Jasmine out loud, squinting at the man as he drew closer.

He was tall and slim and slightly dishevelled. His long, dark hair flopped over his eyes. He was carrying a bottle in his right hand and a satchel was slung across his body.

'Oh, it's Louis,' grinned Chrissie. 'He does like to make an entrance, doesn't he?'

They all seemed to think of Louis as a bit of a misfit, but Jasmine felt her face break into a smile as he approached. She adored him. He sauntered with loose limbs towards her and grinned his lopsided grin.

'Jasmine.' He kissed her softly on each cheek and squeezed her arm affectionately. 'I 'ope you don't mind me coming. I walk along the beach from ze 'otel. The dog next door, he almost bit my bum!'

Jasmine laughed. 'No, Louis, it's a lovely surprise. I wasn't expecting you.'

'None of us were,' muttered Jimmy, as he strode past on his way to the bar. He didn't stop to say hello to the newcomer.

Jimmy wasn't very keen on Louis. He was a bit different from the other guys. He was Portuguese for a start, and much more – how could Jasmine put it? – well, sensitive, than the rest of them. He didn't join in their laddish antics. He didn't drive a sports car. In fact, he didn't seem to own a car at all. He never got so drunk that he was kicked out of a club; he'd never been 'papped' snogging someone else's girlfriend and he didn't frequent Exotica. He didn't dress like the others, either. The footballers had an unofficial uniform of designer jeans, shirts undone to reveal their six-packs, smart suit jackets, gold chains, diamond earrings and the odd tattoo to rough up the image a bit. Their hair was their crowning glory – whether it was cut into a Mohican, shaved, a shaggy rock-god 'do' or just a simple short back and sides – it was always slathered in 'product' and preened to perfection. Quite how they ever got on the pitch in time to play a game of football was beyond Jasmine. Jimmy took longer to style his hair than she did – and his was a good two feet shorter than hers.

But Louis was a law unto himself. Jasmine supposed he was a bit of a geek, really, with his ripped jeans, battered trainers and crumpled T-shirts. He wore a small silver St Christopher around his neck but was otherwise unadorned. His hair was long, dark brown and floppy and he wore black-framed glasses. Despite his millions, he always looked a bit unkempt. That wasn't to say he was an unattractive man. Far from it. Louis Ricardo was tall, dark and handsome in the true sense of the phrase. And if Jasmine was completely honest with herself, she did kind of fancy him a bit. Sometimes she wanted to just lean forward and stroke his flawless brown skin. It looked so smooth and inviting. And she'd even had a dream about him the other night, a dream so naughty that she'd barely been able to look Jimmy in the eye the next day. But no! What was she thinking? She was about to become a married woman.

'Look at those pecs,' whispered Cookie, as Louis was busy kissing Chrissie hello.

Jasmine tried not to stare. Tonight Louis was wearing his trusty old jeans with a white vest. There were acres of perfect tanned flesh on show and it was not wasted on the girls. All the guys were in good shape – it was their job to stay fit. But while the rest of them *looked* as if they'd spent hours in their private gyms (which of course they had), Louis appeared to be exactly as nature intended. It was all so effortless. There was no primping or preening or parading. He had no idea how attractive he was and that made him all the more appealing. The guy just had good genes. It was as simple as that.

'Jasmine,' he said a little breathlessly. 'I 'ave something for you …' He started rummaging around in his leather man-bag.

Jasmine watched him intently. His glasses had begun to slide down his nose and she couldn't help but notice that his eyelashes were impossibly long. God! What was wrong with her? She would have to do something about this silly crush she seemed to be getting on Louis! He would notice her staring if she didn't stop. He was a clever man. He'd been to university and everything. In fact, Jimmy had once told her that Louis had turned down his first cap because he had to finish his final exams. Jimmy told this story to illustrate how stupid Louis was, but it just made Jasmine admire him all the more. And now he studied football with the same passion. The other players were always complaining about the discussions Louis had with the coach about tactics and positions.

'He thinks he's fucking José Mourinho,' she'd once heard Luke Parks snap bitterly. 'He's got his eyes on the manager's job.'

Jasmine was the only one who pronounced his name properly, the Portuguese way. 'You say like this,' he'd explained to her, puckering his full lips. 'Loo-esh. Loo-esh.'

Jimmy hated that Jasmine liked Louis so much. He didn't understand the attraction at all. In fact, he only tolerated the situation because he (along with all the other guys) was convinced Louis was gay. But Jasmine knew different. Yes, Louis was intelligent. Yes, he was thoughtful. Yes, he was gentle and, yes, he was kind. But, no, the man was definitely not gay. She might not have been to university, but there was one subject Jasmine was an expert on and that was men. Louis Ricardo was as red-blooded as the rest of them. Of that she was sure. Not that she'd told Jimmy that, mind you.

Louis was still fishing in his leather messenger bag.

'Oi, Louis!' shouted Jimmy from across the terrace. 'Is that a handbag you've got there?'

The others guffawed loudly and Jasmine frowned at her fiancé. Jimmy could be so childish sometimes. Didn't he know a Mulberry when he saw one?

But Louis just smiled at his team mates and shrugged. Then he continued searching for whatever it was he wanted to give Jasmine.

'Ah, here,' he said, handing her a book. 'Is guide book of Andalusia. Is very good, I think. It has in-depth section on history and geography of area.' He blushed slightly. 'I thought you might like it. You mentioned you were interested in …' he searched for the word in English, '… exploring the region.'

'Oh, Louis, that's so sweet of you,' said Jasmine, genuinely grateful. As she kissed him thank you on his smooth brown cheek, she noticed Jimmy's look of horror. She watched as Jimmy said something to his mates and then all three men stared at Louis and laughed, cruelly. The fact was that the footballers were as bitchy as their wives and girlfriends.

'Right, time to go!' announced Jimmy, clapping his hands and ushering everyone towards the stretch limo he'd booked, now waiting in the drive. The group grabbed designer clutch bags and half-drunk bottles of champagne and climbed in. As the limo pulled out on to the street the flashes started again and the gang could hear the photographers screeching their names. Sometimes Jasmine felt as if she lived in a particularly manic video for some trance track – 'warning, this scene involves strobe lights'. It was just as well she didn't suffer from epilepsy. Cookie winced as the bulbs went off.

'God, it gives me such a headache,' she complained.

Jimmy wound down the window and he and Paul gave the paparazzi the V sign as they sped off.

'Very mature,' muttered Jasmine.

There were even more photographers waiting at the club, fifty of them at least. It was clear to Jasmine that they were expecting a high celebrity turnout at Maxine's event.

'Wow, this place is fucking amazing!' announced Blaine, taking in the sight of the lit-up ship. 'Cruise', he read the blue neon sign above the deck. 'Good name. Good old Maxi, eh?'

Jasmine watched the guys spill out on to the pavement first, and then waited as Madeleine, Cookie and Chrissie slid gracefully from their leather seats, careful not to flash their knickers. Jasmine went last. She took a deep breath, smoothed down her dress and slid from the car into the flashing night. She was blinded by the lights and, as always, her heart was racing with excitement. Did she look OK? Did she have spinach from the canapés in her teeth? Had her mascara run? And then she heard her name being called over and over again and a switch flicked on in her brain and she knew what she had to do.

'Jasmine!' shouted the paparazzi from the other side of the road where they were held back by a barrier. 'Madeleine! Crystal! Cookie!'

As always, the girls did their thing for the cameras. Chrissie waved enthusiastically, Madeleine pouted moodily and Cookie smiled sweetly. But Jasmine put everything into her performance. The others complained about the attention but she was grateful to be there. She knew she was nothing without the press and she liked to put on a good show for them. She flashed her eyes and teeth and smiled with her tongue placed firmly behind her top teeth: a tip she'd picked up from an interview she'd read with Katie Price. She was careful to place her right foot just so, in front of the left, with her knee bent and her bare shoulder turned towards the cameras, hand on thigh. This was the most flattering pose she'd found. Then she leaned forward slightly, to give them the flash of cleavage they'd been waiting for. Jimmy tolerated the photographers because he knew he had to, but he'd soon had enough. 'Come on Mother Teresa,' he muttered moodily. 'I think you've given them enough of an eyeful, don't you?'

Chapter Seventeen

Grace usually hated going to parties alone, but tonight was turning out to be quite fun. It was Blaine who'd suggested she get herself an invite and he'd been right – there would be plenty to interest a celebrity journalist here. Cruise was ridiculously over the top with a zillion fairy lights illuminating the exterior. An army of paparazzi was camped across the road and hundreds of holidaymakers were lined up against the rope barricades, mobile phones held aloft, desperately trying to photograph the arriving celebs.

Inside, the walls were fuchsia-pink with black orchids hand-painted on top; the lights were exquisite glass chandeliers, twinkly rather than bright, and the seating arrangements involved velvet chaises longues in jewel shades and animal-print Louis V chairs. The bar was semi-circular and gold. It was quite dark in the club, but not uncomfortably so. In fact, the atmosphere was almost womb-like.

The staff (who all looked like models) were wearing traditional black and white uniforms but with a twist. The girls had a bit of a French maid thing going on with very short, flirty skirts, low-cut white blouses and black high heels. The boys, who were in black DJs, had their bow ties undone and their collars loose. The overall effect, decided Grace, sipping a glass of complimentary champagne, was relaxed opulence. And sexy. Expensively sexy. Just like Maxine de la Fallaise herself, Grace supposed.

She'd met Maxine many times in the past and, for a celebrity (and a B-list one, at that), she liked her very much. Despite her reputation as a party animal, Maxine seemed extraordinarily media savvy. She always gave interviews when she had something to publicise and would give a few juicy morsels of personal detail, just enough to pique the reader's interest, without actually revealing very much about herself. Yes, Maxine was smart and Grace admired that. And now she'd created this amazing nightclub. Grace was very impressed. The Party Princess had evolved into the Queen of Clubs. There, Grace had her angle already.

She leaned back on her velvet chaise and watched the VIPs pouring in – Spanish soap stars, minor European royals, a handful of British stars who were on holiday in Marbella, the older, ex-pat brigade, ah, and now the footballers and their funny little WAGs. Grace laughed. They reminded her of little girls on their way to a fifth birthday party, all dressed up in their princess outfits, holding hands, giggling and excited. She had to admit they were kind of cute. Except Madeleine Parks, of course; there was nothing cute about that one. Even Grace felt intimidated by her.

Maxi worked the door like a lioness protecting her pride, flicking her golden mane as she kissed and complimented every arriving guest and posed with them for pictures taken by the official photographer. God, she was good. Carlos Russo, meanwhile, chatted amiably with his guests, glancing every now and then at his girlfriend and smiling encouragingly at her as she worked her magic. He looked more like a proud father than a lover, thought Grace.

Grace watched the footballers weave through the crowds and head purposefully towards the back of the room. Jasmine spotted her as she passed and waved hello enthusiastically while Jimmy scowled. Where were they going? Grace followed them at a safe distance, knowing that they must be heading for some secret area reserved for the most famous guests. They disappeared down some stairs. Grace followed. As she got to the bottom of the steps, Jasmine glanced back and noticed Grace.

'Come on,' she called, ushering her to join them. 'This is the VIP area.'

Grace trotted down the stairs, but as she tried to enter the room an enormous black guy in a DJ blocked her way.

'Back upstairs, love,' he ordered in a friendly but firm voice. 'This area is private.'

'She's with us,' explained Jasmine, flashing him her sweetest smile.

The doorman shrugged and allowed Grace through.

Fabulous! The inner sanctum. It was a journalist's idea of heaven. Wall-to-wall celebrities just oozing column inches. Grace stepped inside and glanced around for suitable prey. Her eyes grew accustomed to the half-light and rested on a woman in white. It was Lila Rose, perched neatly on a couch. Grace stopped in her tracks. Shit. She couldn't face the woman. Not after what she'd written about her. She hurriedly made her excuses to a confused Jasmine and skulked back upstairs, wondering why her conscience had begun bothering her lately.

Lila had arrived at the back of the ship by speedboat and had avoided being seen by the press. It had been kind of Maxine to arrange this special secret entrance and Lila was touched by the gesture. In fact, seeing Maxine again had been a much happier event than Lila had anticipated. Maxi had been hovering on the deck as Lila alighted, dressed up to the nines in tight leopard print with her hair blowing in the wind and a mega-watt smile on her scarlet lips. She'd hugged Lila tightly and proclaimed that she'd missed her soooo much! As Maxi clamped Lila to her bosom, Lila had been flooded with a wave of affection for her old friend. She felt safe in Maxi's arms. It was a warm, comfortable sensation, like returning home after a long absence. Yes, it had been good to see Maxi again.

Now Lila and Peter were lounging on a leather sofa in the VIP area, sipping their cocktails, listening to the live music (some achingly hip band from London whom Lila had never heard of) and happily people-watching.

'Oh God, it's *that* woman,' said Lila, horrified at the sight of Grace Melrose.

'What on earth is *she* doing here?' spat Peter in disgust. 'Shall I get rid of her?'

But just as Peter was about to get up, Grace Melrose turned on her heels and disappeared.

'Must have got thrown out,' said Peter.

'Good,' replied Lila. 'Who does she think she is, coming in here?'

All the guests that night were 'somebodies', but this area on the lower deck had been cordoned off for the true elite. Now they were concentrating on the arrival of the footballers and their partners. Maxine had explained that there had been some discussion about whether or not this group was important enough to be allowed into the VIP area. Luke and Madeleine Parks were obviously A-List and Jimmy Jones and Jasmine Watts were borderline. The others were nobodies, really, but in the end a begging phone call from Blaine Edwards had been enough to swing it. That and the fact that Maxine was terrified of insulting Madeleine. 'She is a total witch,' Maxi had explained. 'And if I don't let her in she'll probably make a voodoo doll of me and stick Botox needles in my eyes.'

Peter was gawping, open-mouthed at the sight before him. 'That one there, Princess Frowny Face ...'

'Madeleine Parks,' interjected Lila.

'Yes, her. She is wearing the equivalent wealth of a Middle Eastern oil state around her scrawny neck.'

'Yes, that's certainly a lot of bling,' agreed Lila.

'Indeed. By my estimation,' he whispered, 'between them, we have several million pounds' worth of diamonds, three metres of hair extensions, forty false nails, fifty bottles of fake tan and at least eight silicon implants.'

Lila giggled. 'Peter, don't be such a bitch!' she scolded, but he did have a point. These girls were certainly not as nature had intended them to be, except perhaps for Jasmine Watts, her mum and dad's new neighbour. Lila had to concede that she really was a natural beauty.

'Which one do you think has her own breasts?' asked Lila.

'Oh, Jasmine, definitely,' replied Peter. 'Look, hers are much less spherical than the others and lower too. God never intended a woman's breasts to be worn on the clavicle! I'm not sure whoever did their surgery has ever actually studied anatomy. But look, Jasmine's jiggle … watch! When she dances around like that.'

'For a gay man you certainly know your boobs,' said Lila, amused.

'Oh, but she's lovely, isn't she?' sighed Peter. 'If I could be reincarnated as a woman, I'd like to come back as Jasmine Watts.' And then, too late, he added, 'Or you, darling. That goes without saying, of course.'

But Lila knew Peter had been right first time. Who wouldn't want to look like that? Jasmine was young and unblemished; her dark skin was smooth like a baby's and there was a plumpness to her buttocks and thighs that Lila had lost years ago. It almost physically hurt to look upon such youth and perfection. She felt how the wicked stepmother must have done when the mirror told her that Snow White's beauty had surpassed her own.

'And who the hell is that gorgeous specimen?' demanded Peter suddenly, sitting bolt upright and spilling his Woo Woo all over his lap.

Lila followed Peter's gaze to a slim, dark-haired boy with glasses. He was on the outside of the footballers' group, alone, staring into space.

Lila shrugged. 'I guess he must be one of the footballers, but you know me, Peter, I wouldn't know a premiership player if he turned up in my gazpacho.'

'No, me neither,' said Peter, standing up. 'But I think it might be time for me to broaden my horizons. Excuse me, darling, but I can feel a season ticket coming on.'

Lila giggled to herself as she watched Peter walk brazenly up to the group of footballers and introduce himself. She stood up and looked around for Maxi. She searched everywhere for her friend but the hostess seemed to have disappeared. Eventually the barman ushered her into the men's toilets, where she found Maxi leaning over an unconscious young man in tight leather trousers. She appeared to be waving a cup of coffee in his face.

'Oh, Lila, thank goodness,' said Maxine in a panic. 'You're good at this sort of thing.'

'What sort of thing?' asked Lila, bemused.

'Sobering people up,' replied Maxi. 'JJ here is the lead singer. They've only done half their set and he's so pissed, or stoned or something that I can't bloody well wake the little bastard up!'

Maxi kicked him with her stilettos and shouted, 'Come on JJ, you're due on again in a minute!'

'Let me try,' said Lila, stepping over the body and bending down to floor level. She stroked the singer's stubbly cheek gently and blew in his face.

'JJ,' she said, softly. 'It's time to wake up now. Come on, baby. Wake up.'

She stroked his face some more and then, suddenly – thwack! – she slapped him so hard across the cheek that it made Maxine jump.

'Eh? What the fuck?' JJ opened his bloodshot eyes and stared uncomprehendingly at Lila. 'Lila Rose,' he said in disbelief. 'Am I dead? Is this heaven?'

Maxine and Lila were still laughing uncontrollably ten minutes later with a rather embarrassed JJ safely back on stage.

'I can't believe you slapped him that hard,' said Maxine. 'He's got a bright-red hand print on his face!'

'I know,' giggled Lila. 'I do feel a bit guilty.'

'No, don't,' said Maxi. 'You saved my party. The DJ's not here yet. I'd have had to get up and sing and, as you know, karaoke is not my forte!'

The two women sat together, their bare knees touching. Maxi smiled broadly at her friend and proclaimed, 'It's so good to see you, Lila; you have no idea.'

Lila grinned back. Perhaps she'd been wrong to push Maxine away for so long. Peter was wonderful, but sometimes a woman needed another girl around. Just being here with her tonight reminded Lila of the fun they'd used to have and for the first time in ages Lila didn't feel lonely at all. Or old. Or past it. In fact, her heart was racing and she couldn't wipe this stupid grin from her face.

'I do have an idea,' said Lila. 'Because I feel exactly the same, Maxi. I'm sorry it's been so long.'

'Let's try and see more of each other from now on,' suggested Maxine hopefully.

'Yes, let's do that,' agreed Lila. And she meant it. She really did.

'I'd better get back to mingling,' said Maxi, reluctantly standing up. 'But we'll catch up again later, won't we?'

'We will,' confirmed Lila. 'I'd better save Peter from himself. He's pestering the footballers.'

'Lila, Lila!' called Peter, spotting her heading in his direction. 'Come and meet my new friends. This is Jasmine, and Crystal – fab name, isn't it? And Cookie and her bump! Cookie's going to have a baby. Isn't that wonderful?'

'Great,' said Lila, bemused, nodding hello to the pretty little WAGs, who were bouncing around Peter like excited puppies.

'Jasmine here has just explained the offside rule to me. And I get it!

Aren't you impressed? I never in a million years thought I'd understand the offside rule. Go on, Jasmine, explain it to Lila too. She can show off to Brett … if he ever turns up.'

Lila shot Peter a warning look and then smiled, patiently, at the fragrant young glamour girl.

Jasmine blushed, obviously embarrassed. 'Oh, I'm sure Ms Rose isn't interested in my silly story,' said Jasmine.

'No, no, no, it's fine,' insisted Lila, touched by Jasmine's modesty. 'I'd love to understand the offside rule. My dad will be amazed.' She smiled encouragingly at Jasmine.

'Go on,' urged Peter.

'OK,' began Jasmine. 'You're in a shoe shop, second in the queue for the till. Behind the shop assistant on the till is a pair of shoes you have seen that you *must* have. The shopper in front of you has also seen them and is eyeing them with desire. Both of you have forgotten your purses. It would be rude to push in front of the first woman if you had no money to pay for the shoes. The shop assistant remains at the till, waiting. Your friend is trying on another pair of shoes at the back of the shop and sees your dilemma. She prepares to throw her purse to you. If she does so, you can catch the purse, then walk round the other shopper and buy the shoes. At a pinch she could throw the purse ahead of the other shopper and whilst it is in flight you could nip around the other shopper, catch the purse and buy the shoes! BUT, you must always remember that until the purse has actually been thrown, it would be plain wrong for you to be in front of the other shopper and you would be offside!'

Peter dissolved into a fit of hysteria. 'Isn't that the most brilliant thing you've ever heard?' he demanded.

Lila giggled. 'Yes, that's pretty good, Jasmine. How did you work that out?'

'Oh, it's just something I read on the internet,' Jasmine blushed again.

Suddenly Maxi burst on the scene, dragging the official photographer by his arm. 'We have got to get a picture of this,' she announced. 'Britain's two favourite pin-up girls together. New best friends!'

She thrust Jasmine and Lila together and then draped herself over both of them from behind. All three smiled automatically as the flash went off and then quickly detangled their arms. Lila and Jasmine took a step back from each other and smiled shyly at each other like the virtual strangers they were.

Then Maxine rushed off again. 'Meet me on deck in five minutes,' she called to Lila. 'I could do with a break.'

Lila noticed the enormous diamond heart-shaped ring on Jasmine's engagement finger. 'Gorgeous ring,' she said politely, although it was way too flashy for Lila's taste. 'Is the wedding soon?'

Jasmine nodded. 'Next week.'

'Where are you having the ceremony?' asked Lila, an expert in the art of small talk.

'Tillydochrie Castle,' she said. 'In the Highlands.'

'Oh, wow, that place is beautiful,' Lila enthused. 'I filmed there once. It's such a magical setting. I'm sure your big day will be wonderful.'

'Why don't you come?' blurted out Jasmine.

Lila was taken aback. She'd only just met Jasmine. 'Well, I'm not really sure what our plans are. Brett's still in LA and I don't know when he's arriving ...'

'Oh, we'd love to!' Peter interrupted, even though Lila hadn't actually noticed him being invited. 'Wouldn't we, Lila?'

Jasmine smiled hopefully. 'It would be great if you could make it,' she urged. 'And Brett too, of course.'

'I'll see what I can do,' said Lila, although she wasn't quite sure how she felt about it. Tillydochrie Castle really was an exquisite place, and she had always hoped to visit it again, but at a footballer's wedding? Hmm. She'd have to think about this one.

Lila was waiting on a bench, gazing out to sea, when the door flew open and Maxine tumbled on deck.

'Hi, hun!' she gushed, throwing herself beside Lila. 'Phew! This hostess lark is exhausting and my feet are killing me.' She slipped off a four-inch stiletto and began rubbing the sole of her foot.

'Where's Carlos?' asked Lila, suddenly realising she hadn't seen Maxine's lover all evening.

'He's gone home already,' giggled Maxi. 'He can't take the pace at his age.' She glanced at her watch. 'He'll be in his dressing gown watching the golf highlights on Sky by now.'

'Doesn't it bother you, the age difference?' asked Lila, thinking that it must.

Maxine shook her head. 'Nope. I love Carlos. He's my soul mate. It wouldn't matter if he was a hundred; he'd still be the man for me.'

'Really?' Lila found it difficult to believe. Maxine was such a big kid.

'Really,' Maxine nodded. 'The only thing that bothers me about Carlos is his frigging ex-wife. She's a nightmare!'

'She still won't divorce him, then?' asked Lila. They'd chatted about the wife problem at New Year before Maxine had got so drunk that she'd stopped making sense.

'No. I mean, it's ridiculous, isn't it? Everybody knows me and Carlos are a couple, but Esther refuses to let him go.'

It was true. Even the press referred to Maxine as Carlos Russo's 'constant companion'.

'Their marriage has been over for fifteen years!' continued Maxi. 'The whole thing is farcical. Have you seen their house in Beverley Hills?'

Lila shook her head.

'It's insane! They've basically split the property in two. They have separate entrances and separate staff but they still share the same address – as if that's going to fool anybody that they're still together! Esther is completely freaking crazy. I can't bear being in the same city as any of my exes, let alone under the same roof.'

'Why does Carlos put up with it?' asked Lila.

'Because Esther is a good Spanish Catholic and Carlos doesn't want to insult her devotion to the church.' Maxine rolled her eyes to show that she thought this was nonsense.

'But doesn't she care that her husband is so publicly unfaithful?' asked Lila, thinking of Brett and the nightmares she had about his nubile young co-stars.

'No. It's not like I'm the first,' explained Maxine. 'Carlos has had loads of girlfriends before me. Anyway, I think she just uses her faith as an excuse to keep hold of him.'

'But she hasn't got any hold over him, has she? He lives with you most of the time.'

'Yeah, that's true. I have the man, but Esther still has the title of Mrs Carlos Russo. That's what she's married to, not the man himself. It's the kudos that comes with having a famous husband that she loves. You know what LA is like, Lila. You lived there long enough. Celebrity status gives you power in that town. Esther isn't about to give that up without a fight. But I tell you what: I'm up for the fight. I really am.'

'So you want to marry him?' asked Lila. She was a bit surprised that Maxine hadn't tired of trips up the aisle.

'Oh yeah. Definitely,' Maxine nodded enthusiastically. 'Like I said, Carlos is the one. Esther knows I want to marry him too and she's not happy about it.'

'Really?' Lila was intrigued by her friend's tumultuous love life. 'Have you met her?'

'Oh yeah,' giggled Maxine. 'Loads of times in LA. We even had dinner together as one big happy family last time I was over. Me, Carlos, Esther and the two youngest kids. It was very cosy, I can tell you.'

'I bet it was,' shuddered Lila. 'Was she civil to you?'

'Oh yes, while Carlos and the kids were around it was all, "Would you like some wine, Maxine?" and "Could you pass the cream, please, Maxine?" but when the kids went off to play with their Playstation and Carlos disappeared off to take a phone call she turned into the crazy woman I always knew she'd be!'

'Really? What happened?'

'She said, "You are nothing to heem, you harlot! You weel marry my Carlos over my dead body!"'

Lila couldn't help but laugh at Maxine's bad Spanish accent.

'Then Carlos came back in and she was all, "Would you like a coffee, Maxine, my dear?" again. The thing is,' continued Maxi, cheerfully. 'I would kill her if I thought I could get away with it. I mean, I might have youth on my side but I'm not going to wait for her to die of old age before I get that ring. God, I have got to find a way to beat that crazy woman!'

'Still the same old Maxi,' grinned Lila. 'You still have to win.'

'Damn right!'

'And you're sure it's Carlos you want?'

'Of course it is! What do you mean?'

'Well, sometimes, when you're hell bent on winning you can lose sight of the prize,' Lila mused.

Maxi shook her head. 'No, Carlos is a catch. I'm lucky to have him. I'd have preferred to have him twenty years ago but, hey, even I can't win 'em all, eh?'

Lila grinned at her friend and then remembered something she'd been meaning to bring up with her for ages.

'Actually, Maxi, I've got a bone to pick with you.'

'Yes?' Maxine looked slightly concerned. 'What have I done now?'

'Well,' said Lila. 'I was reading in a magazine the other day that you had just celebrated your thirtieth birthday.'

Maxi grinned mischievously, knowing what was coming next.

'And I just thought that that was a bit odd, considering you're only two years younger than me and, unless I've lost track, I was thirty-six on my last birthday. You've shaved off four years, you jammy cow!'

'I know, I know, but everybody's at it, aren't they?'

'I'm not,' said Lila.

'Well, sack your bloody agent then, girl,' teased Maxine, tickling her friend in the ribs. 'What did you think of Jasmine Watts?' she asked suddenly.

Lila shrugged. 'She seemed nice enough. A sweet girl. Far too good-looking for us old hags to be seen with, of course, but we can't hold that against her, can we?'

'Hey, don't you go getting jealous of the young guns coming up behind,' teased Maxine. 'You do all right for yourself, Mrs Sexiest Woman on the Planet as voted for by *GQ!*'

Lila smiled and conceded, 'Yes, I suppose I do OK for a woman of my age. But that was 2005. I have a feeling I'll be behind the fragrant Jasmine these days.'

'Maybe,' shrugged Maxine. 'But I wouldn't complain if I woke up in the morning and found myself trapped in your body! Anyway, the reason I asked is because Blaine Edwards – you know that Australian tosser, her manager?'

Lila nodded grimly. She knew Blaine Edwards. Or, at least, she knew of him.

'He asked if I could persuade you and Brett to go to Jasmine's wedding next week. They could do with upping the celeb count, apparently.'

'Oh, what is this?' asked Lila, rolling her eyes. 'Rent a celebrity?'

Maxine nodded. 'Something like that. The Beckhams are going. It should be a pretty good bash.'

Lila shrugged. 'I don't know,' she said. 'I'll see what Brett thinks.'

When they finally got home, long after midnight, Lila found the house in silence. It had been such a lovely night Lila didn't want it to be over yet. She and Peter decided to have one final glass of wine under the stars. They sat side by side on a wooden swing under the gazebo, and rocked gently back and forth listening to the crickets and the lull of the waves. Lila had surprised herself tonight. She'd actually had a pretty good time and it had been lovely to catch up with Maxine. Come to think of it, she'd barely given Brett a thought all evening.

'It was a good party, wasn't it?' she said to Peter.

'Certainly was,' he agreed. 'Shame I didn't meet the love of my life, but then I never do, do I? Always the bridesmaid, me ...'

'I take it you didn't get very far with that footballer, then?'

Peter shook his head. 'My gaydar must be on the blink,' he said. 'Straight as a die, that one. Unfortunately. What a waste. He had such beautiful long fingers, too. Just like a pianist I once met in Vienna ...'

'Oh, Peter, you didn't go propositioning a straight footballer, did you? They're Neanderthals, aren't they? I'm surprised you didn't get taken on deck and thrown overboard.'

Just then, the peace of the night was broken by shouting from the other side of the hedge.

'What's going on?' asked Lila.

Peter shrugged.

The sound of more shouting drifted over the hedge, but it was too far away for Lila and Peter to make out the words.

'Do you think they're OK?' asked Lila.

'Don't know,' replied Peter. 'Shall I have a look?'

He shoved Lila up on to her feet and then stood on the swing, straining to see above the hedge. 'I. Can't. Quite. See. Over,' he complained, straining on his tiptoes.

Lila giggled. 'You're going to fall,' she warned him, just before he toppled forwards and fell head first into the hedge.

'Shit!' exclaimed Peter, from somewhere in the foliage. 'I think I've lost an eye!'

'Shhh,' said Lila, fishing her friend out from the hedge. 'They'll hear us.'

She brushed the twigs and leaves off Peter's face and tilted his face towards the moonlight.

'You're OK,' she said, gently. 'Just a little scratch on your eyelid.'

'Oh no!' cried Peter. 'Do you think it will scar?'

'I'm sure you'll be as handsome as ever in the morning. Now shoo! Let's get to bed before we trash Mum and Dad's garden.'

As they started to head towards the house, they heard the shouts again. Louder this time.

'Jasmine, you get here now, you wee bitch!' came an angry Scottish cry. 'I mean it, Jazz. You've been bang out of order tonight! Where are you? Get here now!'

'Gosh, that sounds pretty nasty,' said Lila, suddenly concerned.

'I fear all is not well in WAGland,' said Peter melodramatically, as he danced across the lawn towards the house.

'No, I don't think it is,' agreed Lila. 'Should we do something?'

Peter shook his head. 'I'm sure they're fine. Everybody has arguments, don't they?'

'I suppose so. But he did sound very angry.'

'Come on,' urged Peter. 'It's their business. Not ours.'

Chapter Eighteen

Jasmine's back was jammed against the wall and Jimmy's angry face was inches from hers. His features were contorted, his eyes full of bitterness and suddenly it struck Jasmine that Jimmy didn't look so handsome any more. His breath stank of beer. He couldn't handle his drink. Jasmine knew that. Too many pints turned Dr Jekyll into Mr Hyde and God knows how many pints of complimentary Spanish beer he'd had this evening. Jasmine was scared. It wasn't the first time he'd got cross with her when he was drunk. Christ! Jimmy could have a fight with a brick wall when he'd had a few too many. But tonight was different. When she looked in his eyes she swore she could see hatred.

He was spitting out his words. 'You behaved like a fucking wee tart tonight.'

'I don't know what you're talking about,' said Jasmine, trying to keep her voice calm. 'I hardly saw you all evening. I've no idea what I've done to annoy you like this.'

'Oh, you've no fucking idea, have you? Playing the stupid card, are we?' he slurred his words. 'Love me, love me, I'm thick!' He mimicked her voice. 'I'm just a stupid, fucking, wee slapper. I don't know what I've done. Eh? Is that it, Jazz? Too thick to know what you've done?'

Jasmine had tears running down her face. She didn't know if she was crying because of his words, or his actions, or because the boy she loved seemed to have vanished into the warm Spanish air.

'I'm sorry if I've upset you, baby,' she sobbed. 'But I honestly don't know why you're so angry with me.'

'I'm angry with you because you made a fool of yourself and you made a fool of me!' he announced, full of righteous indignation.

'How?' asked Jasmine desperately, still baffled by Jimmy's rage.

'Och, I saw you with Louis. Kissing him and rubbing yourself against him. Little slapper! He's no' even interested in you, Jasmine. The boy's a fucking queer! What did he give you anyway, that made you so fucking desperate to rub your fanny up against him?'

Now Jasmine was getting angry. She could feel the red mist rising. She'd always believed in justice and this just wasn't fair!

'He gave me a book, you drunken tosser!' she shouted back. 'Just a book. A guide book about Spain because he thought I might like to read it.'

'Aye, well he's as daft as you are, then. Everybody knows stupid wee strippers can't read!'

There was nothing Jasmine hated more than being called stupid. OK, so she was no intellectual, but she was no idiot either. How dare he! Jasmine tried to push Jimmy's arm out of her way but he grabbed her wrists instead. He squeezed so tight that she could feel the blood draining from her fingers. She'd had enough of this. He was just ranting for the sake of it, throwing wild accusations that he wouldn't remember in the morning. But she would. And she didn't want to hear them. They had a wedding coming up next week and she wasn't about to let Jimmy ruin everything.

'Let me go,' she warned. 'I mean it. Just let me go to bed. You can sleep in the spare room. We'll discuss this in the morning when you're sober!'

'You're going nowhere, sweetheart,' said Jimmy, through gritted teeth. 'If I'm going to marry you, you need to learn a thing or two about how to be a fucking wife, eh? Like a bit of respect for your husband. All that business with that journalist bitch earlier. What was that about, eh? Saying you were going to keep taking your kit off. As if!'

'Oh, shut up, Jimmy. This is ridiculous! It's my career and I'll decide what I will and won't do.'

Jasmine struggled against his grip. She was pretty strong but Jimmy was stronger.

'And all that fucking flashing your tits to the photographers. I never knew you were such a slag. I wouldn't have looked twice at you if I'd known.'

'You met me at a flipping strip joint! The only thing you did know about me was that I took my clothes off for men. It didn't seem to put you off then, did it?'

He looked her up and down, his top lip curling as if he was disgusted by what he saw. 'I only wanted a shag, love. I didn't plan to marry you. That was all your idea. I just went along with it to keep you quiet.'

That was it. Jasmine was ready to kill the little bastard. With all her might she pulled one hand out of his grip and then fought with him to prise his fingers off the other wrist.

'Let me go, you bastard!' she shouted. 'Let me go!'

Eventually she managed to free her other hand and she ran as fast as she could away from Jimmy. She could hear his feet pounding behind her on the tiles and hear his breath panting closer and closer to her ear. She was running past the pool when he caught her. His hand felt like a lead weight on her shoulder as he grabbed her and swung her round to face him. They stared at each other for a moment. Jasmine was sure she knew what was coming next. She'd been hit often enough as a child to recognise the look on a bully's face and Jimmy was wearing that same dead expression right now.

'Don't do it,' she warned, quietly. 'If you hit me it's over. There's no going back.'

His eyes bored into hers. She could feel her heart pounding in her chest. She was scared. Scared of getting hurt and scared that Jimmy would go too far this time. If he struck her, she'd have to leave. There would be no choice. And then he swung his arm slowly above his head. He hesitated for a minute, as if deciding what to do and then he pushed her hard in the chest so that she tripped backwards, teetered on the edge of the pool and then fell with an almighty splash into the cold water. By the time Jasmine came to the surface, coughing and spluttering, Jimmy had gone. As she pulled her exhausted body out of the water she heard the car engine rev. Jimmy was going for a spin in his sports car. He was so pissed he'd probably wrap it around a tree. Right at that moment, part of Jasmine hoped that he would.

Blaine watched the proceedings from his bedroom window. Silly little fucker, that Jimmy Jones. He wouldn't find another bit of skirt like Jasmine Watts in a hurry. There was a celebrity marriage destined for the scrap heap. Blaine had seen enough A-list divorces pan out to be sure of that. Never mind, he'd make sure those two walked up the aisle together next week. He had far too much money riding on the event to let anything go wrong now. And then when the whole thing fell apart? Well, good old Blaine would be there to pick up the pieces … and to sell the exclusive interviews to the highest bidder. Blaine yawned and stretched. He was tired. He glanced one more time at Jasmine, sitting sobbing on the edge of the pool, took a final sip of his whiskey nightcap and climbed into bed. Blaine Edwards would sleep like a baby tonight. He always did.

When Jasmine woke up in the morning it took a few moments for the horrible events of the night before to seep back into her brain. But then she felt the gritty sting in her eyes and the damp patch on the pillow and she remembered sobbing herself to sleep. She wanted to hate Jimmy, but her first thought was whether or not he'd got home in one piece after driving off in that state. She ran downstairs to the living room and was relieved to find him there, crashed out on the sofa, still wearing his clothes from the night before. He looked beautiful again. Sleeping peacefully with the face of an angel.

He looked like the real Jimmy again. Jasmine's Jimmy. The gorgeous boy she was going to marry next week. She didn't know whether to kiss him tenderly on the cheek or smother him with a pillow. She loved this Jimmy, but what about the one she'd met last night? Drunken Jimmy was a monster who reared his ugly head from time to time. She'd thought she could handle him. She'd certainly handled worse. And it wasn't as if he'd actually hit her or anything. All he'd done was thrown a few drunken insults at her and then push her in the swimming pool. Jasmine knew what extreme physical abuse felt like and this wasn't it. But he had scared her. And he had been seriously out of line. She'd have to talk to him about it later. Explain that things were going to have to change. Perhaps they could make a deal – she would stop the topless work if he stopped drinking. It seemed a fair exchange.

On the floor was an enormous bunch of lilies. She picked them up and padded through to the kitchen to make herself a coffee and put her peace offering in some water. It was going to take more than a few withered flowers to make up for last night. No doubt Jimmy would be hopelessly apologetic when he woke up. Of course, Jasmine knew already that she would accept his apology. But she would make him sweat first. It was the least he deserved.

She opened the French doors and was greeted by a perfect Mediterranean morning. It was barely seven o'clock and the air was still cool from the night before. Jasmine breathed in the smell of dewy grass and smiled to herself. It was a beautiful day.

She perched on a stool at the breakfast bar, sipped her coffee, munched on her honey and toast and scrolled through her emails on her laptop. It had been a couple of days since she'd checked them and her inbox was full. Amongst the junk mail was an email from Alisha, with some cute pictures of her baby, Ebony, attached, and another from her old mate, Roxy, keeping her posted on the comings and goings at Exotica. A couple of designers had been in touch offering her free clothes for her honeymoon. They knew about the magazine deal, of course, and their offer was all about getting free publicity rather than any generosity towards the bride. There were about twenty emails from the wedding planner, Camilla Knight-Saunders, firing questions at her about final decisions on floral displays and asking her what colour of ribbon she wanted on the wedding car. Ooh, and the hotel in the Seychelles where they were spending their honeymoon had sent some more information through. They were getting their own private cottage on the beach with a waterfall and a plunge pool and a four-poster bed both inside and out. How lovely was that?

Then she came to an email from an address she didn't recognise. She was about to report it as spam but something about the title, 'Read me', made her curious. She opened the file.

See attached. 70,000 euros in cash to be left in a plastic bag in the phone box opposite the aquarium by twelve noon Saturday. Or this goes public.

Jasmine had to read the email several times before it began to make any sense. And even then, it made no sense. Was someone trying to blackmail her? She frowned at the screen, not knowing whether to delete the email as a hoax or open the attachment and see if it was genuine. The longer she stared at the words on the screen the more frightened she began to feel and by the time she double-clicked on the attachment her hands were shaking. But nothing could have prepared her for the shock she was about to receive.

A grainy video played before her. It was black and white and a bit shaky and it took a while for Jasmine to make out what was going on. And then gradually, a queasy feeling rose in her stomach as she recognised the room, and the girl in the video, and with a gasp of horror she realised exactly what she was watching. Holy fuck! It showed events that Jasmine had been desperately trying to force from her memory for years. 'No!' she screamed at the screen, hitting the delete button over and over again. 'No!' Finally the screen went blank, but the dreadful scenes wouldn't stop playing in her head. Now somebody wanted to go public with it. She knew she could never let that happen. She'd be ruined. Jasmine tried to catch her breath but she couldn't. She ran outside and tried to breathe in the fresh morning air, but still her heart pounded in her chest. And then her mouth filled with bile and she was sick – violently, horribly, painfully sick all over the fresh, dewy lawn.

It took a while for Jasmine to get her head together, but as her fingers hovered over the keyboard she knew what she had to do. She had to make this situation go away as quickly as possible.

I'll do as you ask on one condition. I'll give you the money if you give me the film footage, every single copy, and delete it from your computer. This is a one-off payment for that tape. Understood?

The reply was almost instant. It read simply, *Deal.*

The truth was, Jasmine knew perfectly well who had emailed her. There was only one man who could have got his hands on this film. She could picture him now, grinning to himself as he typed. Oh, he must be loving this. He'd always got off on having power over those less fortunate than him. Jasmine had thought about going to him, turning up on his doorstep and sorting it out face to face. But it was too risky. He was a dangerous man. He would get what he wanted one way or another and this way she wouldn't have to see him in the flesh.

Jasmine wasn't quite sure how she'd got into town in one piece, her driving had been so erratic, but somehow she was there, waiting at the bank when it opened at ten. She still didn't know if she was doing the right thing. What was the right thing in these circumstances? Jasmine prided herself on being streetwise, but this was something else. This was terrifying. She'd taken Jimmy's car – it was blocking her own – and left him a note saying she'd had to pop out. He would probably still be asleep when she got back, anyway. He need never know anything about this whole sordid deal. As she entered the building on wobbly legs she hid her tears behind her sunglasses. Most of her money was tied up in the joint account she shared with Jimmy, but she'd put some aside in a private account. It was money she'd been paid for a swimwear campaign earlier in the year. Money she'd saved for an emergency. And if this wasn't an emergency then she didn't know what was.

The young, female bank teller didn't bat an eyelid when Jasmine asked to draw such a huge amount. This was Marbella. Everybody had money here and not all the business done in these parts was legitimate. Cash was still king in many circles. But surely the girl must have been suspicious. Jasmine could feel her hands trembling as she reached for the cash. She shoved the brown envelope full of hundred-euro bills into a carrier bag inside her Balenciaga bag and hurried shakily back to the car. Now what? She had almost two hours to kill before the drop-off. She had seriously considered calling Charlie and asking for his advice. She'd have felt much safer with him by her side. But then she'd have to tell him about the video, and about the horrible thing she'd been involved in. And she wasn't sure she could handle the pain in his eyes when he realised that his little Jasmine wasn't quite as innocent as he'd believed. And there was no way she could confide in Jimmy. He would freak out. Oh, Jimmy thought he was 'street' and cool but he was just a baby. He didn't have a clue about the things Jasmine had seen in her past. No, she had no choice. Jasmine had to deal with this thing on her own.

Her hand shook so much that she spilled coffee all over the table as she tried to stir in the sugar. She was killing time in a cafe overlooking the marina, nursing a skinny latte, hiding her bloodshot eyes behind her huge sunglasses and avoiding the gazes of curious British holidaymakers who recognised her from the papers. Jasmine realised that she must be wearing her misery like a sign around her neck because, unlike on any normal day, nobody approached for an autograph. And then, at precisely three minutes to midday, she walked as calmly as she could to the phone box opposite the aquarium. She thought her knees would buckle beneath her. Her head felt tight and she was short of air. She guessed she was close to hyperventilating and she had to lean against the phone booth to stop the world spinning before she could drop her carrier bag full of money on the floor. By now she didn't care about losing the money. Money meant nothing to her. Not when she considered the alternatives.

Jasmine knew that the sensible thing to do would be to run back to the car and disappear for a while, then to return for the tape when the coast was clear. But what if someone else found it first? No, she needed to stay close, so that she could grab the package immediately. Nobody else could see that footage.

There was only one person who could be doing this to her. But why now? When everything was going right? She'd made a name for herself, found a good man, was about to get married. Why would he do this to her now? He'd never disappeared from her life completely. He was always lurking in the background, reminding her that he was there, watching. There was the annual Christmas card with the loaded greeting every year. What had last year's one said? Oh yes, that was it. 'Wishing you a prosperous and safe New Year'. Who wished anybody a 'safe' New Year? He always signed off with 'All my love'. And then there had been the housewarming card, waiting for her on the doormat, on the day that Jimmy had got the keys to Casa Amoura. It had been hand-delivered.

But now she wanted to see him. To confront him. To ask him why. She was terrified but she needed answers. Jasmine ducked between two parked cars and waited. She could see the phone box quite clearly from her hiding place as she crouched uncomfortably between the vehicles, her heart pounding in her chest. And then she saw her. A tall, glamorous blonde woman, dressed in a sheer black kaftan and denim hotpants appeared from nowhere, strode confidently towards the phone box. She placed a red canvas holdall on the floor, grabbed the plastic bag, and then walked briskly towards the entrance of the aquarium. Jasmine was confused. Who was this girl? And how had she got hold of the tape? She didn't *look* threatening. She was young, maybe even younger than Jasmine, and she had a pretty, approachable face. Jasmine watched the young woman enter the aquarium and disappear. No, she didn't recognise her. She was not a face from her past or a girl she knew from London. Who the hell was she? And why had she just walked off with seventy-thousand euros of Jasmine's hard-earned cash?

On her way home Jasmine parked the car in a clifftop lay-by and slid down the steep path to the beach below. She threw the video tape on to the wet sand and stamped on it as hard as she could, over and over again, until the plastic shattered into a thousand pieces. She pulled the tape out, metres of the stuff, ripping it desperately through tears of anger and fear. And then she threw the mess of plastic and tape into the sea and watched, patiently, until it disappeared for ever under the waves. If only memories could be washed away so easily.

Chapter Nineteen

Jimmy came to slowly. It took a few moments for him to get his head round where he was and what he was doing there. His cheek was stuck to a leather cushion with dribble and sweat. He had to peel it off his skin, wincing as it caught his lip. His mouth tasted as if something was decomposing in there, while his clothes stank of BO and stale beer. Jimmy's head felt as if it were too small for his brain and, Christ!, as he dimly recalled snatches of last night's antics, he realised it wasn't much of a brain. Sunlight poured through the floor-to-ceiling windows. He squinted at his surroundings. He was in the living room. Why was he on the couch? Why was the place so quiet? Where was Jasmine?

Jimmy stood up, but the sudden movement proved too much for him. His head span, white lights flashed in front of his eyes and he immediately fell back down on to the couch. Ouch. The hangover was worse than he'd first thought. He pulled a cushion over his eyes to block out the daylight and searched his brain for clearer memories of the night before. And then it all came back to him in full Technicolor glory. Holy shit! He cringed, remembering how he'd shouted at Jasmine. Jesus fucking Christ! He winced, seeing the look on her face as she'd fallen into the pool.

'You're such a fucking arsehole,' he told himself as he curled back into a ball on the couch. 'Just like your fucking father.'

He could still see his mother now, crouched in a corner, hands raised above her face, trying in vain to protect herself from the blows of the drunken monster in her front room. She was shouting at Jimmy, pleading with him through blood and tears: 'Run, Jimmy. Just run. Don't let him touch you.' Oh, and how Jimmy had run. He was always the coward. Over and over again he'd left his poor mother to be beaten senseless while he sought refuge in the park, kick, kick, kicking that precious football, imagining it was his old man's head. Knowing it was his ticket out of there. Dreaming of a better life. Swearing he would never be anything like his father.

'Jazz?' he called, tentatively. 'Are you there, baby?'

Silence.

'Jasmine?'

Nothing.

Jimmy felt his bottom lip begin to wobble. What if he'd gone too far? What if she'd gone for good? He hugged the sticky leather cushion and listened for signs of life in the villa. There were none. Jimmy was alone. Alone with his guilt and his self-pity.

He'd been running away for years, but somehow the monster had followed him. 'You're just like me, son,' his dad had said, every time Jimmy had brought another trophy home from the club. 'A chip off the old block, eh?' And no matter how much he hated that man, somewhere deep inside he'd always believed it was true. One day Jimmy would turn out just like his father.

And now the monster had grown inside him, fed by success and excess, roused by insecurity and fear. It was Jasmine's fault, really. She was too beautiful. Too perfect. Too good for Jimmy Jones, that was for sure. When the fear gripped him and the red mist came down he was no longer in control. And that was what Jimmy craved more than anything: control. He wanted no less than total ownership. But somehow he knew he could never own something as lovely as Jasmine. He bought her diamond rings, designer dresses, villas in the sun, but he couldn't buy her soul. She said she loved him; she was marrying him for fuck's sake! But somehow, sometimes, it wasn't enough.

He would watch her with other men, the way she threw her head back when she laughed at their jokes, the way her eyes flashed and her tongue darted out from behind those perfect white teeth as she spoke. She would touch the man's hand or brush his arm accidentally with her breasts and Jimmy would feel the air drain from the room; his head would tighten and his fingernails would dig into his palms. Jasmine had no idea of the power she had over men, but Jimmy knew. Even his best mates. He was well aware that they'd all give their scoring foot for one night with Jasmine.

Jimmy wished he could put her in a cage like an exotic bird. He would keep her safe. She would be just for him. Not for public consumption. But, of course, that was stupid. He couldn't keep her in captivity. He couldn't even stop her from getting her kit off in the lads' mags, for fuck's sake! Sometimes he felt like he could see into the future. And already he knew Jasmine wasn't for keeps. One day a bigger man than Jimmy would show her how to fly.

A door creaked somewhere. There were footsteps getting closer. Jimmy sat up straight.

'Jasmine?' he called, hopefully.

The door swung open and Blaine's enormous form cast a shadow over the couch. He was naked but for his favourite thong.

'Sorry mate, just me,' grinned Blaine, lifting one chubby leg and farting loudly in Jimmy's face. 'Scuse me,' he guffawed.

Jimmy turned his head away, swallowing the bile that filled his mouth. Blaine really was rank. Bloody good at his job, but rank all the same.

'Don't know where the princess is,' continued Blaine cheerfully. 'She wasn't here when I got up. Shopping, probably. Abusing your plastic as punishment for last night, no doubt!'

'Last night?' Jimmy narrowed his eyes at Blaine. So the Aussie git had heard them fight. Shit! Jimmy hated that. Wasn't it enough that the guy managed their public life, without spying on their private life?

'Yeah, quite a ding-dong you two had, eh?' Blaine threw himself down on the couch beside him. 'Oooh, but she's lovely when she's angry—'

'Shut up,' snapped Jimmy.

'What's wrong? Hangover?' Blaine continued, patting Jimmy playfully on the head. 'Bit of a headache this morning have we? Or ...' he glanced at his Rolex, ' ... this afternoon, I should say.'

'Afternoon? She's been gone a while, then?'

Blaine shrugged. 'Guess so.'

'Wonder what she's up to?' mused Jimmy, more to himself than to Blaine.

'Like I said, she's punishing you, mate,' replied Blaine, knowingly. 'She's probably sipping a mojito and bitching about you with Cookie and Crystal as we speak. She'll be back later, weighed down with shopping bags. You mark my words. If anyone understands the complicated world of the female brain it's the Blainemeister.'

'You reckon?' said Jimmy. 'Well, you're a wiser man than me because I don't have a fucking clue about birds.'

Jasmine and Charlie sat side by side in silence, bare shoulders almost touching, both staring out to sea, each lost in their own thoughts. A waiter collected their abandoned lunch plates. Jasmine had barely touched her salad.

'Would you like another drink, *señorita*? *Señor*?'

'Hmm?' Charlie gazed up at the waiter, dragging his mind back to the moment, to the beachside restaurant, to his lunch date with Jasmine. 'Oh, yeah, please,' he said eventually. 'Another San Miguel.'

Jasmine continued to stare into space, oblivious to the waiter.

'Jasmine,' said Charlie, gently. 'Another drink?'

'Pardon?' Jasmine looked lost today. She'd been quiet. Strangely quiet. Her sparkle was missing.

'Drink?' repeated Charlie.

She shook her head. 'No thanks, Char. Think I'd better be getting home.' She stood up, picked up her bag from the table and kissed him on the top of his head.

'You sure you're OK?' he asked again, slipping his arm around her waist and hugging her. 'You're a bit quiet today.'

Jasmine smiled weakly. 'I've just got a lot on my mind. Wedding plans. There's a lot to do still.'

Charlie nodded. 'Well, I haven't exactly been swinging company either, have I?' he said. 'I'm a bit distracted myself.'

'Anything I can help with?'

Charlie shook his head. 'Just work, babes. Nothing for you to worry about.'

'Thanks for lunch, Charlie. It really is lovely to have you around.'

'Lovely to be around,' he replied.

He squeezed her hand and then let her go. Back to Jimmy. Was he making her happy? Charlie watched her meander through the restaurant towards the street. Her head was down. Her shoulders slumped. Had Charlie missed something important? He'd been too caught up in his own troubles to pay much attention to her. But what he did know was this: if Jimmy Jones hurt that girl, Charlie Palmer would break his scrawny little neck.

By the time Jasmine got home to Casa Amoura she had all but forgotten Jimmy's outburst from the night before. She had bigger problems now. Had she given enough money? Would the blackmailer go away? Had the tape she'd destroyed been the only copy? She wanted, desperately, to believe it was over, but a nagging voice at the back of her mind kept whispering that her problems had only just begun.

Her wedding was looming large and Jasmine wanted nothing to get in the way of the big day. This was more than just a wedding to her: it was the end of the nightmare and the beginning of the dream. A new husband, a new name, a new life! Jasmine firmly believed that the moment she said, 'I do', something fundamental would change in her world. She would put the horror and the pain of the past into a box and bury it deep in the darkest part of her brain and then, as she walked out of that church into the light as Mrs Jasmine Jones, she would stride towards a future filled with happiness and sunshine. It was her time to shine and nothing, not even blackmail, was going to spoil that moment.

As she pulled past the paparazzi and swung into the drive, the gates automatically closed behind her. Jasmine switched off the engine and sighed with relief. Home. The best place in the world. Home to her Jimmy, who, despite his drunken rantings, was the one who made her feel loved. She'd got rid of the past. Now it was time to concentrate on the future. She would make up with Jimmy. It was time for a fresh start.

He was waiting for her, loitering at the door sheepishly, kicking the ground with his bare feet and glancing shyly up at her through his blonde fringe. One look at her fiancé told Jasmine that he was mortally ashamed of his behaviour and that he would be eating huge slices of humble pie today. The sight made her smile despite herself. There was no point in huffing. She'd stayed out all morning and half the afternoon; she'd been ignoring his calls. She'd punished him enough. He was not a bad man. God, not compared to some! No, Jimmy was not like them.

He smiled weakly at her as she approached and shrugged his shoulders with his arms outstretched. He looked vulnerable and terribly young. He was flawed, like everyone, but he was no monster. Jasmine felt sure of that.

'What can I say, babe?' he ventured tentatively. 'I'm so sorry. It'll never happen again. I love you more than—'

'Oh shut up, you plonker,' grinned Jasmine, throwing herself into his open arms and snogging him full on the lips.

'Take me inside and make it up to me properly,' she whispered in his ear.

Jimmy looked confused.

'Now!' ordered Jasmine. 'I mean it. Take me to bed or lose me for ever!'

And then Jasmine was tripping up the stairs with Jimmy, clutching his arm, laughing at the look of relief on that handsome face, kicking off her shoes and heading for the bedroom as if she didn't have a care in the world.

Chapter Twenty

Lila had butterflies. It was ridiculous. She'd been married to the man for most of her adult life and he'd seen her give birth – twice! – so why was she so nervous about meeting him at the airport? Well, partly she was worried that he wouldn't actually arrive after the incident last week. OK, so she'd spoken to him two minutes before he boarded the plane this time, but in Brett's world things could change fast. Anything could have happened in those last hundred and twenty seconds before the doors closed. Until she saw him with her own eyes, she wouldn't actually believe he was for real.

But then the thought of seeing him and, more importantly, of him seeing *her*, was also a bit scary. She knew already that she would be searching his face for signs of disappointment. Was he as shocked by the thirty-something woman who greeted him as she was when she faced that same woman in the mirror every morning? He was so used to getting up close and personal with very young actresses, surely the sight of his wife was something of a let down these days.

And then there were other concerns. What would they say to each other? Would the conversation still flow? It had been almost three months since their last brief meeting in Paris (thirty-six hours while he was on a whirlwind promotional tour of France) and although they spoke on the phone most days, it was almost always about the kids. Brett was beginning to feel to her like an outsider. He had become a kind of soft-focused, shadow husband, who inhabited the dream part of Lila's mind but seldom stepped into her reality. She barely knew him anymore. She certainly had no clue what he got up to while she wasn't there. She hated thinking about it. And so, in a way, her husband was becoming a stranger. And strangers could be dangerous. She resolved to stay cool during his visit. If she kept him at arm's length he wouldn't be able to hurt her.

The kids were jumping up and down in their seats with excitement. They were trying to spot aeroplanes landing, guessing which one might be Daddy's. Peter didn't join in the game. Instead he flicked through the on-board TV channels with a slightly bored expression on his face. Lila smiled to herself. She liked the fact that Peter was totally on her side in the silent little Rose v Rose battle that was being waged (in her head at least). Peter had never pretended to be Brett's biggest fan, but these days he was becoming increasingly outspoken on the subject. He was always telling Lila that she would be better off without Brett. 'And you'd get a tidy divorce settlement,' he'd add. 'Clever girl, refusing to sign that prenup!'

Lila had refused the prenuptial agreement that Brett's lawyers had been so keen on, but not for any financial reasons. When she'd married Brett she'd been one hundred per cent sure that it was for keeps. The prenup had seemed irrelevant. Unromantic. Wrong. And Brett had agreed. 'Whatever you want, honey,' he'd shrugged nonchalantly. 'It's no biggie.' But was their marriage for keeps? Lila was no longer so sure. She wanted it to work out with all her heart. She prayed that this was just a passing phase, a bad patch that they'd look back at and laugh about in years to come. Surely it was salvageable? And there were the children to think about, too. Lila did not want her kids to come from a broken home. Their life was extraordinary enough already. How many children had to deal with being hounded by the press? And Daddy spent most of his time on another continent, in a different world. No, she wanted some sort of normality for Louisa and Sebastian. And yet … Lila stared out of the window. And yet the nagging doubts were getting louder and louder. She still loved her husband. What Lila was uncertain of was whether or not he still loved her.

Lila watched heads turn in every car they passed as the black limo sped towards the airport. They strained to see who was inside, but were foiled by the blacked-out windows. God, she hated these ridiculous vehicles, but Brett would expect to be picked up in style and he would want something flashy. He was like that. Unlike Lila, he loved the attention that came with being a somebody. Brett would never sneak out a back door. He preferred the main entrance and the crowds of admirers every time.

The limo pulled up at a coned-off area outside arrivals and the door was opened by a fawning member of airport security who bowed at Lila as she stepped out. She smoothed the front of her classic red Diane von Furstenberg wrap dress, shook her shiny hair and placed her oversized Chanel sunglasses firmly on the bridge of her nose. *OK, here we go*, she thought.

'Hold my hands,' she told the children firmly. 'And don't let go. Come on, Peter. We're in a hurry!'

Holidaymakers stopped in their tracks as they spotted Lila Rose hurrying through the airport with her entourage. She was faking a smile as usual, but inside she was screaming out to be left alone. Mobile phones were being held aloft all around and it wasn't long before a couple of professional photographers joined the throng. They were young, greedy and ambitious. They practically lived at Malaga airport during the summer months, just waiting for days like these when a fleeting celebrity encounter would boost their reputations and their bank balances. Lila's heart sank. Her cover had been blown. From now on her stay in Spain would involve a cat-and-mouse game of hide and seek with the press. Peter had long arms and he seemed to envelope Lila and the kids in a protective hug, keeping the tourists and paparazzi at bay.

Lila knew how it would work. It was always the same. Brett would come out through the gate while the rest of the passengers were left waiting at the luggage carousel, or perhaps even still on the plane. By now he would have been whisked off the aircraft and hurried through a private route of secret corridors reserved for VIPs. He would have flashed his passport briefly at a grateful official and been accompanied to the gate by a burly security guard or two. He might have flashed a smile as he passed the queuing cattle from previous flights, still waiting to go through security. If they were lucky.

The automatic doors opened. The two photographers jumped in front of Lila and started flashing before she could spot her husband. They were so bloody rude! It might be their job, but this was her life.

'Excuse me,' she said curtly, as Peter pushed them aside. And then there he was – Brett Rose – striding towards them, grinning from ear to ear, gold aviators firmly in place. He was wearing faded blue jeans and a white T-shirt with his favourite hand-stitched crocodile-skin cowboy boots. Lila could see his tattoo of a raven-haired mermaid curled around his muscular left bicep. It had been her wedding present to him. Her hand brushed her right buttock automatically. Underneath her dress a wild stallion reared. That had been his wedding present to her. Brett's golden-brown hair was perfectly mussed up beneath his LA Lakers baseball cap and his skin glowed bronze from the Californian sunshine. Lila felt her stomach lurch. Brett was such a handsome bastard. How could she fight when the enemy looked like *that*?

The children ran, screaming, into their father's arms as he dropped his leather holdall. He scooped them up with his strong arms, smothering their cheeks with stubbly kisses. All the while the paparazzi cameras flashed, recording this private scene for the world to devour over tomorrow's breakfast. Lila held back a little, watching the look of sheer, unadulterated adoration on Louisa's face as she gazed up at her daddy. Then Brett placed the kids gently back on the ground, pushed his shades up on to the peak of his cap and levelled his sexy green eyes straight at Lila.

'Well hello there, Mrs Rose,' he drawled, doffing his cap. 'Looking mighty fine, if I may say so.'

'Will somebody please pass me a sick bag,' deadpanned Peter in her ear.

But she ignored him. Brett was smiling lopsidedly at her, his eyes twinkling, and her resolve to stay cool was melting faster than an ice-cube under the Mediterranean sun. She found herself running towards him, falling into his arms, kissing his large, warm mouth, feeling the roughness of his cheeks and the firmness of his hand as it cupped the back of her head. He pulled her into him, until her nose was filled with his manly scent, and her heart was filled with longing and joy and a need so strong that it made her knees buckle. Lila belonged to Brett. No matter how badly he behaved, he had her in the palm of his hand.

'So, guys, what plans have you got for me?' asked Brett as he lounged in the limo, stretching his impossibly long legs in front of him. He squeezed Lila's hand affectionately.

'Sandcastles,' squealed Louisa.

'And paragliding,' shouted Seb.

'And pedaloes and rock-pooling and flamenco dancing. I'm a really good flamencoer—' Louisa babbled excitedly. 'Me and Granny were practising at Grandpa's party yesterday.'

'And a wedding in Scotland,' added Peter curtly. 'If you're staying until Saturday.'

'Scotland, geez,' drawled Brett. 'That sounds awesome. Who's getting hitched?'

'We're not definitely going,' interjected Lila quickly.

'Yes we are,' insisted Peter. 'I RSVP'd yesterday.'

'But I hadn't made up my mind,' Lila tutted.

Peter shrugged. 'Well, you'll have to sack me then, because I'm not missing the nuptials of Jimmy Jones and Jasmine Watts for anyone, even you, your Royal Highness.'

Lila hit him over the head with a copy of *Grazia* with faux annoyance.

'Who are the lucky couple?' asked Brett. 'Anyone I know?'

Peter opened the magazine and showed Brett a picture of Jimmy and Jasmine on the beach.

'Hmm, that girl looks familiar,' mused Brett. 'I think I've met her somewhere before.'

'You probably have,' replied Peter. 'She used to be a stripper.'

Brett ignored the dig. 'And who's the guy?'

'He's a footballer, darling,' explained Lila. 'Nobody you would have heard of.'

Brett grinned enthusiastically. 'Soccer! Jeez, I love soccer. It's my new favourite thing,' he insisted. 'I've been to see Galaxy play a few times. In fact, I met David Beckham and his lovely lady wife at a party on Saturday. Soccer's really hot back home right now and—'

'Saturday?' said Lila suddenly. 'But weren't you in Montreal on Saturday?'

Brett didn't miss a beat. 'Oh yeah, you're right. Must have been Friday, I guess,' he shrugged. 'It's the jet lag, honey. I'm a bit disorientated.'

'Sure,' said Lila.

She let go of his hand. Brett didn't seem to notice.

'So, d'you think David will be at this wedding? Because he's a really cool guy. I wouldn't mind hanging with him some more.'

'I should think so,' mused Peter. 'This will be the WAG wedding to end all WAG weddings.'

'What's a wag?' asked Brett.

'You'll see,' promised Peter. 'You'll see.'

Jasmine soon discovered that the best way to blank out her problems was to throw herself head first into the final preparations for her wedding. No, it wasn't just *her* wedding. It was *the* wedding. The wedding of the year. At least, that's what *Scoop!* magazine were calling it and with that kind of pressure on her shoulders, the bride had little time to worry about a minor case of blackmail.

Despite the army of people involved in staging this monumental event, there just seemed so much more to do. Jasmine thought her head might explode with the decisions she was constantly being asked to make. There were now only a few days to go until the big day and she was having an emergency meeting with her wedding planner, Camilla Knight-Saunders.

From Hollywood to Bollywood, via Mexico and Mauritius, Camilla had planned some of the 'It' crowd's most exquisite nuptials. Jasmine had spent so much time in Camilla's company lately that she felt she knew the woman better than her own mother. Oh, if only Camilla *was* her mother!

Now she was prancing back and forth across Jasmine's deck in kitten-heeled court shoes, gesticulating wildly with perfectly manicured hands. She was pencil-thin, with shiny, cropped, silver hair. She always wore black clothes – today it was a beautifully tailored shift dress – and red lipstick. There was something of the ageing ballerina about her; her neck was impossibly long and her toes were always a little turned out. She called herself a dying breed. She'd told Jasmine (many times) how she'd come from old money ('one can't buy good breeding, darling'), and had attended the finest Swiss finishing school. Then she'd been the most beautiful deb on the circuit the year she'd 'come out'. She'd married well ('naturally, darling') and had spent the next three decades being the perfect trophy wife – producing three strapping sons and heirs while looking ravishing, and organising the best soirées, dinner parties and charity balls in the Home Counties.

And then her husband had died. Just like that. ('Dropped dead of a heart attack in the bar of the House of Lords, darling'). Camilla had been shocked and heartbroken to find herself a widow in her prime ('I was only fifty-one, darling') but not as shocked as she had been to find herself bankrupt. It turned out her husband had been better at spending the family fortune than he had been at making it and after death duties, inheritance tax and the cost of the lavish funeral ('I couldn't let poor Monty down at the last hurdle, could I, darling?') Camilla had been left with nothing. And so she sold the family pile, gave most of the (substantial) profit to her three boys and started her own business with the rest. ('I mean, I'd never worked, darling. One just didn't. But I knew what I was good at. I was the perfect hostess.') She'd started off small, organising the local hunt ball, that sort of thing, but then she'd got her big break: a friend asked Camilla to plan her daughter's wedding. The daughter just happened to be the tabloid's favourite 'posh totty' that year and the wedding got national coverage. The marriage only lasted a few months, but Camilla's reputation was sealed. There was rarely a wedding featured in *Hello!* these days that Camilla hadn't organised.

'We have a major catastrophe regarding the ice sculptures,' Camilla was announcing melodramatically.

'Our sculptor is the best in the UK, but he's based in London, naturally, and his schedule simply won't allow him to travel to Scotland. It will take him three days to do the work and we had planned to fly them up to Inverness on the Saturday morning. Except now, we discover, that the hold isn't tall enough for the statue of Boadicea.'

'Couldn't she lie on her side?' asked Jasmine.

'No, no, no,' Camilla shook her head. 'She's far too fragile. But don't you worry about it, darling. I've put a call in to Richard—'

'Richard?'

'Branson, darling. An old family friend. He's trying to find us a plane with a bigger hold.'

'Oh,' said Jasmine. 'Right.'

She was constantly amazed by Camilla's connections.

'And the bridesmaids' dresses are a disaster.' Camilla continued to pace. 'Crystal's breast enlargement has thrown things completely out of propor-tion. Why must you all insist on being so well-endowed these days?'

Jasmine folded her arms protectively across her chest.

'In my day we believed that the perfect breast fitted neatly into a champagne glass,' Camilla announced.

'But—' Jasmine stared quizzically at the glass of champagne on the table. It was barely big enough for a nipple.

'Don't be silly, darling,' scoffed Camilla. 'That's a *flute*. I'm talking about a champagne *glass*.' She cupped her hand to demonstrate the proportions. 'Anyway, breasts are the least of our problems when we consider Cookie's bump. What a time to start a family! In the middle of your wedding, darling. Some people really are very self-centred. Well, at least your sister will look divine. She has such a perfect little figure. No lumps and bumps to get in the way. As long as she doesn't open her mouth Lisa will do you proud.'

'Alisha,' said Jasmine. 'Her name's Alisha.'

'Alisha? A-lee-sha? Is it really? How very strange. I've been calling her Lisa. I've never heard of such a thing as an Alisha before,' laughed Camilla. 'Oh well, horses for courses and all that, darling.'

Jasmine nodded, although she really had no idea what Camilla was banging on about. She'd never worried about her younger sister's name before. Alisha's behaviour, on the other hand ... well, Jasmine would have to keep an eye on that at the wedding. Alisha might only be sixteen, but that girl was a man-eater. Her little sis had been over the moon when Jasmine had asked her to be a bridesmaid.

'Are you sure, Jazz? Me? You want me to be a bridesmaid? And be in all the magazines and get famous and, oh my God, this is soooo going to be the start of my glamour career and ... and ... and ...'

Jasmine wasn't sure how she felt about Alisha wanting to be a glamour model. But Alisha seemed dead set on the idea, even refusing to breastfeed poor Ebony in case her pert little titties sagged.

'Nah, it ain't natural, is it?' she'd exclaimed when Jasmine had suggested breastfeeding for a few weeks at least.

'None of you lot was breastfed and it ain't done you no harm,' their mum had chipped in. 'Mind you, I s'pose you might have been, Jazz. Before I got you, like. P'raps that's why you got them huge knockers, innit?'

Jasmine despaired of most of her family. Her mum was a lost cause and her brothers were a waste of space but Alisha ... Perhaps there was still a glimmer of hope for her. If only she wasn't so hell bent on following Jasmine's career. It wasn't as if Jasmine was exactly ashamed of her work, more that she just knew there were other things she'd rather be getting paid for – like singing. But to Alisha, glamour modelling was 'it' – the ultimate goal. It was all she wanted. That, and a famous boyfriend. She was pretty enough, all right. She was slim with great legs, but the fact was, if she was going to succeed she would need to have surgery on her A-cup boobs. And, wild as Alisha was, Jasmine didn't particularly like the idea of her baby sister going under the knife.

'Are you concentrating, darling?' Camilla was demanding. 'I need to confirm the order of the music. We have the Queen's own Highland pipe band to march you from the chapel to the castle. The Proclaimers will kick things off with 'Let's Get Married' as requested by James ...'

Camilla always called Jimmy 'James'. It made Jasmine giggle.

'And then KT Tunstall is doing a set and then possibly Carlos Russo to finish things off, but I wondered if he might be a little last-century for you youngsters.'

'No, that all sounds perfect,' enthused Jasmine.

Actually, she thought the preparations seemed to be going pretty amazingly. The bridesmaids' dresses had been altered in record time, the florist had the final list for the various bouquets, church flowers and table centrepieces; even the seating plan had finally been done, and my God, had Jasmine had sleepless nights over that! And as for her dress ... ah, the dress ... it was beyond her wildest dreams.

Chapter Twenty-One

Maxine stared at the package in front of her. It was a baby-pink box, tied with black velvet ribbon. The card attached read, 'For my Venus. Enjoy. All my love, Carlos xxx'. They'd had an argument a couple of days ago and she'd been ignoring him ever since. Huffing. Trying to teach him a lesson.

The problem was that Maxine had been feeling increasingly fidgety. She had an itch that needed scratching. Ants in her pants. Big time. For a while now, she'd had a sense that she needed to be doing something – something bigger and more substantial than she was used to. Launching Cruise had kept her occupied for a while, but now the opening night was over – and a roaring success even by her high standards – she was no longer nervous about the club. Cruise would fly. Maxi had ensured her 'baby' had the finest staff, the best press coverage and the most impressive guest list possible. As long as she showed her face and flouted her hostess talents every weekend then she had no worries there. No, she had made up her mind. Maxine needed a new project in her life and this time she had her heart set on a *real* baby.

The only problem with the plan was Carlos – the reluctant father-to-be. He'd never been particularly horny, preferring good old-fashioned romance to the full-on, rip-your-pants-off action that Maxi craved. Until now she'd made allowances for his age and waning libido, but if she was going to conceive, Maxine knew she would need Carlos to take his coital duties more seriously. What's more, if she was honest with herself, Maxine was beginning to feel sexually frustrated. And so she'd spent the weekend working on him.

When she'd got back from the club on Friday, she'd found him sleeping peacefully in his checked pyjamas, with an empty mug of hot chocolate and a Sevi Ballesteros autobiography on the bedside table. Maxi had sighed deeply. She'd never found seducing men a challenge before, but Carlos really was quite hard work. She'd stripped off to her scarlet, lacy underwear, slipped under the sheets beside him and got to work, slipping her hands under his pyjamas and massaging his skin. Nothing. Carlos had slumbered soundly. And so Maxi had tried harder. She'd turned him over on to his back, straddled his sleeping body, unbuttoned his top and begun kissing his chest, his stomach, his …

'Carlos,' she'd whispered breathlessly. 'Carlos, baby. I'm horny as hell and I need you to wake up.'

Carlos had snored loudly and turned back over on to his side, throwing Maxine off the bed on to the shagpile carpet in an inelegant heap.

'Damn you!' Maxine had cursed with frustration.

Eventually, she'd given up. Carlos had been out for the count. Maxine had gone through to the kitchen, poured herself a Martini and watched the sun rise over the mountains before retiring to the guest bedroom.

'Tomorrow,' she'd decided. 'Tomorrow will have to do.'

On Saturday, Maxine had tried a couple of times to get Carlos in the mood by sitting on his knee in nothing but her panties. But he hadn't taken the hint and she'd been too tired and hungover to persevere.

On Sunday, Maxine and Carlos had been enjoying a lazy day by the pool. It was Isabel's day off, so they had the villa to themselves. Maxine was naked but for a teeny silver thong.

'Carlos, honey,' she'd asked in her best breathy voice. 'Could you rub my oil on me, please.'

Carlos had peered at her over his glasses, shrugged and then placed his newspaper on the ground, a little reluctantly. Maxi lay on the sun lounger on her back, eyes closed, basking in the glory of the sun on her naked skin, shivering with anticipation at the thought of what was to come. By now she really was feeling hot. She'd been thinking of nothing but sex for days and she could feel her pussy tingling with excitement. If Carlos didn't fuck her soon she felt sure she'd explode.

'Oh God, baby, that's so good,' she'd whispered, as Carlos rubbed her naked breasts with oil. 'Oh Jesus, Carlos, that's divine,' she'd cooed as his hands had worked lower, over her stomach and hips. Then he was massaging her thighs, fingertips brushing her thong, teasing her with every firm stroke. Maxine's eyes had remained closed. She'd opened her legs as wide as they would go, aching for Carlos to touch her there, or to just dive right in. Hell, she didn't need any more foreplay now. Maxi was raring to go. Carlos was teasing her, working his way down her legs, rubbing oil into her shins and even her feet.

'All done,' he'd said matter-of-factly.

'I think you missed a bit, baby,' Maxine had breathed. 'Just here.' She'd touched herself where it tingled. Her thong was already damp. Her eyes were still closed. She'd felt sure Carlos was standing above her, as turned on as she was, ready to make beautiful love under the sun.

But Carlos didn't respond. Maxine opened her eyes just in time to see Carlos diving into the pool.

'What the hell?'

Maxine sat bolt upright. Carlos proceeded to swim lengths of the pool, completely oblivious to his girlfriend's burning desires.

'No way are you getting out of it now, daddio!' Maxine had announced more to herself than to Carlos, whose head was underwater.

She'd stood up and dived straight into the pool, even though this was against her own rules – normally Maxine avoided putting her head under the water as it messed up her hair and make-up. But she was a desperate woman. She'd swum straight up to Carlos and thrown her arms around his body mid-crawl.

Carlos had floundered, disappeared under the water for a few moments and then reappeared, coughing and spluttering.

'What the hell are you doing, Maxine?' he'd demanded, almost angrily. 'You almost drown me!'

'Oh God, I'm sorry, honey,' Maxine had soothed as she patted his back, making sure he'd coughed all the water out of his lungs. 'It's just … I need you, baby.'

'Need me?' Carlos had looked confused. 'I am just here, chica.'

'I know, Carlos,' Maxine had explained patiently. 'But when you rubbed my oil in it felt good.'

'Good?' said Carlos, getting his breath back.

'As in *good*.' Maxine had done her best to convey how horny she felt in that one word.

'Good?' Carlos was obviously still confused.

Maxine's sexual frustration had turned into a more general frustration. 'I feel horny, Carlos!' she'd snapped. 'I want a fuck, for fuck's sake! It's been weeks. I have needs, you know.'

'Ah, I understand,' Carlos had nodded, looking serious suddenly. He'd pulled himself up on to the side of the pool and drawn his hand through his wet hair. He'd gazed down at her benevolently, like a schoolmaster surveying a keen but unruly pupil. 'Maxine, my dahling. You very beautiful woman. You young. I have been worrying that this might become problem,' he'd said, calmly.

'What? You don't want me? Don't you find me attractive?'

It was a new feeling for Maxine. She had been hurt and insulted many times in her life, but she had never felt rejected sexually. Tears merged with the chlorine and stung her eyes.

'Maxine, Maxine,' Carlos had soothed. 'You know I find you the most beautiful woman alive. You are my Venus. I tell you this every day but—'

'But what?' Maxine had shouted. 'But you just want to look at me, like a beautiful painting?'

'In a way, yes,' Carlos had said gently. 'I enjoy our lovemaking but once, twice a month is enough for me. I have been your age. I do understand. But I am not there anymore. I am calmer now. My brain is more awake than ever but my ...' he indicated his penis, ' ... he is less so. It is not you, chica. It is me. I am sorry.'

Maxine could feel hot tears pouring down her face.

'But I want lust, Carlos,' she'd explained. 'I need to be desired.'

'I desire you, dahling. You must believe me. But I desire your smile, and your laughter, and your kind heart too. Not just your body. When I was twenty-five, then I would have lusted after you, but I would not have loved you. Not properly. Now I love all of Maxine. I desire whole package. This is better, no? This is better for you?'

'I don't know, Carlos,' Maxine had replied. 'I really don't know.'

And now, as she looked at the present in front of her, she was still confused. She loved Carlos, adored him. She wanted to be his wife and to have his baby, but a seed of doubt had been planted and she wasn't yet sure how big that doubt would grow. Could she live without lust? Maxine wasn't sure it was a sacrifice she was willing to make. Not yet, anyway. She was still young.

But, what the hell. Maxi loved presents and if Carlos felt guilty enough to leave her a little treat by the bed then who was she to ignore it? He was at the golf club. Isabel had gone to the supermarket. Maxi was alone. She ripped off the black ribbon and opened the box. The gift was wrapped in pink tissue paper. What was it? The box was no bigger than a shoe box. A pair of Louboutins? A necklace? Diamonds? She dived into the tissue paper like a five-year-old at Christmas.

'What the ... ?'

Maxi picked up the gift and turned it round in her hands. It was about twelve inches long and three inches in girth. It was pink and smooth and solid. It felt cold to the touch, like fine china, although Maxine guessed it was made out of plastic. And there were diamonds, twelve perfect little diamonds set into the tip. It was quite beautiful in its own way. She pushed the 'on' button. It whirred into action. The thing had so much life in it that Maxi nearly dropped it on the floor.

A vibrator. Carlos had bought her a vibrator. It was a very beautiful, expensive-looking vibrator but a vibrator all the same. Maxine didn't know whether to be offended or relieved. She switched it off and stared at it for a few moments. What was she supposed to do with it? Maxine had never been one to fly solo, so to speak. There had always been a willing guy on hand to service her needs whenever she was in the mood. But now? Carlos wasn't satisfying her and he was offering a solution. Maxi stood up and walked to the bedroom door. She locked it, returned to the bed and picked up her present. She switched it back on and watched it vibrate for a while. Slowly, Maxine slipped out of her knickers and lay down on the bed. This gift wouldn't give her the baby she desired, that was for sure, but her new friend sure as hell would get rid of those ants in her pants. Maxine closed her eyes and let the delicious sensations flood through her body. The relief was unbelievable.

When Carlos got home from the golf club he found Maxine in a delightfully upbeat mood.

'You like your gift?' he asked, a little shyly.

'I *love* my gift,' said Maxine, winking at him saucily. 'In fact, I've been enjoying it all afternoon.'

'Really?'

'Really. I could barely drag myself away.'

'Oh good. I am pleased you like it. In fact, I was thinking, dahling, that later I could see you enjoy the gift for myself,' suggested Carlos.

Maxine was surprised. Surprised but delighted. 'Sure, baby. I would love to show you how much I'm loving my new toy!'

'And then, perhaps, I could try my new toys too …' Carlos put his hand in his trouser pocket and pulled out a small bottle of pills.

Maxine peered at the label on the bottle. 'Viagra? But I thought you said you'd never try it. You said it was for dirty old men.'

Carlos slipped his arms around Maxi's waist and pulled her towards him. 'Dahling, if it means keeping my Venus happy I am willing to try anything.'

'Thank you,' said Maxi gratefully. Viagra meant sex, and sex meant babies, and babies meant wedding rings, and wedding rings meant happily ever after …

Chapter Twenty-Two

Charlie was restless. He'd packed and unpacked his leather holdall three times and laid out two different sets of travelling clothes. His hands shook slightly as he smoothed his jeans down on the hotel bed. The truth was, he was bricking it.

It wasn't the wedding in the afternoon that was worrying him. Jasmine's wedding planner had organised Savile Row morning suits for all the men in the wedding party and Charlie had endured three fittings for that. No, his wedding suit was pukka. He'd look the business when he walked Jasmine down the aisle. And his speech was written, folded neatly in his wallet, memorised, word for word. He was feeling a bit jittery at the prospect of speaking in front of all those famous people, but he reckoned as long as he didn't catch Katie Price's or Sir Alex Ferguson's eye during the speech he'd be all right. He was going to talk directly to Jasmine. He'd look her in the eye and let her know that he meant every single word of it – how proud he was of her and how chuffed her old man would have been if he'd been there to see her get married. He'd convinced himself that the wedding would be fine.

It wasn't even the journey there that was making him nervous. OK, maybe he was a bit intimidated by the idea of travelling with Hollywood royalty, but it was nothing he couldn't handle and, to be honest, he was quite excited by the prospect. Jazz had arranged for Charlie to travel with Brett and Lila Rose. No joke. How mental was that? Charlie Palmer was going to fly from Malaga to Inverness in a private jet chartered by Mr Hollywood Megastar and his wife, who just happened to be the most beautiful woman in the world bar none. Only a week ago he'd sat behind Lila on his flight to Spain; now he was going to be her guest. He would get to talk to her, on the level, one to one. What's more, Maxine de la Fallaise and her boyfriend Carlos Russo were going to be on the flight too. Charlie had always liked the look of that Maxine, whenever he'd seen her in the papers. She had one of those smiley, approachable faces. A body to kill for, but a face like the girl next door. Still, not a patch on Lila Rose.

No, it wasn't the flight that worried him, either. What scared the living

135

daylights out of Charlie was setting foot back on British soil. If it wasn't for Jasmine's wedding there wouldn't be a snowball's chance in hell of him going anywhere near the place, not for years. McGregor had made no bones about it after the Donohue job. He had to get away and stay away. The place wasn't safe. And that was before Nadia went missing.

Jeez. Charlie breathed in sharply. He hoped she was OK. There'd been no news from Gary. The kid had been asking around as best he could, but nobody seemed to know anything. Not that anyone would talk even if they did know something. Everyone in London was shit scared of the Russians and Dimitrov was the scariest of the lot. Charlie was grateful for the fact that Nadia's old man hadn't been in touch again and his boys had left Gary alone too. Charlie was hoping that they must know he had nothing to do with her disappearance. He wished he'd had the balls to bring her with him to Spain. At least that way he'd have been able to keep her safe.

Safe? Who the fuck was safe? Charlie's heart was beating too fast in his chest. Was Marbella safe? Would Tillydochrie Castle be safe? Was it far enough away from London? Was anywhere far enough away? Charlie took a deep breath and sat down on the bed. Maybe he should call Jasmine and just check that everything was OK in Scotland. She'd probably be with her mates now, having their nails done or something. He shouldn't bother her. But …

Jasmine was sprawled across her lavish antique four-poster bed on her tummy, in stripy pink boy pants and a purple camisole, surveying her lovely French manicure, when there was a knock on the door

'I think it's time for …' Chrissie opened the door in her dressing gown and let a smartly dressed young waiter in. 'Bubbles!'

'Oo, lovely jubbly,' said Jasmine. 'Pink champagne. Thanks, darling.' She winked at the waiter, who blushed and hurried back out of the room.

'Not any old champagne, either,' Chrissie pointed out. 'It's Cristal.'

'Well, natch,' said Jasmine.

'Not for me,' said Cookie, patting her little baby bump protectively. 'Makes me want to barf, that stuff!'

'And I don't think you're old enough yet, are you, Alisha?' Crystal teased Jasmine's little sister.

'Fuck off!' cried Alisha. 'I'm old enough to have a baby. I think I can handle a bit of bubbly!' She grabbed a glass from Chrissie and took a big slug.

'Wait!' cried Crystal. 'That stuff costs almost a grand a bottle. Sip it, Alisha. It's not an alcopop! Anyway, I'm going to propose a toast.'

The girls all stood up, each in various states of undress, and Chrissie announced, 'To Jasmine. The most beautiful bride in the world. May all your dreams come true!'

'To Jasmine!' shouted the others, and then they all clinked glasses and giggled as the bubbles tickled their noses.

'Is that your phone, Jazz?' asked Alisha, looking around. 'Better get it. Might be Jimmy and the lads wanting to meet up.'

'Nah, I'm not seeing them tonight, Lish,' said Jasmine, picking up cushions and rifling around her bed for her phone. 'It's bad luck.'

'We could just sneak over to their hotel for a bit, though. It's just there, look.' She pointed out of the window to the hotel about half a mile away, over the castle grounds. 'All the footballers are there. I could line up a bit of talent for tomorrow, innit?'

'No, we're having a girlie night, Lish,' said Jasmine patiently, finally finding her phone in her handbag. 'Oh look, it's Charlie. Hi, Charlie! What do you mean is everything OK?' she laughed into the phone. 'Of course everything's OK. We're drinking pink champagne!'

'Stop stressing! You're not our dad Uncle Charlie!' shouted Alisha loudly.

Jasmine wandered out on to the balcony and closed the French doors behind her. She could barely hear herself think with the girls squealing inside. Dusk was setting in and a strange haze drifted across the loch before her. The ancient house where Jimmy was staying was situated on the other side of the loch. It had once been the gatehouse for the castle but had recently been turned into a boutique hotel – a nice little money-spinner for the laird to go with the celebrity weddings he hosted. The hotel's interior was cool and contemporary enough to have been featured in *Elle Decoration* but from the balcony it looked old, creepy and ghostly in the half-light.

'Char?' said Jasmine. 'That's better; I can hear you now. Yes. I'm fine. Uh-huh, the castle's lovely, beautiful, it's perfect … Security? It's the best. The magazine won't let anyone in or they'll lose their exclusive and Camilla's stalking the joint like a bloody Rottweiler in case there are any undesirable gatecrashers …

'No, honestly, Charlie, I feel quite happy with all the arrangements. Mm-hmm, the security guards are big guys. Now, stop worrying about me and let me get back to my bubbly … So, I'll see you tomorrow then. Yeah, love you too, Char. Sleep tight.'

Jasmine sniffed the air. It was sweet and damp and smelled of freshly cut grass. No doubt the grounds had had a manicure too, ready for tomorrow's wedding. Camilla would have seen to that. She was about to go back into the room when she spotted a figure strolling casually beside the loch about fifty feet away. She peered through the mist, trying to make out who it was. There was something familiar about the way he walked. It was definitely a man. Too tall for Jimmy. Too slim for the laird. (Jasmine had been introduced to him when she arrived. He'd been very friendly and jolly but he was not a slim man.) Now the man had his back to her. He was skimming stones and as her eyes got accustomed to the light she could make out the pebbles dancing, once, twice, three, four, five times across the surface of the still water. He turned sideways and ran his fingers through his long dark hair. Jasmine recognised his profile immediately. It was Louis. He didn't have his glasses on.

She was about to call out to him, but something stopped her. She preferred to watch him for a while, secretly. She found Louis intriguing; he was so different from the others, and it was nice to have an excuse to study him like this. Louis sat down on a rock by the water's edge and looked around him. Jasmine followed his gaze as he watched a hawk hover above the trees. Then he got up and faced the castle. Jasmine ducked down behind the stone balcony wall and peered through the gap. She felt like a spy. She didn't know why she was doing it and she certainly didn't want to get caught. How embarrassing would that be?

Louis approached the castle, staring up at the magnificent building, no doubt admiring the architecture. Jasmine wondered, briefly, why he wasn't with the others at the hotel. She hoped they hadn't been mean to him. Then she heard a sharp female voice shout, 'Who's there?'

Jasmine's heart pounded as Camilla strode out from directly beneath her balcony. The entire area had been cordoned off by the police – the castle, its grounds, the hotel – and there were security guards at both entrances to the estate. Camilla would go mental if she thought her security had been breached.

'Who are you?' she demanded. 'This is private property. What are you doing here? How did you get in?'

Louis stepped forward with his hand outstretched. 'I am Louis Ricardo,' he introduced himself with a polite nod of the head. 'I stay at hotel with Jimmy.'

'Oh, oh, right, I see,' blustered Camilla. 'I'm Camilla Knight-Saunders. I'm the wedding planner.'

From her hiding place Jasmine could see Camilla practically swooning over the handsome young intruder.

'Is a big wedding to plan,' said Louis.

'Yes, yes, it is. And there's a lot still to do so you really shouldn't be here until tomorrow.' Her voice was a lot less stern now. 'But I suppose you're not doing any harm.'

'No, I was just looking. The castle, she is beautiful, no?'

'Magnificent,' agreed Camilla. 'Aren't the young men having some sort of bash at the hotel tonight?'

Louis nodded. 'Is not my scene,' he shrugged. 'They are all, how do you say it? Peessed!'

'You don't drink?' asked Camilla.

'Oh, no, I do. I enjoy a glass of wine with a meal but I don't like all this, this, shouting and this, how you say it? Showing off.'

'No, I can't say I'm a big fan of all that nonsense either, Louis.' Jasmine noticed that Camilla pronounced his name properly. The Portuguese way. 'Are you a friend of James?' she asked.

Louis shrugged his shoulders and raised his palms heavenwards. 'A leetle,' he said. 'We play football together but Jimmy is not exactly my friend. I would say I am more friend of Jasmine.'

'Yes, Jasmine is a delightful creature, isn't she?

Jasmine couldn't help smiling to herself.

'Mr Jones is a very lucky man,' added Camilla.

'I think, sometimes, Jimmy not know how lucky he is,' added Louis, just loudly enough for Jasmine to hear.

Jasmine felt her cheeks burn. Not with indignation at what Louis had said about her fiancé, but with pride that he regarded her so highly.

'Well, goodnight, Louis Ricardo,' said Camilla. 'I'll look forward to seeing you again tomorrow.'

Louis bowed his head and stepped backwards. 'Goodbye,' he called politely over his shoulder as strolled slowly back towards the loch and the path to the hotel. He didn't appear to be in any hurry.

Jasmine heard Camilla close the door to the castle behind her, back to her table settings and her name cards.

'Bye, Louis,' Jasmine whispered into the night. And then she stood up, took a deep breath and opened the French doors.

'Jasmine!' shouted Chrissie. 'It's your last night of freedom. Have another glass of champagne.'

Louis glanced back at the castle. A light was on in a first-floor room and although he didn't have his glasses on he could make out the shapes moving through the windows. It must be Jasmine and her friends. He wasn't by nature a nosey man, but Louis rummaged in his pocket for his glasses and perched them on the bridge of his nose. The silhouette of a perfectly curved female figure was framed by the window. She was dancing, slowly and provocatively with her mane of hair swinging behind her. Louis was transfixed. He sighed, a little sadly, and dragged his eyes away. Jasmine. Beautiful, perfect Jasmine ...

And then he felt immediately guilty. Only last week he had proposed to his childhood sweetheart, Maria. She was a clever girl, attractive too, and she was kind and loyal. His parents adored her and Louis admired her a great deal. But did he love her? Louis wasn't sure. He certainly didn't feel passionate about her. He glanced guiltily up at the window once more and felt the familiar tingle in his groin that he always experienced when he allowed himself to feast his eyes on Jasmine. Maria didn't get his juices flowing that way. No woman did.

He walked reluctantly back towards the hotel. His team mates had been behaving like animals when he left. They had all been snorting cocaine. The football season was over and there would be no drug tests for a couple of months.

Jimmy's friend Paul had organised some girls for the evening – mainly groupies, wannabes and cling-ons. He'd had them flown in especially for the stag do. They all looked the same to Louis with their dyed blonde hair, short skirts and high heels. He'd seen them all before, or at least a thousand girls who looked just like them, hanging about outside the football club, flaunting their flesh in the footballers' favourite nightclubs. They were easy to spot. Easy to find. Easy to seduce. In Louis's eyes they were just plain easy. He wondered how Paul's wife Cookie would feel if she knew.

He'd seen his team mates have sex with girls like these in toilets, in limos, in alleyways and even, once or twice, in public bars. To the foot-ballers, earning tens of thousands of pounds a week, these girls were as disposable as dirty socks. And cheaper to replace, too. They didn't even talk to the girls. They just stuck their tongues down their throats and their hands down their tops. But the girls didn't complain. The spectacle made Louis despair. Where had all the intelligent girls gone? All these girls wanted was to sleep with a footballer. To sell their story to the papers. To be famous. Why? Louis would never understand.

Some of the wives were no better, Louis thought. In fact, they were just prettier, richer and more successful than the groupies. OK, so most of them came from pop groups, or modelling careers, but they were still groupies of sorts. They went after that wedding band like hounds after a fox. They thought they'd made it once they'd marched their footballer up the aisle. But that wedding band meant nothing to their husbands. Louis was sure about that.

Paul had organised professional girls for the evening's entertainment too – strippers and expensive 'escorts'. One of them was a girl called

Pamela from their favourite strip club in London. She'd been lap-dancing naked for Jimmy when Louis had left. Even the normally faithful Calvin had been trying to impress a group of girls at the bar by setting fire to fifty-pound notes.

Louis knew that a girl like Jasmine was wasted on an idiot like Jimmy. She wasn't well-educated but she was clever. It was her mind that excited Louis as much as her body. Although, man, was that some body …

Jasmine was loving her hen night. The four girls had swapped sex secrets, shared shopping tips and polished off three bottles of Cristal. Jasmine knew she should stop soon. Her head was spinning and she didn't want to be hungover on her wedding day. But she was having such a great time in this fairytale castle, with her four-poster bed and antique furniture and, of course, her two best friends and her little sister. Now she was showing Cookie and Crystal how to be a stripper (God, she must be drunk).

'More! More! Show us how to lap-dance!' Chrissie was clapping her hands with glee as she watched Jasmine's burlesque performance.

Cookie tried to copy her but ended up falling backwards on to the bed in a hysterical heap. 'It's the baby,' she laughed. 'Knocking me off balance. Normally I'd make a brilliant lap-dancer, honest!'

Jasmine danced over to the bed and helped her pregnant friend back to her feet.

'My mum says I got kicked out of my ballet class when I was seven because I had so little poise and grace,' giggled Crystal, wobbling as she tried to twirl around like Jasmine had done. Her cheeks were flushed and she was getting out of breath.

'Yeah, not exactly Darcy Bussell are you, babes?' agreed Cookie.

'Actually, you do look just as graceful as a ballerina, Jazz,' said Crystal, stopping suddenly and gazing at her friend in awe. 'You look … you look …' She pushed her damp hair out of her eyes. 'You look so hot that if you weren't my best mate I'd want to scratch your eyes out!'

'I can do it too,' Alisha jumped in, pushing in front of Jasmine and wiggling her tiny bottom manically.

Jasmine stepped aside and let Alisha take the floor. The girl had rhythm. She could certainly move, but it was all too obvious, too in your face. Jasmine thought Alisha was trying too hard, but she knew her sister didn't want constructive criticism; she was looking for praise and approval. It wasn't something their mum handed out freely.

'That's brilliant, Lish,' enthused Jasmine. 'You're a natural, sweetheart.'

But Cookie and Crystal had lost interest in the strip show and were giggling together on the bed.

'Shall we?' Cookie was saying.

'Oooh, I don't know,' Crystal replied. 'She really should wait until tomorrow.'

Alisha stopped dancing. Jasmine saw that she was disappointed at the lukewarm reception.

'You were great, Lish,' she said.

'Yeah, but not as great as you, eh?' she snapped. 'I've never been as good at anything as you, have I?'

'Alisha!' said Jasmine, taken aback by her sister's outburst. 'Don't be so touchy. I'm just older. I've had years of practice.'

'Yeah, I know, but it's not just dancing, is it? It's everything. Look at you. Think about what's happening tomorrow. This place,' Alisha swung her arms around the magnificent room. 'Stuff like this doesn't happen to normal people.'

'I'm just lucky.' Jasmine squeezed her little sister's arm affectionately. 'Good things will happen to you too.'

'Nah,' Alisha shook her head. 'You're special. You always have been and sometimes it's hard following behind you.'

'It hasn't always been easy for me,' Jasmine reminded her. 'I've always been the outsider, remember? I've never been Mum's little baby, like you.'

Alisha raised a sceptical eyebrow. 'Oh, what? And sharing DNA with Mum is a good thing, right?'

'We-ell ...' Jasmine had to accept that Alisha had a point. Cynthia was not a glowing role model.

Alisha was on a roll. 'I tell you what, sis, you are soooo lucky not to be properly related to us lot. Look at the rest of us – a bunch of lowlifes and fuck-ups. I dunno where you come from, but it's somewhere better than me, that's for sure.'

Jasmine glanced over at Cookie and Crystal. They were pretending to be deep in conversation, but she could tell from their faces that they were listening in.

Jasmine lowered her voice. 'Listen, Alisha,' she said, putting one hand on each of the girl's cheeks and staring straight in her eyes. 'We might not be related by blood, but you're the only sister I've got. I love you. Never forget that.'

Alisha blushed and pulled away from Jasmine. 'Blooming heck, Jazz. How much champagne have you had? Don't go getting all slushy on me, girl. Forget I opened my big trap. It's not your fault you're so fucking per-fect, is it? Right, I'm going for a smoke.' She tossed her hair defiantly, but Jasmine noticed the glimmer of a smile on Alisha's lips as she disappeared through the French doors and out on to the balcony.

'Little bit of sibling rivalry going on there?' asked Crystal.

'Normal family stuff.'

'Hey, shall we give her the pressie now?' asked Cookie excitedly.

'I told you, she really should wait until after the wedding ...' teased Crystal.

'But then she won't have the pleasure of showing it off tomorrow, will she?'

'That is true ...'

Cookie was swinging a black bag from her fingers provocatively. She let Jasmine catch a glimpse of the white logo. The intertwined Cs were a dead giveaway.

Jasmine gasped. 'You got me something from Chanel?' Jasmine didn't have anything from Chanel. She'd always considered the label too grown-up and sophisticated for her.

'Well, you're going to be an old married woman tomorrow, so it seemed appropriate,' Crystal grinned.

'Oh my God. You haven't gone and spent a fortune on me, have you?'

Cookie and Crystal glanced at each other and both burst out laughing. 'Of course we've spent a fortune on you,' said Cookie. 'But it's the boys' fortunes so I shouldn't worry about it too much. They can afford it.'

That was true, Jasmine conceded. 'Oh, come on, then, stop teasing me. You're going to have to let me have it now.'

'Shall we?' Cookie hid the bag behind her back.

'Oh, go on then,' said Crystal eventually. 'Let her have it.'

Jasmine untied the black silk ribbon at the top of the bag and opened it very slowly. Inside was a large white box. She took the lid off and glanced at her friends. They were giggling with excitement. The contents were wrapped in tissue paper. Carefully, she unpeeled the layers of tissue to reveal the most exquisite butter-soft cream leather bag she'd ever seen. It was a classic Chanel quilted number, with gold chain straps and diamond-encrusted catch. Jasmine gently took the bag out of the box and hugged it to her chest. 'It's the most beautiful bag I've ever seen,' she cried.

'Look inside,' urged Crystal. 'Look at the craftsmanship.'

The bag was lined with dark red leather.

'It's called a two fifty-five,' explained Cookie. 'And it was designed by Coco Chanel herself in nineteen fifty-five. You can wear it across your body to avoid 'WAG Elbow'. That Chloe Paddington you lug around must be giving you RSI. And look, here, there's even a secret compartment for love letters!'

Jasmine opened a zipped compartment in a second hidden flap and found a card inside.

'To the best friend any girl could have. Happy wedding day! From your biggest fans, Cookie and Crystal xxxxxxxxxxx,' it read.

Jasmine had tears streaming down her face as she hugged her friends and kissed their cheeks. Not in a pretentious celebrity-best-friends kind of way but in the true, heartfelt way best friends embrace in bedrooms all over the world.

'But the best thing is,' said Crystal, 'that this little beauty is a limited edition number with nine-carat gold handles and real diamonds on the clasp. There's a waiting list for it the length of Bond Street, and guess who thought she was top of the list?'

'Who?' asked Jasmine, wide-eyed. 'Not Victoria. I don't want to upset Victoria.'

'No, not Mrs Beckham, you fruitcake, way better than that.'

'Madeleine!' shouted all three girls in unison and then they collapsed on the bed in hysterics.

'Have I missed something?' asked Alisha, walking back in from the balcony.

But the others couldn't answer, bent over as they were with laughter.

Chapter Twenty-Three

Charlie's 'wanker' antennae were buzzing. After decades of doing business with London's dodgiest wheeler-dealers, his inbuilt bullshit radar was a finely tuned piece of equipment. It had taken Charlie less than five minutes to work out that Brett Rose was a tosser of the first degree. The Hollywood megastar was a huge disappointment to Charlie. OK, so he looked the part with his perfectly crumpled designer clothes, his permatan and his megawatt smile, but his 'sparkling' personality was way too much for Charlie to swallow this early on a Saturday morning. Sad as it might be, he'd been really looking forward to hanging out with the A-list. And nervous, too. He'd thought he might feel inferior and awkward. But no, there was no reason to feel inferior to Brett. The guy was an idiot. It was as simple as that.

Brett liked the sound of his own voice. He'd been talking non-stop since the group had assembled in the VIP lounge of Malaga airport. While Maxine and Lila had chatted quietly to each other and Carlos Russo had engrossed himself in a newspaper, Brett had talked to, no, not to, Brett had talked *at* Charlie. And he'd kept on talking and talking and talking – about himself, his last movie, his new movie, his gym programme, his dietary requirements, his cars, his houses, his sexy co-stars, his kissing technique, his nudity clauses. Now, he was sitting next to Charlie on the plane, still talking, an hour into the flight. He hadn't asked Charlie one question about himself. Not that Charlie particularly enjoyed talking about himself, but a 'How are you?' might have been polite.

Brett dropped his voice to a conspiratorial whisper and glanced over his shoulder to check that his wife wasn't listening from her seat two rows behind. 'And you know, Charlie, some of those young actresses have awesome bodies,' he said, grinning wickedly. 'So why would I get a stunt double to do my nude scenes, man? Jeez, I get paid millions to rub up against the finest female flesh on the planet. And I get me some serious action after the cameras have stopped rolling, if you get me.'

Charlie 'got' him. He thought the man was a complete arsehole for bragging about his extra-marital conquests while being married to the most beautiful woman in the world, but Charlie understood Brett loud and clear.

Brett licked his lips and continued his soliloquy. 'People wonder how my marriage survives long-distance, but I tell you what, man, five thousand miles away is just about the best place I can think of keeping a wife. She's so far from the action she ain't gonna get a whiff of any juice from LA. I mean Lila's a fine woman, but she ain't no spring chicken these days and a man has needs, no?'

Charlie shrugged. 'If you don't mind me saying, I think you're a lucky man to have such a gorgeous wife.'

Brett grinned. 'Hell Charlie, I do love my wife. That is a fact. She's kind and smart and she does a real good job of taking care of my kids. And I guess, she still is a fine-looking woman for her age. But she's a real woman – she's had two kids; she's gotten stretchmarks!'

Brett seemed to recoil at the thought. He curled his top lip and shuddered a little.

Yeah, from having your children, you plonker, thought Charlie, although he said nothing.

'If I'm honest with you, man, women don't do it for me. I'm still into girls, you know what I mean?' Brett sighed and seemed lost suddenly in some sordid memory or other.

Charlie did know what he meant. Some young girls were pretty, that was for sure. And in Hollywood *most* young girls were pretty. But Charlie often found younger women a little irritating. They talked too much about frivolous things; they had bad taste in music; they giggled; they were insecure about their bodies and obsessed with their looks. He thought of Nadia briefly – twenty-seven, and still too much of a girl for Charlie. He hoped she was safe. It would never have lasted, but he was fond of her and it scared the shit out of him to think she might be in danger.

No, Charlie preferred women over thirty. He found them sexier, more alluring. He glanced back at Lila. She had her head bent towards Maxine, listening intently to whatever it was her friend was saying. Her glossy hair was bobbing up and down as she agreed to some unheard comment. She glanced up for a moment and caught Charlie staring. He blushed and turned back towards Brett. Christ, if he had a woman like that ...

'The young ones are so green.' Brett was still talking. 'Inexperienced and easy to manipulate. They will do anything I ask them, and I mean *anything*, man.'

Brett leaned right back in his seat, placed his hands behind his head and grinned. He was so fucking pleased with himself. Charlie would have loved to give him a smack right in that cheesy grin of his, but of course he didn't. Instead he deliberately changed the conversation.

'So, how do you know Jasmine?' Charlie asked.

'Who?' asked Brett uninterestedly.

'Jasmine,' repeated Charlie in disbelief. 'My goddaughter. We're on our way to her wedding.'

'Oh jeez, yeah, the chick that's getting hitched to the soccer player,' Brett laughed, but not with embarrassment. 'Man, I take so many flights I'm never sure where I'm going. Brandy, my assistant there, takes care of all that.' He nodded his head towards the back of the plane where two personal assistants (one belonged to Brett, the other to Carlos), a hairdresser (Maxine's) and a huge black guy who Charlie assumed was a bodyguard (also Brett's) were sitting.

'No, haven't had the pleasure of meeting the bride,' Brett continued. 'But I have seen the pictures and she sure looks hot. You're her godfather, right?'

Charlie nodded.

'Not a blood relative?'

Charlie shook his head.

'So, have you had her?' asked Brett, wide-eyed.

Charlie shook his head and glanced out of the window. He could feel a vein pulsing in his right cheek. It did that when he was really angry. It wasn't something he could control. The plane was somewhere over France. Inverness seemed a very, very long way away.

Jasmine felt like Cinderella in the Disney film, when the birds and animals make a dress for her to go to the ball. There were so many people fluttering around her that she felt dizzy. The hairdresser was tweaking her hair while the make-up artist touched up her lip gloss. The stylist had tried pulling the bodice tighter and tighter with a bare foot on the small of Jasmine's back; now she'd decided to hand-sew her into the dress. This seemed crazy to Jasmine – she was only wearing the wedding dress for the ceremony and the first photographs, then she was changing into her outfit for the reception (a Vivienne Westwood number with a Scottish vibe) and then her 'going away' outfit (a Roberto Cavalli maxi-dress in a hot tropical print had seemed suitable for jetting off to the Seychelles). The photographer's assistant held the light monitor up to her face and set off an eye-watering flash. Jasmine was used to all this. It was what she did for a living (but usually with far fewer clothes on).

The women from *Scoop!* magazine were running around like ants, flapping and flustering with clipboards and mobile phones, tripping over their high heels in their hurry to get everything done just perfectly in time.

Camilla, the art director of the magazine and the celebrity photographer were having some sort of heated debate about which angle was the best to capture the dress in all its glory. Jasmine could hear Alisha squealing that her pink mini-dress was too long and Cookie complaining that her bump made her look fat. She'd barely had a chance to glance out of a window, but everyone insisted that it was a perfect, sunny day outside. Crystal came over and handed Jasmine a glass of champagne.

'You look gorgeous,' exclaimed Jasmine, taking in the pale-pink, strapless bridesmaid's dress. 'That colour suits you perfectly, babe.'

Crystal smiled. 'Thanks, love, but I think we're all going to pale in comparison with you today. You look …' She took a step back and surveyed her friend. 'You look absolutely fan-fucking-tastic.'

'Really?' asked Jasmine. She was nervous. She couldn't see herself. Her dress, her make-up, her hair – they were all in the hands of the professionals and they weren't letting her anywhere near a mirror until they were completely finished.

Crystal stood open-mouthed and nodded. 'Just amazing, Jazz,' she confirmed. 'The best. I can't even put it into words. You are so totally—'

'Can you get out of the shot, bridesmaid?' called the photographer, impatiently. 'I just want Jasmine.'

Camilla shooed Chrissie away.

'Are we almost done here?' she demanded of the hairdresser, make-up artist, stylist and photographer. 'I think Jasmine could do with a few minutes to herself now. Please remember that this is the girl's wedding, not just a magazine shoot.'

Jasmine felt very grateful to Camilla for that. The morning had been so hectic that she hadn't had a minute to stand back and think about what she was about to do.

'Is Charlie here?' she asked Camilla, worrying suddenly that his plane might have been delayed. As long as she had Charlie by her side she knew everything else would be all right.

'Of course Charles is here, darling,' Camilla said. 'He's waiting for you in the library. He's a charming man and he looks devilishly handsome in his morning suit. One would never guess he's from Essex.'

Camilla clapped her hands loudly twice and shouted, 'Right, everybody, time to get out. Shoo! Shoo!'

She pushed the assembled mob towards the door.

'Bridesmaids, wait downstairs with the godfather of the bride. You …' She pointed at the photographer. 'You wait outside the drawing-room doors. We'll leave from there as discussed previously. Everybody else … get to the chapel. Now go!'

Suddenly the room was very quiet. For the first time a wave of nerves crashed over Jasmine and her legs felt wobbly. She was about to get married. It seemed unreal, like something that was happening to someone else.

'Are you ready to see yourself?' Camilla asked. She was smiling warmly, taking Jasmine's elbow and leading her towards the full-length mirror in the corner of the room. Jasmine's legs weren't working properly and she struggled to walk across the room, pulling the heavy train. However would she make it to the chapel and up the aisle?

And then there she was – the girl in the mirror. Jasmine stared and stared but she barely recognised her own reflection. The girl staring back at her was not a stripper from Dagenham, but a princess from another world. She had to blink back tears.

Jasmine thought the dress was the most exquisite creation on the planet. It had been designed by Elie Saab himself and was made of the finest ivory silk. The bodice was strapless, figure-hugging and encrusted with twenty-five thousand hand-sewn pink diamonds and eighteen thousand pink pearls. Even the laces that criss-crossed up her back were finished with real pink pearl beads. The skirt was so full that it had taken thirty metres of fabric to create it. Around her neck was a priceless platinum and pink diamond necklace that Camilla had borrowed from DeBeers, and a matching tiara was perched on top of her head. Her hair was pinned up at the front with soft tendrils left loose at the temples. The rest bounced loose and long in cascading curls down her back. Peeping out from beneath Jasmine's skirt were her specially commissioned Jimmy Choo stilettos – strappy silver sandals decorated with another two hundred diamonds per shoe.

'Are you happy?' asked Camilla.

Jasmine nodded, but she couldn't get any words out. She was beyond happy. She was living the dream.

'Don't cry,' warned Camilla. 'Remember those close-up shots and save the tears until we're closer to a make-up artist! It would be a travesty to smudge your eye make-up at this juncture.'

Charlie paced the grand library, glancing from his watch to the door and back again. Jasmine was already five minutes late and the waiting was giving him sweaty palms.

'She'll be here any minute,' said Crystal. 'Brides are supposed to be late. It's the law.'

And then finally the posh old bird who'd organised the wedding entered the room. 'May I introduce the bride,' she announced, rather formally.

And then there in front of him stood this ravishing young woman in the fanciest gown Charlie had ever seen, and it took his breath away that this could be Jasmine, his lovely little Jasmine. Because somehow, over the years, while the rest of the world watched her transform into a breathtaking beauty, Charlie had only ever seen his best friend's girl. Sweet, wide-eyed, always smiling, but just Jasmine. And even now, as she stood there in all her glory, Charlie could see that cute little five-year-old, jumping off her dad's lap, running towards him with her arms outstretched with a smile that could melt a hard man's heart. If only her dad could see her now. Charlie felt himself welling up.

Pull yourself together, man, he told himself sternly.

'Do I look OK?' Jasmine was asking, tentatively.

Charlie stepped towards her, took her hand and kissed the back of it. 'You look sensational,' he said. 'It will be an honour and a privilege to walk you down the aisle.' He couldn't have been more proud if he had been her old man.

As they stepped outside, arm in arm, Charlie could hear the press helicopters buzzing overhead. They'd been circling the castle all morning, desperate to get shots of the wedding for the Sunday tabloids, but Camilla had foiled them. The bridal party exited the castle from the French doors in the drawing room, straight into a tunnel of pink and white flowers that extended all the way to the chapel some two hundred metres away. The walkway had been purpose-built and completely shielded them all from the press.

Charlie squeezed Jasmine's arm gently as he led her down the path. Behind them Crystal, Cookie and Alisha were following, stopping every now and then to straighten the train. In front of them a pipe band played, marching them towards the church in full Highland dress. Weaving in and out of them all was the official photographer. He pranced backwards, stooping and then stretching, capturing every moment for the magazine. And then they were there, at the chapel. The photographer took a few more pictures and then disappeared inside. Charlie paused outside the heavy wooden door to the church and turned to Jasmine.

'Are you ready?' he asked.

'Are you ready?'

Charlie's words swam in Jasmine's mind.

Am I ready? she wondered to herself. *Oh, fuck! Am I really ready? This is for ever. Am I ready for that?*

She swallowed hard. She knew she loved Jimmy. She knew she'd always dreamed of this day. And so why did she feel so terrified about walking through that door?

Charlie was staring down at her, starting to look concerned. 'Jasmine,' he was saying. 'Is everything all right?'

'Come on, Jazz,' whined Alisha. 'My feet are killing me in these shoes. I need a seat.'

Jasmine closed her eyes and took a deep, deep breath. She counted to ten and waited for her heart to stop beating so loudly in her ears. There was no choice. It was just last-minute jitters.

'Right,' she said, eventually. 'Let's do this!'

'Thank fuck for that,' muttered Alisha as they entered the chapel. 'I thought you were going to—'

And then Alisha's words were drowned out by the gasps of the guests as they watched the bride start her long walk down the aisle.

Jasmine could feel hundreds of eyes boring into her, hushed voices whispering to their neighbours, the gospel choir singing 'Oh, Happy Day'. The congregation was just a mass of blurry faces; she couldn't make out anyone – not her family, her friends or the famous guests. Her head felt odd, kind of light, as if it might fly right off her shoulders and through one of the stained-glass windows in to the pale-blue sky beyond. Although she was moving towards the altar she wasn't quite sure how, because she had no feeling in her legs at all. Thank God for Charlie. He was holding her arm tightly, keeping her upright.

And then she spotted Jimmy, peering back at her from the front right-hand pew, grinning like a kid at Christmas. He looked so happy. He looked happier than she felt. Why? But what struck her most was how much like a little boy he looked. A little boy who'd borrowed his dad's suit. Oh God, was she doing the right thing?

Jasmine's heart was thumping in her ears again and the blurry guests were swimming in front of her eyes. *Focus! Focus!* she ordered herself, terrified that the panic in her chest was showing in her face. *Focus on anything*, she ordered herself. She was almost at the end of the aisle now, getting closer and closer to Jimmy and the minister and the words, 'I do.' Jasmine forced herself to focus on the nearest face. Dark hair and fine features appeared in front of her eyes and Louis was there, smiling kindly, mouthing the words, 'Good luck.'

Lila couldn't take her eyes off the bride. Yes, Jasmine looked devastatingly beautiful (if a little princess-like) in her confection of a dress, but that wasn't it. No, it was the look of sheer terror in the girl's huge brown eyes that was intriguing Lila. She felt herself sigh, and then regretted it, hoping that no one else had heard. Weddings were not the place for regretful sighs. But the bride looked so scared!

Lila glanced up the aisle towards the groom who, in stark contrast to his bride-to-be, was clearly delighted with his lot. Lila thought that Jimmy looked all wrong in his groom's attire. He wasn't carrying the look off at all. He had his hair gelled back off his face; his pale-silver cravat and shirt were made of the same silk; his eyes and teeth looked too white beside his deeply tanned skin. He was cute, but he had no charisma. And it was obvious to Lila that he was still more boy than man. This worried her. She'd married a man/boy like that herself and now, ten years later, he still refused to grow up. She glanced briefly at her husband sitting beside her, and cringed. Americans never knew how to behave in British churches. Brett was lounging backwards in the pew, legs splayed, taking up way more room than was necessary. His hands were tapping on his thighs to the sound of the gospel choir. He was also chewing gum loudly and, even more mortifying for Lila, he was still wearing his shades! She couldn't tell where his eyes were wandering, but she suspected it might be all over the bride's cleavage, which was threatening to spill out of her dress as she passed.

Lila had woken up in a bad mood with Brett. It wasn't anything he'd done. In fact, he'd been his usual attentive, charming and sexy self since he'd arrived in Spain. They'd cuddled, chatted and made love. He'd played with the kids, talked golf with her dad and even helped her mum with the cooking. But she'd had one of her dreams again last night and that always made her feel distant with him in the morning.

Lila had had these dreams for as long as she could remember. Not the same dream every time: different places, changing scenarios, shifting time frames. In fact the only constant in the dream was a man (he'd been a boy when she was young, but he'd grown up with her). During the dream she knew exactly what he looked like and his face was as familiar to her as her own. But when she woke up she could never, for the life of her, remember his face. In her dreams this man was her partner. No, more than that, he was her soul mate. Whatever adventure they were having together in this dream world, they were a team. It was as simple as that. He was just the man who made her feel at home. The final piece of her jigsaw. All those corny clichés.

Lila did make love to this man. Indeed, she'd made love to him when she was a girl and he was a boy, long before she'd done the deed in real life. Their lovemaking was always delicious, but that wasn't the crux of their relationship. The most important thing about him was that he made her feel like … like what? How could she describe it? Yes, that was it. He made her feel like Lila. Like Lila should feel. Comfortable in her own skin, truly loved and cherished for the person she was, and had been, and would become.

When she woke up and realised he wasn't there, that he would never really be there, Lila always felt bereft. The truth was she missed him. She felt lonely and cold when he wasn't there in the living world. And so this morning when she'd opened her eyes and found Brett in her bed instead of the man from her dreams it had been a major disappointment. Brett was a gorgeous, charismatic and talented man, but he was not Lila's dream lover. He was her husband. He was real. And, like all real people, he was flawed. She knew it was irrational to feel cross with Brett for falling short in comparison with a man she'd dreamed up in her own head, but cross she was. Maybe if she'd waited longer before marrying she'd have met a man who really was the final part of her jigsaw. Perhaps she'd been too young.

Lila dragged her mind back to the moment. Jasmine and Jimmy had their backs to Lila now as the minister spoke about love, commitment and marriage. She barely knew Jasmine, let alone Jimmy, but Lila doubted theirs was a marriage made in heaven. She'd seen it in Jasmine's eyes. Christ, she'd heard them arguing. The bride was having doubts already. Lila sighed again. Audibly this time. Maxine turned round from her pew in front and mouthed, 'Cheer up. It's not a funeral!' Lila smiled back at her friend, but she didn't feel happy. Weddings were supposed to be about pure, perfect love. But everywhere she looked were 'make do' relationships full of compromise. Look at Maxine and Carlos. Maxi was on her fourth serious relationship and she was still making do with 'almost there' rather than 'happily ever after'. Did no one meet the man of their dreams? she wondered.

When the minister asked the congregation if anyone present knew of any reason why Jasmine and Jimmy should not be joined in holy matrimony Lila was sorely tempted to stand up and shout, 'He's not the man of your dreams, is he, Jasmine? You're young. You still have time. Keep searching for the dream.' But, of course, she said nothing. And once the couple had been pronounced man and wife, and Jimmy had snogged Jasmine for far too long, Lila clapped along with everybody else, in her cameo role in this great big charade of the wedding of the year.

Chapter Twenty-Four

Grace Melrose was a child in a sweet shop. She didn't know many of the guests at the wedding, and most of those she had met before had only been people she'd interviewed. The guests on her table were sitting with their partners, but Grace was alone (a downside of being the perpetual mistress). After the initial polite conversation, the others had retreated back into the comfort of their own relationships and seemed to have forgotten all about the lone woman at their table, sipping her champagne quietly. Most women would have felt awkward in her situation, but Grace was loving it. With no one to interrupt her train of thought, she was taking in every tiny detail of Jasmine and Jimmy's wedding and storing it up in her mind to use at a later date. And, boy, was there a lot going on around here.

The top table was a hilarious site to behold. Jasmine and Jimmy had changed into matching outfits for the meal. He was in a kilt, which Grace supposed was fair enough, what with him being Scottish and everything, and Jasmine was now wearing a matching green tartan dress. It looked very Vivienne Westwood (and it probably was one of her designs) with an alarmingly tight, cleavage-enhancing bodice, a fitted knee-length skirt with a bustle at the back and the most amazingly high, platform, peep-toed, green satin shoes Grace had ever seen. It looked sexy, and trendy, but not a comfortable outfit to wear while eating a five-course gourmet meal.

But even Grace had to admit that both the bride and groom were positively radiating excitement. Jimmy kept squeezing Jasmine's hand and kissing her bare neck, which made Jasmine giggle and swat him playfully away. They appeared to be genuinely, completely and blissfully happy. Something deep in Grace's heart stirred as she watched the newlyweds. What was it? Hope? Hope that true love really did exist? Hope that one day Grace too might find 'the one'? Nah! The cynical voice of reason took over. This wasn't true love. Jasmine and Jimmy Jones wouldn't last. How many celebrity marriages lasted the course these days? And as for Grace finding true love? Pah! Who needed love? It was always such a messy business. Grace dragged her eyes away from the happy couple.

Jimmy's father appeared to be a rather angry gentleman with a drink problem. He had the florid cheeks and misshapen nose of a chronic alcoholic and he was now digging into his fifth glass of whiskey (Grace had been counting). Mr Jones Senior was sitting beside the mother of the bride. But there was no tasteful lavender-blue pencil skirt, jacket and matching hat combo going on here. No, no, no. Cynthia Watts had chosen to wear red satin and leopard print to her daughter's wedding. The Essex gangster's moll, noted Grace, who was acutely aware of who Cynthia's boyfriend was. There was no sign of Terry Hillman, which was both a relief and a disappointment to Grace. He wasn't someone she wanted to meet, but she was well aware that he was a big story just waiting to break. She wondered if Blaine had banned him from the wedding to protect Jasmine's reputation. Or perhaps it was Jasmine who had told him not to come.

Cynthia had the air of someone who had once been attractive, but her girlish good looks had long since been eroded by years of poverty, misery, drug-addiction and a forty-a-day cigarette habit. She was the wrong side of skinny, wasted rather than waif-like, and her face was lined far beyond her years. How old must she be? Forty-five at most, concluded Grace. Her hair was too long and too bleached blonde for a woman of her age. She looked ill. Frazzled. As if life had chewed on her for a while and then spat her out with a loud 'Yuk!' Grace might have felt sorry for the woman had it not been for the cruel snarl on her lips and the jealous glint in her eye whenever she glanced in her daughter's direction. If Cynthia Watts had been a pantomime character the audience would have booed every time she walked on stage.

Jimmy's mother, on the other hand, looked like a very nice lady with pink cheeks and a shy smile. She was at least two stone overweight and clad in a horrendously unflattering peach dress and jacket. She appeared to be scared witless by the company she was suddenly keeping, but she had the good fortune to be sitting beside Jasmine's godfather. Charlie Palmer turned out to be the handsome man Grace had spotted arriving at Casa Amoura as she had left that day and from where she was sitting she could tell he was making it his duty to look after Mrs Jones – topping up her champagne glass and laughing at whatever it was she was saying. Nice bloke, thought Grace.

Also on the top table were the head bridesmaid, Crystal, and her husband the best man, Calvin, who were amusing themselves by throwing scallops at Madeleine Parks's head as she sat below them at the 'second' table. Their behaviour was adolescent and inappropriate but Grace couldn't help tittering as she watched. After all, Madeleine Parks was a right royal pain in the butt. Grace had had the misfortune to interview her a couple of times and had found her vain, self-important and rude. The thought of her wafting around the reception smelling of fish was hilarious.

Actually, thought Grace as she watched the second table, Madeleine must be having a miserable time of it. She was sandwiched between Jasmine's brothers, Jason and Bradley, who wore cheap, shiny suits, accessorised with tattoos, scars and skinheads. The pair were leaning into her on either side, talking too close to her face. Madeleine looked seriously disturbed and was obviously trying desperately to catch her husband's eye, from across the table. But Luke Parks was happily chatting to another member of the bride's family – the youngest sister, Alisha – and he seemed oblivious to his wife's pain. Alisha had turned her chair towards Luke, hitched her already very short bridesmaid's dress right up her thighs and was now sitting in front of him. Grace couldn't quite make out whether or not Alisha was wearing any underwear from her seat across the room, but she was sure that Luke Parks would know one way or the other.

The second table had another couple of footballers on it (including the heartbreakingly handsome Louis Ricardo), one of Jasmine's fellow glamour girls and an empty seat where Jasmine's aunt had been sitting, very briefly, before bursting into tears and running out of the room before the starter had been served. Grace had made a mental note to find out what that had been about. Jasmine had mentioned something about her aunt being a bit 'funny' and Grace smelled a story.

The next table was the most celeb-packed in the marquee, with Brett and Lila Rose (Grace was still avoiding making eye contact with her), Maxine de la Fallaise and Carlos Russo, the Beckhams and Elton John and David Furniss all rubbing designer-clad shoulders with one another. Grace was disappointed, if not surprised, to see that they were all behaving impeccably. These were the A-list. They rarely made mistakes.

From there the tables fell away from the top table in descending order of importance. Katie Price and Peter Andre were at table four with Jimmy's football manager. Peter Stringfellow had wangled a place on table five with Blaine Edwards and Piers Morgan. Table six appeared to be full of businessmen – Richard Branson, the chairman of the football board, a Russian oligarch and McKenzie. Yes, *Grace's* McKenzie. Of course they could never be seen together in public and she understood why he ignored her at these events. But did he have to look so interested in what the weather girl on his left was saying? Grace sighed. Couldn't he just pop over to her table briefly, say hello, and tell her she looked nice? No, she supposed not. She had no right to expect that. She'd known what she was getting involved in from the start.

Grace herself was on table twelve, nearest the exit, furthest away from the bride and groom, wedged between a lesbian lap-dancer called Bunty and Jasmine's accountant, Clive. But she wasn't complaining. She was enthralled to be here.

'Time for more photographs,' whispered Camilla in Jasmine's ear as she crouched behind her at the top table.

Jasmine looked at her untouched summer-fruit mousse with regret and excused herself from the table. She had work to do. Jimmy followed. Camilla ushered them through a tunnel into a smaller marquee behind. The room was set up as a photographic studio with a white backdrop, strategically placed wedding flowers and wrought iron love seat, festooned with yet more flowers.

'Sit,' said Camilla to Mr and Mrs Jones.

'Isn't this a bit ...' started Jasmine as she climbed on to the seat.

'What?' asked one of the magazine women.

'Cheesy?' suggested Jasmine.

Jimmy grinned and nodded.

'Of course it's cheesy,' replied the woman impatiently. 'It's what the readers will expect.'

'Of course,' said Jasmine. She knew she had to do exactly what they were told. They had sold their big day for several hundred thousand pounds and now she had no choice. But it didn't stop her feeling like a prize lemon as she perched on her ridiculous love seat and smiled cheerily for the photographer while the magazine woman, who looked frighteningly witch-like in her black dress, barked orders.

'OK,' said the witch. 'Now let's get some shots of you and your friends.'

Jasmine turned round expecting to see Chrissie, Cookie and co, but instead Camilla was ushering Maxine de la Fallaise, Victoria Beckham and a rather reluctant-looking Lila Rose into the marquee. Jasmine felt her cheeks burn with embarrassment. She hardly knew Victoria and Lila and now she was being thrust into fake friendships with them just to sell a few extra copies of a celebrity gossip magazine. This was her wedding day. She had wanted to feel like a princess but instead Jasmine felt like a cheap fraud. She was prostituting her big day for a few pounds. And the sad truth was she needed that money. Or at least her share of it. The blackmailer had cleared her out of savings and even though they were now married, she couldn't live entirely off Jimmy's earnings.

As she was squeezed between Victoria and Lila, Jasmine felt the shame creep up her neck; a lump formed in her throat and her eyes filled with tears. Nothing felt real anymore. Nothing *was* real anymore.

Every now and then the young blonde magazine assistant would scurry out of the studio on her high heels and reappear with another famous guest. Next Jasmine found herself sitting on Elton John's knee. After that it was Jasmine lying on her side, being held aloft by eight premiership footballers (five of whom she'd never met before). Jimmy was allowed to rejoin the party at this point, but not Jasmine. No, Jasmine had more work to do.

It was while she and Katie Price were toasting each other, ample chests almost touching, that the commotion started outside.

'What's going on?' asked Jasmine. She could hear raised voices and see a burly security guard blocking the entrance.

'I'm her fucking mother!'

It was Cynthia. Jasmine's heart sank even further. Now there was going to be trouble.

'Don't ya want me in your precious fucking magazine?' Cynthia screamed, stamping on the security guard's toes and elbowing her way into the marquee.

Jasmine had always been amazed by Cynthia's physical strength. She was barely five foot tall but she'd always been able to push people around.

'Tell 'em, Jazz,' she ordered, yanking up the straps of her red satin dress so that her gnarled old nipples weren't on show. 'Tell 'em who I am. I'm your fucking mother!'

The magazine witch stared open-mouthed from Jasmine to Cynthia and back again as the older woman shoved past Katie Price and flung her arm around her daughter's waist. Jasmine could see that Cynthia was drunk. And when Cynthia was drunk, there was no point in arguing with her.

'We'll get some nice family shots, won't we, love?' she grinned at Jasmine, showing her yellow teeth and receding gums. 'Boys! Alisha!' yelled Cynthia. 'Knock that flaming monkey's teeth out if he won't let you in.'

'It's OK,' said Jasmine to the security guard who was attempting to keep Bradley, Jason and Alisha from entering. 'They're my family.'

I wish they bloody weren't, she sighed to herself.

Alisha sauntered into the room with her baby, Ebony, casually slung on her left hip and a cigarette burning in her right hand. She was followed by her brothers who looked for all the world as if they'd just escaped from an asylum. Bradley had a black eye from the previous weekend's escapades and Jason was sporting a new scar on his forehead that was still red raw. They both had the wild-eyed look of substance-abusers about them and Jasmine wondered whether they'd been smoking crack in the toilets. She was mortified.

'Now, take some nice pictures of the family or I'll shove that camera where the sun don't shine!' shouted Cynthia at the photographer. Jasmine noticed he'd turned rather pale. He was a rather well-known celebrity snapper. He was obviously not used to dealing with people like Cynthia Watts and her brood. They were more likely to get photographed outside Dagenham Magistrate's Court. He glanced quickly at the magazine woman, who nodded curtly and then left the room. Probably, thought Jasmine, to have a good cry. Oh, how she wished she could join her.

Jasmine could hear music playing in the main marquee and wondered how her wedding was going without her. It seemed as if hours had passed since the meal and the speeches. She felt tired and deflated. Cynthia, Alisha and the boys had finally been kicked out of the studio and the photographer looked as if he was about to pack up.

'You haven't taken any photographs of me with my godfather or my aunt,' said Jasmine tentatively.

She'd had so many set-up shots done, but few that really mattered to her. She wanted a photograph with Charlie and Auntie Juju. Then she would be done.

'Oh, I don't think that will be necessary,' said the magazine witch.

Jasmine took a deep breath. She knew that her entire wedding had been bought and paid for by *Scoop!* magazine and that they would only publish the pictures they liked, but she also knew that she wouldn't get this chance again. She wanted a nice photograph with Charlie and Julie. It was one of the few shots she would like to put in a frame and have on the mantelpiece at home.

'No,' she said as firmly as she could. 'I just want one or two shots with my closest family. It will only take a minute.'

The photographer rolled his eyes. The magazine witch shrugged her shoulders and then they shared a look that read, 'Diva!' Jasmine couldn't care less what they thought of her.

Eventually the little assistant scurried off and reappeared a few minutes later with Charlie.

'So this is where you've been hiding,' smiled Charlie. 'You're missing all the fun.'

'Nearly done,' said Jasmine, hugging Charlie. 'Then I'll be strutting my funky stuff on the dance floor, I promise.' Jasmine peered towards the door. 'Where's Juju?' she asked.

'Ah,' said Charlie.

'Ah, what?'

'Well, we've had a bit of a problem with Julie,' explained Charlie. 'She wasn't feeling very well so she had to go.'

Jasmine felt herself deflate even further. 'Did she have one of her funny turns?' she asked.

Charlie nodded. 'Not quite sure what upset her this time. She was fine at the church and when she got into the marquee she seemed quite chipper at first. Next thing I knew she looked as if she'd seen a ghost. Poor old thing burst into tears, started shaking, all sorts. Don't worry about her, though. I've arranged for her to get home safely.'

'Oh, God. Poor Juju,' sighed Jasmine. 'I didn't even get a chance to talk to her.'

'I know, love,' said Charlie. 'But you know what she's like. Crowds aren't really her scene. She probably just got freaked out by the scale of the whole thing.'

'I know,' said Jasmine. 'But it's a shame. It's a real shame.'

And so, Jasmine and Charlie posed as a twosome for the last shot.

Chapter Twenty-Five

Charlie surveyed the dance floor from his seat at the top table. The vein in his cheek was pulsing again and it had nothing to do with the polite conversation he was attempting to make with Jimmy's mother, Maureen. She was a sweet woman, shy and conservative, who had latched onto Charlie during the meal and who now seemed reluctant to talk to anyone else.

'I always knew my Jimmy was special,' she was saying. 'Such a beautiful, talented wee boy. Even when he was three he could dribble a ball like Kenny Dalglish. And he's been really good to me, you know. Bought me a house in Newton Mearns ...'

Charlie wasn't really listening. He was nodding his head every now and then, adding a polite, 'Yes,' and 'Oh, really? That's interesting,' once in a while but his eyes were locked on the floor below.

He'd been halfway down the aisle when he'd first spotted him; sitting at the end of a row in a black suit with his silver hair slicked back off his face and a look of sneering superiority on his face. What the fuck he was doing there Charlie didn't know, but his presence changed everything – ruined everything. It was as if, at that moment, a black cloud had filled the sky and taken the light out of the day.

Charlie surveyed the room, trying to make sense of the scene. Now he was talking to Jimmy at the back, near the door. Towering over the footballer with a famous Russian supermodel on his arm and two burly bodyguards flanking him on either side. Jimmy seemed uncomfortable. Uncomfortable but awestruck. What was he doing here? How did Jimmy know him? What was going on? Not for one moment had Charlie even considered the idea of Dimitrov being a guest at Jasmine's wedding.

His mind was buzzing. It was too much of a coincidence and Charlie didn't believe in coincidences. He'd been around long enough to know that everything happened for a reason and that everyone had ulterior motives. What had he missed? Had Frankie known Dimitrov would be here? Was that why he'd asked Charlie to do the job? He wasn't used to feeling like this. Charlie had always been ahead of the game. It was the only reason he'd stayed alive all these years. But now he was confused.

And, if he was brutally honest, he was scared. Dimitrov glanced up at the top table and raised his glass to Charlie with a cold sneer. Charlie felt his blood run cold.

For a split second Charlie regretted getting rid of his gun. For years it had been his constant companion. Now it was buried under three metres of concrete somewhere in West London and Charlie felt vulnerable. Maybe he should have taken Frankie up on his offer. That way he would have had a gun. He could easily have got rid of Dimitrov here. There was a plane waiting at Inverness airport to take him back to Malaga tonight. There was a lake in the grounds. A body could go missing here for quite some time. Long enough for Charlie to escape, anyway.

He shook his head and tried to clear his mind. No, it was crazy thinking. This was Jasmine's wedding. Besides, Dimitrov had his heavies with him and Charlie had no idea how he would get past those giants. They looked like retired hammer-throwers from the USSR Olympic team of 1982. And if he was honest, Charlie knew Dimitrov was too big even for him. He'd heard the rumours about Russian mafia connections, uranium smuggling and arms dealing. He'd heard tales that Dimitrov had the ear of the Kremlin. Charlie knew what happened to guys who crossed men like that. Marbella was not far enough away to escape their clutches. Hell, the moon was too close for that.

Besides, as sinister as the man was, he was also Nadia's father. How could he even contemplate killing Nadia's old man? She was quite the Daddy's girl. Nadia would be devastated if anything happened to her dad and Charlie couldn't live with that on his conscience. He sighed and cracked his knuckles under the tablecloth. He was still worried about Nadia. It all came back to her. If it wasn't for her disappearance Dimitrov would have no problem with Charlie. But Nadia had vanished and, as far as her father was concerned, Charlie was in the frame.

He excused himself and left Maureen with Paul. The footballers weren't the brightest bunch Charlie had ever met, but they did have respect for their mothers. Maureen would be OK. He weaved his way through the dancing bodies and caught hold of Jimmy's arm. Jimmy turned round, looking surprised at the sudden interruption.

'Watch it, Char,' he said, rubbing his arm. 'You don't know your own strength, man.'

'Sorry,' said Charlie, trying not to sound flustered. 'I just need to ask you something.'

'What?'

'That bloke. Dimitrov. The Russian. What's he doing here?' Charlie tried to keep his tone casual.

Jimmy looked confused. 'He's a businessman. A billionaire or some-thing. My governor said I should invite him. Why? What's it to you?'

'Nothing really, Jimboy. I just know him vaguely from London, that's all.'

'Oh, right.' Jimmy lowered his voice and whispered conspiratorially in Charlie's ear. 'Don't tell anyone I said this, but I heard he's thinking about buying the football club. An aggressive takeover, or whatever it's called. Big scandal. You heard it here first.' Jimmy tapped the side of his nose and then disappeared back into the throng.

Charlie's shoulders relaxed and he could feel the vein stop throbbing in his cheek. So Dimitrov wasn't here for him. Maybe it *was* a coincidence. Another one. There seemed to be a lot of that going on lately. Charlie smiled to himself. It was almost funny when you thought about it. He'd been getting his knickers in a twist for nothing. Still, he would avoid Dimitrov today. With Nadia still missing, it was probably the safest thing to do.

Jasmine appeared by his side.

'Have you seen Jimmy?' she asked. 'I haven't had a chance to dance with him yet.'

'He was here a second ago, love. Not sure where he's slipped off to.'

Jasmine's face fell as she looked around, trying to spot her new husband in the crowd.

'Will I do?' asked Charlie. 'I'd like to dance.'

It was a lie. Charlie hated dancing. But he hated seeing Jasmine unhappy even more. Especially today of all days.

Lila sipped her champagne and surveyed the scene in front of her. She was sitting quietly with Carlos, making occasional and polite chit-chat while their respective partners tore up the dance floor together – a modern-day John Travolta and Olivia Newton John. Brett and Maxine shared a love of the spotlight and they were both formidable dance partners. Brett had recently starred in a movie set in New York's infamous nightclub, Studio 54, during its seventies heyday and the critics had raved about his snake-hipped performance as a disco king. There was no denying her husband looked like hot stuff out there in his sharp black tux. He'd discarded his jacket and tie and undone a couple of buttons on his shirt. His hair was starting to curl in the heat, just like it always did.

And Maxi ... well, the girl just knew how to move. She was sex on legs. Thirty-six-inch, mahogany-tanned, firm, full-thighed legs. Needless to say Maxi's electric-blue Versace dress was indecently short and as Brett spun her around it flared up and gave onlookers a flash of matching electric-blue knickers. Her wild golden hair blazed around her head as she span and twirled and threw herself into Brett's arms. If it had been anyone else dancing with Brett like that Lila would have been green with envy. But this was Maxine and during these last few days Lila had come to appreciate what a good friend she truly was. She felt sure she could trust her. For all her loud, brash, sex-siren ways, Lila knew that Maxine's heart was steadfast and pure. She felt lucky to have such a loyal friend.

'Ah, she is beautiful, no?' said Carlos suddenly.

'Oh yes,' agreed Lila. 'She's spectacular.'

Lila turned her head to watch Carlos as he gazed adoringly at Maxine. He really did seem to love her. Perhaps Lila had judged their relationship too harshly before.

'You must think me a silly old fool to fall in love with such a young woman,' mused the Spaniard.

'Of course not,' said Lila, although she had thought exactly that many times in the past. 'You both seem very happy. And that's all that matters, isn't it?'

Carlos turned towards Lila. It was, she realised, the first time she'd made eye contact with him. For all his wealth and success he was a shy, almost reclusive man, who was always polite and charming but never particularly warm or forthcoming. Now she met his gaze and for a moment she felt like she was staring into his very soul. It was the eyes. Such beautiful, deep, chocolate-brown eyes. The eyes that had sung a thousand love songs and broken a million teenage hearts in their prime. When she stared into those eyes Lila no longer noticed the deep laughter lines around them, or the leathered skin, and she understood suddenly what Maxine saw in Carlos.

'You know, Lila, that I will never divorce my wife,' he said, still holding her stare.

The statement took Lila by surprise. It was none of her business.

'Um, oh, right,' she murmured, snatching her eyes away from his. 'Well, that's between you and Maxine, Carlos. Nothing to do with me.'

'I tell you this because I'm not sure Maxine listens when I say it. And I do say it. Often. She hear the words but she does not really believe it, I think.'

'I'm not sure you should be telling me this,' ventured Lila, getting nervous about the direction the conversation was taking. 'Maxi is one of my oldest friends.'

'And that is exactly why I tell you.' Carlos continued to stare at Lila and somehow managed to drag her eyes back to his. They looked full of concern and sincerity. 'I love my Maxine. I want to be with her for ever.

But I am, how you say it? I am set in my ways. I don't like fuss. I can't divorce Esther now, after these years have passed.'

'Why not? If it will make Maxi happy? You and Esther are history, aren't you?'

Carlos shook his head. 'My wife and I will never be history. We are Catholic. We have children.'

'But I thought your kids were grown-up,' responded Lila. It sounded like an excuse to her. Brett said a divorce would cost Carlos too much. That that was why he stayed married. Perhaps he was right.

'Oh, they are. But I owe it to Esther, as the mother of my children, not to disgrace her. And divorce would be a disgrace for her. She is a different generation to you and Maxine. If I divorce her she will be ruined. She is not bad woman. She does not deserve that.'

'And what about what Maxi deserves? Doesn't she deserve commitment?'

'She has my commitment,' Carlos nodded with certainty. 'She has all of me.'

'But not a ring.'

'No, not a ring.'

'Carlos, why are you telling me this?' asked Lila, still bemused.

Carlos smiled warmly and the corners of his eyes crinkled. 'Because I like you, Lila. You are sensible woman. Different from Maxine's other friends. And I hope when you talk ... I know how you girls talk ... that it will help Maxine for you to know this.'

Aha. Carlos was asking for her assistance. Maxi wasn't listening to him, so maybe Lila could get through to her. Well, perhaps it made sense. Maxi wasn't a great listener. She did tend to hear what she wanted to hear and ignore the rest. But did Lila want to accept this role of intermediary? Not bloody likely! It made her feel awkward and complicit in Carlos's attempt to have his cake and eat it. Wasn't that what he was doing? Staying married to Esther but living with Maxine as his common-law wife? It just seemed plain greedy to Lila.

'Well, Carlos, I'll bear what you've said in mind whenever Maxine talks about your relationship, but I won't act as your spokeswoman. I don't agree that you should stay married to Esther. Not if you really love Maxine. I think Maxine deserves the whole package. She deserves all this.' Lila gestured towards the wedding extravaganza surrounding them.

Carlos laughed and patted Lila's hand with almost fatherly affection. 'She has had all this three times already, remember. This does not make her happy. This does not make anyone happy. This is just a public show of affection. It is not love.'

He sat back in his seat, averted his eyes from Lila and went back to surveying the dance floor. He looked very wise. Lila shrunk down in her seat. Carlos had made her feel naive, unsure, stupid. For the first time in a long time she felt young. But not in a good way. She watched Brett strut his stuff for all the other women in the room. Hell, what did she know about love, anyway? Who was she to preach about the virtues of a happy marriage?

'Hey, you two look cosy!' laughed Maxi, spinning around and throwing herself down on Carlos's knee. 'Isn't this the best fun ever?'

'It's great,' said Lila, although Maxine noticed her friend didn't look too cheerful.

Maxine was having a ball. She'd met so many interesting people and she thought the bride and all her friends were awesome. They were so little and cute and beautifully dressed. They reminded Maxine of living Barbie dolls. She'd already made up her mind that she was going to play with them some more. What was it Lila called them (a bit snootily, Maxine thought)? Oh yes, that was it. The WAGs. Whatever they were called, Maxi loved them. If they wanted guest passes to Cruise they'd be welcome any time.

And as for the footballers, they were deeply cute. Not in the same league as her lovely Carlos, of course, but they sure were nice to look at and admire from a distance. And she was having a gas dancing with Brett. Whoa! What a mover Mr Rose was. Carlos didn't like to dance. Well, only slow dancing to slushy, old-fashioned stuff, and that really wasn't Maxine's scene. It was great to get the chance to go wild on the dance floor with a guy like Brett.

Phew! Maxi was hot. Hot and dizzy. Why was she dizzy? She wasn't drunk. She'd been taking it easy with the champagne just in case her little plan had started to work already. She and Carlos had been going at it great guns since he'd got hold of that Viagra and who knew, perhaps she was pregnant already. That would be perfect, wouldn't it? They'd have a baby, they'd get married ... Maybe she would be just like Jasmine soon. Oh, she did hope so. She already had it all planned in her head. They would get married at the Alhambra Palace in Granada, not too far from their home, and Maxine would wear a flamenco-inspired white dress with red roses in her hair. The baby would wear a cute little mini flamenco dress if she was a girl and a blue suit if he was a boy. Yes, Maxine had it all planned.

'D'you wanna dance, honey?' Brett asked Lila.

Lila shook her head and excused herself to go to the ladies'.

'I'll dance again!' announced Maxine.

Brett grinned. 'Cool,' he said.

'You don't mind, do you, Carlos?' she asked her lover.

Carlos smiled and his brown eyes twinkled. 'You dance, Maxine. I watch you. I am happy.'

She kissed his tanned forehead, took Brett's hand and spun back on to the dance floor. No, she had no idea why she was so dizzy. Maybe she really was pregnant already.

Charlie had eventually started to enjoy himself. He'd danced with Jasmine for a while and then they'd swapped partners with Brett Rose and Maxine de la Fallaise, so now he was dancing with a famous 'It' girl. It was mental! Maxine was every bit as friendly and chatty as Charlie had imagined she would be and she was some dancer, too. Since relaxing over the whole Dimitrov problem, he'd allowed himself several glasses of bubbly and it had gone straight to his head. Christ! Maxine had him wiggling his hips and clapping his hands in the air like a right plonker. But it was fun. Charlie was actually having fun.

He glanced over to where Jasmine was dancing with Brett Rose just in time to see Alisha cut in and wriggle her little body in Brett's face. Jasmine didn't seem at all bothered. She wandered off, still looking for Jimmy no doubt, and left the Hollywood actor at the mercy of her little sister. Alisha couldn't have looked more delighted if Brad Pitt had fallen in her lap naked. Come to think of it, Brett didn't look too upset either.

Carlos Russo tapped Charlie politely on the shoulder and asked if he could cut in. Maxine kissed him on both cheeks and said, 'Thanks for the dance, handsome,' with a saucy wink. Charlie's cheeks were still burning as he made his way through the crowds towards the gents'.

Grace Melrose had had enough of discussing the merits of setting oneself up as a limited company with the crushingly boring accountant, Clive. He was still wittering on about beneficial tax breaks but Grace had long since stopped listening and was busy people-watching instead. It was her plan to write a book one day about all the bizarre celebrity behaviour she'd witnessed during her years as a journalist. This WAG wedding was full of prime book fodder.

The wedding had reached the tipping point, where polite conversation turns into raucous misbehaviour and best dresses and smart suits start to look crumpled and sweaty. Yes, even here, where most of the guests were household names, the jackets had come off, the stilettos had been abandoned and the dance floor had filled up. Grace half-expected a conga line to form at any moment.

Now The Proclaimers were singing 'Five Hundred Miles' and everybody was jumping up and down so enthusiastically that it felt as if the entire marquee might take off at any moment. Scantily-clad WAGs clung to each other, giggling, as their enhanced cleavages spilled out of their dresses. Footballers in kilts flashed their muscular thighs (and every now and then their crown jewels) proudly. Even Jimmy's mother was up there, bouncing with the young boys. Jasmine's brothers were gesticulating at each other angrily at the next table to Grace and looked as if they were about to come to blows. Jasmine's mum, meanwhile, was licking the naked ice sculpture of Adonis for reasons known only to her. Grace noticed that Blaine Edwards had his fat arms draped around the neck of the youngest member of a famous girl band. The girl looked as if she was about to throw up, but whether she'd had too much to drink or too much of Blaine was anybody's guess.

And then Grace spotted the bride, catching sight of her new husband and running over to him. The newlyweds threw their arms around each other's necks and kissed passionately for a few moments before Jimmy's team mates dragged them apart and pulled Jasmine into the centre of the floor. Even Grace found the scene quite touching. The group formed a circle around Jasmine and took turns in dancing for her while she giggled with embarrassment.

Grace decided to go for a wander to see if she could spot any illicit snogs, or eavesdrop on any private celebrity conversations. She removed herself from Clive as politely as she could and headed towards the ladies'. She pushed the door open and found herself face to face with Lila Rose. Grace felt her mouth move into an involuntary 'Oh' shape.

Lila's eyes widened as she recognised her and it seemed to take her a while to decide how to react. 'Hello,' she said eventually. Her tone was not friendly, but neither was it full of spite. 'Grace, isn't it? You're a journalist. We've met.'

Grace nodded. 'Hello Lila,' she said.

And then she didn't know what to say. She didn't normally have to deal with meeting interviewees again. Not ones she'd been nasty about. They tended to refuse her any more interviews and then that was that. Their paths never crossed again and Grace was on to her next victim. But here was Lila Rose, two inches away from her nose, looking as serene and elegant as she had done the day they'd met in the Covent Garden Hotel.

The two women locked eyes for a moment and, against her better judgement, Grace felt compelled to say something, *anything*, about the article she'd written.

'I'm really sorry if I upset you with my feature,' she blurted out and then immediately regretted it.

Lila stared at her dispassionately and shrugged her shoulders as if she had no idea what Grace was talking about.

'Why would I be upset? I don't read my own press, good *or* bad,' she replied. 'Peter, my PA, mentioned something about you being catty.' Lila flicked her hand and looked beyond Grace towards the marquee. 'But these little stories really have no effect on me. Now you must excuse me. I'm going to rejoin my party.'

Grace stepped back out of the way and let Lila Rose waft past. What a class act. She was lying, of course. She had definitely read the piece. Celebrities were tabloid junkies. They thrived on column inches. But Grace had to admire Lila's style and there was no denying she was a good actress. Such a shame she had no career left to speak of.

But Grace had no time to dwell on Lila Rose because as she entered the ladies' she was greeted with a gob-smacking sight. Madeleine Parks had a pregnant Cookie McLean pinned against the tiled wall. She was so swept up in her anger that she didn't even notice Grace enter. Grace weighed up the situation quickly and decided that Cookie didn't actually seem to be in any imminent physical danger and so she sneaked quickly into a cubicle and locked the door. What was going on here? She listened intently.

'That bag had my name on it, you little bitch,' she could hear Madeleine spitting. 'You and Chrissie knew it was being held for me. What the fuck were you thinking getting it for Jasmine?'

Cookie sounded terrified. 'It's her wedding, Madeleine. We wanted to get her something special.'

'But it was mine! They promised me.'

'You're next on the list. We told them you wouldn't mind because it was for Jazz.'

'I can't be seen with that bag now, can I? I'm not having Jasmine Watts's sloppy seconds. Who do you think I am? I'm a leader, not a follower of fashion. That bag is dead to me now. I can never carry a Chanel again.'

'Jones,' said Cookie in a shaky little voice. 'She's Jasmine Jones now.'

'Whatever,' sniffed Madeleine, who sounded on the verge of tears. 'I can't believe you and Chrissie would do this to me after everything I've done for you. I could have made your life hell on the team, but I didn't. I put up with you silly little cows. I took you shopping. I even let you have your picture taken with me.'

'I know, Madeleine,' replied Cookie. 'And we're really grateful to you, but it's just a bag. There are lots of other bags.'

'But I wanted that one!' screamed Madeleine. 'How do you think I'm going to feel every time I see Jasmine carrying *my* bag? I'm devastated, Cookie. Devastated.'

Grace couldn't believe her ears. These women were fighting over a designer handbag. She knew they were shallow, but this? This was ridiculous.

'I'm sorry,' whispered Cookie, still sounding terrified. 'It will never happen again.'

'It had better not,' spat Madeleine. 'Now you listen to me. There's a new Balenciaga coming out next month and it's mine, understand? If any of you little bitches turn up with it I will single-handedly make sure that you never set foot in Chinawhite again, OK?'

'OK.'

'Because I have power, Cookie. Remember that. If you want your ugly little face to keep turning up in those magazines you'd better keep me sweet.'

'I know.'

'And that bump there,' continued Madeleine. 'What's that little brat going to be worth when it's born? You get good money for baby pictures. I could ruin that for you.'

'Don't,' pleaded Cookie. 'Stop it. I get it. I won't disrespect you again. I promise.'

'Good,' snapped Madeleine menacingly. 'And remember. Next month, stay away from the Balenciaga. Or else.'

Grace heard high heels clipping on the marble floor and then the sound of the door swinging open and shut. She flushed the toilet and let herself out of the cubicle. Cookie McLean was wiping smudged mascara from under her eyes in the mirror. Her shoulders were still shaking a little bit from the ordeal.

'Are you OK?' asked Grace.

Cookie nodded without meeting Grace's eye and then she too clipped out of the ladies' in her heels.

'What a strange old world,' thought Grace to herself.

She was just washing her hands when the mirrored wall in front of her shook suddenly. The thump that accompanied it made Grace jump. What was that? And then there was the sound of an almighty crash from the other side of the wall and then another. She thought she heard a deep voice cry out in pain. Things were getting very weird around here.

Charlie hadn't seen it coming. What an idiot he'd been. He'd let his guard down, allowed himself to relax and enjoy himself. What had he been thinking? Now the Russian hammer-throwers were pummelling into him. Smashing him in the ribs, punching him in the groin, but avoiding his face. They would leave no outward trace of their visit. They were professionals.

Dimitrov stood blocking the door, watching his henchmen beat the shit out of Charlie while he kept his hands clean.

'Where is she, Charlie?' he asked calmly. 'Where is my Nadia?'

'I ... don't ... know ...' spluttered Charlie between punches. 'I'm telling ... argh! ... you ... Jesus! ... the truth.'

'So, you know nothing about her whereabouts now?'

'No!' shouted Charlie, curling into a ball to protect his already-broken ribs. 'She was there, in bed, in my flat when I left. She was fine.'

Dimitrov strode towards Charlie, bent down and stared him straight in the face. 'What happened?'

'My assistant, the boy, the one you beat the shit out of ...'

The hammer-throwers grinned at each other as they remembered with glee the damage they'd done to poor Gary.

'He saw Nadia leave in a black cab,' explained Charlie.

'Tsk!' Dimitrov tutted. 'Keep going, boys. My Nadia, she no take taxi. She never take taxi.'

Wham! Bang! The boots were in his ribs again. The pain was so excruciating, Charlie had lights flashing before his eyes.

'It's the truth,' he shouted. 'Get these monkeys off me!'

Dimitrov said something in Russian and the hammer-throwers took a step back.

'Continue,' ordered Dimitrov. 'She took taxi. Alone?'

'No,' said Charlie, trying to catch his breath. 'With a man. A dark-haired man. That's all Gary saw. She looked happy. It must have been someone she knew. She went on her own accord.'

Dimitrov bent down again. Charlie heard the familiar click of a safety catch being let off and suddenly the cold steel of a gun was against his left temple. He'd done this to others, but had never felt the sensation himself. He felt the blood drain from his face and heard his heart beat in his mouth. Was this it? Was this how he was going to die?

'You tell me truth, Charlie Palmer?' demanded Dimitrov. His hand held the gun absolutely still. The Russian was not fazed by the situation. It was all in a day's work.

'It's the truth. I swear,' replied Charlie, trying to sound strong, although he felt sickeningly weak inside.

'OK,' said Dimitrov. 'I believe you.'

Slowly, very slowly, the Russian removed the gun from Charlie's temple, stood up and walked towards the door. He looked as if he was about to leave when he spun round.

'But is still your fault, Charlie,' he said. 'Nadia was in your care. You left her. You let this happen and you must pay. Now is your job to find her. You have six weeks. I'll be in touch.'

He mumbled something else in Russian and then left Charlie alone with the animals. As they threw him against the urinals, the whole wall shook.

Chapter Twenty-Six

Jasmine had persuaded Carlos to sing a few of his most famous love songs at the end of the night. Lila supposed, a little grudgingly, that although his line of schmaltzy ballad wasn't to her taste, he was rather good. He dedicated the first song to Maxine, who was up on stage beside him, swaying along to his velvety smooth voice. Lila looked around for Brett. She hadn't danced all evening. If she was honest it was because she could never dance like Maxine, never let her guard down properly. She always felt self-conscious and a little bit silly when she danced. But a slow dance like this might be quite nice, romantic even. If only she could find Brett. She wandered round the marquee looking for him but he was nowhere in sight.

Now Carlos was on his second number. The wedding was drawing to a close. Most of the big names had already left by helicopter or limousine. The bride and groom had sped off on their honeymoon in a blacked-out Mercedes, and the marquee had an air of dishevelment about it. The ice sculptures had melted to the point where it was impossible to tell Boadicea from Adonis; the flowers were wilting; the champagne had lost its fizz. One of Jasmine's brothers was slumped unconscious on the floor. Lila stepped over him and carried on her search.

'Excuse me, I don't suppose you've seen my husband, have you?' she asked a handsome young man, sitting alone at a table, nursing a whiskey and a faraway look in his eye. She'd been introduced to him earlier but she couldn't remember his name. He was a footballer. Portuguese.

The footballer shook his head mournfully. 'I no see him,' he replied. 'Sorry.'

God, there was nothing more depressing than the dreg ends of a wedding. It was fine for the loved-up couples but anyone left alone at the end of the evening felt wretched. And now Lila was alone too. Alone, and ready to go home. Where the hell was Brett? She wandered out of the marquee and into the gardens. The day had been warm but it had given way to a clear, chilly night. Lila shivered as she stepped down into the grounds. She spotted a figure sitting at the bottom of the steps. It was a man. A big man.

As she got closer she recognised him as the nice guy from the plane that morning. It was Jasmine's godfather, Charlie.

'Charlie?' she said. 'Hi, it's me. Lila.'

Charlie smiled up at her, but his eyes looked strange.

She sat down beside him, close for warmth, but he winced as her elbow brushed his arm.

'You OK?' she asked. The man looked sick.

'To be honest, I've got terrible stomach pains,' said Charlie. 'I'm not feeling too bright.'

'No ...' Lila surveyed his pale face. 'You don't look too bright. We'd better get you to the plane.'

She looked around. 'I don't suppose you've seen my husband, have you?' she asked. 'I can't find him anywhere and it really is time to get going.'

Charlie stood up slowly with a pained expression. He clutched his side and took a deep breath. It looked serious. Lila hoped that they all weren't about to go down with food poisoning.

'I'll find him,' offered Charlie. 'It might do me good to stretch my legs. You go back inside and wait with Carlos and Maxine. Has Carlos finished?'

Lila listened for a moment. 'Yes, I think so,' she said. 'Are you sure you're OK to walk around?'

Charlie nodded but his face looked grim.

Something told Charlie that Brett was up to no good and, despite the fact his broken ribs were killing him, he couldn't let Lila Rose go looking for her husband. His job had made him a good listener. He'd had to stalk men through endless dark alleys before now and once he'd had to track his prey through London's disused underground tunnels. He had an instinct for these things and, as he headed deeper into the gardens of the castle, it wasn't long before he heard noises coming from a secluded gazebo. There was a female voice ooh-ing and ah-ing, and a low male voice, grunting.

Charlie crept towards the gazebo and crouched behind a bush to look. It was a clear, starry night and his eyes had become accustomed to the dark. He could clearly make out the shape of a naked male bottom, bobbing up and down in the moonlight. The man hadn't bothered to get undressed. He was still wearing a white shirt and his boxer shorts and black trousers were round his ankles. It was Brett all right; Charlie recognised him from his clothes. And he knew who the girl was too. She had her dark legs wrapped around Brett's waist and her pale-pink bridesmaid's dress yanked up around her waist. Charlie had known Alisha since the day she was born. He'd watched her grow up with Jasmine. But she had none of Jasmine's charm. Charlie might have guessed she'd end up here, being screwed and used by some tosser at her sister's wedding.

Jasmine would be mortified if she knew. Charlie would make sure that she never found out. And he would make sure Lila didn't catch sight of this either. There was no point in saying anything to Alisha and Brett. That would only cause a scene and Charlie hated scenes. Anyway, he needed to let this piece of information sink in before he could decide what to do with it. Charlie liked to think things through before acting. He wasn't a man to make rash mistakes. He retreated silently back towards the marquee where he found Lila waiting at the door.

'Any sign of him?' she asked.

Her huge blue eyes gazed up at Charlie hopefully as she bit her quivering bottom lip. God, she was so astonishingly beautiful that Charlie could barely believe what he'd just seen. Why would any man be unfaithful to a woman like this? And with a girl like Alisha. It was madness. If Charlie had a woman like Lila he would never leave her side. But Charlie would never have a woman like Lila Rose. She was way out of his league. Just breathing the same air was a treat enough.

He shook his head. He was not going to be the one to break Lila's heart. Not here. Not now. Perhaps later he would let Brett know that he'd seen him with Alisha. He would tell the bastard to confess what he'd done to his wife or he would do it himself. But for now he would keep Brett's secret from Lila.

Charlie's entire body was throbbing but his mind was still alert. 'I can't find him anywhere,' he lied. 'But there's a hotel over there, where most of the footballers are staying. Perhaps Brett's gone back with them to have a drink.'

Lila nodded. She seemed convinced. 'Probably. That sounds like Brett. And he was so impressed by all those "soccer" players.' She mimicked her husband's American accent. 'Well, we're not waiting for him,' she announced. 'He can find his own way to the airport and if he's not there by the time we're ready to leave, then he can bloody well make his own way back to Spain.'

She smiled, but Charlie could tell she was hurt. Still, the woman had balls. Despite her fragile beauty she was obviously no walkover. Charlie was even more impressed by Lila Rose than ever.

Blaine hadn't missed a trick. He'd hoped this wedding would be a smorgasbord of scandal but the reality had surpassed even his wildest dreams. He'd noticed the bride's jitters, and heard about the WAGs' handbag dispute. He'd seen Jasmine's mother collapse unconscious in a drunken stupor and then her sons following suit. He'd heard about Dimitrov's takeover of the football club and he even knew some guy had been beaten up in the toilets by the Russian's heavies (although he didn't know why and was wise enough not to ask).

But this ... wow! This was a classic piece of gold-plated celebrity filth. He held his tiny digital camera aloft and snapped away, then checked to make sure he'd got the shots. Oh yes, there he was – Brett Rose knobbing Jasmine Jones's teenage sister. It was definitely his firm white Hollywood butt drilling into the little bridesmaid. What a fucking cracker! This was the big one he'd been waiting for. These shots were priceless. Totally fucking priceless. Blaine sneaked off while Brett was doing up his trousers and Alisha was still searching for her knickers. They didn't have a clue they'd been caught. But they'd find out soon enough. When the time was right. It might be the making of Alisha, Blaine mused. She could make a killing out of publicity like this and Blaine would be just the man to help her. Yes, it had been a very good day for Blaine Edwards.

Brett Rose stumbled on to the plane at the last minute with a half-drunk champagne bottle in his hand and, as Charlie noted ruefully, his flies still undone. He grinned and shouted, 'Well howdie, y'all! Let's paaaartay!!!'

Lila tutted and looked out of the window. Maxine continued to sleep, her head resting on Carlos's shoulder as her lover stroked her hair tenderly. The Spaniard nodded politely in Brett's direction and then he too turned to look out of the window wearing a hint of mild disgust on his handsome face.

Charlie flinched. The last thing he needed now was that pissed-up, philandering yank irritating the hell out of him. He felt as if he'd been hit by a train. His head throbbed and his ribs ached. The painkillers Lila had given him hadn't even touched the sides. Brett's eyes were wide, his pupils dilated. *Coke head*, thought Charlie scathingly. He hated druggies. They all looked the same, whether they were beating up prostitutes in Dalston or flying on their own private jets. They all caused trouble. And Charlie had had enough trouble for one day.

Brett raised his champagne bottle in Charlie's direction and yelled, 'You'll have a drink with me, won't you, my good man!'

Charlie's heart sank. He couldn't tell Brett Rose to fuck off, tempting though it was. But the thought of sitting next to that man, making polite conversation with him, made his skin crawl. He knew what Brett had done and where he'd been.

Brett staggered forward. Charlie didn't see a Hollywood hotshot approaching him anymore, just a cruel, filthy lowlife. And Charlie had seen enough of those to last him a lifetime.

A fake smile froze on his face as he resigned himself to a couple of hours of Brett's company. 'Please stop him,' Charlie pleaded in his head to whichever God might be listening. And then, suddenly, his prayers were answered. With a loud crash, Brett tripped over Maxi's handbag and tumbled onto Lila's lap, covering her with champagne.

Brett giggled. Charlie winced. Lila just tutted and pushed her dishevelled husband on to the carpeted aisle. Brett landed in a heap, hiccuped and then immediately fell unconscious.

'He needs to be strapped in a seat for take-off,' said the air hostess. 'He can't stay there.'

'Yes he can,' replied Lila icily. The air hostess didn't even try to argue.

Charlie smiled to himself through the pain. At least he'd have some peace for the trip back to Spain.

Chapter Twenty-Seven

The girl is back in the cold, dark cell with her back against the wall. Back to the damp and the rats. In the silence, every tiny noise is amplified a thousand times. The scratching of the rodents' feet, the sound of her heart beating in her chest, her mouth, her ears. All she can taste is blood. She's so cold that she can no longer feel her feet or her fingers. She tries to wriggle her toes but they won't move.

The skirt he made her wear is so wet that it clings to the skin of her thighs and she doesn't know if it's water, or cold sweat, or blood. The man has done unspeakable things to her. Things so disgusting that she knows she will never be able to put them into words. But then will she ever put anything into words again? Will she ever get out of here? The girl starts singing to herself, though her voice is little more than a sobbing whisper, just so that she can hear her own words. She thinks she might be losing her mind.

He's gone, for now, but when she closes her eyes all she sees is his face. She tries to stop the film playing in her mind, but it keeps going, round and round, showing her what he did, what he's going to keep doing. He said he'd be back. Please don't let him come back. Perhaps it would be best just to lie down here and never wake up. Sometimes the best thing to do is to stop fighting. Is she ready to stop fighting?

Her voice goes quiet. She doesn't have the energy to sing anymore. She lies down on the hard floor and waits. For what? For Charlie to save her? For death to come? Or for … no! … not that … Footsteps. A lock. The door is opening. Rough hands are grabbing her arms, calloused fingers digging into her bruised flesh, dragging her into the light, up the steps, back to his lair. And then she's lying on her back again like a piece of meat and she knows he's going to butcher her some more.

He's on top of her now, and his big hands are ripping at her clothes, and she can barely breathe, and then she sees it. The gun. Just a glimpse of metal glinting in the light. He's holding it in his right hand. The girl tries to keep fighting. She struggles to push him off her but he's too strong and then the gun is raised above her head and it's coming towards her, smashing against her skull and then it's all gone. Darkness falls. Everything is gone.

Chapter Twenty-Eight

'Char? Is that you?'

Gary sounded edgy and scared.

'Yeah, it's me, mate. Any news your end?'

Charlie steadied himself on the hotel balcony and narrowed his eyes at the ocean. Such a beautiful view. Such a shitty old world.

'Nothing,' Gary was saying. 'But I've been keeping my head down, to be honest. I'm still at my mum's.'

'Well, get back to town and do some digging,' barked Charlie. 'Pronto.'

'But, but, but, you said to lie low,' stammered Gary. 'It's not safe.'

'Forget what I said before and find out what the fuck has happened to Nadia.'

Charlie knew he was being harsh on the boy. None of this was Gary's fault and what he was asking the kid to do was dangerous. But Charlie had no choice. He couldn't go back to London himself and he needed somebody there to find out what was going on. Gary was the only one he could trust. It was time for the boy to become a man.

'All right, boss.' Gary sounded unsure. 'If that's what I've got to do ...'

'It is,' replied Charlie firmly.

'What about Nadia's old man?' asked Gary. 'He thinks we've got her.'

'Not anymore he doesn't. I've spoken to him,' said Charlie. 'But he's still got me in the frame for it. He says it happened on my watch so it's my fault. You know how these things work, Gary. Until she's found, it's my head on Dimitrov's plate. We've got six weeks. Problem is, I can't come back, so you're going to have to find Nadia, kiddo. I'm relying on you.'

'I'll do it,' promised Gary. 'Where do I start?'

Charlie sighed. Gary was such a great kid. And loyal. So fucking loyal. But what Charlie was about to ask him to do could get him killed.

'Talk to Nadia's friends,' he told the boy. 'Talk to her enemies. Talk to Dimitrov's enemies. Talk to the fucking filth if you have to. McGregor owes me and you know where to find him.'

'The boozer?'

'Correct.'

'Righto, boss.'

'And turn the flat upside down. She might have left something – a diary, a ticket, I don't know, anything.'

'OK,' said Gary, sounding fired up now. 'I won't let you down.'

'I know you won't,' Charlie said. 'And Gary ...'

'Yes, boss?'

'When this is all over, I've got something lined up for you. Something here. With me.'

It was a lie, of course. Charlie had nothing lined up in Spain – no flat, no job, no plans for the future. But something would happen. It always did. That was the one certainty in Charlie's world – there was no such thing as a quiet life.

'Thanks, Char.' Gary sounded pleased. 'Where are you, anyway?'

Charlie watched a couple of topless babes playing beach tennis by the shore. Their tanned breasts bounced up and down in the morning sun. 'Paradise, mate. When Nadia's found you can join me in paradise.'

After the phone call, Charlie washed down a handful of painkillers with a glass of neat Jack Daniels and lay gingerly on the bed. His ribs were screwed. One of his balls had swelled up to the size of a grapefruit. He had a bruise the size of Epping fucking Forest on his back. He'd planned to go house-hunting this week, but instead he was laid up in his hotel room barely able to walk to the balcony and back. He didn't even have a tan yet. 'Paradise, my arse,' he thought, wincing with pain. 'Paradise Lost, more like.'

Maxine squinted at the pregnancy test. It was one of those new ones that could tell if you were pregnant really early on. Her period wasn't even due until tomorrow but she couldn't wait another minute to know if she was carrying Carlos's baby. She crossed her fingers and waited. She had a funny feeling that it was going to be positive. She'd been feeling light-headed for days and she'd been even more emotional than usual – she'd even cried at Isabel's Spanish soap opera last night and she didn't even understand most of what was going on in that because they spoke far too fast. Her breasts were tender and her tummy was more rounded than it had been only a week ago. Plus there was that low dull ache in her abdomen. Yup, she had all the symptoms. She *must* be pregnant!

A clear straight blue line appeared in one of the boxes. Right, what did that mean? Maxine took the instructions from the box. Oh crap! They were all in Spanish. She could understand most of what Carlos said these days, but her grasp of the written language was still pretty poor. She tried to make sense of the pictures. OK, so if there's a cross ... no she didn't have a cross, just a line ... so, if there's a line ... tsk ... this was too complicated.

She could hear Isabel vacuuming outside the bathroom door. It was putting her off. Maxine couldn't hear herself think. She was getting frustrated and shouted, 'What does *no embarazada* mean anyway, for Christ's sake!?' just as the vacuum cleaner went quiet.

There was silence for a moment and then, 'It mean no pregnant, Miss Maxine,' came Isabel's voice from the other side of the door.

The vacuum cleaner started up again and Maxine was left sitting on the side of the bath feeling mortally embarrassed and deeply disappointed all at once.

She lay on her bed for an hour before reaching for the phone.

'Lila? Are you there? Pick up if you are. I'm having a *bad* day ...'

Maxine sighed. Where was Lila? She hadn't heard from her all week. Not since the wedding. Now she could think of nothing better to do to commiserate her lack of fertility than getting smashed with her friend. She tried her mobile instead. It rang and rang until finally the phone clicked and a male voice came on the line.

'Maxine? Hi honey, it's Peter,' said Peter breathlessly. 'Sorry, I was upstairs. Lila's having a swim at the moment. Are you OK, hun?'

'No, I'm having a crap old time of it this week and I feel like getting drunk with Lila. How's her diary looking for this afternoon?'

'We're in London.'

'But you said Lila's having a swim?' Maxi was confused. Why would Lila leave without telling her?

'She's swimming in her pool here. In London.'

'Oh,' Maxi replied, completely deflated. 'She could have told me she was leaving.'

'Sorry, but Brett's gone home to LA and the kids are back at school. Lila won't be in Spain again until October half term.'

'Well, get her to ring me later,' she said, unable to keep the disappointment from her voice.

The ache in her abdomen had turned into the familiar, gnawing cramp of period pain. By the time Carlos got home from the golf club, Maxine was curled up on the couch with her dog, Britney, and a pink, fluffy hot water bottle, feeling very sorry for herself indeed.

Carlos kissed her forehead and threw a handful of post on to the coffee table. 'You OK, chica?' he asked.

Maxi nodded forlornly.

Carlos frowned. 'You no look OK, dahling,' he said.

'Just one of those days, honey,' she replied. 'It's nothing important.'

At least, it was nothing she could tell Carlos about. He patted her head affectionately and started sorting through his post.

'What's that?' asked Maxine. She'd spotted a bright-red card with black embossed lettering. It looked like a rather swanky invitation and Maxi could smell a party at a hundred paces. And there was nothing like a good party to cheer a girl up.

'Oh, is just something from Juan,' said Carlos dismissively, tossing the invitation on to his 'to be recycled' pile.

Maxine leaned forward and picked up the invitation. Juan was Carlos's oldest son. He was twenty-five and a shit-hot Latino singing sensation. Maxine had only met him once, very briefly, last year. Juan looked just like Carlos had done in his prime – only with piercings and tattoos rather than beige slacks and tasteless seventies shirts. Juan was seriously hot property across the pond at the moment. He'd collaborated with all the hippest producers, rappers and R&B divas on his first album and he'd won an MTV award for his trouble.

Carlos and Juan had a difficult relationship. Carlos said his son had always been a mummy's boy and that the problem was they had nothing in common, but Maxine begged to differ. She thought that Juan was a chip off the old block and the two were just too alike to get on. She suspected that Juan's success, and his good looks, and his infamous way with the ladies (according to the *National Enquirer* he had worked his way through most of Hollywood's bright young things) made Carlos feel uncomfortable, envious even. It must have been hard for a man of Carlos's age to watch the limelight being stolen by his son.

'This sounds great!' Maxine enthused. 'It's a party to celebrate his second album release.'

'Yes,' said Carlos patiently. 'In Los Angeles.'

'Cool!' Maxine continued. 'I haven't been to LA in months. It'll be fun. We can make a holiday of it.'

'I am not going to LA,' said Carlos firmly. 'Anyway, the party is next weekend. I have a celebrity golf tournament.'

'Oh, Carlos …' She could hear the whine in her voice. 'Please, honey. What's more important? Supporting your son's career or playing *another* game of golf, huh?'

Carlos stared at her. He looked angry. Carlos rarely lost his cool. She knew she'd touched a raw nerve.

'Drop it,' Carlos warned her. 'I am not interested in going to Los Angeles. I am not interested in Juan's type of music and I am not interested in this party.'

'Oh, that's mean,' Maxine continued, although she knew she was pushing her luck. 'Juan would love you to be there.'

What she really meant was that *she* would love to be there; she didn't know Juan well enough to second-guess what he might be thinking at all.

'Juan will not care if I am there or not,' Carlos snapped. 'He has just sent this to be polite!'

He snatched the invitation out of Maxine's hand and threw it back on the reject pile.

'Well, maybe I'll go without you …' She reached forward and retrieved the invitation for a second time. She didn't even know why she was saying that. She wouldn't know anyone there and it was Carlos's invitation, not hers. But the fact was, she was bored. Bored, and not pregnant. She needed something to look forward to. Some excitement in her life.

Carlos frowned. 'You will not go. Do you hear me? I forbid you to go to this party.'

Oh dear. Now he'd blown it. This was not the reaction Maxi had expected. He was usually very reasonable and fairly easy to persuade. She'd thought if she kicked up enough of a fuss that Carlos would agree to go with her, not ban her from attending like some Victorian father. The problem was that beneath her airbrushed exterior, the teenage rebel lived on inside Maxine. If someone said, 'No, you can't do that,' her automatic reaction was to reply, 'Just watch me.' Carlos was forbidding her to go. Well, she'd have to bloody well go now, wouldn't she? Just to show him that he couldn't push her around. It looked as though she'd talked her way into a solo trip to LA. She couldn't back down now.

Chapter Twenty-Nine

Jasmine closed her eyes and lost herself in the bliss of the moment. She was lying on her back in the chalk-white sand, as the gentle waves licked her toes. She could feel the hot afternoon sun on her bare skin and hear the exotic birds singing in the palm tress. She had never felt so relaxed. Earlier, she'd enjoyed a wonderful aromatherapy massage at the resort spa, which was perched on the top of a cliff, overlooking the turquoise Indian Ocean. Then she and Jimmy had enjoyed a delicious fresh fish lunch in the Michelin-starred Creole restaurant before heading back to their private wooden villa on the beach for some gentle lovemaking (it was too hot for anything more exerting) and then an hour-long siesta in their four-poster bed, under the gentle breeze of the ceiling fan.

The Seychelles were utterly idyllic and Jasmine couldn't have dreamed of a more perfect honeymoon destination. Paradise Island was a private island resort of just twelve villas, each with its own secluded garden, complete with freshwater plunge pool and jacuzzi and, naturally, a stretch of empty, white beach out front. The wooden villa had a thatched roof and was full of Colonial-style furniture in mahogany and teak, and the enormous bed was draped in metres of white voile. The staff kept the room filled with wild, exotic blooms and huge baskets of fresh fruit. If it hadn't been for the sixty-inch plasma screen on the wall opposite the bed, and the mini-bar stocked with champagne, Jasmine might have felt she been transported back a hundred years, the daughter of some wealthy Plantation owner.

Jimmy had gone for a workout at the hotel gym, but Jasmine didn't feel like doing anything more energetic than lounging by the sea. Every now and then a white-suited waiter would wander down the beach from the main building and leave a fresh melon daiquiri on the table beside her lounger. Other than that, Jasmine was utterly alone. This peace was exactly what she needed after the stress of the wedding and the upset of the blackmailing incident. Now she pushed those things to the back of her mind and soaked up the tranquillity of the here and now. Ahhh! Bliss!

After a while she decided to go for a gentle swim. She wouldn't go far.

She'd had three cocktails already, after all. But a little swim to those rocks over there to see what lay beyond them would be nice. Jasmine plunged into the cool water and felt her hot skin tingle as she swam towards the rocks jutting out into the ocean. When she reached them, she pulled herself up out of the water and shook out her hair. So what lay beyond her own private beach? Jasmine stood up and stepped gingerly over the rocks until she could peer round into the next bay. What she saw shocked her so much that she almost fell back into the water. There, as bold as brass, about twenty feet from her nose, was a small fishing boat filled with photographers, their long lenses pointed straight at her. Jasmine gasped and folded her arms protectively across her naked breasts. She recognised some of them as the usual suspects from London and Marbella.

'What the hell are you lot doing here?' she demanded. 'How did you find us?'

'Ask Blaine Edwards,' called back one of the photographers. 'Now give us a smile, Jasmine! Flash us some flesh for the guys back home!'

'Oh, bugger off!' she snapped, retreating as quickly as she could back over the rough rocks. 'Ouch!' She stubbed her toe. 'Bastards,' she muttered to herself.

Usually she tolerated the press. Hell, she was good to them. She always gave them a smile and a wave and a hint of cleavage. She'd even taken trays of tea and biscuits out to them on one particularly cold London night. She understood that she had to play the game. But here? On honeymoon? Was nothing sacred anymore? She would kill Blaine when she got home. She would bloody well ring his fat neck.

It was raining in London. Raining and way too cold for June. Grace tutted as the rain lashed the windows of her Mews house. Her cat, Moriarty, kept wandering to the cat flap, poking one paw outside and then retreating to the comfort of his basket. Now he was throwing accusing glances in Grace's direction, as if she were somehow responsible for the dreadful weather.

Grace was working from home today. She'd managed to convince Miles that she needed peace to write up her feature about the Joneses' wedding but the truth was she'd got no further than the title – 'Nice Day For A WAG Wedding'. The truth was she was feeling dreadful. The truth was she'd been dumped. And dumped in the most inelegant and humiliating way possible – by text!

Alarm bells had started ringing yesterday morning in the office when Gerald, the theatre critic, had shared his latest piece of gossip with her. Gerald was an ageing queen, with wavy silver hair, an astonishing array of Savile Row suits and a tongue so sharp it could cut glass.

'We-ell,' he'd confided. 'You will never guess who I saw at the Adelphi last night.'

'Who?' Grace had asked, not uninterestedly. Gerald's gossip was normally pretty enlightening.

'Munroe himself, sitting beside Paige Richardson.' Gerald had beamed proudly.

'Munroe? Munroe who?' Grace had asked.

'Our esteemed proprietor McKenzie Munroe, you slow coach.' Gerald had rolled his eyes. 'Our extremely *married* esteemed proprietor with a twenty-two-year-old weather girl no less.'

Grace had felt a lump form in her throat and she could barely get her words out. *Her* McKenzie with Paige bloody Richardson? It didn't make any sense. McKenzie liked intelligent women. He said that's what had attracted him to Grace in the first place. Paige Richardson was a fluffy bimbo who gesticulated wildly in front of a weather map on some cheesy morning TV show. There had to be some mistake.

'I can't believe there's anything going on there,' Grace had said to Gerald, desperately trying to pull herself together. 'There must be some explanation. He's married.'

'Oh, yes, and of course we all know that married men are immune to the fragrant delights of pretty little weather wenches, don't we?' Gerald had sneered. 'No, no, no. There was nothing innocent about it. I saw his hand on her bottom during the interval.'

Gerald had widened his eyes and nodded to confirm his gossip as fact. Grace had swallowed hard and forced herself not to cry. McKenzie had never taken her to the theatre. He'd never taken her anywhere public. Even last week at Jasmine's wedding he'd ignored her 'just in case' anyone got suspicious. Come to think of it, Paige Richardson had been a guest at the wedding too. Grace remembered seeing her there in some hideous frothy white number. Everyone knows you don't wear white to a wedding. Not unless you're the bride. It had stuck in Grace's mind because it was such a schoolgirl error to make, even for a lowly weather girl.

'What on earth must he see in her?' Grace had found herself saying.

'Pardon?' Gerald had shot her a look that said, *Are you crazy?* 'What does *he* see in *her*?' he'd spluttered. 'Don't you mean what does *she* see in *him*? Can you imagine anything less pleasant than sharing a duvet with McKenzie Munroe?'

Gerald then pretended to vomit while Grace stared at her shoes, her cheeks burning.

'The man is a vile, rodent-like creature with halitosis. Believe me,' Gerald continued. 'I had to sit next to him at last year's Press Association Awards.

I'd rather sleep with *her* than *him* and I haven't touched a woman since nineteen sixty-seven. A redhead called Janet Evans, if you're interested; she practically mauled me behind the coconut shy at the village fete. I was fourteen. I believe that may have been the moment I turned ... Anyway, darling, don't quote me on the whole Munroe thing, obviously. This is one story we won't be seeing in print. Oh, the power of owning the media. One could do exactly what one wanted and never pay the consequences. Ta ra!'

And with that Gerald had minced his way towards the lift leaving Grace with her heart in her mouth and her life in tatters. What sort of man cheated on his mistress? The sort of man who cheated on his wife in the first place, of course. God, she hadn't seen this one coming. What an idiot. What a silly, naive, blinkered idiot.

When she'd got back to her desk, Grace had noticed that she'd missed a text on her BlackBerry. It was from McKenzie.

Not wrkng. Thnk shld cll it a day. Thxs 4 evrythng, M.

He hadn't even had the decency to call. Grace wondered if he'd got his secretary to send the bloody text. Somehow she didn't see McKenzie using text-speak.

And so today she was working from home. Away from Gerald and his gossip, Miles and his unreasonable demands and away from the job and the newspaper and the building that McKenzie Munroe owned. She was daydreaming about leaving her job. She could sell the Mews. Highgate was a desirable location. Property prices had quadrupled since she'd bought the place ten years ago. Despite the slump in the market, she'd still make a killing if she put it on the market now. She could buy a pretty cottage in the country somewhere. Dorset was nice. She liked the beaches there and London wasn't too far away if she needed a fix of Selfridges. She could live the good life with the equity she'd made. She could get some more cats. Write that book she'd been planning and forget about men altogether. She'd met a literary agent at a book festival a couple of weeks ago. They'd exchanged numbers. She might give her a call ...

The phone was ringing. Grace dragged her mind back to the present and glanced at the caller ID. Blaine Edwards. What the hell did that fat toad want?

'Hello, Blaine,' said Grace, picking up the phone reluctantly. She couldn't ignore it. Blaine would have a story and, for now at least, she still had her day job to do.

'Grace, my gorgeous girl,' boomed Blaine down the line. 'Have I got a scoop for you! I am about to make your career!'

Grace groaned inwardly. Blaine was always making such promises.

She really wasn't in the mood for it today. Today, she wasn't particularly bothered about her career.

'What is it?' she asked, without enthusiasm.

'Oh, do try to sound at least a little bit excited,' said Blaine. 'This one's going to blow you away. But I'm only going to give you it if you promise to be nice and grateful to your Uncle Blaine.'

Grace sighed. 'I am eternally grateful for all the scoops you've given me, Uncle Blaine. Now, what's the story?'

'It's not just the story.' Blaine's voice cracked with excitement. 'I've got exclusive pics, too.'

Grace's ears pricked up with the words 'exclusive' and 'pics'. Pictures were good news. Pictures meant proof and proof meant no risk of lawsuits.

'How do you know they're exclusive?' she asked.

'Because I took these ones with my own fair hands, dear Grace,' replied Blaine, smugly. 'No one else in the world knows about this story except me.'

'OK, you've got me hooked. Let's hear it.'

Blaine squealed with delight. He sounded like a piglet who was about to get some scraps. 'I don't even know where to start.'

'Well, do try. I haven't got all day.'

'Right. So I'm at the JimJazz nuptials—'

'Blaine, half the world was at that wedding. *I* was at that wedding. What could you possibly have unearthed that the rest of us missed?'

'I unearthed the biggest piece of gold-plated, five-star, celebrity filth since Hugh Grant was caught with his pants down on Sunset Strip. Believe me. It's *that* good.'

'OK, talk,' said Grace.

'So, I'm taking a moonlit stroll in the gardens towards the end of the evening and I stumble across a couple going for it hammer and tongs in the gazebo ...'

'Uh-huh.'

'He's got his trousers round his ankles and she's got her dress up round her waist and he's drilling into her like nobody's business and—'

'I get the picture,' said Grace. 'Who was it?'

'Are you ready?' he teased.

'I'm so *over* ready.'

'It was— God, I'm so excited to be telling you this ...'

'Just fucking tell me, Blaine!'

'It was Brett Rose and Jasmine's little sister. The young, mixed-race girl. The bridesmaid.'

'Oh. My. God!' Grace was dumbstruck.

'Isn't it fantastic?' giggled Blaine.

Grace was silent for a moment while she took in the enormity of the story. For some reason the first person she thought of was Brett's poor wife.

'It's not too fantastic if you're Lila Rose,' replied Grace.

Jesus, this really was a huge story. She'd heard rumours about Brett Rose's behaviour before, but none of it was in the public domain. None of his alleged conquests had spilled the beans and his lawyers were the best in LA. No newspaper had ever dared publish even the hint of a rumour about his infidelity. She thought about the interview she'd done with Lila. She remembered how fragile the actress had seemed. She thought about how she'd felt yesterday, when Gerald had told her about McKenzie's affair, and she couldn't even begin to imagine the pain this story would bring to poor Lila. The woman had been married for a decade. They had children. This story would rip her world apart.

'I can't touch it,' said Grace reluctantly, after a few moments of silence.

'Wha-at?' Blaine screeched incredulously. 'But this is the ultimate front-page splash, Grace. You're never going to get a chance like this again. I'm offering you the world exclusive with photos. Photos of them at it. Are you mental? Have you got a journalistic death wish or something? I could have given this to *anyone*, but I thought you'd appreciate it. I thought you were the best.'

Grace bit her lip and stared at the rain outside. Every bit of her professional being craved this story, but something else inside her, something real and compassionate and good that had been lying dormant for years, told her to say no. It felt like a light switching on in her brain. A moment of clarity. An epiphany, even.

'No, Blaine,' she repeated, firmly this time. 'I can't do it.'

'Why the hell not? I have all the proof you need.'

'It's not that I don't believe you,' Grace tried to explain. 'It's just I've met Lila Rose and I don't think I can be responsible for destroying her. I couldn't live with myself.'

'Jesus, woman, you've lost it. You've gone soft in the bloody head!'

'And I was there, at the wedding, as Jasmine's guest,' Grace continued. 'Can you imagine how upset she's going to feel about this coming out? She knows Lila. And this is her little sister we're talking about.'

'Exactly!' shouted Blaine in exasperation. 'That's what makes it such a good story. It's so deliciously incestuous *and* it involves celebs from every walk of life. It's a transatlantic tale from Hollywood, California to the Hollywood Nitespot, Essex. It's love – or at least sex – across the great social divide. It's the perfect fucking scoop.'

Grace rubbed her forehead with her hand. What was she doing? This was the Big One. The one she'd been waiting for. A promotion would be in the bag. Why was she walking away? But something inside her was stronger than her ambition.

'I can't do it,' she said adamantly.

'Grace, these people are not your friends. It's not your job to worry about their feelings. It's your job to tell the public what they get up to.'

'And I thought it was your job to look after Jasmine,' added Grace tartly. 'This is hardly good news for her, is it?'

'Oh, Grace, Grace, Grace ...' Blaine sounded bitterly disappointed in her. 'I thought you were wiser than that. It's not my job to look after Jasmine. It's my job to get *press* for Jasmine. There's a big difference. The only one I need to look after is Mr Blaine Edwards Esquire. And that, my dear, is exactly what I'm doing now.'

'I understand. You're just doing your job. But it's still a no from me.'

'Miles will kill you.' Blaine had a snigger in his voice now. 'If I take this to one of your rivals, you'll get sacked.'

'I'm aware of that,' she said flatly.

'What's going on with you, Grace? Are you having some sort of mental breakdown or something?'

Grace smiled to herself. 'No. Maybe I'm just finally coming to my senses.'

'Oh well, your loss.' Blaine finally stopped trying to persuade her. 'But you can be sure that you'll be devouring this fabulous tale of celebrity sleaze along with your breakfast on Sunday morning. No one else will turn it down.'

'I know that. I'll see you around, Blaine.'

'I doubt it,' he replied. 'You'll be on the next train to Losersville, girl. Your career is over. O ... V ... E ... R!'

Grace hung up on Blaine and stared at the blank screen on her computer for the longest time. Then she dumped the WAG Wedding feature in the waste bin and opened a fresh document. Save as ...

Resignation letter, she typed.

It was time to turn over a new leaf. She felt a weight floating off her shoulders as she typed. God, she'd barely seen it coming, yet here it was, the end of her career. It felt like a slightly mad thing to do, but it also felt good, liberating even. She would be free of Miles, and McKenzie, and the likes of Blaine Edwards and she would be free of the guilt that she'd carried around all these years. She realised now it had always been there in the background, gnawing away at her conscience, even while she told herself it was OK to make a living from other people's dirt. Now she could see things clearly. It wasn't OK. It wasn't OK at all. From now on Grace would do things differently.

She started by trying to get hold of Jasmine Jones to warn her about the story. Maybe Jasmine could then get word to Lila. Surely it would be better if the poor woman didn't digest the news of her husband's affair alongside her egg white omelette on Sunday morning. It would not be easy getting hold of Jasmine, because Blaine was her manager. But Grace had contacts. Photos had been printed in the papers that morning of the glamour model honeymooning in the Seychelles. Grace knew one of the photographers who'd taken the shots. They'd worked on stories together in the past. She called his mobile.

'Jeff? It's Grace Melrose,' she said. 'I'm after a favour. You don't have the hotel details where Jasmine and Jimmy Jones are staying, do you?'

'I certainly do,' he replied, chuckling. 'In fact I'm staring at the place right now. Jimmy and Jasmine are just getting jiggy in the jacuzzi ... Wait a second, let me just get this shot ... You still there, Grace? Sure. I'll text you the phone number now. Bye.'

Grace called the Paradise Island Resort and Spa and left a message for Jasmine to ring her, but she wasn't confident of getting a reply. Why would the girl return a call from a tabloid hack?

Next, Grace turned her attention to tracking down Maxine de la Fallaise. She and Lila were close. Carlos Russo was an extremely private man and tracing the phone number for his Spanish home proved impossible, but Grace did have the number for Cruise – Maxine's floating club in Marbella.

'Hola! Cruise,' said a woman.

'Oh, hello. I wonder if you can help me,' started Grace. 'I'm a good friend of Maxine's and I was wondering whether she might be there at the moment. She doesn't appear to be answering her mobile phone.' Lying came too naturally to her these days.

'Her mobile no work because she on plane to America,' came the response.

Bollocks! Another dead end. Maxine was on her way Stateside and Grace had no way of getting hold of her mobile number. There was only one more number to try.

'Hello, is that Peter?' she asked as politely as possible.

'This is he,' came the reply. 'And to whom am I talking?'

Grace had Lila's PA's phone number stored on her BlackBerry. He'd rung her on the day of her interview with Lila and had forgotten to block his caller ID. Grace had caught many a PA and even the odd celebrity out that way. Her contacts list was bulging with A-list numbers. Grace knew that Peter was more than the usual celebrity Chore Whore. He and Lila were genuinely close. If anybody could break this sort of news to her it would be him.

'Peter, it's Grace Melrose—' she started.

'Grace Melrose,' said Peter. His tongue rolled uncomfortably around her name as if it was a rather offensive swearword that he'd rather not repeat. 'What the hell do you want? Do you have any idea of the damage your article did to poor Lila? You can just take your grubby little Dictaphone and shove it where the sun don't shine, lady!'

'Wait,' pleaded Grace. 'I need to tell you something. I'm trying to help—'

But the line had gone dead. When she tried Peter's number again the phone had been switched off. Grace had run out of numbers. Ruining people's lives had always proved easy. Trying to help them was a lot more difficult.

Chapter Thirty

Jasmine and Jimmy were sipping champagne in the jacuzzi while they watched the sun set over the Indian Ocean. Jimmy had his arm thrown casually over Jasmine's shoulder and was tickling her nipple as they played footsie beneath the water. Jasmine was just on the edge of horny.

'Jimmy!' squealed Jasmine. 'That tickles. Stop it!'

Jimmy started kissing her neck. 'Sorry Mrs Jones,' he whispered.

'That's OK, Mr Jones,' she giggled. It still sounded funny – Mrs Jones. Mrs Jasmine Jones. It would take a while for her to get used to it.

The phone rang in their room and they could hear a voice leaving a message on the answer machine.

'This is hotel reception here. We have a message for Mrs Jones. A Grace Melrose has been trying to get in touch. She asked if you might call her back as it's a matter of some urgency. Her number is—'

'Fucking cheeky wee bitch!' said Jimmy. 'What the fuck's she doing calling you here?'

Jasmine shrugged. 'Maybe I should phone her. It might be something important.'

She started to stand up but Jimmy shook his head and pulled her back into the water. 'When will you learn, sweetheart?' he said. 'She'll just be wanting a quote to go with those bloody pictures. Blaine probably set her up to do it. Sleazy cun—'

'Jimmy!' Jasmine hated the 'c' word. She never used it and couldn't stand it when Jimmy did.

'Sorry, babes, but Blaine is a total wanker. Why did we bother paying the hotel staff to keep them quiet when our own manager tips off the press, eh? And don't even think about phoning that stupid wee journalist cow. Do you hear me?'

Jasmine nodded. Jimmy was right. She didn't need to make a phone call. All she needed was this glorious starry evening, the warm bubbly water and her gorgeous new husband. Finally they had some peace and quiet, away from the press. The photographers wouldn't be able to see them here in the jacuzzi.

'Now where was I?' asked Jimmy as he started to kiss her neck again. His hand cupped her breast as she curled her leg around his and his lips met hers and they were lost in each other's embrace. He pulled the string of her bikini bottoms and they floated up to the surface, leaving her naked. Jasmine pulled herself round to face her new husband and sat on his lap. She was just lifting herself on to him when his mobile rang.

'Leave it,' she whispered breathlessly into his ear.

Jimmy held her at arm's length for a moment as he picked up the phone that was perched by the side of the jacuzzi. He glanced at the number. 'I've got to get this, babe,' he mumbled.

He pushed her away and stood up, shaking the water from his hair.

'I'm here,' he said quietly into the phone. 'What do you want?'

And then he padded barefoot into the villa and out of earshot.

Jasmine lay back in the pool and sighed with frustration. She fished for her bikini bottoms and tied them back on. What was wrong with him? Why did he have to take that call? What were these secret little discussions about? Who was he talking to? She stared into the dark night. The stars had lost their magic.

Almost an hour passed before Jimmy reappeared, stepped back into the pool and tried to pick up where he'd left off.

'Come here, baby,' he cooed, kissing her behind the ear, groping for her breasts.

She swatted his hand away. 'Piss off, Jimmy,' she said. 'I'm not some machine you can switch on and off when you feel like it.'

'Oh, don't be so touchy. It was just a bit of business, that's all. It couldn't wait.'

'But I could?' she demanded.

'Oh, don't get your knickers in a twist, Mrs Jones,' teased Jimmy, trying to untie her bikini bottoms again.

'I mean it. Don't touch me. I'm not in the mood. Tell me what's going on with those phone calls. I'm your wife now. I've got a right to know if you're in trouble or something.'

'Jazz, it's just football business. It's nothing to do with you.'

'Tell me who you were speaking to.'

'No!' snapped Jimmy. 'It's none of your damn business, all right? Now come here. I thought we were in the middle of something.'

'We were. But that was an hour ago. Before you had to have your precious phone call. I'm not in the mood anymore, OK?'

'Oh, here we go again,' said Jimmy, rolling his eyes. 'Little Miss Prick Tease …'

Jasmine couldn't believe her ears. It was déjà vu. Practically the same argument they'd had in Marbella the week before the wedding. 'Jimmy, we've talked about this—' she started to say, but he was out of the jacuzzi now and heading back indoors.

She jumped out and followed him, her bare feet slipping on the wet floor. Jimmy was rubbing himself dry with a towel, pulling on his shorts and T-shirt, running some gel through his hair.

'What are you doing?' she asked. 'Where are you going?'

'Out,' he snapped. 'I'm going for a drink. On my own. Away from you, you annoying wee bitch.'

As the door slammed Jasmine threw herself on to the bed with a great gulping sob. Why did he do this? How could he change from her sweet, tender Jimmy into this monster in a split second? She spent the evening alone in bed watching soaps on the plasma TV and crying into her pillow. It was not the honeymoon she'd planned.

Much later, when Jimmy crept back into the villa, she pretended to be asleep. He crashed around drunkenly, falling over as he tried to get out of his shorts, stubbing his toe on the bed as he tried to climb in. He swore loudly but Jasmine kept her eyes firmly shut. The room smelled of booze. He seemed to fall asleep the moment his head hit the pillow, but Jasmine lay awake for a long time, listening to the crickets and wondering if she'd made a terrible mistake.

Maxine knew she shouldn't be feeling so excited about her trip to Los Angeles. Carlos was quietly livid about her leaving. It was clear that he hadn't believed she would actually pack her suitcase, order a taxi and make her way to the airport. He had barely looked up from his book when she'd said goodbye. But she had left and now here she was, running away to Hollywood. As she lay back in her first-class seat, listening to the Red Hot Chilli Peppers on her iPod and staring down at the Atlantic below she could smell freedom.

She'd had the same sensation before, when she'd run away from boarding school. She remembered sitting alone in one of those old fashioned compartments, chewing gum and listening to Duran Duran on her Sony Walkman, still in her school uniform as the train made its way slowly towards London, stopping at every little village en route. She'd known then, as she knew now, that the time would come to face the music. But not yet.

The journey was always the best bit. Nothing could beat the delicious taste of anticipation. Who knew what adventures lay ahead? She was going where she shouldn't be going. Doing what she'd been told not to do. Breaking the rules. When would she grow up? 'Californication' was playing in her ears. Maxi sipped her chilled white wine and smiled. Not yet. Maybe never.

It was the last night of their honeymoon and Jasmine and Jimmy were swinging gently together in a double hammock, strung between two palm trees on the beach. Their limbs were comfortably entwined. Jasmine's head lay against Jimmy's chest as he stroked her hair. All arguments had been forgotten. The last couple of days had been idyllic. Some big Hollywood story had whisked the paparazzi away and the young couple had spent long, lazy hours sunbathing and dreaming about their future.

'I like Destiny for a girl,' Jimmy was saying now.

Jasmine wrinkled her nose. 'No, I knew a stripper called Destiny once,' she said. Anyway, I prefer more old-fashioned names – Olivia, Amelia, Sophia, that sort of thing.'

'A bit posh,' mused Jimmy. 'But then our kids probably will be posh, won't they? We can buy them class. We can send them to the best schools, get them the best nannies. They can horseride. Play the fucking piano! God, it's mental, isn't it? You make a bit of money and you can change the future. I never thought in a million years that I'd be able to give my kids a life like that.'

'Me neither,' agreed Jasmine. 'It's quite a responsibility, really. We've got the power to give them the best start in life, but we could still get it wrong. Having money doesn't stop you from getting screwed up.'

'No, but it helps,' said Jimmy.

'It's not just the poverty you have to kill, though,' Jasmine continued. 'It's the lies and the violence and the hatred.'

Jimmy nodded solemnly. 'I know all about that. I'll never be like my dad,' he promised.

'I don't even know if I'm anything like my *real* dad,' mused Jasmine. 'Or my mum …'

'Do you want to find them?' asked Jimmy. 'I mean, I'll pay for a private investigator if you want …'

Jasmine shivered, even though it was a hot, balmy night. 'I don't know, babe,' she said. 'It's something I think about all the time, but what if they're not what I'm expecting?'

'What are you expecting?'

'Nothing amazing. Just something better than the Watts, I suppose.'

Jimmy laughed. 'Believe me, Jazz. Anyone's going to be an improvement on the Watts.'

She smiled. 'Yup, I suppose that's true.'

'So?'

'So what?'

'Are you going to do it? When we get home, are you going to look for your family?'

'Maybe,' said Jasmine quietly. 'It's definitely something I'd like to do before I have children. I'd like my kids to know who their grandparents are. I'd like to give them a past as well as a future.'

Jimmy's arm tightened around Jasmine and she snuggled down into his warm, smooth chest. He kissed the top of her head and she sighed with sheer satisfaction. She was so lucky to be here with this man in this paradise. She could hear the waves lapping gently to shore, the cricket's evening song, Jimmy's breath on her cheek ... and a mobile phone ringing somewhere in the distance.

Jimmy sat bolt upright. 'That's mine,' he said. 'Shit, I've left it in the villa. I'm going to have to get it.'

Jasmine sat up too. She couldn't believe what she was hearing. 'Don't you bloody dare,' she warned. 'This is the last night of our honeymoon. I'm not going to put up with you spending all night on the phone.'

'I'm sorry, babe,' said Jimmy, hurriedly scrambling off the hammock. 'But I've got no choice. I need to take the call.'

And then he was running up the wooden steps from the beach two at a time and disappearing into the black night.

Jasmine didn't cry this time. She was beyond tears. She was just plain livid. She stormed up the steps after her husband and found him sitting on the bed, listening intently to his iPhone.

'Give me the phone,' she demanded.

Jimmy shook his head, stood up and walked out into the garden at the back.

Jasmine followed him again. 'Jimmy Jones,' she said, her voice getting louder. 'Give me that bleeding phone now or I'll shove it up your—'

Jimmy spun round towards her and she saw immediately that the monster had returned. 'Piss off,' he whispered angrily.

'No, no, no, not you mate,' he stammered into the phone. 'I'm just trying to get rid of the Mrs.'

Jasmine felt her blood reach boiling point. How dare he talk about her like that? He'd gone too far and she'd had enough. With all her strength she lunged at Jimmy and prised the phone out of his hand. He tried to grab it back and for a moment they stood locked in an arm wrestle and then somehow the mobile was free. It was flying through the air in slow motion as both Jimmy and Jasmine reached out to catch it. Jimmy got his fingers to it. The phone bounced back up into the air. Jasmine swatted at it but missed. Jimmy's mouth gaped open in horror as he watched the phone's trajectory. He threw himself towards it like a goalkeeper and almost got his fingertips to it again but, no, it was too late. Splash! His beloved iPhone drowned in the jacuzzi.

For a minute there was silence as the pair stared into the bubbling water. Jasmine giggled a little nervously. It was funny, wasn't it? Surely Jimmy would see that.

Slowly, oh so slowly, he turned towards her and Jasmine could see immediately that she'd made a terrible mistake. Jimmy's eyes flashed with rage.

'What the fuck have you done, you little bitch?' he spat, taking a step towards her.

'Jimmy, it's only a phone,' she giggled again. Why was she giggling? This wasn't funny. He was scaring her.

'It's not the phone,' he said coldly. 'It's the person I was speaking to on the phone that matters. He'll think I've hung up on him. He's not a man you hang up on! Jesus, Jasmine. What the fuck have you done?'

'But you wouldn't tell me who you were talking to. How was I supposed to know it was *that* important?'

Jimmy's nose was almost touching Jasmine's as he replied menacingly, 'It's none of your fucking business. You don't need to know. You're my wife, not my frigging keeper.'

For a moment they were locked together, eyes blazing, hot breath on each other's faces, then Jimmy turned and walked away.

'I'm going inside to make a phone call from the landline. If you know what's good for you, you'll stay out here, out of my way, and let me get on with my business,' he warned.

Jasmine sat down on the side of the jacuzzi and thought hard. Her heart was thumping, her blood pulsing through her veins. She felt lost but still she wasn't crying. She was too angry for that. What should she do now? Stay out here as he'd demanded? Why? Why should she? He had no right to treat her like this. She wasn't a walkover. She wasn't some puppy who would roll over and play dead whenever he wanted. This was her marriage, her honeymoon, her life. Jasmine decided it was time to make a stand. If she took this now, he'd expect her to take it for the rest of her life. No, Jimmy, it wasn't going to be like that.

She strode purposefully into the villa. Jimmy looked up with his hand hovering over the phone. His eyes narrowed.

'Go back outside.' His voice sounded strange. Low and strained. Not like Jimmy's at all.

But Jasmine stood firm. 'No,' she said, as bravely as she could. 'Your phone call can wait. This is the last night of our honeymoon and I want us to spend it together. Nicely. Romantically.'

Now it was Jimmy's turn to laugh. But there was no mirth in his laughter. He sounded like a villain from a horror movie.

'You want to be romantic, do you?' he asked. 'Don't you think it might be a bit late for that, sweetheart?' There was nothing affectionate about the way he said 'sweetheart'.

'OK, I'm sorry your phone got broken, but can't we just forget that? Let's go to the bar, have a drink, celebrate our last night in paradise ...'

Jimmy stood up.

'Jasmine, this is the last time I'm going to say this ... get out. Get the fuck out! Do you hear me? Leave me alone, you annoying wee cow!'

'No,' said Jasmine defiantly, standing firm in the doorway. 'And don't you dare speak to me like that, Jimmy Jones. I want an apology.'

'*I want an apology!*' mimicked Jimmy menacingly. 'She wants a fucking apology!'

And then something seemed to snap.

'I'll give you an apology,' he promised, running towards her and grabbing her by the scruff of the neck. She heard the fabric of her thin summer dress tear as he lifted her up and threw her on to the bed.

She saw that his face had turned crimson and veins were pulsing in his neck and forehead. Then she saw him raise his hand and she knew what was coming. Suddenly, she understood what a terrible mistake she'd made. But it was way too late.

The first blow was to her right cheek. The second caught her on the left eyebrow. The third was to her stomach and then she stopped feeling anything anymore. She let her mind drift to the dream place where she'd always gone as a child when her mother used to beat her. Or when Terry came home drunk and couldn't find Cynthia to vent his frustration on. Jasmine would always do. She'd spent years as the family punchbag. Even her brothers had had a go now and again. And there had been others, of course ...

She'd learned long ago to detach herself from the pain. It was as if she was watching herself being beaten from a safe distance. Except this time it was her darling Jimmy laying into her and it looked so very, very wrong.

Physically there was nothing Jimmy could do that others hadn't done before. But mentally? Emotionally? These were bruises that would never heal. He'd been her hope for the future. Her great escape. Her knight in shining armour who'd scooped her up out of her dungeon and carried her to a better life.

As Jimmy's fists pummelled into her, Jasmine felt her dreams float away into the tropical night. She tried to hold on to them but they fluttered out of reach and melted into nothing. Now, as she stared into the future she saw a reflection of her past. Tonight, everything had changed. Or perhaps nothing had changed at all.

Blood dripped on to her white Chloe dress, trickled down her legs and splashed her Jimmy Choo shoes. Her Tiffany diamond engagement ring glinted in the half-light of the bedroom, mocking her with promises that had already been broken. She owned so many pretty things. She had jewels and gowns and designer handbags to disguise the shame of where she'd come from. But Jasmine wasn't fooling anybody – especially not herself. Jimmy smashed one last punch into her mouth before storming out of the villa. As she lay there on the blood-splattered white sheets, Jasmine had never felt more like a cheap piece of meat.

Chapter Thirty-One

Maxine had spent forever deciding what to wear. Now she had it down to two dresses laid out on her bed. She'd taken a suite at the Bel-Air up in the Hollywood Hills. A limo had been waiting downstairs for an hour now, ready to whisk her off to Juan's party at the Chateau Marmont hotel in West Hollywood, but still she couldn't make up her mind. This party would be filled with gorgeous, fashionable young creatures. The other girls there would have Rachel Zoe on speed dial for last-minute styling tips. Maxi had gotten far too used to going out with the middle-aged wives of Carlos's cronies. Tonight she would have some serious competition and she needed to get her look right. It had to be more 'hip' and less 'hip replacement'.

The Los Angeles look was difficult to pull off – it was a crime to appear as if you'd tried too hard in this town and yet it was essential to look utterly flawless at the same time. Like minimal make-up, this pretence of not trying took hours to prepare. Maxine's usual uniform of legs, tits and heels wouldn't cut it tonight. Juan had collaborated with the hottest Hip Hop and R&B stars on his latest album. They would all be there in their track pants with their gold teeth and their hoodies. Juan himself favoured baggy designer jeans, gold jewellery and sneakers. Maxi didn't want to look too old – or too old hat!

So she'd whittled it down to a bright tangerine-coloured Versace dress and a tight black body-con number. She tried the black dress on for the seventh time. It made the most of her killer curves and tapped into the eighties retro vibe but was it too safe? Too black? And could she possibly wear it with sandals rather than courts? She thought not. What's more, she'd done the eighties the first time round. Did that mean she should avoid going there again?

Maxi pulled on the floaty wisp of orange Versace. Yes, that was better. The dress was fresh, youthful, sexy *and* it looked great with her gold gladiator sandals. It was short, of course, but for once it didn't show off her boobs. In fact, the neckline was quite high. The back, however, was so low that it showed off her bum cleavage instead. And this was the problem.

Even her hipster thong peeked out above the fabric and there was no way she could wear a bra with it. This was a dress that required no underwear. Did Maxi have the nerve to go and party with a bunch of strangers wearing nothing beneath her dress? She eyed herself once more in the mirror. The dress was a knockout and she had just had a Brazilian wax. At least if she flashed accidentally, her bits would look well groomed. Maxine slipped off her La Perla knickers and bra and discarded them on the floor. She fluffed up her hair, reapplied her lip gloss one last time, picked up her gold clutch and was good to go.

There was a queue halfway down the block outside the Chateau Marmont and several huge beefcake bouncers were keeping the crowd under control. An exquisitely beautiful girl with white blonde cropped hair and a pierced eyebrow was in charge of the guest list. Maxi didn't usually suffer from nerves, especially when it came to getting into parties. Hell, she was normally the one deciding who was getting in. But she felt herself gulp as she stepped a little gingerly past the queue and up to the door. Why hadn't she called Brett? He would probably be here anyway. It would have been so much cooler arriving on his arm, rather than having to do this lonely little catwalk.

'Hey, who the hell is she?' came a whine from the front of the queue. 'How come she gets in? She's nobody.'

The white blonde girl chewed her gum and looked Maxi up and down. 'Yeah?' she drawled. 'You are?'

'Maxine de la Fallaise,' answered Maxi, flicking her hair and pulling herself up to her full height. She was used to killer heels. Despite being almost six foot tall, she felt short in her sandals.

'Gotcha,' said the girl eventually, ticking off Maxi's name from the list. 'I guess you better go in then.'

Phew! She'd got past the fashion police on the door; now she just had to get her entrance right. She'd been directed through the hotel lobby and down a corridor and now she stood before a white silk curtain. She could hear music pumping and voices laughing from beyond it. It was an intoxicating sound to Maxi's ears. Without a second thought she was drawn through the curtain, into the party and towards her spiritual home.

The party was rocking. Actresses danced provocatively with glazed eyes while rampant young rock stars eyed them hungrily from their booths. Bottles of vintage Perrier Jouët Belle Epoque (which Maxine knew cost a thousand dollars a bottle) littered the tables. She spotted many familiar faces. Some she'd met before; others she'd seen only in magazines or on screen.

Maxine ordered herself a lychee Martini and surveyed the scene. She couldn't see Juan but she had spotted Brett. He was squeezed into a booth with a young actress on either side. Maxine recognised the actresses as the Houston sisters – child stars who'd recently graduated to adult movies. He had one arm draped casually across each of the Houston girls' shoulders and he was laughing heartily at what they were saying. At first, Maxine thought nothing of her friend's husband's behaviour. This was Brett, for Christ's sake. The man lived and breathed to flirt. She was just making her way towards him to say hello when she stopped dead in her tracks.

Brett was kissing the girl on his left and not in a platonic way either. He had his tongue firmly down her throat and his hand clearly down her dress. What was worse was that he was fondling her sister at the same time with the other hand. Then he turned directly from one Houston sister to the other and started snogging her instead. Still he kept one hand down each girl's dress. Maxi stood frozen on the dance floor, gawping at the scene. Now the younger Houston was climbing on to Brett's lap while the older girl nibbled his ear. These girls obviously shared everything! The younger Houston girl slithered down Brett's legs and disappeared under the table. Her older sister laughed and then slipped her tongue back into Brett's mouth. Brett had his eyes closed and a look of sheer, unadulterated bliss on his face. Maxine didn't have to guess what was going on beneath the tablecloth. She wanted to march right up to him and knock his veneered teeth out. How the hell would she explain this to Lila? And she would have to tell Lila. She'd have no choice. She was her oldest friend.

Maxine felt sick. She couldn't stay here and do nothing. Neither could she stay and cause a scene. There was only one thing for it. Maxi necked her martini, turned on her heel and headed for the door. She wasn't sure if Brett had even seen her there, watching him. Sure, it had been a long way to come to stay for five minutes, but she couldn't be in the same room as Brett Rose while he was behaving like that. She couldn't trust herself not to murder him!

Maxi was in sight of the white curtain when a strong hand grabbed her arm. She swung round, expecting to see Brett, but instead she came face to face with Juan. His handsome face broke into a wide grin and his huge brown eyes (his father's eyes) sparkled with delight.

'Maxine! You made it!' he said, hugging her warmly and kissing her cheeks.

Maxine was thrilled by this warm welcome. He seemed genuinely blown away that she'd made the effort. Perhaps she should stay. Just for five more minutes.

Juan peered over Maxi's shoulder. 'Where's Dad?' he asked, puzzled. Suddenly, Maxi understood why Juan looked so pleased to see her. He was expecting his father to be with her. Of course he was! How stupid of her not to realise it.

'Juan, I'm sorry, he couldn't make it,' she apologised.

Juan shrugged casually, but Maxine could tell he was disappointed. She knew how it felt to be let down by a father. It had happened to her often enough.

'He had a prior commitment and he tried really hard to move it but you know how these things are; he was stuck in Spain,' Maxi lied. 'So, he asked if I could come and represent him. I know I'm not as good as the man himself but, hey, imagine me in golf slacks …' Maxine smiled sheepishly at Juan. 'Will I do?' she asked hopefully.

Juan grinned. 'Maxine, you will more than do. Come on. I'll introduce you to some people.'

She was relieved when he took her by the hand and led her in the opposite direction from Brett's table.

A few lychee Martinis later and Maxine had all but put Brett out of her mind. That worm could wait. For now, there was fun to be had. She'd met so many new people, heard lots of new music and picked up a few new dance moves along the way. Juan's LA set were wild. They drank hard, partied hard and danced hard. It was just Maxine's scene. Now Juan's new track was playing and there was a collective whoop of joy as the entire room poured on to the dance floor and started grinding their hips.

Maxine felt a hand slip round her waist.

'Dance with me,' said Juan. It felt like more of a challenge than an invitation. His eyes bored right into her soul, just like his father's. Maxine felt her stomach lurch.

'Of course,' she said, taking his hand.

'You dance good,' said Juan, drinking in her body with those eyes.

'So do you.'

She was confused. She felt at once very comfortable dancing with Juan (they seemed to be naturally in rhythm) and yet very uncomfortable at the same time (was it wrong to bump and grind with your boyfriend's son?).

Now he was behind her, holding her hips. She could almost feel his eyes on her butt.

'My old man's one lucky son of a bitch,' he whispered in to Maxi's ear.

'Is he now?' she laughed.

Juan was flirting with her outrageously. It felt good to have such a gorgeous young guy flattering her but, at the same time, she was wary. She hoped he wouldn't push it too far.

'You're way too young for him,' he added, spinning her round to face him. His head was cocked to one side and his eyes sparkled with mischief.

'Says who?'

'Says me. Besides, he'll never leave Mom. You're wasting your time.'

Maxine felt the smile freeze on her face. So that's what he was playing at. Perhaps he was still the mummy's boy Carlos said he was.

'Let's not go there,' she warned. 'You love your mother. That's nice. But don't do her dirty work for her, OK?'

She turned away from Juan and left the dance floor.

He followed her, jogging to keep up. 'Maxine! Maxine! Wait up!' he called. 'You've got me all wrong,' he said, sitting down beside her at an empty booth. 'I couldn't give a flying fuck whether my mom and dad divorce. I'm an adult. I'm my own man. My parents stopped being married in my eyes a long time ago. I'm not saying you're too young for my dad because I want him to get back with my mom.'

'Then why did you say it?'

'Because it's true,' Juan grinned. 'You're way too hot to be wasting your time with an old-timer like my dad. It just seems like such a waste!' He shrugged. 'I was trying to pay you a compliment, that's all.'

Maxi felt herself blush. A compliment from the sexiest, most smouldering twenty-five-year-old hunk in the room. Oh well, who was she to ignore it?

'Sorry,' she said. 'And thanks. For the compliment, I mean.'

'You're welcome. Jeez, I think that might have been our first family argument. Shucks, let's kiss and make up, Stepmommy.'

Those eyes were sparkling again and as he leaned in to kiss her Maxi had to turn her head to stop his lips landing on hers. God, that boy was cheeky! He made her feel all funny. She wasn't quite sure if he was genuinely flirting with her or just winding her up. Whichever, he'd raised her blood pressure, that was for sure.

'You need another drink,' announced Juan.

'I do?' Maxine wasn't so sure. She'd lost count of how much alcohol she'd had and everything was going a bit fuzzy around the edges.

She watched him slide through the crowds like a messiah. It was his party and everybody wanted a piece of him. The guys high-fived him or knocked knuckles, the girls giggled, simpered, wiggled their boobies and licked their teeth. He gave everyone a moment of his time but nobody his undivided attention.

At the bar an actress Maxine recognised squeezed up beside him and whispered something in his ear. Juan threw his head back and laughed. Then she started stroking his arm with her fingers. Maxi couldn't see his face but she watched the girl intently. She was still talking, glancing up at Juan every now and then, still stroking his skin. Maxine wondered if the actress was his girlfriend. They certainly looked cosy. Now the girl was standing behind Juan as he ordered drinks. She wrapped her arms around his waist and leant her head on his back. Maxi felt herself deflate. The actress was obviously Juan's girlfriend. She was beautiful and young. She looked like the right type. She and Juan would make a great cover of *Rolling Stone* magazine.

Maxine suddenly felt very old and very stupid. She'd allowed herself to feel attracted to Carlos's son. It was wrong and she felt guilty. It was time to leave. She picked up her purse from the table and headed for the door, glancing over at Brett as she passed. He was still embroiled with the Houston sisters, but this time he looked up as she went by. She glared at him as he took a double-take. Maxine could practically hear the cogs of his mind trying to figure out why she was there and what she might have seen. She thought she heard him calling her name, but walked right past him towards the door.

'Maxine!' came another shout, louder this time.

It wasn't Brett. She hesitated for a moment. Juan had followed her. What did it mean? She stopped, although she knew that she should just keep walking out of the door.

'Where are you going?' he asked. 'I've got a drink for you at the bar.'

'I'm tired,' lied Maxi. 'And I thought you were with your girlfriend.'

'My girlfriend?' Juan looked confused. 'What girlfriend? I don't have a girlfriend.'

'But the girl at the bar ...' Maxi felt silly saying it. As if she were letting him know she'd felt ... Felt what? Jealous? God, this whole situation was insane. She must be drunk.

'She's just an old friend,' said Juan. 'Come here.' His arms were outstretched.

'I don't know,' she said. 'I think I should leave. I think we're—'

What? She wondered. What were they doing?

'Just dance with me again. Please.'

Just looking into Juan's face made her feel dizzy. How could she resist?

And then they were on the floor again, and his arms were around her and she could feel his strong, muscular young body push against hers. Some powerful urge inside her was stirring: she was a lioness waking from a long sleep. She pushed her body back against his, breathed in his intoxicating scent and lost herself in his deep, chocolate eyes. Of all the men she'd ever danced with, she'd never felt desire like this. His hand stroked her bare back and brushed against the cleft of her bottom.

'Jesus, you're not wearing any underwear, are you?' he groaned in her ear.

Maxine felt as if she was holding her breath and now she knew that Juan felt the same way too. They were hot for each other. Christ, they were on fire. The music pumped in their ears, their hips ground together, their lips brushed but didn't quite meet.

'We gotta get out of here,' said Juan urgently.

'I know,' she said.

They both knew what they needed to do. Then they were in the back of a limo and Juan was reaching for her and she was kissing the boy who was her boyfriend's son. She knew it was wrong, but it felt so damn right. And then they were back at his Malibu penthouse, kissing in the lift, ripping each other's clothes off in the hall. They were naked now, up against the wall, so hungry for each other that foreplay wasn't even an option. He slipped inside her and she gasped with delight as she remembered how lust was supposed to feel. Then they were making love as rhythmically as they had danced, perfect partners, totally in synch. At last, they climaxed at exactly the same time and Maxine felt as if she might explode with relief. It was the fuck of a lifetime.

'You're so beautiful,' said Juan, breathlessly. 'From the moment I first laid eyes on you I thought you were the sexiest woman I'd ever seen.'

'You did?'

'Christ, yeah. 'I can't believe I'm here ...'

He gazed at her with what seemed to be genuine awe and Maxine's heart melted. He was such a beautiful boy. How could she ever have resisted him?

Later they made love again, slowly this time, exploring each other's bodies in a deliciously indulgent fashion. It was so much better than sex had ever been with Carlos. So much better than sex had ever been with anybody. Maxine found herself wondering how she would ever make love to Carlos again. But that was tomorrow's problem. Tonight she was Juan's.

Chapter Thirty-Two

Jasmine winced as the daylight hit her swollen eyes. She had lain awake for most of the night before, wondering how it had come to this and worrying about when and if Jimmy would return. Eventually she'd fallen into a fitful sleep full of nightmares. Now it was morning. Jimmy's side of the honeymoon bed remained empty and the villa was silent. He hadn't come home.

She padded stiffly to the bathroom. Her stomach ached where he'd hit her. She had bruises on her arms, her collar bone and her thighs. She stared at her reflection in the mirror. A battered, haunted face stared back. Jasmine looked pale despite her tan. Her right cheek was swollen and her left eyebrow had split. Both her eyes had dark rings around them and her top lip had burst right open. So this was what marriage looked like? It was an ugly sight.

Jasmine felt nothing but tired. She'd fought all these years to keep her optimism alive despite the shit that went on all around her. But last night Jimmy had beat that optimism right out of her. Now, she got it. This was her lot.

She heard footsteps. A quiet knock on the door.

'Jasmine?'

'Jasmine, baby?'

'Can I come in?'

She ignored him. He could come in if he liked. Or not come in. She didn't care. This must be what they called beyond caring.

She heard the door creak open and his footsteps on the wooden boards. The bathroom door was ajar. She heard him stop outside and wait for a moment. He obviously didn't know what to do. What could he do? He couldn't make last night go away.

'Are you in here?' he asked, slowly pushing the bathroom door open.

Jasmine levelled her eyes at him in the mirror as he entered. She watched as he flinched at the sight of her.

'Jesus fucking Christ, did I do that to you?' he asked, clearly appalled at the state of her face.

'No, the fucking Honey Monster did it,' replied Jasmine, coldly.

Jimmy gawped open-mouthed for what seemed like minutes. It was obvious that he couldn't believe how much damage he'd done.

'I really hurt you, didn't I?' he said.

Jasmine nodded and then looked away from his gaze. She splashed cold water on her face.

'Shit! That stings!' she cried out.

Jimmy crumbled. He fell to the floor and dissolved into tears. He wrapped his arms around her ankles and sobbed on to her bare feet. 'I'm so sorry, Jasmine. I don't know what came over me. I'll never, never do anything like that again, baby. You've got to believe me. I love you. You're the best thing that ever happened to me—'

'Have you swallowed a book of clichés?' asked Jasmine, stepping out of his grip and leaving him sobbing in the bathroom.

Jimmy crawled after her, tears pouring down his face. 'What can I say to make it better?'

'You can't.'

She was taking her clothes out of the wardrobe, folding them neatly and putting them in the suitcase. Jimmy lay pathetically on the floor.

'Are you going to leave me?' he asked, with a look of desperation on his face.

Jasmine shrugged.

'Please don't say you're going to leave me!'

He scrambled to his feet, collapsed on to his knees before her, threw his arms around her waist and cried inconsolably into her stomach.

Jasmine sighed. She looked down at the top of his head and his shaking shoulders. He looked genuinely heartbroken. But still, she felt nothing.

Was she going to leave him? Probably not. She knew she wasn't that strong. And anyway, what was Jasmine without Jimmy? Nothing but a cheap stripper from Dagenham. She needed him more than he needed her. Their relationship had never been balanced in her eyes.

He gazed up at her with his turquoise eyes full of remorse.

'I am so sorry, princess,' he said. 'If I ever do this again, you can shoot me. I mean it. I'd rather die than hurt you again, baby.'

Something stirred in Jasmine's broken heart. Love? Forgiveness? Pity? She wasn't sure, but it was something. Not much, but it was enough. She wrapped her arms around his shaking shoulders and stroked his damp golden hair.

'Shush ...' she whispered. 'Shush, Jimmy. Stop crying. Everything will be all right.'

*

Maxine watched Juan as he slept. It was light outside and she knew she had to leave him now. But she just needed a few more precious moments of gazing at his beautiful face. His eyelashes were impossibly long and his lips outrageously full. His smooth brown chest was rising and falling as he breathed deeply in his sleep. A slight smile danced on those plump lips as he dreamed. She wondered if he was dreaming about her. She hoped so. Dreams would be all they had of each other from now on. Maxine sighed. Every fibre of her body longed to stay there, under the crisp white sheets with Juan, but she knew she had to go.

She noticed the empty condom wrapper on the floor and felt relieved. Last night she'd been so caught up in the moment and, if she was honest, so crazily drunk, that she was impressed that they'd remembered to take precautions. She slipped silently into her dress and sandals, picked up her clutch and left a lingering kiss on Juan's gently parted lips. And then she let herself quietly out of the door. The lift was mirrored. There was no escaping her reflection. The woman in the mirror brushed a stray tear from her cheek.

She knew she should feel bad. She should be filled with remorse. What she'd done to Carlos was unforgivable. But instead all she felt was bereft. It was crazy. She barely knew Juan. They'd spent one drunken night together. What she was feeling wasn't real. It couldn't be. She fished her sunglasses out of her bag and covered her watery eyes.

She wasn't too familiar with Malibu. It was barely seven a.m. on a Saturday morning and the boulevard was deserted. There were no cabs to be found. Juan's penthouse was right by the ocean and Maxi found herself wandering along the footpath by the beach. A well-groomed woman of around Maxine's age jogged past with her equally well-groomed dog following behind, getting on with her clean, wholesome life. Maxine looked down at her creased party dress and felt grubby in comparison. She sat down on a bench and stared at the calm sea. The beach was empty but for a lone guy practicing t'ai chi in the early-morning sun.

'Good night?' came a gruff voice.

'Pardon?' Maxine looked up and saw a homeless bum approaching, wheeling an old-fashioned bicycle.

He looked like the ghost of a hippie from the summer of love. He had a long, crumb-filled grey beard, a faded red bandana on his head and he wore round mirrored shades. His clothes were dirty and ragged but must once have been bright. He wore a full-length patchwork coat. He carried all his worldly possessions in two plastic bags, hanging from the handlebars of his bike. And yet there was something almost Biblical about his appearance – the beard, the kind expression on his face, the theatrical clothes. He was Joseph in his technicolour dreamcoat.

The bum smiled benevolently at Maxine, leant his bike carefully against the bench and sat down beside her.

'May I join you?' he asked, although he already had.

'Sure,' replied Maxi. For some reason the ragged man didn't feel like any kind of threat.

'I asked if you had a good night,' he reminded her. 'I couldn't help noticing that you're still in your party clothes.'

His words were punctuated by a painful-sounding cough and there was a wheeze in his chest. Every now and then he held a grubby handkerchief to his mouth.

'I had an *interesting* night.' Maxine tried to smile.

'Interesting good? Or interesting bad?' He was staring at her intently as if he really wanted to know.

Maxi shrugged. 'I'm not quite sure,' she said, honestly.

'I'm guessing you spent the night with someone you shouldn't have, huh?'

Maxine nodded and then, on hearing what she'd done put into words, she started to cry. She had no idea why she was opening up to a tramp.

'Oh, honey, that's a tough one,' sighed the tramp. He really sounded like he knew what he was talking about.

'God, you have no idea. I am such a bitch,' sobbed Maxine.

'You're not a bitch, honey. A bitch wouldn't be sitting here breaking her heart over what she'd done.'

'No, you're wrong. What I've done is … God, it's … it's just the worst thing imaginable.'

'Why? Did you kill somebody?' He sat back, dug into his pocket and started rolling a joint. 'D'you mind?' he asked.

Maxine shook her head. Who was she to judge anyone else's behaviour?

'Well, did you?' he asked. 'Kill someone?'

'Of course not.'

'Then it's not so bad, is it?'

'I've been unfaithful,' she explained sheepishly.

'Yeah? You and half the population, honey.' The bum took a deep draw on his joint and then spluttered into his handkerchief.

'But this is worse. What I've done is … God! It's so messy!'

The bum winced and drew harder on his spliff. 'It's always messy,' he said. 'Life is messy.'

The ragged man offered Maxine his joint and she found herself accepting it. It had been years since she'd touched drugs, but somehow it seemed like the right thing to do under the circumstances. Could her life get any more surreal? She inhaled deeply and felt the marijuana start to reach her brain. She felt slightly light-headed.

'You'll be OK,' he continued.

Maxine shook her head and took another drag. How could this be OK? She wiped her eyes and sighed deeply. 'What should I do?' asked Maxine. 'I'm flying home today. How can I face my boyfriend?'

The bum took off his mirrored shades and placed them in the chest pocket of his technicolour dreamcoat. His eyes were the clearest, pale-blue colour. They were the wisest eyes Maxi had ever seen.

'LA is the strangest city on the planet,' he said, staring out into the ocean. 'It's the city of dreams. Anything is possible. This is where people come to find themselves and if that doesn't work out, they can lose themselves here instead. Believe me. I should know.'

The man went quiet for a while, lost in his own thoughts. He coughed into his hankie and Maxine noticed that it was splattered with blood. She hurriedly handed the joint back to him. Sharing it had probably not been the wisest thing she'd ever done.

He continued; 'You see, honey, nothing here is real. Not if you don't want it to be. If you get on that plane, go home and behave like nothing happened, then maybe in time you'll start to believe that nothing *did* happen. What happened in LA can stay in LA.'

'Do you think?' asked Maxine hopefully.

The man sighed, a little sadly. 'If that's what you want ...'

'I don't know what I want,' said Maxine wistfully. 'I thought I did but now I'm not so sure.'

Maxine pictured Carlos's face. She thought about her safe, comfortable life in Spain. She remembered the Viagra, the vibrator, the forced lovemaking. It made her shudder. Then she let her mind wander to the events of last night – how she and Juan had danced and made love and it had seemed like the most natural thing in the world. Tears streamed down her face.

'What have I done?' she sobbed. 'I've ruined everything.'

'There, there, honey.' He patted her knee gently. 'Shush now. In time, it will all become clear.'

'How? How do I fix this?'

'You don't. Only time can fix it. You just have to wait.'

Maxine watched his wise face relax into a smile and she nodded. He was right, of course.

'Nothing's over,' he mused. 'Nobody died.'

'No, you're right.' Maxine wiped her tear-stained face on her Versace dress. 'It could be worse, eh?'

The bum nodded, smiled at her and then started to cough again.

'I guess I'd better be going,' said Maxine, standing up a little unsteadily on her feet. 'Thank you, though, for taking the time. For listening and for talking. I needed that.'

'No problem,' he replied with an easy smile. 'I have all the time in the world.'

Juan woke up to realise that Maxine had gone. He wasn't surprised. Why would she hang around? He looked at the clock. It was barely eight o'clock. Her side of the bed was empty and cold but the pillow was still moulded to the shape of her head. Juan could smell her perfume on his bare skin. Boy, that was one sexy lady. Maxine intoxicated him. She was like a drug. There was no way he could have resisted. Not that his dad would see it that way if he ever found out. Christ! It was best not to think about that. Better just to think about last night and the fact he'd just had the best fuck of his life. The truth was Juan had been fantasising about Maxine for months. And now he'd tasted that perfect flesh for real. He didn't regret last night for a moment.

The first time he'd laid eyes on her he was lost. That mane of wild hair, the curve of her top lip, the arch of her back, the way her nose turned up a little at the tip. She made him feel weak with lust. Juan had never had a problem attracting girls – blonde girls, dark girls, famous girls, models – they were all easy. But Maxine was something different. She was all woman.

Why the hell did she have to be his father's girl? This was one seriously messy situation. Juan got out of bed and threw on some old running gear. He needed to clear his head. There was no point in hanging around here now that Maxine had gone.

It was a perfect morning – clear and not too hot yet. Juan's feet pounded the sand to the drum of his beating heart. He couldn't stop thinking about Maxine and about what they'd done last night. Usually once Juan had slept with a chick the feeling of desire disappeared. It was as if, once the chase was over, there was nothing left to do. But this time he'd been left wanting more.

There was a tight feeling of panic in his chest. What if his dad found out? The old man would kill him! Adrenalin pumped through Juan's veins. What he'd done was terrible but, boy, was it exciting. Maybe that was the attraction with Maxine: she was so totally off limits that it made her desirable beyond belief. But there was no denying the chemistry between them. Fuck! What had he done?

He ran along the beach until it started to fill up with weekend sun-worshippers and then turned on to the footpath and headed home. Halfway along Juan spotted an old bum on a bench. From a distance, the guy looked as if he was sleeping, but as Juan got closer he realised something wasn't right. People were just walking past, not noticing him, like he was some sort of nobody. But Juan couldn't take his eyes off the bearded dude in his weird, multicoloured coat. The bum was totally still and his eyes were wide open, staring out at the ocean beyond. Juan ran up beside the old guy and stopped. The tramp had died with a smile on his face.

'Holy shit!' said Juan, crossing himself. He was a very lapsed Catholic but some habits died hard. 'Well, at least you picked a beautiful morning to go,' he said to the dead guy. Weird! The dude was definitely smiling. 'And you died happy, my friend. That's something.'

Juan called 911 from his cell phone and reported the death. As he waited for the cops, he picked the butt of a joint out of the bum's hand and buried it in the sand. It seemed the right thing to do. This poor man had probably been judged all his life; Juan saw no reason for him to be judged harshly in death.

A crowd had gathered now, but they all stood back from the corpse as if they might catch something if they got too close. A couple of young girls shouted, 'Hi Juan! Love your work!' He nodded and smiled politely but kept his distance. This was no place to be signing autographs.

Juan sat down on the bench right beside the stiff and waited. The poor dead guy shouldn't be alone at a time like this, right? Juan stared out at the ocean and appreciated the old guy's final vista. It must have been a good way to go – a fat reefer and a sea view. There was nothing like the ocean to put things in perspective and make you feel part of some bigger picture. The water lapped the beach gently, ebbing and flowing, like it always had for a million years and more. The waves were calm today and they seemed to soothe Juan's troubled mind.

He turned to look at his companion. He was dead, that was for sure, but it felt to Juan as if his soul was still there, hovering above the bench somehow. Juan felt sure the guy had been a righteous old dude and he felt sad that he'd never had the chance to sit here with him when he was still breathing. He wondered if there had been other mornings when he'd run past without noticing him.

The old guy was still staring at the ocean, still smiling, looking wiser than any living soul Juan had ever met. Juan had never been much of a believer. His mom had had to drag him kicking and screaming to mass every Sunday. But this morning he felt sure he'd met an angel. An angel, in a City of Angels.

Chapter Thirty-Three

Christ, Maxi felt like death by the time she arrived in London. She and Juan had been so busy with their bedroom gymnastics that she'd barely slept the night before and now she was suffering. By the time she'd made her way back to the Bel-Air to shower, change and fetch her things and then caught a cab to LAX it had been mid-morning. She'd actually had to beg (and flash her cleavage) to be allowed on the eleven a.m. flight because the gate had already closed. Thanks to a rather cute guy on the BA desk she'd scrambled on to the plane just in time. But, exhausted as she was, Maxi couldn't sleep. She made a point of never sleeping on planes. It was a superstitious thing – if she was going to die in a plane wreck she sure as hell wanted to know about it.

Instead, she'd watched three movies (two of which she'd already seen at their London premieres) and tried her hardest to stop thinking about Juan and Carlos and about what the hell she was supposed to do next. There was so much adrenalin pumping through her veins that she could barely catch her breath the whole flight. Plus, the time difference was a killer. In her head it was time to hit the sack, but the clock on the wall in Arrivals said it was only half past two at Heathrow. This was going to be the longest day ever.

Maxi stopped to grab a coffee and consider what to do next. She *should* catch the first available flight to Marbella, but that would mean facing Carlos and she wasn't sure she was ready to do that yet. The fact that she'd have to face him some time soon was scary enough. Or she *could* go and visit Lila and break the bad news to her friend that her husband was a dirty philandering bastard, but that was hardly an appealing prospect either. Shit! Her head ached. People were looking at her, recognising her. Usually Maxi loved to be the centre of attention but today she needed to hide.

Someone had left a newspaper on the next table. Maxi picked it up and used it to shield her face from prying eyes. A grainy coloured photo of a half-naked man swam in front of her eyes. Maxine squinted at it. 'Brett Bonks Bridesmaid' screamed the headline. What?! She sat bolt upright and took a closer look at the photograph. Oh. My. God! It was Brett's butt on the front page all right, and underneath him was Jasmine's kid sister. Her stomach churned as she hurriedly read the article. It turned out what she'd seen in LA was nothing compared to what he'd been doing right under all their noses at Jasmine's wedding.

'Oh, Lila. You poor, poor thing,' she whispered to herself.

Well, there was no choice now, was there? She had to get to Lila – and fast. Minutes later she was in a black cab headed for Lila's Kensington townhouse.

Peter was not a violent man. He had always proclaimed himself to be a lover, not a fighter. But if Brett Rose had walked into the house at that moment, Peter would happily have picked up his prized Oscar from the mantelpiece and smashed the actor's head in with it. How dare he do this to Lila! How dare he ... How dare he ... Peter's shoulders began to shake again, his lip wobbled and then he was crying like a baby again. He folded his arms protectively across his heaving chest and stared out of the first-floor drawing-room window at the sea of paparazzi crowding outside. Bastards! They were spilling in from Kensington Square, climbing the gate, scrambling over the hedges, knocking over the potted bay trees he'd given Lila for Christmas; some were even standing on the window ledge below trying to scale the front of the house. Every few moments the front door bell rang. Peter had ordered the housekeeper to ignore it but every time it rang he felt his nerves fray further.

Peter sniffed back his tears and saluted the troops of press with his middle finger. 'Piss off!' he mouthed. The army had invaded Lila's hallowed territory. This was all Brett's fault. The war of the Roses was underway.

Peter loved Lila like a sister. Her pain was his pain. He had been the one to break the news this morning. Oh, there had been other members of staff who had been keen to tell her – they would have got some vicarious thrill from watching her crumble – but Peter had insisted that he should be the one. He'd waited until the nanny had taken the children to their riding lesson. The poor little things would get hurt by flying shrapnel soon enough. There was no point in them witnessing their mother's ruin.

She'd taken the news in a remarkably dignified manner, but she was visibly shocked.

'Show me the paper, Peter,' she'd said calmly.

Peter had held it behind his back, reluctant to let her see it.

'Give me it,' she'd demanded.

She'd read the newspaper quietly with an open mouth and wide eyes. There had been no tears at first, just silence – a painful, deafening silence that Peter longed to fill with words of comfort. But what could he say to make this better? There were no words. And then the tears had come, fast and free, cascading down her cheeks and dripping on to the open newspaper, smudging the words that were breaking her heart.

'The thing is, I knew,' she'd sobbed, staring up at Peter with a haunted expression. 'Deep down I knew he was doing it. Not with her, necessarily...'

Lila had prodded the 'glamour' photograph of Alisha Hillman on page two.

'But with someone.'

'I don't know how he could stoop so low,' Peter had said, supportively. 'I mean, look at her. Why would he touch *that*?'

Lila had shaken her head sadly. 'Why not? She's young. She's pretty.'

'But she's hardly in your league. He's an idiot!'

'No, I'm the bloody idiot!' Lila had thrown the paper across the room. 'I saw it coming and I did nothing.'

'What could you have done? None of this is your fault.'

'I got old!' Lila had screamed. 'I got old and ugly and now I've lost him. I've lost Brett ... I want Brett!'

'No you don't. He's a complete fucking shit and you're better off without him.'

'And the children,' Lila had wailed. 'How do I explain this to my children?'

'You don't have to,' Peter had said, more gently. 'Not now. Not today. We'll all take care of Louisa and Seb. We'll protect them.'

But Lila had stopped listening. She was locked in her own private hell, rocking backwards and forwards on the floor, wailing like an injured animal. She'd stayed like that for so long that Peter had had to call the doctor. Now she was sedated and sleeping while the press trampled all over her front garden. It was officially the day from hell.

Peter narrowed his eyes at the journalists and photographers below. TV crews had joined the throng and they were all jostling for position on the garden path, on the lawn, on the street ... Now, there was some sort of commotion going on. A tall blonde woman seemed to be even more determined to get to the front than the others. She was hitting people over the head with her handbag, pushing them from behind so that they tripped over wires and tripods, elbowing news reporters in the kidneys. Peter squinted at the blonde as she fought her way through the crowd. He hadn't got round to putting his lenses in this morning and he couldn't make out her features from this distance. Now she was literally climbing over the competition. Quite a feat as she appeared to be wearing killer heels and carrying a suitcase! Eventually she made it to the front door, stood up straight and tossed her blonde hair defiantly.

'Maxine,' whispered Peter to himself. 'Thank God, it's Maxine!' He ran downstairs as the front door bell rang for the hundredth time that day. 'It's Maxine! Let her in! Let her in!'

At last, he thought, an ally has arrived.

'Alisha, what the fuck have you done?' Jasmine could hear her voice breaking with anger as she left the message on her sister's voicemail. 'I will never forgive you for this,' she spat. 'Do you hear me, Alisha? Never.' And then she hung up.

'I can't believe she did it,' said Jasmine, staring at the pile of last weekend's newspapers that the maid had left for them on the kitchen island. 'And at our wedding, too.'

Jimmy nodded, half in agreement, but he was reading the sports pages and munching on some toast at the same time. He was obviously less outraged by Alisha and Brett's now very public bonk than Jasmine was.

'Alisha's a slapper,' he said half-heartedly. 'What d'you expect? Thought Brett Rose might have better taste, mind.'

'Hmm, yes,' Jasmine mused. 'Lila's such a lovely woman, isn't she? God, she must be in pieces.'

'Och, he probably does it all the time. I bet they've got one of those Hollywood marriages of convenience. She's probably a lipstick lesbian.' Jimmy looked quite excited at the thought.

Jasmine tutted and walked through to the open-plan living room of their London apartment. She pushed her oversized sunglasses up on to her head and examined her face in the mirror. The bruises had turned yellow and the cut on her lip had scabbed over, but her face was still a mess. They hadn't talked about what had happened. Jimmy had been extra sweet and attentive on the journey home, clinging to her arm, treating her like his princess by carrying her bags of designer duty-free. They'd stopped off in Paris for a couple of days on the way home and he'd taken her to Cartier to choose an eternity ring. Jasmine had gone through the motions of picking out a beautiful platinum band, encrusted with heart-shaped diamonds and sapphires, but she knew it meant nothing. The shopping trip was just a way for Jimmy to purge his guilt. What else could he do under the circumstances? If in doubt, throw money at the problem; that was Jimmy's motto. But Jasmine had quickly learned that when a man earns eighty thousand pounds a week, it's hard to take any financial gesture too seriously.

Jasmine sighed and replaced her sunglasses. It would be a couple of days yet before she could be seen in public without them. She'd had to walk around Paris with a Pucci silk scarf wrapped around her face and she'd arrived at the airport in one of Jimmy's sweatshirts with the hood up. She must have looked ridiculous, but at least nobody had noticed the bruising.

'Have you been through the post?' Jasmine called to Jimmy.

He'd flicked on the Plasma TV in the kitchen and was catching up with Sky Sports News. He shook his head.

She sorted the letters into three piles – his, hers and junk mail. There were three packages too. The biggest contained prints of some of the wedding photos from the magazine. Jasmine glanced at them briefly and then put them to one side. She wasn't in the mood for romantic reminiscences. Not yet. Maybe one day, but certainly not yet. The second package was addressed to Jimmy. She tossed it on to his pile. The third was for her. She opened it half-heartedly while glancing out of the window. London looked grey and dreary from up here in the penthouse. Jasmine missed the sunshine. A DVD fell out of the package on to the polished limestone floor. She picked it up uninterestedly. The cover was blank – no title, no picture, no explanation. Must be a wedding DVD from one of our friends, she thought. It couldn't be the official DVD. They'd paid a fortune for that to be made like a Hollywood movie with a soundtrack. No, this looked amateur. She fished around inside the padded envelope and found a short printed note.

Oops, I remembered about this copy. Another 100,000 euros should help me forget. Ladies' toilet, ground floor, Natural History Museum, third cubicle on the right, 11 a.m. Wednesday.

Jasmine dropped the letter and the DVD on the floor. Her hands were shaking. She stared at them, willing them to be still, but they wouldn't stop. She felt the blood drain from her face. So, he hadn't gone away. She bit her lip until her teeth broke through the skin and she could taste blood. Jasmine was scared. Hell, she was terrified. He'd found her in Spain; now he'd followed her to London. Her head span and the room seemed to lurch under her feet. This was the last thing she needed. First Jimmy, then Alisha and now this. Jasmine had thought this summer would be perfect. Now her whole world was being torn apart.

Chapter Thirty-Four

Charlie Palmer thought his time had finally come. He was being chased by giant dogs with razor-sharp teeth and foaming mouths. It was a dark but hot night. He was panting, out of breath. Sweat dripped down his forehead and stung his eyes. He was trying to scramble over a high, barbed-wire fence but the dogs were snapping at his heels and the barbs were tearing his flesh. Voices shouted behind him somewhere and lights flashed in the dark. They were getting near now. Soon, they would catch him. Charlie had no idea where he was or what he was doing there. All he knew was he had to get out.

Somewhere in the back of his mind he heard a phone ringing. The dogs stopped barking, the voices fell silent, the fence melted under his limbs and Charlie opened his eyes. He was still panting; it remained dark and hot; the sweat continued to drip down his face, but now he realised he was in his hotel bed. The sheets were soaked through. It was just a nightmare. Too many painkillers, he thought to himself. Time to lay off that shit. It was messing with his head.

He glanced at the clock – two a.m. it said. What kind of sick joke was this? It was the third night in a row that it had happened. His phone had rung at exactly two o'clock in the morning. He'd answered it the first time, through a fog of sleep, expecting it to be Gary with some news. Instead, there had been nothing. Well, not nothing exactly. There was heavy breathing and the sound of industrial machinery in the background, but nobody spoke. Last night he'd answered it again, convinced that the timing must be some warped coincidence. But the same thing had happened – the psycho heavy breathing routine, the sound of metal against metal. Charlie had had enough. He took the call.

'Who the fuck is this?' he demanded angrily. 'Speak, for fuck's sake. Speak or piss off.'

The breathing continued, deep and husky with a slight wheeze. 'What are you, some kind of coward?' Charlie barked. 'This is schoolboy be-haviour. Be a man – tell me what you want!'

The breathing got deeper and then it broke slowly into a hoarse, throaty laugh that reverberated in Charlie's ears. But still the caller said nothing. Charlie listened to the clanging noises behind the laughter, trying to work out what it might be. There were voices now too, shouting somewhere far behind the caller. Charlie listened intently, trying to make out the words. Slowly it dawned on him that they were speaking Russian.

'Oh, fuck off then!' shouted Charlie.

He threw his phone across the room. It hit the wall opposite and crashed to the tiled floor. The battery fell out and slid across the room. Damn! What was going on? Was it Dimitrov trying to scare him? It didn't make any sense. Why would he bother? Dimitrov had made himself perfectly clear already. Charlie had the broken ribs to prove it. Was it Nadia's captors? If she'd been kidnapped it would make sense for them to get in touch. But why not speak? Why not demand a ransom? And why call Charlie rather than Nadia's old man? OK, so Charlie had a few bob put away, but that was nothing compared to Dimitrov's billions. Besides, Charlie wasn't in love with Nadia. He was fond of her, but his feelings didn't come close to the love that a father could have for a child. No, any kidnapper would be crazy to get in touch with him rather than Dimitrov. So, who the fuck was it?

Charlie pulled his aching body out of bed and gathered up all the bits of his phone. The screen was cracked but miraculously the thing was still working. He poured himself a JD from the mini-bar and walked out onto the balcony. He needed some air. Some space to think. But it was a close, sticky night and clouds were obscuring the stars. There was no air in Marbella tonight.

It had been ten days since Dimitrov had made his threat and Charlie was still no closer to knowing what had happened to Nadia. Gary had managed to piss off some important people in London with his digging around but he'd got no answers – just a beating in a back alley in Soho. No one had seen Nadia. Nobody knew where she'd gone or who she was with. There wasn't long left now and Charlie was getting desperate. It was the middle of the night but he dialled McGregor's number anyway. It rang and rang for the longest time before the line went dead.

'Bastard,' muttered Charlie to himself. 'He owes me. He fucking owes me.'

As Charlie stared ahead he became aware of a light on the beach. It looked as if someone was carrying a torch. He tried to make sense of the blackness. A shadowy figure emerged from the darkness, about fifty metres away. Charlie couldn't tell who or what it was. Suddenly the light spun towards him, blinding him, hurting his eyes. It stayed there, locked on his face. Whoever was holding the torch must have had a clear view of the fear in his eyes, but Charlie had no idea who was watching him.

He rushed back inside, closed the glass door and drew the curtains. He was panting, out of breath. Sweat dripped down his forehead and stung his eyes. The nightmare continued, but this time Charlie was awake.

Frankie Angelis felt sure he was getting close to breaking Charlie. The phone calls had been a work of genius, even if he did say so himself. He'd made the calls from the warehouse at the docks and held the phone aloft so that Palmer could hear the Russian voices in the background. It had just been his delivery boys, shouting as they'd unloaded their human cargo, but Charlie wouldn't know that, would he? Actually they weren't even Russian – they were from the Ukraine. But Charlie bloody Palmer wouldn't know the difference, would he? He'd think it had something to do with Dimitrov's girl. And that was the point of the exercise. He had to get Charlie so shit scared that he'd do anything to save his skin – even if that meant shooting Dimitrov. And Frankie needed that Russian out of the way. It was the only solution to his cash-flow problems.

Frankie had been at the docks to oversee a delivery of new girls from Eastern Europe. He was replacing some of the stock. When they hit twenty-five he sold them on to an old mate in London, who put them to work in his brothels. Frankie preferred them young. The problem was he could barely afford his girls anymore. Not with Dimitrov on his back. That was where Charlie came in to the equation.

There was a knock on the door. Yana entered wearing men's clothes.

'Everything OK?' asked Frankie.

Yana pushed back the hood of her sweatshirt and revealed her beautiful Slavic bone structure. She nodded and grinned before replacing the torch in its drawer.

'He was frightened. Like bunny rabbit. He ran into his room and closed doors!'

'Good girl,' said Frankie, unzipping his flies. 'Now, come over here and I'll give you your reward.'

Getting the cash out of the bank in London was a bit trickier than it had been in Spain – but not that tricky. Jasmine was ushered upstairs to a private office and offered a seat at a polished wooden desk. A young girl in a pinstriped trouser suit brought in a tray of fresh coffee and biscuits while the Premium Account Manager – a guy in his fifties also wearing pinstripes – examined Jasmine's bank accounts on his computer screen. Jasmine kept her largest Oliver Peoples sunglasses firmly in place to cover the bruises on her face.

'I normally deal with your accountant, don't I?' He seemed suspicious.

But maybe Jasmine was just being paranoid.

'And it's a lot of money to take out in cash, Mrs Jones,' he continued, glancing at her over his wire-rimmed spectacles. 'And you say you want the funds in euros ...'

Jasmine nodded, trying to look confident and upbeat. It was her money. There was enough in there. She'd got her half of the wedding money through from the magazine now. She had every right to withdraw it.

'You know the pound is weak against the euro at the moment, Mrs Jones,' continued the bank manager. 'I wouldn't advise taking out such a large sum in that currency at present.'

'I'm buying a speedboat for my husband,' lied Jasmine. She'd spent ages coming up with this story and she thought it was a pretty good one. 'It's a surprise for him. A late wedding present. I'm buying it from a Spaniard. He wants euros. I think I'm getting a good deal. That's OK, isn't it?'

The bank manager sighed deeply and frowned. 'Well, it is quite irregular, but I suppose you know what you're doing ...'

'I do,' Jasmine jumped in. 'And it *is* my money.'

The bank manager sighed again and nodded. 'It is your money,' he agreed solemnly. 'But at this rate it won't last very long. You young girls do like to shop, don't you?'

Jasmine flashed him her best smile. 'Shoes, bags, speedboats ...' she giggled, patting her Chanel bag and swinging her delicate pink Jimmy Choos. 'Once I start spending, I just can't stop!'

'I am quite concerned about you walking out of here with such a large sum in cash,' he said.

'Oh, that's OK. I've got a bodyguard waiting for me downstairs and my driver is parked on a double yellow right out front.' The lies were flowing now. 'In fact, if you don't mind speeding this up a bit, I'd hate him to get a ticket. The traffic wardens are vicious round here, aren't they?'

Five minutes later Jasmine was walking down Threadneedle Street with a hundred thousand euros in cash folded neatly into a manila envelope, wrapped in a Topshop carrier and tucked snugly into her Chanel bag. She hailed the first black cab she saw and asked the driver to take her to The Natural History Museum straight away.

The museum was packed with kids on school trips, Italian students on exchange and Japanese tourists taking pictures of their grinning wives in front of the giant dinosaur in the entrance hall. Jasmine's heels click-clacked on the floor. She didn't glance up at the magnificent Tyrannosaurus Rex (although she would have loved to), or meet the eyes of the school kids who recognised her. She just stared at her feet and made her way deeper in to the building. She heard her name whispered as she passed.

There were two signs for ladies' toilets on the ground floor. Jasmine bit her lip and wondered what to do. Should she turn right or left? She couldn't go leaving a hundred thousand euros in the wrong loo. The ladies' on her left was closer. It seemed to make sense. There was a long queue – it trailed out the door. Jasmine took her place patiently behind a group of pubescent girls in short school skirts and frosted pink lipstick. She kept her eyes down, still hidden behind her shades, but she could sense the girls nudging each other and feel their stares. Even these enormous sunglasses couldn't disguise her identity. Sometimes Jasmine longed to be anonymous again.

At last she reached the front of the queue, then waited until the right cubicle became free. She locked the door, fished the Topshop bag out and placed it neatly between the toilet and the sanitary bin. She hesitated before letting herself out. What if someone else picked it up first? What if this was the wrong loo? How would she know the money had got in to the right hands? What if this money went missing and they wanted more? There wasn't much more left.

Christ! Perhaps she should forget the whole thing. Maybe she should put the cash safely back in her bag and get the hell out of here. She could put it back in the bank, tell them that the speedboat deal had fallen through. But then what? Would the blackmailer follow through with the threat? If she thought her life was going off the rails now just wait until *that* news got out. Then it really would be game over.

She glanced one more time at her hard-earned cash (Christ, she'd sold her bloody wedding for that) and let herself out of the cubicle. The queue had miraculously disappeared. Just one blonde girl was waiting to go in. Was that her? The girl from the aquarium in Spain? She didn't look the same. Her hair was longer and she looked younger, less sophisticated. This girl was wearing jeans and trainers and she had a battered old backpack slung over her shoulder. Her face was free of make-up. She looked like any other foreign exchange student. But there was something familiar about her, wasn't there? As she brushed past, Jasmine couldn't help herself grabbing the girl's arm.

'Do I know you?' she demanded.

The girl pouted at Jasmine and withdrew her arm.

'I do know you, don't I?' Jasmine continued, her heart thumping in her chest.

'Excusey?' The girl shrugged innocently and shook her head. 'I no speak Eengleesh.'

She wriggled past and locked herself in the cubicle that Jasmine had just been in. Was that her? Jasmine didn't know what her next move should be.

224

Wait here to see what happened? And then do what exactly? She started to splash cold water on her face but suddenly there was the sound of shrieking and footsteps approaching. The gang of teenage girls who had been in front of her in the queue reappeared from outside the toilets, their faces flushed with excitement. They'd brought a group of boys with them in to the ladies'.

'See!' shouted one of the girls. 'I told you it was her. It's Jasmine Jones!' Jasmine smiled at them politely and tried to push her way past.

'Can we get your autograph, Jasmine?' asked one of the girls.

'Can you autograph my bum?' shouted one of the boys.

'Can I see your tits?' guffawed another.

Jasmine muttered something about being in a hurry and pushed her way past the baying gang of kids. But their screams had been heard by other groups and soon Jasmine was being followed towards the door like the Pied Piper. Her shoes click-clacked faster and faster until she was running through the revolving doors, down the grand stone steps outside and on to the Cromwell Road. Tears streamed down her cheeks, merging with the cold rain that was now lashing from the sky. She lost her sunglasses halfway down the road but didn't stop to retrieve them. Her feet pounded the pavement and filthy rainwater splashed her clothes as she ran straight through the puddles without a thought for her Jimmy Choos.

Jasmine's mind was racing as fast as her feet. Who could be doing this to her? But, deep down, she knew the answer. Over and over just one name came to her mind. Nobody could know about it except for *him*. It had to be him. This girl, the other girl, or were they the same girl? Jasmine didn't know. But she ... they ... must work for him. Why had he decided to do it now? After all this time? There were so many questions and nobody to turn to for answers. Jasmine was lost.

She kept running until she found herself in Hyde Park and didn't stop until she reached the banks of the Serpentine. There she stood, heart pounding, and watched the rain bounce on the water, making perfect circular ripples that met and linked, broke and then reformed. A swan swam elegantly on the horizon. Jasmine opened her mouth and let out an ear-splitting scream of anger and frustration. The swan startled and rose up out of the water with its wings spread wide. Jasmine's shoes had turned from palest pink to murky brown. Her Chanel bag was sodden and mud-splattered. She lifted her hand and felt the scab on her lip. Everything was ruined. Nothing was beautiful any more.

Chapter Thirty-Five

'Charlie?' said the familiar voice. 'It's Frankie.'

It was the first contact Charlie had had with The Angel since their argument on the beach.

'Frank,' said Charlie warily. 'How's life?'

'Good, my boy, good,' said Frankie. 'You? Enjoying the Costa del Sol, are you?'

Charlie sighed. His life was shit and he'd barely been out of his hotel room for days, but he sure as hell wasn't going to let Frankie Angelis know that. 'I'm doing fine,' he said, keeping his guard up.

'Really?' said Frank. Charlie could hear the mirth in the old man's voice. 'Because that's not what I heard, my boy. I heard you'd been getting yourself into some bother with a certain Russian gentleman we both know.'

Charlie clenched his fists. How did The Angel always seem to know everyone else's bloody business?

'It's nothing I can't handle, Frank,' Charlie deadpanned. 'But I appreciate your concern.'

'Oh, I'm not concerned,' said Frankie with a chuckle. 'I just thought you might want to reconsider that proposition I made to you.'

'No thank you. I meant what I said. I'm not interested.'

'Oh, I think you are, my boy. I think you're very interested indeed. I tell you what. I'll give you until tomorrow to reconsider. I'll call again then.'

'Frankie, there's no point. I've made up my mind. I'm—'

'I hear you, Char. I hear you. But do you know what? I don't believe you. I'll call tomorrow.'

The line went dead. The thing was, Frankie was right. If Dimitrov disappeared, then all Charlie's problems would disappear too. And if anyone could make a man disappear, it was Charlie Palmer ...

Later, Charlie woke up to the familiar sound of his phone ringing again. It was two a.m. Charlie hadn't had a decent night's sleep in days and suddenly he realised he'd had enough. He picked up the mobile with the cracked screen, threw it on the floor and stamped on it with his bare feet until all that was left were shards of plastic on the cold tiled floor. He picked a few shards out of the sole of his foot. Now nobody could call him. Not Angelis, not Dimitrov, nobody. Charlie needed some peace and quiet to get his head straight. That, and some sleep. He collected up the pieces of broken phone, dropped them into the bin, climbed back into bed and waited for sleep to come. It was a long wait.

'What d'you mean you're going back to Spain?' Jimmy demanded as he stood at the door, watching Jasmine pack. 'We only just got back to London. I thought we'd be going home for a bit.'

Home? Where was home? Jasmine really wasn't sure. They had three properties – this place in town that was handy for the football club and their favourite clubs and shops, the villa in Spain and the sprawling mansion in the country that impressed their mates and was close to the airport. Jasmine guessed that's what Jimmy meant by home – the country pad. It had cost the most money and it had the most rooms. Fifteen blooming bedrooms! Jasmine had always felt that was ridiculous – she only needed one. She had no desire to go back there. It wasn't a home; it was a statement. An empty, hollow, flash of cash that looked great in magazine spreads.

'I want to go back to Spain,' repeated Jasmine, calmly folding a sarong. 'I feel happier there.'

The truth was Jasmine was as surprised as Jimmy by her desire to return to Marbella. She'd been relieved to be leaving for the wedding and honeymoon after the first blackmailing incident. But now he'd found her here too, in London, and she realised nowhere was out of his reach. Besides, who could protect her from him here? Jimmy? Not bloody likely! Blaine? As if! But Charlie was in Marbella and he always made her feel safe.

'But you can't go.'

'Watch me,' replied Jasmine. She was in no mood to give in to Jimmy's demands. He still had a lot of making up to do.

'But I'll miss you.' Jimmy was whining now.

'So, come with me,' she said.

'I can't. I've got some business to do here.'

'More mysterious business.' Jasmine glanced up at her new husband. 'Nothing you can tell me about, I suppose.'

Jimmy shook his head. 'It's nothing for you to worry about.'

Jasmine shrugged and got on with her packing. 'Who's worried?' she said. 'Come with me; don't come with me. It makes no difference to me.'

'Jasmine, why are you being so horrible to me?' Jimmy was pouting and gazing up at her forlornly from behind his floppy fringe.

Jasmine indicated her bruised face. 'Why do you think?'

'Och, I thought we'd forgotten about that.'

Jasmine snorted. 'I think it'll take more than a couple of nights in Paris and a poncy ring to forget about you beating the shit out of me.'

It was the first time she'd mentioned what had happened on their honeymoon and Jimmy seemed keen to change the subject.

'It's OK,' he muttered. 'You go back to Spain. I'll stay here for a couple of days, sort out my business and then I'll join you.'

'Fine,' she said, closing the suitcase. 'Whatever makes you happy.'

'*You* make me happy,' he said, walking up to her and trying to kiss her neck.

Jasmine shrugged him off. 'Right, I'm out of here,' she said. 'There's a cab waiting downstairs.'

'What? You're going now? Right this minute?'

'Uh-huh,' she replied, swinging the suitcase on to the floor and wheeling it towards the door.

'Can I at least have a kiss goodbye?' asked Jimmy, sadly.

Jasmine stopped as she passed and offered him her cheek.

'That's it?' he asked. 'A cheek? No lips! That's all my wife's offering?'

'For now, Jimmy,' she said patiently. 'You should be grateful you're even getting that.'

Jimmy sighed and kissed her softly on the cheek. 'I love you, Jazz,' he said tenderly as she headed for the door.

'I know,' said Jasmine a little sadly. But is that enough? she wondered to herself.

As she opened the door she came face to face with the grotesque sight of Blaine Edwards about to let himself in.

'Blaine!' she said, crossly. 'Do you have keys to all our houses?'

'Sure do, baby,' he grinned.

'But how?' she asked. The guy was more like a squatter than a manager.

'It's all part of my job, gorgeous. Nothing for you to worry your pretty little head about.'

'I'd say I'm more disturbed than worried,' retorted Jasmine. 'Anyway, you've got a nerve turning up like this after you invited the press on our honeymoon. What were you thinking?'

Blaine shrugged with faux innocence. 'I just wanted to keep you in the headlines, honey,' he said. 'Anyway, you looked amazing in those topless shots.'

Jasmine glared at him. 'You're such a shit, Blaine. If you weren't so good at your job I'd—'

'Oh, don't be cross with me, Jazz baby,' said Blaine, squeezing past her into the apartment. 'Everything I do is with your best interests at heart.'

Jasmine snorted with indignation. 'You are so full of crap. What about my privacy?'

'Pah! Privacy is overrated. It's publicity that counts, baby.'

'It was our honeymoon.'

'Jazz, honey,' said Blaine patiently. 'Those people created you. You'd be nothing without the press. Remember that. Without your pretty picture on the front pages, you wouldn't exist. You were begging me to get you into the papers when I first met you, so don't go getting all high and mighty about it now.'

Jasmine sighed. In a way he was right. She knew he was. Uncomfortable as it made her feel, she needed Blaine and she needed the press attention he created for her. There was no point in getting angry with him. He was just doing what she paid him to do.

'Let's forget about it,' she said. 'Anyway, it's good you're here. You can keep Jimmy company while I'm gone.'

'Gone?' Blaine looked confused. His eyes fell to the suitcase. 'Where are you going? You've got to clear these things with me first.'

'No I don't,' she said flatly. 'I'm going back to Spain.'

'You're staying here, young lady,' warned Blaine. 'I've set up interviews for you. The people need to get a response from you about your sister's scandalous behaviour at your wedding.'

'The people can fuck off!' said Jasmine sweetly. 'Bye-ee!' She pushed past Blaine's enormous belly and towards the lift.

'What's got into her?' she heard Blaine ask Jimmy.

'Probably just the time of the month.'

Men! Who needed them?

The door to the lift opened.

'You'll still have to do those interviews!' Blaine shouted after her. 'You can do them on the phone!'

Jasmine ignored him and stepped into the lift.

'I'll join you at the villa in a couple of days,' he called.

The doors closed behind her and suddenly everything was blissfully quiet. Jasmine needed space to find herself again. It was time to look to the future, but first she would have to delve into the past. Recent events had left her feeling vulnerable and alone in the world. She had become consumed by a need to know who she really was and so she'd decided to try to track down her real parents. It was a big move, but she felt the time was right. The Watts were useless – all Cynthia cared about was making money out of her daughters (she was having a field day with Alisha's new-found notoriety). She had never been a real mother to Jasmine. And Jimmy? Well, was he any better than the scumbags she'd left behind on the estate? Probably not. No, what Jasmine needed was *real* love. Perhaps her birth parents could give her that? It was a long shot but somewhere, deep down, Jasmine still believed in happy ever after.

Lila wasn't saying much but Maxine could tell she was dying inside. She hadn't bothered to put on any make-up for the trip and she was wearing black sweatpants and a comfortable old cashmere hoodie. This from a woman who did the school run in Chanel! Lila's skin – so often complimented for its iridescent alabaster perfection – had a grey tinge to it and there were deep, dark circles under her eyes. And despite Maxi and Peter's encouragement she'd downright refused to take a shower or wash her hair. For the first time in her life, Lila Rose looked properly rough! It broke Maxi's heart to see her this way.

Now Lila was curled up in a chair in the VIP departures lounge. She had her knees drawn up to her chest with her arms crossed on top and her chin resting on the back of her hands. Her hood was up, covering the greasy hair at least, and her eyes were cast downwards, staring at the carpet.

The other First Class passengers must have seen the weekend's papers but they had the decency to keep their distance. Nobody whispered. Nobody stared. Maxi watched Peter pace up and down in front of his charge and realised that it was just as well everyone was giving their party a wide berth. Peter would have decked anyone who'd come within three feet of Lila. Maxine had never seen him so angry.

'Oh Christ! I don't believe it! What the fuck is *she* doing here?' he muttered, stopping suddenly and staring at the door.

Maxine followed his eyes and spotted Jasmine Jones entering the lounge. She looked extraordinarily sexy in sprayed-on designer jeans, a red silk camisole and enormous sunglasses. She was even more tanned than usual and her luscious black hair bounced in perfect ringlets as she strutted across the room in killer heels. Every head in the lounge turned to watch her arrival. Every head except Lila's. Lila seemed to be lost in her own world.

Maxi sighed. Sure, Jasmine was an unfortunate choice of travel companion. It was *her* sister who'd been caught in flagrante with Brett and *her* wedding that had facilitated the unfortunate event. But was any of it Jasmine's fault? Maxine thought not. Not for one minute.

Peter was glaring at Jasmine from across the room, his eyes flashing with hatred. Maxine placed her arm gently on his.

'No, Peter,' she said, softly. 'I know you're angry but none of this is Jasmine's fault. Don't take it out on her.'

Jasmine hadn't noticed them. She'd sat down on the other side of the lounge and got a Spanish guide book out of her bag.

'I'll go over and say hello,' said Maxine.

'Don't you dare,' hissed Peter. 'OK, so maybe she's not exactly to blame for this mess but she's the last person Lila needs to see right now.'

They both glanced at Lila's bowed head. She didn't seem to be aware of anything.

'Peter, she lives next door to Lila's folks. You can't ignore her.'

'Yes I bloody well can,' he retorted childishly.

'No you can't!'

'Yes I can!'

'Please stop fighting,' came a weak voice from behind them.

Maxine and Peter spun round and stared at Lila's haunted face. She looked up at them with a pained expression.

'This is Brett's fault, not Jasmine's,' said Lila quietly. 'I have no hard feelings towards her. Why would I?'

'Oh ...' said Peter.

'Good,' said Maxine, flashing Peter an 'I told you so' look.

'Anyway, she's seen us now,' added Lila. She sounded exhausted. 'You'd better go and say hello.' And with that she disappeared back under her hood and into her private hell.

Maxine caught Jasmine's eye, smiled and waved. Jasmine waved back, tentatively. Poor kid, thought Maxine as she made her way over. We're probably the last people on earth she wants to bump into as well.

'Jasmine, hi!' said Maxine in her friendliest voice, kissing her on each cheek. 'You look wonderful. It must have been a good honeymoon.'

'Yes, yes, it was fine. How's Lila?' Jasmine bit her lip and glanced over at Lila huddled in her chair.

'Not so good,' admitted Maxine. 'She's gutted, obviously.'

'I am so sorry about Alisha's behaviour,' said Jasmine. 'I had no idea she'd do something like that. I mean, I've never been so ashamed in my life. Oh God ... it's so dreadful. What can I do? Lila must hate me. My sister destroyed her marriage!'

'No, of course she doesn't hate you. I'm not sure she even hates your sister. She just hates Brett.'

Jasmine nodded but she still seemed worried.

'If it makes you feel any less guilty,' Maxine lowered her voice and whispered in Jasmine's ear. 'Your sister's at the end of a very long line of Brett's conquests.'

Jasmine's eyes widened and her full mouth made a perfect 'Oh' shape.

'Peter's been tipped off. There are other stories coming out next weekend – actresses, models, make-up girls; you name her, Brett's done her!'

'That's horrible,' gasped Jasmine. 'How's Lila taking it?'

'Peter hasn't told her yet. He says he's waiting for the right time. But there's never going to be a right time, is there?'

'No, I guess not.'

'Makes my troubles seem insignificant, that's for sure,' said Maxine, trying to push Juan's gorgeous face out of her mind.

'And mine,' agreed Jasmine.

Maxine smiled. Bless her! What problems could lovely young Jasmine have? Freshly married to that sexy young soccer star and every schoolboy's favourite pin-up. Jasmine Jones couldn't have a care in the world, surely.

Chapter Thirty-Six

Grace pulled up at the security gates of Cynthia Watts' new 'executive' home in Chigwell. Urgh! She'd experienced better taste in a Pot Noodle. The newbuild was an identical copy of all its neighbours, except that it was the only house on the estate to have a brass fountain in the front garden and carved stone lions on either side of the porch. An undernourished Dobermann paced the drive impatiently, with the kind of bored yet angry expression Grace had only seen before on a tiger in an Afghani zoo. The white BMW convertible in the drive had the number plate 'Sin1'. It was classy stuff.

Jasmine had called Grace unexpectedly the day before and asked her if she was interested in trying to track down her birth parents – for a generous fee, of course. The call had come at a good time for Grace. She'd left the newspaper immediately on paid gardening leave and had planned to spend her free time redecorating the Mews with a view to putting it on the market as soon as possible. In reality, she hadn't got much further than drooling over the pages of *Homes and Gardens* and perusing the odd Farrow and Ball colour chart while watching daytime TV from the comfort of the sofa. No, the truth was that Jasmine's call had saved her from terminal boredom.

So, here she was, Chez Cynthia.

'Yeah? What d'you want?' barked a voice through the intercom.

'Is that Mrs Watts?' asked Grace politely.

'Depends who's asking …'

'Grace. Grace Melrose. I'm a journalist. I want to ask you a few questions about your daughter. I'll pay.'

Jasmine had told Grace that this approach would work best. 'Pretend you're trying to dig up some dirt on me. She's not exactly into family loyalty. Just pay the greedy bitch enough and she'll sing like a canary,' she had promised. 'She's done it often enough before.'

'How much?' demanded the voice.

'Enough,' replied Grace.

'And you just want me to tell you about Alisha, yeah?'

'No. Not about Alisha. I want to ask a few questions about Jasmine.'

'Oh?' There was a pause. 'I thought my youngest was the biggest star in the family these days.' Cynthia let out a throaty laugh. 'Brett Rose trumps Jimmy Jones, don't he?'

'Yes, well, they're both very talented girls,' Grace continued patiently. 'But it's Jasmine I'm interested in.'

'You better come in then. But just to the garden. I don't let no journalists in my house, d'you hear?'

The gates opened and Grace parked beside 'Sin1'. The Dobermann licked his lips hungrily.

'Come here, Saddam, you evil fucker,' bellowed Cynthia, appearing from the house in a denim mini-skirt and pink Playboy bunny vest. Grace noticed that the woman looked even more rough than she had done at the wedding.

Cynthia grabbed the dog's collar, kicked its rump with her high heels so that it yelped and flung it into a kennel in the front garden. Grace winced. She would make an anonymous call to the RSPCA later.

'I'm Cynthia. Sin to my mates, but you can call me Mrs Watts ...' She laughed at her own bad joke. 'What d'you want to know about our Jazz, then?'

'I want to know who her real parents are,' replied Grace boldly.

Cynthia paused and Grace noticed a shadow cross her face.

'Do you now?' she said slowly. 'Well, I'm not sure you can afford *that* information.'

At first, Maxine overcompensated for her indiscretion by fawning all over Carlos. She felt so damn guilty about sleeping with Juan that she thought treating him like a king might ease her guilt. Not surprisingly, Carlos had started to get suspicious. Normally, Maxine was the one who expected to be treated like royalty.

'You are too kind, Maxine. But I don't need another Rolex!' he'd exclaimed at the gift she'd brought him back from London. 'Chica, chica! I am trying to watch this movie!' he'd shrugged her off as she'd attempted to give him an aromatherapy shoulder massage the following evening.

'Breakfast in bed!' He'd been visibly shocked as she'd presented him with a tray of fresh croissants and coffee the next morning. 'But it is not my birthday!'

'No, no, no, Maxine! I am too tired to make love again!' he'd protested as she'd appeared from the bathroom wearing nothing but a black g-string and a purple feather boa. 'And anyway, we have been so busy, I have run out of my Viagra.'

'Oh.' Maxine had stopped in her tracks. 'Are you sure?'

Carlos had peered at her over the gold rims of his reading glasses and nodded with certainty. 'Quite sure. I am at a very exciting point in my book,' he'd confirmed.

The truth was, Maxine was relieved not to have to make love to Carlos again. She'd only been doing it out of guilt. She'd figured that if she made a big deal out of *wanting* Carlos, he'd never guess that she'd played away. But when he touched her it felt all wrong. His skin was too dry, too rough, too old. His hands felt cold, his touch was clumsy, his breath smelled all wrong and she couldn't bring herself to kiss him on the lips or look him in the eye. She felt like a prostitute. All she could do to make it bearable was close her eyes tight and remember that delicious night with Juan. God, it was all such a mess!

All she wanted to do was to lie on her bed and dream about Juan, but what was the point in that? She couldn't allow herself to wallow in this insane situation. She had to shake that boy right out of her mind. Forget him. But how could she do that when she lived with his father? There was a picture of Juan on her mantelpiece, for Christ's sake!

Maxine was trying really hard to erase the memories by keeping herself manically busy. She'd been rushing around all over town, finding imaginary errands to do, having endless beauty treatments, running miles on the treadmill at the gym. Anything to keep her mind off Juan. It wasn't working, of course. She tried to swat him out of her brain but he kept buzzing around there like a fly. He was the first thing she thought about when she opened her eyes in the morning, his face was the last image she saw when she closed her eyes at night and in her dreams it was his name on her lips.

Maxine could feel the gulf widening between herself and Carlos. She was on one side, he was on the other and no matter how hard she tried she couldn't keep hold of him. Could he feel the gap too? She wasn't sure. How could he not see the guilt written all over her face? Fawning over him hadn't made her feel any better about what she'd done, so now she was avoiding him instead. She realised it was remarkably easy to share a house with someone but never actually see them. He had his rituals – his golf, the clubhouse, his poker nights with his cronies – and it was easy to be out when he was going to be in. Hell, it was easier just to be out, full stop.

Of course, she had had to find a partner in crime. Poor Lila had locked herself up in her parents' villa and refused to see anyone – even Maxi now. It wasn't as if Maxine hadn't tried to see her friend. She rang and spoke to Peter on the phone at least once a day, but Lila was always unavailable – sleeping or swimming.

Thankfully, Maxine had found a new playmate in Jasmine Jones. Jimmy had been caught up in London on some business or other and Jasmine, too, was alone in Marbella. As glorious summer's day followed glorious summer's day, the two women had fallen into a comfortable habit of meeting for lunch on the beach, a little light shopping or evening cocktails at Cruise. Jasmine was a sweetheart. She helped take Maxi's mind off Juan (not that Maxi had told her new best friend about him, of course). And she lived next door to Lila. Which meant Maxine could grill her for information.

'Have you seen her yet?' she asked Jasmine as they settled down for lunch on silk cushions in their favourite Moroccan rooftop bar in the old town.

Jasmine bit her lip and nodded. She looked concerned. 'Yes, I saw her yesterday afternoon and then again this morning. I mean, I wasn't spying or anything but I do get a good view of their property from my bedroom ...'

'No, of course it's not spying. We've got to look out for her, haven't we? She's our friend. So what was she doing?'

'Swimming,' replied Jasmine. 'Just swimming and swimming and swimming. It's quite frightening, really. She swims so far out to sea.'

'She's a strong swimmer,' Maxine said, reassuring herself as much as Jasmine. 'How did she look?'

'It's hard to tell from a distance. She's lost weight, though. And she's got a tan. I've never seen her with a tan before.'

Maxine frowned. 'No, Lila usually wears, like, factor fifty or something. That can't be a good sign. God, I don't understand why she won't see me!'

'I suppose she just wants to hide from everyone. Mind you, the press are everywhere. She can't hide. I can hear them even in the middle of the night; there are at least two helicopters buzzing around. We've had a couple of photographers in our garden, trying to climb the wall.'

'That's horrible. Poor Lila. And poor you. Aren't you scared, having them crawling all over your garden with Jimmy away?'

Jasmine shook her head. 'Blaine's come back,' she explained. 'I mean, usually I hate having that fat tosser under my feet, but he has his uses. He knows most of the photographers so they listen when he tells them to piss off.'

'Peter says she's hardly speaking. Not since all those young girls started coming forward, saying they'd slept with Brett too. I've lost count! Alisha, the make-up artist in New York, three Hollywood actresses, a Vegas show-girl ...'

'And the au pair,' sighed Jasmine. 'That must have been the worst. I mean, Lila let that girl in her house. She looked after her children!'

Maxine nodded solemnly. 'And all that sex-addict stuff. He says he can't help himself, that he's got a problem and he needs help. That's pathetic, isn't it?'

Jasmine grimaced. 'I know. What an absolute bastard. He won't even take responsibility for what he's done. He has to claim it's some medical problem that he's got no control over. What a pile of crap. The problem's not in his head; it's in his boxer shorts!'

'Well, that's Hollywood for you,' said Maxine. 'It's poor Lila who needs help, not Brett. I'm not sure she's strong enough to cope with this. Not on her own.'

Chapter Thirty-Seven

Lila pushed the plate away. She'd only had one tiny bite of her sandwich, but she didn't feel hungry. She barely felt anything anymore. Her head was permanently fuzzy and her hearing wasn't right. Everything was muffled – the phone, the intercom, the helicopters overhead. When Peter or her parents talked to her it was as if she was hearing them from inside a goldfish bowl. They kept telling her she had to eat. Over and over again her mother would try to tempt her with old favourites – she would wave champagne truffles, pieces of mango or chunks of farmhouse cheddar (flown over from home) under Lila's nose, almost pleading with her to take a bite – but nothing tempted her. Peter said she was getting too thin, losing too much weight, but if that was true, why did her limbs feel so heavy?

She stood up from the kitchen table, slowly, painfully. Three sets of concerned eyes followed her. God, it was like being under house arrest. Lila winced. Her head was killing her. She felt as if she'd been shot between the eyes. Thank God the kids couldn't see her like this. Their nanny had whisked them off to her parents' dairy farm in Devon while the dust settled. Lila felt guilty palming them off like that but they seemed to be enjoying themselves, bottle-feeding calves, eating ice-cream and playing on the beach. More importantly, they seemed to be blissfully unaware of the scandal that had ripped their family apart.

'Are you all right, darling?' asked her mum.

Lila nodded, although she was anything but.

'Sit down, love,' urged her dad gently.

Lila ignored them and stepped gingerly towards the French doors and the daylight beyond.

They liked to keep her indoors where they could protect her and although Lila understood what they were trying to do it was downright infuriating. They didn't want her to be hurt anymore and they thought that if they kept her wrapped up inside then nothing and no one could inflict any more damage. It was a nice idea but it wasn't going to work. Lila needed to breathe fresh air.

'Where are you going?' asked Peter, jumping to his feet, putting his body between Lila and the door.

She knew she was worrying him to death. She could see the concern etched into the frown lines on his forehead. She didn't want to upset him. But what else could she do? She was just surviving this hell the only way she knew how.

'Swimming,' she muttered, brushing past him towards the door. She couldn't be bothered with too many words anymore.

'But Lila, the helicopters are out there. 'Please don't go outside.'

'Peter's right, darling.' Her mum's voice cracked with emotion.

She ignored them. It didn't matter what they said. It wouldn't change anything. What did she care about the press? Let them photograph her. What harm could that do compared to what had happened already? So what if they printed photographs of her looking dreadful? What did she care what strangers thought of her now? How could that hurt her more? Her husband didn't want her. It was clear now that he hadn't wanted her for a very long time. That was what hurt. The harm had been done long ago. The die had been cast by Brett. The rest, all this, was just how it had to be. These were the consequences.

She could hear Peter following her out of the house, down the steps, on to the sand. He was calling to her, telling her to swim in the pool instead, but she filtered his voice out of her head and listened to the waves calling to her instead. Peter didn't follow her into the sea. He wasn't a strong swimmer. No, she could be alone in the cold water. The salt stung her skin and it felt good. Good to feel pain somewhere other than in her heart. Her heavy limbs began to feel weightless as she swam. The water was such a relief. All she could hear was the water rushing around her ears. All she could feel was the pull of the tide, helping her out, out, out into the ocean. Lila didn't glance backwards to see how far she'd swum from shore. She just pounded the water with all her strength until her tears merged with the salt water and she was too tired to picture Brett's face anymore. Then, eventually, once she was too exhausted to know or care whether she'd make it back, she turned round and slowly, somehow, she was washed back on to the beach.

She lay there, flat on her back on the sand, letting the midday sun burn her flesh. Peter was standing above her, casting a shadow over her face. He was talking to her; she could see his lips moving but couldn't make out his words. Then he gave up and slumped down on the sand beside her. He reached out and squeezed her hand. Lila was grateful for the gesture. She appreciated Peter's loyalty. One day she hoped she'd be able to tell him that. But, for now, her head was too full of images to think about words. She'd stared for hours at their pictures in the newspapers – Brett's conquests. Those girls' faces haunted her. So fresh-faced, so pretty, so young, ever so bloody young. She stared straight at the sun until she was blinded by the light and those beautiful young faces were burned to oblivion. Sometimes it was good to burn.

Blaine watched Lila through his long lens and clicked away. This stuff was priceless. Lila Rose, the great British beauty, was no more. The woman he was watching was a haggard mess, lying there in the sand with no one for company but that limp-wristed assistant of hers. She looked wretched, weak, insane. Over the last few days he'd watched her skin burn, turn lobster red, peel and blister. Now it was brown and leathery. Through his powerful lens, Blaine could clearly see Lila's hollow cheeks and scrawny body. She'd aged ten years in the last two weeks. Or maybe she'd always looked like this under her make-up. You never knew with women. They could trick you like that. Blaine had lost count of the times he'd gone to bed with Beauty and woken up the next morning with the Beast. Hmmm … well, Lila Rose was certainly no beauty today. Was it any wonder Brett Rose had had all those affairs? No man in his right mind would blame him when his wife looked like this.

Cruise was buzzing tonight. Maxine had persuaded a hot young band of shaggy-haired boys from New York to squeeze in an extra gig at the end of their European tour and everyone who was anyone on the Costa del Sol had turned up to see them play their thrashing guitars. Jasmine was more angry than disappointed that Jimmy hadn't managed to get back in time for the gig. What was he playing at? What the hell was going on in London that was keeping him so long? And it was a shame that Charlie hadn't been in the mood to come out this evening. She'd barely seen him recently. He seemed even more distracted than Jimmy. Well, she had Maxine for company, at least. And what company! Jasmine adored her new friend.

Maxi was such a whirlwind of energy and enthusiasm. It was no surprise that Cruise had become such a major success. Doing anything with her was fun. And Jasmine needed fun in her life right now. She'd almost told Maxi about the blackmailer a couple of times after a few too many cocktails. It would have been a massive relief to share the burden and she felt sure she could trust Maxine to keep it to herself. But how could she explain the whole story to anyone? She thought that even someone as warm as Maxi would be horrified by the truth. She hadn't mentioned anything about Jimmy hitting her, either. Maxi was such a strong, independent woman; she couldn't imagine her putting up with a man who abused her.

Jasmine would have felt ashamed, pathetic even, to admit that Jimmy had done that to her – and worse, that she'd let him get away with it. So she kept her secrets to herself.

After the band had finished their set, Jasmine and Maxine joined the boys in the VIP lounge for a post-gig drink. The lead singer – a guy called Jamie with floppy black hair and dangerously come-to-bed eyes – seemed to have taken a shine to Jasmine. He'd flopped his arm casually over her shoulder and was trying his best to chat her up.

'So, you're married, then?' he pouted. 'That's a real shame. Breaks my heart to hear that a chick like you is off the market.' He ran his finger along her bare arm. It tickled. He was seriously cute but Jasmine wasn't in the least bit tempted. She laughed and pushed his arm off her.

'That's right. I am completely off limits so there's no point wasting your energy on me. Look, there are loads of gorgeous girls here and I bet most of them are single. Why don't you go and talk to them?'

Jamie shook his head and said, 'Nah, I prefer a challenge.'

'I'm not a challenge. I'm a non-starter. Honestly, you're wasting your time.'

She smiled at him politely and then excused herself to go to the ladies'. That's where she found Maxine, fixing her face.

'He is sooo into you,' giggled Maxi. 'It's kind of cute.'

Jasmine pulled a face. 'It's kind of annoying,' she said. 'God, what part of married does he not understand?'

'Flattering, though,' said Maxine, touching up her lip gloss. 'To have such a handsome, young dude fawning over you.'

'I suppose so but I'm a one-man woman. I'd never be unfaithful. It's the worst thing you can do, don't you think? I mean, look at what it's done to Lila.'

Maxine put her lip gloss back in her bag slowly and deliberately, but she said nothing.

Jasmine continued. 'No, there's never any excuse for infidelity. You should always finish one relationship before you start another.'

Maxine stood up straight and fluffed up her hair. 'In an ideal world, everyone would be faithful, nobody would ever get hurt and we'd all live happily ever after,' she said.

'Exactly!'

'But unfortunately we don't live in an ideal world.' Maxi caught her eye in the mirror. The older woman looked very wise and Jasmine suddenly felt a bit silly and naive.

'Sometimes life is complicated, imperfect ...' Maxine trailed off and looked away.

Jasmine wondered for a moment whether Maxi was speaking from experience. Maybe she should ask her. But, no, something in the firm set of Maxi's jaw told her to drop the subject.

'Shall we get out of here then?' asked Maxine, suddenly. 'I fancy a change of scene. I spend half my life here these days. And you can escape Jamie's advances!'

'Yeah, sure. Where shall we go?'

'Oh, just for a quiet drink somewhere.'

They sneaked out without saying goodbye to the band and jumped into Maxine's private car. The driver took them to the old town and dropped them off at a boutique hotel that Jasmine had been to before a couple of times. It had an amazing candle-lit rooftop bar and the staff were very discerning about who they let in.

'We'll get some peace here,' promised Maxine. 'No annoying little Rock Gods to paw at you!'

The bar was popular rather than packed and the atmosphere was intimate. Couples and small groups of friends chatted quietly to each other under the starry sky. The sound of chinking glass and muted laughter merged with gentle Spanish guitar music. Jasmine glanced around to see if there was anyone there she recognised. She waved hello to a couple of models she knew from home and then her eyes fell on a lone man in the far corner. He was slumped at an angle in his chair, staring into a bottle of beer. Jasmine couldn't see his face clearly but he was obviously drunk. She thought he looked terribly out of place. This wasn't the sort of bar where people fell off their bar stools after one too many San Miguels. It was far too classy for that.

The waiter seated them two tables away from the lone man. Maxi ordered a bottle of champagne and started chatting about the bands she had lined up to play at Cruise for the rest of the summer, but Jasmine couldn't take her eyes off the drunken man. There was something familiar about his dark hair and tall, skinny frame. His clothes were well-cut and obviously expensive but his shirt was creased and untucked and he'd spilled beer on his trousers. He had an unlit cigarette dangling from his mouth. It wasn't until he picked up a pair of glasses from the table and placed them lopsidedly on his nose that Jasmine realised who he was.

'Isn't that Peter? Lila's Peter.'

'Where?' Maxi followed Jasmine's gaze. 'Oh my God, yes! I've never seen him out without Lila before. I was beginning to think they were surgically joined at the hip. God, he's in a bit of a state, isn't he? Come on. Let's go and see if he's OK.'

Jasmine nodded, but her heart fell. She knew Peter didn't approve of her. She'd sensed at the airport that he blamed her for Alisha's behaviour. And he was drunk. Jasmine was always wary of drunk men. She knew what they were capable of. Reluctantly she followed Maxine to Peter's table. He looked up at them but it seemed to take a while for his eyes to focus.

'Maxine!' he said almost cheerfully when he eventually recognised her. Then his eyes fell on Jasmine. 'Oh,' he said, less enthusiastically. 'And the WAG.'

'Well, you're obviously pissed as a fart,' said Maxine, slipping into the seat next to Peter. 'What's up? I didn't have you down as an old lush.'

Peter shrugged and swilled back some more beer. Most of it missed his mouth and dribbled down his white shirt. 'Needs must!' he announced loudly, banging his beer bottle back down on the table. 'Waiter! Waiter! More beer!'

Jasmine took a seat with her back to the rest of the bar. The truth was that Peter was being loud enough for people to stare and she was embarrassed to be seen with him in this state.

'So this is your new BF is it, Maxine?' he slurred as he pointed a finger accusingly at Jasmine. 'Forgotten all about poor Lila, have you? Too busy drinking with the enemy!'

'Oh, don't talk nonsense,' said Maxine in her usual cheerful tone, as she swatted Peter's finger out of Jasmine's face. 'Jasmine is not the enemy and you know perfectly well that Lila won't see me. How is she, anyway?'

Jasmine's cheeks burned with embarrassment. She wished the floor would open up and swallow her.

'How do you think she is?' demanded Peter loudly. 'She has been destroyed by the likes of your sister!'

He was pointing at Jasmine again and now everybody on the rooftop had turned to see what was going on.

'Now, listen to me,' said Maxine sternly. 'This behaviour is not helping Lila, is it? Now, you will apologise to Jasmine for being so rude and then you will explain to us exactly what is going on with Lila and we will try to help. Do you understand?'

Peter nodded his head like a chastised schoolboy and belched. The unlit cigarette fell out of his mouth on to the table.

'Where did that come from?' he asked distractedly.

'Peter,' warned Maxine. 'I think you owe Jasmine an apology.'

'Sorry, Jasmine,' he slurred. 'I know it's not your fault that your sister is the spawn of Satan.'

'It's OK,' said Jasmine, quietly.

She felt as if she was intruding. She barely knew Lila and thought perhaps she should go and leave Maxine and Peter alone to talk. She half stood up and began to say, 'I think I might head home ...' But Maxi shot her a warning glare and whispered, 'Don't you dare leave me with him in this state!' Jasmine sat down again reluctantly.

'Lila is dying!' announced Peter dramatically, sweeping his arms across the table and sending his empty beer bottle crashing on to the tiled floor. 'I honestly don't think she can survive this.' His head slumped down on the table with a bang.

Jasmine glanced at Maxine. Was he being serious? Or was it just the drink talking? Maxine was frowning and chewing her lip. She asked the waiter, who had rushed over to clear up the broken bottle, to bring Peter a strong coffee.

'OK, Peter, I need you to pull yourself together and quietly ...' Maxine glanced around. 'Because you never know who's listening. *Quietly* explain what's happening with Lila.'

Maxine coaxed Peter into having a few sips of his black coffee and lit his cigarette for him. He inhaled deeply and then, at last, he spoke.

'She won't eat,' he explained more calmly now. 'She doesn't sleep. I mean, she spends hours lying in bed but I can hear her pacing around her room, even in the middle of the night. She's not even crying anymore. She's like a zombie. She barely speaks. The only thing she does is go swimming in the sea, for hours on end. Then she lies on the beach, in some trance or other, and just stares into space. I can't get her to wear any sunscreen so she's burned to a crisp. She hasn't washed her hair in two weeks and her face is like this ...'

Peter sucked in his cheeks until he looked skeletal.

'I don't know what to do,' he whispered. 'I'm really scared. I don't know how to fix her.'

Jasmine listened and her heart felt heavy. It was so sad. She'd been really impressed by Lila Rose when they'd met. She had seemed so elegant and poised. She was sophisticated in a way that Jasmine knew she would never be. It was heartbreaking to hear that such a lovely woman was in such a bad way.

'You've got to persuade her to see me, Peter,' Maxine said. 'I can help her. I know people she can talk to. I had an amazing counsellor when I split up with, well, all my exes, and it does help. But she's got to let me in. There's nothing I can do if I can't see her.'

Peter sipped his coffee and stared out over the rooftops. 'But she doesn't listen to me. It's like someone's switched the lights off. And the frightening thing is, I don't think she's hit rock bottom yet. I really think it's going to get worse before it gets better.'

'I wish I could do something to help,' said Jasmine.

'No offence, Jasmine,' replied Peter flatly, 'but what on earth could you do to help Lila?'

Chapter Thirty-Eight

Charlie woke up with a clear head. It was the first good night's sleep he'd had in ages and as he stood up and stretched he realised that his body felt strong again. About bleeding time! It was time to stop hiding away in this godforsaken hotel room and get on with the rest of his life. Wasn't that the reason he'd come here? To start afresh and leave the demons behind? OK, so Nadia was still missing. What could he do? He wasn't God, for fuck's sake. He was just a bloke trying his best to do the right thing.

Today he would start looking for an apartment. He would begin to put down roots. He'd wasted thousands of euros on this bloody hotel room and it had made a dent in his wad of cash. Perhaps he should think about getting some sort of job. Nah, Charlie had had enough of doing what other people told him to do. He could set up his own business with the money McGregor had paid him. Maybe he could buy a nice little bar on the beach somewhere. He knew enough about running clubs and pubs in London. How hard could it be in Spain? Charlie imagined himself on the beach, making cocktails for pretty girls in bikinis, chatting to the lads on holiday from back home, bantering with his local clientele. Yes, he could see himself doing that. Lovely job. But first he would go and visit Jasmine. He'd hardly seen the little darling since she'd got back from London and with Jimmy away she was probably a bit lonely. He'd been so busy worrying about Nadia that he'd neglected his number one girl right under his nose.

It was a beautiful, clear morning. The sky had lost its haze, a slight breeze blew in from the sea and the temperature had dropped a few degrees so that it was nicely warm rather than stiflingly hot. As he drove along the coast road towards Jasmine's place, Charlie felt the wind in his face and the sun on his skin and he let himself smile for the first time in ages. His problems were not insurmountable, he decided. Nadia would be OK. If anyone could save her it was Dimitrov. She had a powerful family on her side. And if she didn't turn up? Or worse, if she turned up dead? No! Charlie shook the idea from his head. Dimitrov wouldn't let that happen to his beloved daughter. What father would? Everything would turn out all right. Charlie had made up his mind to be positive. Nothing was going to ruin this lovely day.

'I saw Maxine last night,' said Peter, placing some toast in front of Lila, although he knew already that she wouldn't eat it.

She nodded uninterestedly.

'She was with Jasmine Jones.'

Still no response. Peter sighed and pushed the plate closer to her. 'Eat,' he urged.

Lila stared out of the window towards the beach below.

'Maxi's really worried about you. She's desperate to see you. Do you think you might feel up to having her visit today?'

Lila shook her head and kept staring out to sea.

'Oh, come on, Lila. Maxine's your friend. Surely it would be good to see her.'

She didn't reply. Peter felt desperate now. He'd done all he could to pull Lila back from the brink, but nothing was working. Her parents were worried sick. The kids called every night but Lila wouldn't speak to them. He knew it was because she didn't want to upset them, but it was too late for that. Louisa cried to Peter that she wanted her mummy and, although Seb was trying to be grown up about the whole situation, when he said he wanted to 'kill Daddy', Peter was shocked by the venom in the little boy's voice.

Peter placed his hand gently on Lila's cheek and turned her face towards his. Her eyes stared over his head. They looked glazed and cold.

'Lila,' he said, trying to break her trance. 'Lila, you have to start helping yourself. Don't let Brett destroy you. He's not worth it.'

She jerked her head away and stood up. The cold toast remained untouched on the plate.

'I'm going for a swim,' she murmured, almost inaudibly.

Peter was sick of chasing her down to the beach. This time he let her walk out of the room without calling her back. He barely had the energy to fight this black cloud anymore. His head hurt from drinking too much beer last night. He wasn't Superman. Today, he would let her swim without a fight.

Jasmine was delighted to have Charlie all to herself. It was such a gorgeous morning that they'd taken their breakfast down to the beach. The maid had prepared a delicious feast of fruit salad, soft rolls, cheese and ham and freshly squeezed orange juice and Jasmine had just finished spreading it out on a rug on the sand.

'You're so lucky to have this beach to yourself,' Charlie said, leaning back on his lounger. 'If it wasn't for that bloody helicopter it would be idyllic.'

They both glanced up at the sky, where the press helicopter hung around overhead.

'I know,' said Jasmine. 'I wish they'd all piss off and leave Lila alone. It's like a circus round here. Orange juice?'

'Yes please,' Charlie nodded and closed his eyes, soaking in the rays. This was the life.

'Oh look. Lila's swimming again.'

'Hmm?' Charlie opened his eyes and followed Jasmine's gaze. 'Christ! Does she always go that far out?'

He sat bolt upright and shielded his eyes with his hand so that he could see Lila more clearly. She was little more than a speck. She seemed way too far out to be safe.

'She swims for miles,' said Jasmine. 'Every day.'

Charlie dragged his eyes away from the sea. He supposed Lila must know what she was doing and it was none of his business, was it? He leaned down and helped himself to a cheese roll.

'This is lovely, Jazz,' he said.

But Jasmine wasn't listening. She was still staring out at the waves. Her mouth fell open and the juice she was pouring started spilling all over the sand.

'Oh my God, Charlie. I think she's in trouble! Charlie! Do something!'

Lila didn't have the energy to fight. She couldn't be bothered with the constant press attention, with the headlines, the helicopters hovering above, the intercom buzzing, the phone ringing. She couldn't deal with her friend's sympathy, her parents' empathy, her children's tears. In fact, as she lay on her back and let the waves lap around her cheeks, she decided she didn't have the energy for any of it anymore. Not even the energy to swim back to shore. Or to tread water. Not this time. This time she was content to let the waves lap her nose and then her eyes.

And then she was drifting slowly under the waves, but it wasn't frightening. It felt like the most natural thing in the world because Lila had always felt at home in the water. Water could wash away the pain. And as the waves engulfed her the relief was enormous. The pain eased and she was leaving it all behind. Her life didn't flash before her eyes. There was no sudden epiphany. There was nothing but a delicious calm feeling that now everything would be all right ...

Then strong hands grabbed her wrists and dragged her towards the light. She heard a voice shout, 'No!' but she wasn't sure if it was her own, or somebody else's. And then she saw his face and she recognised him from her dreams. He was rescuing her. But where was he taking her? Back to the real world and all its pain? Or to their dream world for ever, where nothing could hurt her again?

Chapter Thirty-Nine

Grace sat in the waiting room, reading and re-reading the letter. Perhaps she should have called Jasmine and told her about it straight away. It felt wrong to be in possession of this sort of information without letting the girl know. But Grace didn't trust Cynthia Watts for one moment. The letter could be a fake for all she knew and she didn't want to go getting Jasmine's hopes up without more proof. And anyway, it didn't actually say who Jasmine's mother was. At least, not in so many words, but ... well, Grace was working on a hunch. No, she would have to talk to Jasmine's aunt Julie first. She was sure that it was Julie who held the key to this whole mystery.

The hospital reception looked like an upmarket hotel lobby with its leather sofas and piles of pristine magazines and yet, Grace noted, the displays of lilies couldn't mask the smell of bleach. The atmosphere was hushed and calm. Nurses in pristine white uniforms walked by quietly in their rubber-soled shoes. Every now and then Grace would hear a muffled cry from the wards, but otherwise she sat in silence. She fingered the letter nervously.

She knew this was one of the most expensive private psychiatric hospitals in the country and she was sure the care was very good, but just being here made her feel uncomfortable. She hoped Julie wasn't too incoherent. Cynthia had mentioned some sort of major breakdown happening at Jasmine's wedding. Well, that wasn't quite how she had put it.

'Stupid fucking cow went totally bleeding mental, didn't she?' Cynthia had said. 'She's always been soft in the head, that one, but she were fine in the church, honest. Then we sat her down for the meal and she just starts shaking like a right nutter. Then she was crying and hyperventilating. It was fucking embarrassing! We was at a posh wedding, for fuck's sake! She didn't half show us up. I think Charlie Palmer sorted her out. I dunno. Next I hear Jasmine's paying for her to go to that nuthouse where the rich loonies are sent. Never been right in the head, that one. Not since she was a girl.'

Grace had found it surprisingly easy to persuade Cynthia to help. She had conveniently 'found' the letter once Grace had offered to pay her a five-figure sum.

'Why didn't you give this to Jasmine when she first started asking about her biological parents?' Grace had asked, perplexed.

'I only found the bleeding thing last year. When I moved. It was in the attic at the old house in a box full of Kenny's crap. I'd never seen it before in my life. The man died years ago, for Christ's sake.'

'But why didn't you give it to Jasmine when you found it?' Grace had asked, dismayed at the woman's lack of compassion.

Cynthia had shrugged. 'Well, it don't say much, does it?'

'It says enough …' Grace had exclaimed. She'd narrowed her eyes at the older woman, knowing full well that she'd held on to the letter waiting for exactly this moment, when someone would offer her money for the information. 'This could explain everything.'

Cynthia had laughed callously. 'I know what you're thinking, love, but hold your horses. Just 'cause Juju had a baby, it don't mean that kid was Jasmine, right?'

'Well, surely, you'd know. You must have known something about where she came from when you adopted her.'

Cynthia had shrugged indifferently. 'Nah, not really. It was all Kenny's idea. I wasn't that bothered about kids. Just wanted one of them bigger flats off the council. He sorted out getting the baby.'

'But didn't anyone interview you?' asked Grace, perplexed. Even twenty-five years ago, there had been pretty strict protocols about adoption. 'Didn't you have to go through some sort of official process to adopt Jasmine?'

'No,' Cynthia had said, amused. 'The social would never have let me have a baby. Anyway, takes years that way, dunnit? As far as I can remember Kenny just came home with the nipper one day. Simple as that. Anyway, it's such a long time ago now. It don't bleeding matter, does it?'

Grace had smelled a rat. Something was seriously wrong here. She stared at the letter. The paper had gone soft over the years and it was torn where it had been folded, but it was quite clear what it said: Julie Watts had had a baby in 1984. The baby was a girl.

'I never even knew Juju had a baby,' Cynthia had continued. 'She went off travelling when she was young. Following some daft dream of hers. I certainly never saw her up the duff, or holding no baby.'

'So what happened to her baby?'

'I don't fucking know!' Cynthia had snapped, getting bored with the conversation. 'It probably died. Juju couldn't look after a bleeding budgie, let alone a baby.'

Grace had felt frustrated. Talking to Cynthia Watts was like talking to a brick wall. Now the woman had her cheque she had no interest in giving anything else away.

'And you swear you have no idea where Kenny got Jasmine?' Grace had asked one more time. 'Your husband just came home one day with a baby and you didn't even think to ask where the child came from?'

'I haven't got a bleeding clue where he got her,' Cynthia had said, starting to walk back towards the house, clutching her cheque firmly. 'A baby's a baby. They're ten-a-penny. Junkies and whores used to sell theirs for a couple of hundred quid in the East End when I was on the game. D'you know how many crack babies are being brought up with double-barrelled names in Holland Park as we speak? D'you think those nippers was 'officially' adopted? You ain't got a clue how the other half live, have you, love?' And with a cynical laugh she'd disappeared back into her hideous house.

Was Julie's child Jasmine? Grace hoped she was about to find out.

A young nurse approached in her quiet shoes and ushered to Grace to follow her. They walked in silence along a long corridor until they reached Room 108. The nurse knocked on the door.

'Come in,' came the reply. The voice was weak.

The nurse indicated that Grace should enter. Grace sighed deeply and pushed open the door.

The first thought that hit her was that Julie Watts must have been stunning in her youth. She was the archetypal faded beauty, with long blonde hair that had started to turn prematurely grey and the most delicate features Grace had ever seen. She had high cheekbones, a perfectly upturned nose, rosebud lips and enormous, clear blue eyes. Julie was sitting in an armchair by the window, wearing a white hospital gown. She was framed by the sunlight that poured in the window, giving her an angelic glow.

'Hello,' she said with a pained smile. 'You must be Grace.'

Julie looked kind but sad. She had the air of someone who had been broken by life. Grace had done her maths and knew that Julie was only forty-three, although it was hard to believe. She looked so fragile and pale that had she not known the truth, she would have put her age at closer to sixty.

'Hello Julie,' said Grace. 'I hope you don't mind me visiting.'

'Jasmine said you'd be nice,' said Julie, patting a seat next to hers at the window. 'And I don't get many visitors so it's good to have some company for a change, although what on earth you'd want to talk to me about I really don't know.'

There was no point beating about the bush. Grace handed the letter to

Julie and sat down. Her heart was pounding in her chest. She had no idea which way this was going to go.

'What's this?' asked Julie, fingering the letter nervously.

'It's something Cynthia Watts gave me. She said she found it in your brother's things.'

Julie tried to hand it back to Grace without unfolding it. 'I don't want it,' she said with certainty. 'Cynthia's not a nice woman. I don't want anything from her.'

Grace took a deep breath, but she didn't take back the letter. This was going to be difficult. There was something incredibly childlike about Julie Watts and Grace was worried about frightening her. The poor woman didn't just look fragile. She *was* fragile. Grace had been told that she was on strong medication and had been warned not to upset her.

'It doesn't have anything to do with Cynthia, Julie. It's about you,' she continued calmly. 'Kenny kept it for you. You should read it.'

Julie's huge blue eyes stared at Grace. She didn't blink. 'Why?'

'For Jasmine,' said Grace, taking a gamble.

Julie's face softened. 'She's such a lovely girl, Jasmine. She's very busy but she comes to see me whenever she can and she always brings me chocolates – truffles; they're my favourite.'

'Please look at the letter,' urged Grace.

Julie turned the paper over in her shaky hands. It seemed to Grace that somewhere, deep down, Julie understood the importance of this letter. It was as if she was deciding whether or not to open a door into a long-forgotten room. Eventually, she unfolded the paper and stared at the words that were typed on it. At first, there was no emotion in her face, and Grace wondered whether Julie even understood what the letter said. And then a lone tear formed in the corner of her eye. Grace watched as it trickled down her cheek, quivered on the end of her chin and then plopped on to her gown. She felt a lump form in her throat. This was more difficult than any interview she'd ever had to do.

'You had a baby,' said Grace, gently.

Julie nodded and kept staring at the letter. 'It was such a long time ago that sometimes it feels like it never happened at all,' she whispered. 'I don't let myself think about it. I'm not very well, you see. I get terribly upset by these things.'

'I know,' said Grace, placing her hand on Julie's knee. 'But perhaps it's time to think about it now. We could talk about it. Maybe that will help you.'

Julie looked up and met her concerned gaze. She looked like a deer caught in the headlamps and Grace felt immediately guilty for dredging all this up.

'I can't let myself go there,' said Julie very slowly but certainly. 'I'm sorry, but I think you should leave now.'

Grace sighed. She didn't want to go. She wanted to dig deeper and get to the truth. But she couldn't risk upsetting Julie too much. She was her only hope – Jasmine's only hope. She stood up and placed a business card on the window sill.

'Just in case you want to talk again.' Then Grace took a deep breath and asked one last question. 'Julie, was Jasmine your baby?'

Julie stood up on shaky legs. A shadow crossed her face and suddenly she looked more like a witch than an angel. She thrust the letter hard into Grace's chest and screamed. 'Take it away! You don't know anything about me! Go away! Get out! Get out!'

Grace clutched the precious letter and tried to back out towards the door but Julie followed her, pummelling her chest with her fists, still screaming, 'Get out! Get out! Get out!' Julie was much stronger than she looked.

A nurse rushed into the room, followed by another one, and Grace watched helplessly as they struggled to restrain Julie. The more they tried to force her to lie down on the bed, the more upset she became. She was howling like a wild animal, and lashing out at the nurses with flailing limbs. Grace stood frozen in the doorway, watching in horror as Julie was strapped to the bed. She felt completely responsible.

'You'd better go now,' shouted one of the nurses to Grace. 'Julie needs her medication.'

Grace nodded, blinking back tears of shame. She half ran down the corridor away from Room 108, but even as she approached the reception she could still hear Julie shouting, 'Get out! Get out! Leave me alone! Go away!'

Grace sat in her car in the car park for the longest time, trying to make sense of what had just happened. There was no doubt about it, she was way out of her depth. Grace was a journalist, not a psychiatrist. All she'd been doing was trying to help Jasmine, but instead she felt as if she'd opened some Pandora's Box. Instead of finding answers, she'd only thrown up more questions. What should she do now?

Chapter Forty

She was floating through the clouds, feeling weightless and carefree. There was nothing troubling her anymore. He was holding her hand, guiding her, and she knew she was safe.

'Lila,' someone was calling from very far away. 'Lila.'

She couldn't decide whether to reply. She was having such a lovely time, just floating here in the sky. She hadn't felt this peaceful or calm for a very long time and it seemed a shame to let someone else in. She squeezed his hand and he squeezed it back. Lila smiled. She couldn't see his face but he was always with her in her dreams.

'She squeezed my hand,' said the voice, excitedly. 'She definitely squeezed it. And look! She's smiling!'

Lila sighed. The voice was disturbing her. It seemed to be pulling her down from the sky. She could feel herself free-falling towards the earth, faster and faster, until the wind howled in her ears and suddenly, she landed with a violent bump.

'Oh my God! She jumped!' screeched the voice. 'Did you see that?'

Lila opened her eyes. The room was very bright. A face swam in front of her, peering down. It had dark hair and glasses and a ridiculous grin on its face.

'Peter,' she whispered, croakily.

'Oh Lila! You're alive!' he shouted and then he hugged her so hard that she thought she would suffocate.

'Give her some air,' ordered a firm female voice. Then a smiling face appeared, wearing immaculate make-up, framed by a mane of rippling blonde hair.

'Maxine,' whispered Lila.

'OK, this is soooo like a movie,' grinned Maxi. 'No. Don't try to talk. Before you ask, you are in the hospital. You very nearly drowned yourself – you crazy woman – but thankfully you were spotted by Jasmine Jones who just happened to have her hunky godfather at hand to jump into the sea and save you.' She paused for breath. 'Of my God, Lila, I'm so happy you're alive!'

'What are you talking about, Maxine?' Lila was more than confused. Drowned? Happy I'm alive? She didn't remember drowning and she certainly didn't remember being anything other than alive. She remembered going for a swim and getting really tired and then … nothing. And Jasmine Jones? And her godfather? What did they have to do with anything?

Peter's face reappeared, still grinning. 'You have totally got your own Guardian Angel now, Lila. Charlie Palmer is the most red-blooded, muscle-bound hunk of hero I have ever seen and if he wasn't so outrageously heterosexual I'd be completely in love with him.'

'I should thank him,' said Lila, in a weak voice.

Charlie Palmer. He was the nice man who'd helped her look for Brett at the wedding. Brett. Oh, Jesus, Brett. Lila's brain was flooded with the memories of newspaper headlines and photos of pretty young girls. What a bastard. Lila felt a ball of anger form in the pit of her stomach. She was not, by nature, an angry person and the feeling was unfamiliar, but somehow it felt good. It made her feel strong.

'Well, you'll be seeing plenty more of Charlie,' Maxine was announcing cheerfully. 'Because Peter's employed him as your bodyguard.'

'My what?' Lila tried to sit up but just at that moment a doctor appeared, shooing Peter and Maxine out of the way.

'Mrs Rose, she need some rest now,' ordered the doctor.

Lila closed her eyes again. A smile played on her lips. She was surprised at how happy she felt to be alive.

Grace had been putting off calling Jasmine and telling her what had happened. How could she explain what was going on when she didn't really understand it herself? OK, so she was pretty sure that Jasmine's adoption had been dodgy in the first place – she could find no official documentation anywhere. And then there was the fact that her aunt Julie had just happened to have an illegitimate baby girl at exactly the same time that Jasmine was born and given her up for adoption. Coincidence? Grace thought not. And of course, there was also the small matter of Grace having tipped Julie completely over the edge, mentally speaking. She wasn't quite sure how Jasmine would take that news either. It had seemed like such a good idea to take Jasmine up on her offer to find her birth parents. A little private-detective work had appealed to Grace. She'd thought it was right up her street. But suddenly journalism didn't seem like such a bad job, after all. What the hell had she got herself into?

She'd been sleeping badly so when her phone rang in the middle of the night she was wide awake and answering it in moments.

'Hello?' said Grace.

Nothing.

'Hello? Is anyone there?' Grace asked.

Silence.

'Hello? Who is this?' she demanded.

'It's Julie,' came the quiet response. 'Julie Watts. I wanted to say sorry.'

Grace sat bolt upright. 'Julie!'

'Yes, that's me. Jasmine's, erm, aunt,' said Julie timidly. 'I behaved badly the other day. I'm not well, you see.'

'That's OK,' said Grace, her head spinning. 'Are you feeling better now?'

'Much better, thanks. But I have trouble sleeping. It's the tablets. They make me jittery. I hope it's not too late to call you.'

Grace glanced at her bedside clock. It was half past two in the morning. 'No, no. It's fine. I was awake anyway.'

'I want to talk to you about that letter you showed me. So I thought you might like to come for tea next weekend,' said Julie so quietly that Grace had to strain to hear.

'That would be lovely. What day? What time?'

'Sunday. Three o'clock. There's something you need to know about Jasmine.' And then the phone went dead.

Lila was sitting up in bed, eating a crayfish and rocket salad and listening intently to her children chatter away about what they'd been doing during their stay at the farm. Peter flapped around the room, topping up Lila's water glass, picking up a magazine from the floor, stroking Louisa's hair and straightening the bed sheets where the kids had been clambering on them. He was still unable to wipe the ridiculous smile off his face.

Charlie watched from his seat at the door. Inside he was smiling too. How was this for a kosher job, eh? Lila Rose's personal bodyguard. OK, so it hadn't been his plan to go back into the protection game but, Christ, was this different from the kind of protection he'd been involved in back home. This time he was looking after the most beautiful woman in the world – and he was being paid handsomely for the privilege. Talk about a cushy little number. And this time he wouldn't have to shoot anybody, either. All he had to do was keep the press off her back. That would be easy. After the lowlifes Charlie had seen off in his time, he could eat the paparazzi for breakfast. In fact, he would enjoy it. Scumbags!

The media circus had become even more frenzied since Lila Rose had almost drowned. Of course the press had pictured the whole bloody thing as it happened and now the entire world was waiting with bated breath to see what would happen to 'poor' Lila next. They were camped out in the hospital car park now, hundreds of them. TV crews, too. Charlie didn't know how she could stand it. A few journalists had tried to get him to give a comment about being the one who'd rescued her but Charlie had quickly made it clear that he wasn't the 'sharing' kind. They'd got the picture and backed off. The last thing he needed was a bunch of hacks looking into his background. He supposed he might have to pay for that camera he'd smashed but, hey, someone had to put those parasites in their place.

They were like ants the way they scurried around, crawling through tiny gaps and getting under everyone's feet. Charlie had already had to see off a couple of undercover reporters who'd slipped past the hospital's own security. A young guy from the *News of the World* had tried to pass himself off as flower delivery boy and a girl from one of the posh papers had posed as a junior doctor. Idiots! Charlie had spotted them both at a hundred paces. They wouldn't be trying those tricks again, that was for sure. But it was all good. It made Charlie feel as if he was earning his keep and Peter seemed happy with his work. And as for Lila? Well, Charlie felt pretty confident she would be OK. Of course, he didn't know her well, but he'd watched a light come back on in her eyes over the past two days.

Lately, the papers had been full of stories about how Lila had lost her famous good looks, but from where Charlie was sitting she was as gorgeous as ever. A bit on the skinny side, yeah, but she was definitely on the mend. She was eating regular meals, chatting to her folks and the kids (who'd been flown in for the weekend) and the doctors were saying they might even let her go home tomorrow. Peter had arranged for Charlie to move into a self-contained apartment at her parents' villa, so he didn't even have to find himself a pad yet. Things were definitely looking up.

'Is Maxine coming today?' Lila was asking Peter.

'No, poor thing's feeling a bit ropey. She's gone to the doctor,' Peter explained. 'She said she's hoping to drop by tomorrow, though. If she feels better.'

'That's a shame. I wanted to thank her for the flowers.'

The private room was full of poncy arrangements of exotic flowers. Charlie hadn't been able to resist a quick butchers at the cards attached. There were flowers from Brad Pitt and Angelina Jolie, Catherine Zeta Jones and Michael Douglas. Christ, even Madonna had sent some!

Charlie sensed this job wouldn't last long. Lila was getting stronger every day and eventually the press would get tired of following her around. They'd move on to some other poor celebrity sucker who was having a hard time and Lila's life would return to some sort of normality. She'd go back to London and Charlie wouldn't be able to follow her there. No, it wouldn't last long, but for now he would enjoy every minute of protecting her. It certainly beat cleaning up for the likes of McGregor and Angelis.

Maxine watched as the doctor re-entered the room carrying a clipboard and tried to read the woman's face. She was terrified that she'd caught something terminal in LA. What the hell had she been thinking sharing a joint with that tramp? She remembered the blood on his handkerchief and winced inwardly. TB? HIV? Maxine was convinced it was something serious. She'd had a terrible fever last night and this barking cough was so painful it made her retch. Now she sat shivering in a pale-green gown in the examination room with her fate in this young doctor's hands.

Maxi was never ill. *Never.* She had the constitution of an ox. Despite the recent frostiness between them, Carlos had also been alarmed by her sudden illness and had sent her straight to this private clinic this morning, where she'd been poked, prodded, relieved of at least a pint of blood and ordered to pee in a plastic bottle. Now the doctor had some results and Maxine was not looking forward to hearing them. She just knew something terrible was wrong. She didn't feel herself at all.

'You have a nasty chest infection,' said the doctor matter-of-factly, peering at Maxine from behind her steel-rimmed glasses. 'So I will give you antibiotics. I do not normally like to give antibiotics to a woman in your condition, but this is a bad infection and I feel it is necessary.'

Maxine frowned. Her condition? What condition? Oh my God, she knew it was something terminal ...

The doctor handed her a bottle of tablets. 'These should not do any harm. How many weeks are you?'

Maxine scratched her head. 'Weeks?' she asked, perplexed.

'Pregnant,' replied the doctor, a little impatiently. She talked to Maxine as if she was stupid rather than just a foreigner. 'You do know that you are pregnant, don't you?'

Maxine felt her jaw drop open. Pregnant. The word seeped into her brain slowly.

'I'm pregnant?' she heard herself asking. 'Are you sure?'

'Quite sure,' replied the doctor. 'I am sorry. I assumed that you were aware of this fact.'

'No,' said Maxine, completely shell-shocked. 'No. I had absolutely no idea.'

'Well, let me be the first to congratulate you,' said the doctor, in the same unemotional manner as before. 'I trust *Señor* Russo will also be delighted. You may get dressed now.' And with that she was gone.

Maxine slipped her dress back on in a daze. Pregnant? She was pregnant!

Her hand fell automatically to her stomach. It was as flat and gym-toned as ever. There was no hint of a bump yet. How could she have known? She and Carlos had barely seen each other lately, let alone made love. For a terrible moment she thought of her night of passion with Juan, but then she remembered clearly seeing the condom wrapper on the floor and sighed with relief. They'd definitely used protection. It was OK. So, it must have happened when she'd first got back from LA then. Maxi did her sums quickly. Yes, that would make sense. She must have conceived about three weeks ago. Her period had been due this week and she hadn't even realised it. She'd been so busy worrying about Lila that she hadn't been thinking about herself. Maxine felt a smile spread across her face and, despite her terrible cough and high fever, a warm, happy glow engulfed her. I'm going to be a mummy, she thought. There was a tiny little person growing inside her. It was magical.

In the chauffeur-driven car on the way home, Maxi stared out of the window and allowed herself to daydream about the future. A baby was exactly what she and Carlos needed to get them back on track. How silly she'd been to have her head turned by Juan. It wasn't as if he'd tried to get in touch since it happened. She must have been just another conquest. Supermodel. Tick. Movie star. Tick. Father's girlfriend. Tick. Yes, he was handsome as hell; yes, she'd fancied the pants off him and, yes, maybe for a while there she'd thought it had meant something but, no, it wasn't real. It can't have been. No, like the tramp had said, what happened in LA could stay in LA It was just a dream and in time it would fade to nothing.

Now it was time for the future. And the future belonged to Maxine, Carlos and their baby. Oh, how should she tell him, the father-to-be? Should she just blurt it out when she got home or wait and make the announcement more of an event? Yes, that would be fun. She would cook him a meal and this time she would get it right. She would show him what great wife potential she had and then she would tell him about this wonderful, glorious baby. She could picture his face now. Carlos adored children. He would be delighted. Delighted enough to divorce Esther and make an honest woman of Maxine? Maxi thought so. She couldn't help but imagine the look on Esther Russo's face when she found out about this child. She rubbed her tummy protectively and silently thanked the little miracle that was growing inside her: this baby would make all her dreams come true.

Chapter Forty-One

Jimmy was back. He was ten days late, but finally he was home. Jasmine didn't ask him about his 'business'. She'd learned her lesson in the Seychelles and she wouldn't go there again. On the surface things were good between the newlyweds. Jimmy was being sweet and attentive. Perhaps *too* attentive. He'd taken her shopping around Muelle Ribera this morning and encouraged her to go mad in Gucci, Lanvin and Jimmy Choo even though she'd insisted she didn't need anything. 'Credit Crunch. What Credit Crunch?' he'd laughed as he flexed his platinum card. Jasmine had cringed. Guilt money, she'd thought. They were papped at The Sinatra Bar enjoying a bottle of champagne together, and to the world they must have looked like the picture of romance. And yet, something was wrong. Jasmine felt uneasy around her husband. He was being a sweetheart, but she couldn't trust him. Every time she looked at his handsome face she could see the monster lurking beneath his skin.

Jimmy seemed to sense her distrust and reacted by smothering her with affection. He wouldn't let go of her hand; he kept kissing her; he told her he loved her approximately once every minute. It was exhausting. Jasmine couldn't lean forward to pick up her handbag without him rubbing himself against her bum. Ugh! It was beginning to turn her stomach. It was nice to be desired, but there was nothing attractive about this level of desperation. The more he pawed at her, the less she enjoyed his touch. Physical attraction had always been such a big part of their relationship, and if that went … God, if that went, what would be left?

Jimmy would become no more to Jasmine than a means of escaping her past. She hadn't married him as a meal ticket to a better life but … but … if she stopped wanting him, stopped desiring him, what more would he be? Last night, when they'd made love, something had been missing. Jasmine's body had refused to react to Jimmy's touch and she'd found herself wishing it was over. She'd slept with him to keep him happy, because that was what a wife was supposed to do. She'd given him what he wanted and now he was buying her shoes. And what did that make Jasmine? A gold-digger at best and at worst? Jasmine felt wretched. At worst, she was no better than Cynthia: a common whore.

Now they were on their way to see Luke Parks's new yacht.

'It cost him over a million euros,' Jimmy told Jasmine excitedly as they walked towards the marina, hand in hand. 'It's going to be fucking amazing, babe.' He was obviously looking forward to the party. Jasmine was not. She hadn't seen Madeleine since the wedding. The woman was always so vile to her.

The yacht was docked in Puerto Banus and the paps had turned out for the event. Jasmine smiled politely when they called her name, but she didn't put on her usual show. Her heart wasn't in it. Lately she had been niggled by a feeling that there must be more to life than this – the shopping, the clubs, the magazine shoots, the paparazzi. What was the point of it all? What was the point of Jasmine Jones? She was famous for what, exactly? Her boobs? Her choice of husband? It was all so empty. She had to do something about her singing career soon.

Maybe she was just churned up about finding her birth parents. She hadn't heard from Grace yet and she was getting jumpy. It was such a huge deal. Chances were that Grace wouldn't find out anything, but there was a tiny flicker of hope that one day soon Jasmine would know where she came from. Just thinking about it gave her butterflies in her stomach.

Jasmine climbed aboard the yacht and accepted a glass of bubbly from the waitress who greeted them.

Jimmy sucked in his breath. 'What I wouldn't do for a bit of kit like this,' he said. 'Honest, Jazz, I'm going to buy us one of these before the end of the summer.'

'Can we afford it?' Jimmy earned a fortune but they'd already bought the villa this year and a million euros was a lot of money, even to the Joneses.

'Not yet, darling, but I'm working on it.' Jimmy winked at her. 'I have plans, baby. Big plans.'

Again, Jasmine worried about the 'business' Jimmy was involved in. She hoped it wasn't anything dodgy. She'd been around enough dodgy deals in her lifetime – her family didn't know any other way of earning money, after all. The last thing she needed was Jimmy up to his neck in it. But she knew better than to push the subject. Anyway, now wasn't the time.

'Jimmy! Jasmine! Good to see you,' said Luke Parks. He was wearing a white linen suit and a smug grin. 'Isn't she gorgeous? She's called Madeleine, of course. The wife would've killed me if I'd called her anything else.'

He swept his hand around to indicate the opulent yacht. It was, Jasmine conceded, lovely, in a James-Bond-set kind of way. And it was enormous.

'Let me give you a guided tour,' offered Luke. 'This is the deck, obviously.

It's solid mahogany, naturally. With the sunbathing area, the hot tub, the bar, and all that equipment stuff that the crew deal with. In here ...' They followed him inside. 'The lounge area. Home cinema, surround-sound speakers, working fireplace. All controlled by one remote.'

Jasmine took in the plush cream leather sofas, the plasma screen and the sheepskin rugs.

'... and the kitchen. We have a chef.'

Gleaming high-gloss units, state-of-the-art appliances and Corian work surfaces.

'Down here are the bedrooms,' Luke continued, taking them down a spiral staircase. 'The master suite has a water bed, a plasma screen, surround-sound speakers and an en suite of course. Then we have the second bedroom, which is a bit less grand but still pretty plush and then over here, out of the way, we have the crew's rooms. They have bunk beds but they don't seem to mind.'

'It's fan-fucking-tastic, mate,' drooled Jimmy. 'You've got great taste, man. Great taste.'

'I know,' Luke said smugly.

Jasmine hated how all the boys fawned over Luke Parks as if he was some kind of superhero. She thought he was an idiot.

They made their way back upstairs and on to the deck which had now filled up with their friends. Jasmine kissed Crystal warmly and patted Cookie's ever-expanding bump affectionately. Then the air temperature seemed to drop a couple of degrees as Madeleine Parks wafted into view wearing a see-through Pucci kaftan over her bikini. She trod on Jasmine's toe in her wedged sandals but pretended not to notice.

'Girls,' she sneered. 'Glad you could make it. Wonderful, isn't she, our Madeleine?'

'It's a beautiful boat,' said Cookie timidly. 'You're really lucky.'

'It's not a boat, Cookie,' Madeleine scolded her. 'It's a yacht. And luck has nothing to do with it. Luke and I have worked very hard to achieve our lifestyle. You should look and learn, girls. Look and learn.'

Madeleine paused, and eyed Jasmine quizzically. 'You're not pregnant too, are you, Jasmine?' she asked with fake innocence.

'No,' replied Jasmine, blushing. 'Whatever makes you say that?'

'Oh, I don't know. You just look even plumper than usual. Oh well, my mistake. You've just put on weight. Right, I must go. We have some very *important* guests here today.' And in a haze of turquoise Pucci pattern she was gone.

'Agh! She makes me so angry!' said Crystal. 'Why does she always have to do that?'

Chrissie turned to Jasmine. 'You look as perfect as you always do, Jazz. You haven't put on an ounce of weight and she's just a jealous old bitch.'

Jasmine grinned. 'I know that, Chrissie. Honestly, I'm getting used to it. I'd start worrying if she didn't feel the need to insult me. Oh look, there's Maxi and Carlos. I'll go and say hello.'

'Yes,' deadpanned Crystal. 'You go and talk to the *important* guests. We know our place, don't we Cookie?'

Cookie nodded and smirked.

'Oh, I didn't mean it like that! I'll be back in a minute.'

'Yeah, yeah,' replied Crystal sarcastically. 'We know you've dumped us for Maxine de la Fallaise. We've heard how you two are joined at the hip these days.'

Jasmine felt herself blushing again. Were her friends really insulted by her new friendship? 'I'm sorry, girls, I didn't mean to—'

Chrissie interrupted her. 'Jazz, I'm pulling your leg, you daft cow. Go and say hello to your mates. We're not going anywhere.'

Maxine had dressed the part. She was wearing navy-blue shorts with gold sailor buttons, a red and white striped vest and a heavy, linked gold chain. Very nautical, but nice. She was always so immaculately turned out. Maxine was talking to (or, at least, being talked at by) Luke Parks while Carlos had his hand gently on the small of her back. She was sipping what looked like a fresh orange juice. She must be detoxing, Jasmine thought. She'd never seen Maxi turn down a glass of bubbly before.

Maxine spotted her friend approaching and backed away from Luke Parks, leaving poor Carlos to listen to him alone.

'Hi babes,' said Maxine, kissing her warmly. 'God that man is a bore, isn't he? He has just told me every detail of his groin operation. Honestly, it's left me with images in my head that will haunt me for ever!'

Jasmine giggled. 'Not drinking?' she asked, nodding towards the orange juice.

'No, I'm on a health kick. Thought it was time to give my liver a break.' And then she stopped suddenly, and smiled. 'Oh, what the hell! I'm going to burst if I don't tell someone soon.' She leaned in towards Jasmine and whispered in her ear. 'I'm pregnant.'

Jasmine almost dropped her glass. 'Oh, that's brilliant! Congratulations!'

'Shhh! Keep it down. It's a big secret. No one else knows. Not even Carlos.'

'You haven't told Carlos?' whispered Jasmine. 'Why not?'

'I'm going to announce it over dinner tomorrow. I can't wait. He is going to be sooo happy.'

Afternoon turned into evening. The sun set on the horizon as canapés were nibbled, endless glasses of champagne were sipped and a local Spanish band played flamenco music under the stars. The only disruption came when Luke and Madeleine smashed their bottle of champagne against the side of the yacht and announced grandly, 'We name this ship *Lady Madeleine!*' Everybody clapped politely and Crystal muttered, 'Lady Muck, more like,' a little too loudly. That caused a ripple of laughter across the deck which, in turn, caused Madeleine to ask, 'What's the joke?'

'You are, love!' Chrissie whispered.

'Shush, Chrissie, she'll throw you overboard if she hears you,' warned Jasmine. But Crystal was too drunk to care.

Jasmine noticed that the atmosphere had started to turn from polite and well-mannered to downright lairy. As soon as the band finished the boys – Jimmy, Calvin, Paul and Luke – took over the microphone and launched into a terrible rendition of 'Born to be Wild'. It made Jasmine and Maxi laugh until they were doubled over with hysterics. 'It's just as well they're good at kicking a ball around,' laughed Maxi. 'Because they sure as hell were never going to make it as rock stars.'

And then suddenly, a stumbling Crystal had grabbed the mike and was bellowing, 'Come on, girls! Get your butts up here! Cookie! Jasmine! Oi, you, Maxine! Come and join me!'

'Oh, what fun!' squealed Maxine. 'I love karaoke.'

And before Jasmine could stop her she'd run off to join Chrissie on stage. And she wasn't even drinking! Now Chrissie was dragging poor Cookie on to the stage too, despite her protestations.

'Jasmine Jones, get your arse up here right now!' demanded Crystal. She was loud at the best of times but with a microphone in her hands she was lethal. The entire party seemed to have stopped talking and turned to stare at Jasmine.

'Go on, babes! Show them what you can do!' Jimmy shouted his encouragement.

Jasmine could feel her cheeks burning with embarrassment. She loved singing. She was good at it. But until now it had been her secret. She'd never actually sung in public before. What if she was kidding herself? What if everyone laughed at her?

'Well, I'm not making a fool of myself,' sniffed Madeleine.

'No one's asking you to,' retorted Chrissie, forgetting that she had a microphone in front of her.

'Stupid little tarts,' Jasmine heard Madeleine mutter.

People were still staring expectantly. Jasmine had no choice. She put down her champagne glass and walked nervously on stage. 'What are we singing?' she whispered to Chrissie, who seemed to be in charge.

'The Spice Girls, of course,' hiccupped Crystal. 'I was their number-one fan when I was a kid.'

Jasmine rolled her eyes. It wasn't exactly her kind of music. 'OK, what song?'

'Wannabe!' announced Chrissie into the mike.

'How appropriate!' Madeleine heckled.

It was a disaster at first. None of the other three could hold a tune, and Jasmine was struggling to remember the words (she'd been thirteen the last time she listened to a Spice Girls track). While Chrissie shouted, Cookie mouthed the words silently like a shy first-former at the back of school assembly. Meanwhile, Maxine was far too busy prancing around pretending to be Geri Halliwell to pay any attention to either the lyrics or the melody. But, as she stared out at the sea of smiling faces below, Jasmine found herself enjoying the moment. The band picked up their guitars and started strumming along to the tune. Jasmine relaxed and sang away contentedly. It took a while for her to realise that the others had stopped singing and were staring open-mouthed at her. Crystal handed her the microphone. The crowd were clapping now and although her cheeks were burning with embarrassment Jasmine carried on. She felt her hips start to sway and now she was centre stage, dancing and singing in front of an audience. It felt so damn good! It felt like her spiritual home.

'I really, really, really, wanna zig-a-zig-ah ...'

Jasmine ended the song with a saucy wiggle. The crowd went wild. And then Chrissie, Cookie and Maxi were all over her.

'I had no idea you could sing like that, Jazz,' Crystal enthused.

'That was amazing,' agreed Cookie.

'I'm going to book you for Cruise,' added Maxi.

As she stepped off stage and made her way back towards her table, everybody congratulated her; they were patting her on the back and telling her how brilliant she was. And when Carlos Russo sought her out and told her what a beautiful 'instrument' she had, Jasmine thought she would burst with pride. 'We should talk,' he suggested. 'I know people who could help you. I think you could be very good indeed.' Maybe her dreams of becoming a singer could come true.

'You were fucking amazing, princess,' slurred Jimmy drunkenly. He planted a slobbery kiss on her lips, squeezed her right breast and then slumped in a heap on the floor. She stepped over him and took a sip of her champagne. Nothing could ruin this moment, not even Jimmy.

She leaned against the railings and stared out at the starry night. Carlos was on stage now, singing one of his dreamy ballads in his velvety-smooth voice. She smiled to herself, feeling happier than she had in weeks. She picked up her bag and checked her phone to see whether Grace had called. She was in the mood for good news. There were no messages from Grace but there was a text message from a withheld number.

It said simply: *Half a million euros by Monday. Or the story breaks. No excuses. Details to follow.*

Jasmine's hands began to shake. She felt the colour drain from her face and began to shiver despite the balmy Spanish air. So he was back. She'd known he would be, somehow. She'd been waiting for him. She knew the game was far from over. And now he wanted half a million euros! How the hell was she going to get her hands on that?

Jimmy staggered to his feet behind her.

'You all right, babe?' he slurred.

'I want to go home, Jimmy,' she said firmly. 'I'm not in the mood to party anymore.'

'Is it good?' asked Maxine hopefully, as she watched Carlos take a mouthful of steak.

He seemed to be having some trouble swallowing and had to take a large swig of water before he could speak.

'Is lovely, chica,' he said. 'A little well done, perhaps, but very nice.'

She watched as he tried to saw through the meat with his knife. Hmm. Yes, perhaps the steaks were a little too chargrilled. Never mind. Even Maxine couldn't burn a salad and the important thing was that she'd done her best. At least the oven chips were a success.

'What is all this for?' asked Carlos, once he'd eventually managed to swallow his next mouthful. 'I thought we decided you were not to cook.'

Maxine took a deep breath. She was excited about telling him the news, but a little bit nervous too. It was such a big deal – telling a man he was going to be a father. Even if the man in question had been a father four times before. What the hell. It was now or never.

'I have some very exciting news,' she announced.

Carlos looked up at her and smiled patiently.

'We're going to have a baby! Isn't that just the most wonderful thing ever?'

She watched him expectantly. At first Carlos began to splutter, and then he started choking and then he was reaching for his water glass with a look of shock and bewilderment on his face.

'Is a mistake!' he bellowed, when he eventually stopped choking. 'You cannot be pregnant, Maxine!'

Maxine felt herself deflate. This wasn't the reaction she'd hoped for.

'No, honey, it's not a mistake,' she replied. 'I've been to the doctor.'

Carlos went very pale and very quiet. He stared at his plate for the longest time.

'Well, say something, Carlos,' Maxine pleaded. 'Say you're pleased.'

She watched as his face turned from white to bright red. He let out a roar like a wild beast, stood up suddenly and pushed the plates of food off the table so that they smashed on to the floor and splattered the walls. 'You are a whore!' he bellowed. 'Nothing but a cheap whore!'

Maxine was confused. Why was he shouting at her? Why was he so angry? She put her hand out to touch his arm but he batted it away. He wouldn't look in her in the eye.

'Who have you slept with?' he demanded. 'Who have you been seeing behind my back?'

'I don't know what you're talking about, Carlos,' said Maxi, tears burning her eyes, streaming down her cheeks. She was scared. She'd never seen Carlos like this before. 'Honey, it's your baby. Our baby,' she told him through her tears.

'That bastard is no my child,' spat Carlos. 'I have vasectomy. Fifteen years ago. After my Federico was born. I cannot have more children, you stupid bitch!'

Now he levelled his eyes at her and she had never seen such hatred in her life. 'I loved you, Maxine,' he spat. 'I treat you like princess. I take you into my home. And this is how you repay me, huh? You sleep with another man behind my back. You get pregnant with his child. Who is he? Huh? Tell me. Who is this man?'

Maxine couldn't speak. She could barely comprehend what was happening. Carlos had had a vasectomy. Why had he never told her? And how could she be pregnant with someone else's child? An image of Juan's face appeared in her mind but, no, they'd been careful. She'd seen the condom wrapper.

'Carlos, I don't understand how this happened …' She tried to say the right thing, but how could she? What was the right thing to say at a time like this?

'Oh, was immaculate conception?' sneered Carlos.

'No, it's … oh God … I can't explain … I'm sorry, I—'

Maxine watched as Carlos's shoulders slumped, the colour drained once again from his face and he sat down in his chair with a thump. He looked old, suddenly, and tired.

'It does not matter who was the man,' he said. 'Is over, Maxine. You must go.'

'But Carlos, maybe there's been some sort of mistake. Perhaps your vasectomy didn't work. You hear about these things happening.'

'It has worked for fifteen years. Just go. I cannot stand to see you anymore.'

'Please. Let's talk this through.'

'There is nothing to talk about. You betrayed me, woman. That is that. Is finished. Over.' He shrugged his shoulders and shook his head. 'Is shame, Maxine. I thought you were classy. But no. You are just whore like so many others.' He stood up and turned towards the door without looking back at her. 'I go to bed now,' he said as he left. 'When I get up tomorrow you will be gone. Understand? Gone.'

He shut the door behind him and left Maxine hunched on the floor, sobbing. What the hell had just happened? How could the baby not be his? She kept thinking about Juan and their night together but it just didn't make any sense. They'd been careful. She'd been so drunk the details of what had happened were sketchy. She tried as hard as she could to remember. They'd kissed in the car on the way back to his apartment, and then in the lift and then, she remembered, they'd made love up against the wall in the hall and then, later, much later, she remembered being in bed with Juan and they'd made love again but much more slowly this time ... Oh Jesus, they'd had sex twice. It was only now that she realised her terrible mistake. They'd had sex twice but there had only been one condom wrapper on the floor. Holy shit! She wasn't carrying Carlos's child; she was carrying his grandchild!

Chapter Forty-Two

'So, Miss Jasmine, do I have some great news for you!' announced Blaine as he entered the living room, licking his lips gleefully.

Jasmine was curled up on the sofa after dinner, trying to read a book to take her mind off her problems. Blaine threw his enormous bulk down next to her and took the book out of her hands.

'Blaine, I was enjoying that,' she complained, although it wasn't strictly true. She wasn't really able to concentrate on anything tonight. Her mind kept wandering back to the problem of getting hold of half a million euros by Monday.

'Listen, Jazz, this is good stuff,' he insisted. 'We've had an offer from *Playboy*. A *big* offer. They want you to pose naked.'

Jasmine looked up, interested. *Playboy*? She'd never done that. They paid well. Really well. Her mind raced.

'She's not doing it,' stated Jimmy bluntly from his chair in front of the TV where he was watching some old Clint Eastwood movie.

'Jim, I'm talking to your wife here,' said Blaine. 'About *her* career. Does she have a say in which team you sign for? I don't think so. So butt out.'

'Well you're wasting your breath because she's not fucking doing it, all right? Are you, Jazz?'

It was more of a warning than a question. Jasmine was thinking hard. She'd pretty much decided to ease off on the glamour work. She wanted to pursue her singing career instead. It was what Jimmy wanted, too. He'd made that very clear. But circumstances had changed. She needed money and she needed it fast.

'How much are they going to pay?' she asked, tentatively.

'It doesn't matter how much they're going to bloody well pay,' Jimmy shouted, standing up. 'You're not doing it.'

'They've offered half a mill, but I reckon I can get more. It's just an opening offer,' said Blaine, ignoring Jimmy's tantrum.

'Pounds?' asked Jasmine, interested now.

'Yes, pounds. I can squeeze them for seven hundred and fifty thousand, easy.'

Jimmy stood facing them with his hands on his hips. 'This conversation is a waste of time. My wife does not pose naked, OK?'

Jasmine could see that his veins were pulsing again, but with Blaine sitting beside her she felt safe. Jimmy wouldn't lose it in front of their manager.

'What if I didn't do full frontal?' she asked. 'What if it was a more arty shot?'

Blaine nodded. 'It's a possibility. There's a lot to discuss. All I know is that they want you on the beach here, in Spain.'

'Is nobody listening to me?' demanded Jimmy, stamping his foot. 'She's not doing it and that's final!'

'Jimmy,' said Jasmine, calmly. 'Loads of big names have done *Playboy*. They do some really tasteful stuff. Don't they, Blaine?'

'They do.'

But Jimmy was having none of it. 'You'll pose for *Playboy* magazine over my dead body, do you hear me? Over my dead body!'

'That could always be arranged,' smirked Blaine.

Jimmy stormed out of the room and slammed the door behind him.

'Hangover,' said Blaine. 'That boy just can't hold his drink.'

'Give me a minute,' said Jasmine. 'Let me talk to him.'

She found Jimmy sulking in the kitchen, opening a beer. 'Hair of the dog,' he muttered.

She took a deep breath. She had decided to ask Jimmy for some money. It was the only way to get the blackmailer off her back. Yes, the *Playboy* offer was good but she needed the money by Monday. She only had a few days.

'Jimmy,' she said a little nervously. 'I don't really want to do the *Playboy* shoot but the thing is ...'

Oh God, how did she put this? She couldn't tell him the truth and she really wasn't very good at lying.

'The thing is, I could do with the money.'

There. She'd said it.

'What do you mean, you could do with the money? You got your share of the wedding dosh, didn't you? And I bought you shoes and dresses yesterday to last you all year.'

'I know, babe, but I'd really like to try and get a record contract and I'll need a voice coach, and a producer and I'll have to hire a studio and none of that comes cheap.'

Jimmy frowned. 'It can't cost that much, can it?' he asked.

Jasmine shrugged. 'It can do. If you do it properly. I want the best people around me, babe. If I'm going to become a singer I want to be a classy singer and class costs, Jim, you know that.'

'So how much do you want?' he asked. She'd played it well so far. Jimmy would do anything to get her to stop modelling.

'Five hundred thousand euros,' she replied as casually as she could manage.

'What?' Jimmy looked at her as if she'd gone mad. 'I can't give you half a million euros.'

'Oh, please. If you don't give me it I'll have to do the *Playboy* shoot.'

'Are you blackmailing me?' asked Jimmy, obviously shocked. He half-laughed, half-frowned as if he didn't quite know how to take her.

'No, babes, don't be silly. I just really need you to help me out, that's all.'

Jimmy shook his head. 'I can't give you it because I don't have it,' he insisted.

'What do you mean, you don't have it?' Jasmine didn't believe him for a second. Jimmy was loaded.

'It's all tied up,' he said. 'In investments.'

'Investments?' Now Jasmine knew he was lying. Jimmy knew more about astrophysics than he did about stocks and shares.

'It's my money. I earned it. It's up to me what I do with it,' he said defensively. 'And I don't have that sort of money spare, OK? If I had it, I'd give it to you, but I don't.'

'And that's your final word, is it?' asked Jasmine, still convinced he was lying to her. 'Because if it is, I'll have to do that shoot for *Playboy*.'

She was playing hardball. She had to. If Jimmy didn't give her the money she was in serious trouble.

Jimmy glared at her. 'No,' he said. 'My final word is this: if you do that shoot for *Playboy*, I will make you sorry.'

Jasmine sensed that the fragile truce between them had been broken. He took a step towards her and pushed his beer bottle up against her throat. It didn't hurt, but the gesture was enough to remind her what her husband was capable of.

'Do you hear me, Jasmine? You take your kit off one more time and you'll wish you'd never been born.'

He stepped away and took a slug of his beer. Jasmine watched him through narrowed eyes. God, she hated him sometimes.

'I hear you,' she replied. 'Loud and clear.'

She turned on her heels and walked out of the room.

'Is that all you want me for?' he shouted after her. 'My money, eh? There's a word for that, Jasmine.'

She ignored him. She was on her own. Jimmy wouldn't help her so she knew what she had to do. She found Blaine sprawled across the sofa, channel-surfing and sharing a packet of crisps with the dog.

'Everything all right with you lovebirds?' he asked, gleefully. He'd probably been eavesdropping again.

'Fine,' snapped Jasmine. She was in no mood for Blaine's warped sense of humour. She needed to talk business. 'Right, this *Playboy* thing. When can they do it? This week?'

Blaine sat up, spilling crisps all over the floor. 'So, you'll do it? Even after what Jimmy said?'

Jasmine nodded. 'I'll do it on the condition they shoot me this week and I want half the money up front the minute the contract is signed. Oh, and I want the contract signed tomorrow.'

Blaine sucked in his breath. 'Jeez, Jasmine, you must have been watching me work. You're turning into a feisty little businesswoman.'

'Yeah, well, get used to it,' she replied. Actually she was quite enjoying this. It gave her a sense of power that she hadn't felt before.

'Don't get me wrong, Jazz. I like it. It turns me on,' Blaine grinned.

'Shut up, Blaine,' she said. 'And there's another condition – if you tell Jimmy I'm going ahead with this shoot I will fire you on the spot, understand?'

'Loud and clear, hot stuff, loud and clear.' He rubbed his hands together with excitement.

'Oh, and I'll also tell Lila Rose that it was you who took those pictures of Alisha and Brett. Her PR team will make sure you never work again.'

Blaine feigned shock. 'Who? Me?' he said. 'Would I do a thing like that?'

'Don't give me any of your bullshit,' said Jasmine. 'I know it was you. Nobody else at the wedding was sneaking around trying to catch celebrities with their pants down.'

Blaine opened his mouth to defend himself but he was interrupted by the intercom buzzing.

Jasmine glanced at her watch. It was almost midnight. 'Who the hell is that?' she asked.

Blaine padded to the window and peered out. 'Looks like a white limo,' he said.

The maid knocked on the door. 'Is Miss Maxine,' she said. 'Shall I let her in?'

'Yes, yes, of course,' said Jasmine, confused. What was Maxi doing here at this time?

She walked down the drive to meet Maxine's car. When the driver opened the limo door she spotted her tearful friend in the back, sur-rounded by several Louis Vuitton suitcases. Her dog, Britney, was on her knee, shivering pathetically.

'Maxi, what's going on?

'Oh, Jasmine. I've ruined everything. I'm pregnant and homeless and it's all gone so horribly wrong!'

The driver unloaded the suitcases and helped Maxi out of the car. He bowed his head and said, 'I will miss you, *señorita*. It will not be the same without you.'

Jasmine watched as Maxine squeezed the driver's hand and gave him a sad smile. And then he got back in the limo and drove away. Maxi stood, clutching Britney, surrounded by her cases on Jasmine's drive.

'Carlos kicked me out and I didn't know where else to go,' she said, wiping away a stray tear. 'Can I stay with you tonight?'

'Of course you can. You're always welcome here. But I don't understand. What's happened? Why has Carlos kicked you out?'

'It's a long story,' said Maxine. 'Help me in with these bags, make me a nice cup of tea and I'll tell you all about it.'

Lila watched Charlie 'helping' her mother in the kitchen. It was quite a sight to behold – this huge hunk of a man being bossed around by her tiny little mum. She had him wearing an apron and chopping onions. It was comical. Lila was sure that cooking wasn't part of Charlie's job description but the poor man had no choice. Her mum had taken a shine to him and that meant that, like it or not, he was now part of the family. Charlie had tears streaming down his face from the onions but he did everything her mum asked with polite good humour. Her mum adored him, that was quite clear, and even her dad said that Charlie was a 'bloody nice bloke'.

'He's quite a find,' said Lila to Peter, who was sitting with her at the kitchen table, nursing a glass of red wine. 'Thanks for sorting that out. I feel much safer with Charlie around.'

Peter grinned wickedly. 'I like having him around too. Have you seen those biceps? And when he stripped off to his swimming trunks earlier … Goodness, I didn't know where to look!'

'Peter, you are such a tart.' She slapped his arm playfully.

'It's good to see you smiling. You're feeling much better, aren't you?'

Lila thought about it for a moment. Well, she certainly felt better than she had done recently, that was true. But she was a long way from being happy. There was still an enormous Brett-shaped hole in her heart. She would wake up in the morning and for a split second she would feel normal, and then she would remember what had happened to her life and she'd have to deal with the loss as if facing it for the first time.

Brett had written her a letter, full of apologies, excuses and promises for some non-existent future he had planned. He said he was having treatment for his sex addiction and that she should pity him, as if he were a drug addict or an alcoholic. But Lila didn't pity Brett. She despised him. He'd even had the nerve to ask her to take him back once he was 'in recovery'. The cheek of the man! She'd taken great pleasure in burning the letter. It had been cathartic. She'd felt as though she was purging herself of some evil influence. But, was she feeling better?

'I'm getting there, Peter,' she replied truthfully. 'I'm definitely on the right track.'

'Have you heard about poor Maxi?' Peter asked, raising one eyebrow.

Lila nodded. 'She called me earlier and told me all about it. Poor thing. She's got herself into a real mess, hasn't she?'

'You can say that again! Did she tell you who the father is?'

Lila shook her head. 'But it must have been someone she really liked. Maxi's never been unfaithful before. She's such a loyal person; it's not like her.'

'It's a messy business, infidelity.'

'You can say that again,' smiled Lila ruefully.

'A moment on the lips, a lifetime in the lawyer's office,' Peter continued. 'Talking of which, I hope you're going to take Brett the Bastard to the cleaners.'

'Naturally,' said Lila, sweetly. 'I plan to make his life a living hell.'

'I'm dying to know who Maxine had a fling with. Do you think she'll tell us?'

'It's none of our business, is it? And don't you go grilling her about it, either. She's coming round tomorrow, so be gentle.'

Peter pretended to be offended. 'Kid gloves, Lila,' he said, raising his hands. 'Kid gloves.'

'And Jasmine's coming too, so be nice. I know you don't like her very much.'

'Oh, you're wrong,' said Peter breezily. 'I've changed my mind about her. I'm totally in love with her again now. I mean, she helped save your life so how can I be cross with her?'

'You're so fickle.'

'And anyway, she's Charlie's goddaughter and I can't go getting on his bad side, can I?' Peter shuddered with mock horror. 'That beast would tear me limb from limb.'

'In your dreams,' laughed Lila.

She sat back in her chair and surveyed the scene. Peter was opening another bottle of red wine. Her father was carving a joint of beef and her mother was taking a tray of perfect Yorkshire puddings out of the oven. But it was Charlie she watched for the longest time. He wasn't doing anything special – just pouring gravy into a jug, wiping his hands on his apron, taking the hot tray from her mum, finding her father a sharper knife. She did like having him around. His presence made her feel so safe. And it wasn't just his size and strength that made her feel protected; there was something else. Something she couldn't quite put her finger on. Charlie glanced up and caught Lila's eye. He smiled at her warmly. There was something strangely familiar about his smile and Lila found herself wondering if she'd met him somewhere before, years ago. For a moment she had the sensation that she was about to remember something – it was the same sensation she often had when she first woke up and tried to recapture last night's dream – but then the thought slipped away, out of her reach and disappeared.

Chapter Forty-Three

Maxine felt like shit and when she looked in the mirror she saw that she looked like shit too. There was nothing like crying for two days solidly to give a girl puffy eyes and a blotchy complexion. And the morning sickness wasn't helping matters. All that retching had caused broken veins in her cheeks. This would not do. It would not do at all.

'Pull yourself together, woman!' she ordered her reflection.

Carlos was gone. There was no point in trying to win him back. He was older and more set in his ways than she was and he was stubborn, too. Maxi knew him well enough to know that once he'd made his mind up about something there was no going back. She was a competitive woman, and she never shied away from a fight, but there was no point in trying to change Carlos's mind. It would be a battle she was bound to lose.

Anyway, did she even want him back? The truth was that somewhere, deep inside, she was a little relieved that the relationship was over. She'd thought she was blissfully happy, but if that was true why had she felt so strongly about Juan? Ever since that night in LA there had been doubts. No, it was better this way. Maxine would just have to get on with her life alone.

She placed her hand gently on her stomach. She would have loved to keep this baby, but she had decided it was impossible. Things were just too complicated. There was no point in telling Juan about the pregnancy. What was he going to do about it? He was a kid and they hardly knew each other. Maybe he would have promised to stick by her, but she didn't think that was fair. If Juan had wanted something serious to happen between them he'd have been in touch weeks ago. Telling him about the baby would just be cruel. She'd be backing him into a corner and that wasn't right.

But keeping the baby and *not* telling him about it would be even worse. That would be downright evil. What would happen eighteen years down the line when Junior wanted to know who Daddy was? The truth would have to come out eventually and then everyone's lives would be messed up. And how would it make Carlos feel to find out that she'd been knocked up by Juan? There was only one solution. This was Maxine's problem and she would deal with it on her own. She'd already made the arrangements.

Maxi had a long, hot shower and pampered herself with beauty products. She dried and styled her hair and then applied her make-up even more carefully than usual. She pulled on her favourite Roberto Cavalli tiger-print bikini and a matching kaftan, and finished the outfit with her highest-heeled mules. There, Maxine was back and ready to take on the world – whatever it might throw at her.

'Switz-swoo!' called Blaine Edwards as she appeared on the terrace. 'You are looking mighty fine today, Maxine.'

She smiled at him warmly even though he was the most vile man she'd ever laid eyes on. Jimmy ignored her. He was like that, she'd realised over the past couple of days. A rude little asshole. She didn't like the way he spoke to Jasmine, either.

'You do look lovely,' agreed Jasmine. 'Are you feeling better today?'

'Oh, I'm absolutely tip-top, hun,' announced Maxi breezily. 'Shall we go and visit Lila?'

'Yes, I'm ready,' said Jasmine, picking up her bag.

'Remember you've got that, erm, meeting later, Jazz,' said Blaine. 'Don't be late. We're leaving here at one.'

'What meeting?' Jimmy looked up from behind his newspaper and scowled.

'I've just lined up an interview for her this afternoon,' replied Blaine. 'Some slushy women's magazine stuff. "Why I love my Jimmy, by Jasmine Jones" or some such bullshit.'

'Oh,' said Jimmy, going back to the sports pages. 'That's fine then.'

Maxine noticed that Jasmine and Blaine shared a conspiratorial look and sensed that they were up to something behind Jimmy's back. It was interesting to see that she wasn't the only one keeping secrets.

'This is ridiculous,' said Maxine as they climbed into Jimmy's sports car. 'We're only going next door.'

'I know,' agreed Jasmine. 'But can you imagine what would happen if we tried to walk past that lot?'

She drove out of the gates and had to beep her horn to move the crowds of paparazzi still camped outside Lila's place.

'You'd think they'd be getting bored by now,' said Maxi. 'Haven't they got something better to do?

'It'll be someone else next week with a bit of luck.' Jasmine drove the twenty metres between the properties very slowly.

'Don't worry about running over their toes,' scoffed Maxine. 'It would serve them right.'

'It's tempting. But I can't afford the lawsuits,' laughed Jasmine.

Charlie was at the gate waiting for them. He ushered the car through and then stood guarding the entrance from the press while the electronic gates swung closed. He glared at the paps menacingly.

Maxine let Jasmine embrace her godfather first and then kissed him hello herself. God, he was a hunk. She could feel his muscles rippling under his thin T-shirt. Lila must certainly be feeling a lot safer with this guy standing guard. It must be like having Russell Crowe as Gladiator on the payroll.

'Lila's by the pool,' he told them. 'I'll be down in a minute once I've had a few words with this lot. I caught one of them trying to climb the wall again earlier so I just need to remind them what will happen to them if I catch them pulling a stunt like that again.' He cracked his knuckles and strode purposefully back towards the gates.

They found Lila lounging under the shade of a parasol in a black bikini. Maxine hated to notice it after everything Lila had been through, but her friend's body looked good. There was nothing like the heartbreak diet to shed a few extra pounds. And all that swimming had left her remarkably toned. She suited being tanned, too.

'Good morning, ladies,' Lila smiled up at them. 'Thanks for coming round.'

'Well, you look much better than last time I saw you,' announced Maxine, flopping on to a sun lounger next to Lila.

'I'd just come out of a coma last time you saw me,' Lila reminded her dryly. 'Anyway, enough about me. How are you bearing up, Maxi?'

'Me?' Maxi shrugged as casually as she could. 'I'm absolutely fine. Carlos wasn't the right man for me anyway. It's all for the best.'

'Is she faking?' Lila asked Jasmine, as if Maxine wasn't there.

Jasmine shrugged. 'She woke up in this sunshiny mood this morning.'

'I'm telling you both, I'm fine, OK?' Maxine insisted. The more she said it out loud, the more it might become true.

'And what about the baby?' Lila looked at her, concerned.

Please don't pity me, thought Maxine. She could just about cope with this situation as long as her friends didn't feel sorry for her. The moment she saw pity in their eyes it made her want to cry. Jasmine was watching her closely too, waiting for a reaction.

'It's all sorted,' she said.

She knew they were gagging to know all the juicy details of her affair but there was no way Maxine would spill the beans. Nobody could ever find out about Juan. And so she changed the subject.

'So, I was thinking, Lila, you should see my therapist, talk through what's happened with Brett. The woman's a genius. You should fly her over from London for a couple of sessions.'

'Yeah, maybe,' said Lila. 'And you could probably do with talking to her too.'

Maxine was relieved when Peter appeared from the house, carrying a tray of drinks. She didn't want to talk about her problems. It was so much easier to concentrate on someone else's troubles.

'Well hello there, gorgeous girlies!' announced Peter, placing the tray on the table with a flourish.

He air-kissed Maxi and Jasmine and then stood back with his head on one side, staring at Maxine.

'What?' she asked.

'No, no, it's nothing,' he said.

'What?' she demanded.

'Oh, I don't know. It's just you look, well, glowing, I suppose. You must have that blooming mother-to-be thing going on. Oh, Maxine, please tell us who the father is. We're all dying to know but Lila and Jasmine are too polite to ask.'

'It's nobody you know,' said Maxine firmly. 'Now, can we drop it please?'

They sat in an uncomfortable silence for a few moments and then Maxi tried again to change the subject.

'I'm going to have a few treatments tomorrow if anybody fancies joining me,' she said breezily.

'What sort of treatments?' asked Lila.

'Oh just a bit of gentle Botox and a few fillers,' she said.

Maxine praised the lord of cosmetic procedures on a daily basis for the invention of Botox. Without it she felt sure she would never have got away with lying about her age for so long. She'd been thinking for a while now that Lila could do with a little 'help' too and hoped that she'd take Maxine up on her offer of a girlie day at the beauty clinic.

'Do you think I need anything done?' asked Jasmine, wide-eyed.

Maxine stared at Jasmine's perfect, line-free face and laughed out loud.

'No!' she, Lila and Peter said in unison.

'Well, I'm not sure if I approve of it,' said Lila. 'It's like cheating.'

'Cheating? Don't be ridiculous!' scoffed Maxi. 'It's just giving nature a helping hand. Anyway, you deserve a makeover after everything you've been through.'

'Well, I'm not having Botox, but I might be persuaded to have an anti-ageing facial or two.' Lila seemed to be warming to the idea. 'Those pictures in the paper haven't exactly made me feel good about myself.'

Maxine seized the idea with both hands. Here was a project to take her mind off her problems. Yes, she would help Lila transform herself like a phoenix rising from the flames. It would be brilliant. Lila could get a new hairstyle, a new wardrobe, maybe even a new face. She was sure she could persuade Lila to have a little jab or two. And then, once the transformation was complete, Maxi would throw her a huge 'Fuck you, Brett Rose' party at Cruise. It was an inspired idea. She could just see the five-page spread in *Marie Claire* now – 'Lila Rose's amazing new look'.

'Do you think I could do with a little work?' asked Peter, pulling his skin back so that he looked like the Bride of Wildenstein. 'Tell me, honestly, have I let myself go? Is that why I can't find a man?'

'You can't find a man because you're already married,' Maxine laughed. 'You've been like a wife to Lila for years.'

'It's true,' sighed Peter. 'Oh, Lila, darling, do you think, while you're having your Botox, you could ask the doctor to just squeeze in a quick sex-change operation at the same time? Then we could both be happy.'

Lila hit him over the head with a rolled up beach towel. 'I'm not having Botox,' she assured him. 'Or any other surgery!'

Charlie checked that the women and Peter were chatting safely by the pool and then continued his rounds. He waved at Eve and Brian sitting on the terrace as he passed and then headed down to the private beach. It felt good to have a purpose in life again. This job made him feel proud. He was earning good clean money and doing something worthwhile in looking after Lila Rose. God, she really was some woman. The more he got to know her the more Charlie admired her. She was clever and funny and kind. Christ, if Charlie was honest he had the biggest schoolboy crush on her. He dreamed about her at night and, even during the day, he found himself having little fantasies about her. He'd watch her sunbathing and imagine how it might feel to stroke that tanned skin, pull his fingers through that dark hair, or kiss those rosebud lips. He had to stop it. What if she noticed him staring? It would freak her out and then he'd get fired. And he really didn't want to lose this job. The truth was he needed Lila more than she needed him.

Charlie tried not to think about what was going on back home. Since he'd broken his mobile he'd called Gary a couple of times from a payphone but there had been no news about Nadia's whereabouts. At least Frankie Angelis couldn't hassle him anymore. He'd felt himself getting weak. He'd been tempted to do that job for the old man. No, it was good that he'd got away. The funny thing was that Lila was protecting Charlie, just as he protected her. This place was like a safe house for him. He had just seven days left before the Russian's deadline ran out, but surely even Dimitrov couldn't touch him here. He strode across the empty beach and checked the sea for bathers. Sometimes the photographers tried to swim ashore. Tourists, too; he'd had to shoo a couple of Japanese kids in a rubber dinghy away the other day.

Today the sea was quiet and still and there was no sign of any intruders. Charlie climbed back up the steps towards the house, enjoying the heat of the midday sun on the back of his neck. Now he checked the far side of the property, out of sight of the swimming pool and the terrace. There was a tall wall covered in thick ivy to his right, which shielded the house from its next-door neighbour. Bushes and palm trees had been planted alongside to increase privacy. As he passed, Charlie heard the sound of a branch snapping. If that was those fucking photographers again ...

Wham! Charlie felt a strong arm grab him around the neck and drag him into the bushes. He lashed out with his arms and tried to turn his head to see who was holding him but the man was even bigger and stronger than he was. He had Charlie's head in a vice-like grip. Suddenly, Charlie felt the cold steel of a gun against the back of his head. What the fuck was going on? How had he let this happen? He felt the blood drain from his face.

'Message from my boss,' the man spat in his ear with a heavy Russian accent. 'You have one week left to find Nadia. Or no one is safe, understand? Not you, not your precious Jasmine, not Lila Rose either. An eye for an eye, a girl for a girl ...'

The man strengthened his grip on Charlie's neck until he could barely breathe. He could hear gurgling noises coming out of his mouth and see stars in front of his eyes. The gun pressed against his skull.

'One week, Charlie Palmer,' growled the Russian. 'One week and then ...'

Charlie heard the click of the gun's safety catch.

'Game over.'

He had made himself perfectly clear. The enormous man threw Charlie on to the ground like a rag doll and kicked him in the kidneys for good measure. Charlie found himself on all fours, with the world spinning around him. By the time he'd managed to catch his breath and struggle to his feet, the man had vanished.

Chapter Forty-Four

Juan kissed his mother on both cheeks and handed her the flowers he'd brought for her.

'Oriental lilies, my favourite! How clever of you to remember, Juan,' she gasped, as if they were a complete surprise.

The fact was he brought her the same bunch from the same florist every week, and every week they went through this ritual. His mother was nuts. LA had got to her after all these years. His dad said she'd gone native. Unlike his father, who still had a strong Spanish accent, Esther had almost lost all trace of hers. She was American now, and proud of it. Esther Russo could host a dinner party, 'do' lunch, gossip and bitch with the best of the Hollywood wives. She looked the part too, in her cream slacks, ivory silk blouse and expensive diamonds. Her thick, dark hair was swept back in a chignon. She looked good. Juan wondered if she'd had another little procedure without telling him.

'What on earth are you wearing, Juan?' his mother tutted, trying to tuck his black T-shirt into his low-slung jeans. 'In my day men wore suits and they shined their shoes.' She glared at his battered sneakers as if they were an affront to her polished marble floor. 'And is that another tattoo?' she gasped, rolling back his sleeve to reveal the shapely form of a naked woman.

The tattoo was a tribute to the gorgeous Maxine. He'd had it done as a reminder of their night together.

'Really, Juan, and to think you used to be an altar boy. What would Father Gonzales say? He must be turning in his grave!'

Juan grinned at her mischievously and kissed her cheek. 'It's just as well I have you, Mom, to keep me on the straight and narrow.'

Juan noticed that Esther smiled despite herself. He could always get around his mother with a kiss and a compliment.

'Come see,' she said. 'I've had some work done on the garden. Walk with me.'

Juan took his mother's arm and led her out into the back garden. They walked arm in arm through the lush tropical gardens, past the infinity pool and up the steps to the gazebo. The maid had iced tea waiting for them on the table, laid out on a crisp white linen tablecloth. It made Juan smile. His mother always had everything just so. She spent her entire life making sure that her clothes, her house and her lifestyle appeared completely flawless to the outside world. It must drive her crazy that she couldn't keep her kids so neat and tidy, Juan thought.

'So, you've heard your father's news, I trust?' asked Esther, raising an over-plucked eyebrow.

Juan shook his head. 'I haven't spoken to Dad for weeks,' he said. 'He's busy, I'm busy, you know how it is.'

The truth was that Juan had not returned his father's calls. How could he? What did he say to the man now that he'd slept with Maxine?

'Tsk,' said Esther. 'A man should never be too busy to speak with his son. Well, it's no surprise, I suppose; he has no family values.'

'So, what's his news?' asked Juan, keen to change the subject. He'd endured years of listening to his mother berate his father and the truth was it bored him now. They were both good people in their own ways.

'Well.' Esther's face lit up and Juan could sense that whatever was coming was a story his mom would enjoy telling. 'You know that young floozy of his?'

Juan flinched. He didn't like his mom talking about Maxine like that. 'Maxine,' he said patiently. 'Her name is Maxine.'

'Whatever.' Esther waved her hand as if this fact was irrelevant. 'She's pregnant! Can you believe it?'

'Pregnant?!' Juan hoped that his mom hadn't noticed the look of utter horror on his face. Maxine was pregnant. She was going to have his father's child. This was terrible news. Juan felt as though he'd been punched in the stomach.

'I know, it's quite a thing, isn't it?' Esther's eyes glinted. 'Because, you see, your father had the snip fifteen years ago. I insisted he got himself done after Federico was born. So, you see, the baby's not his. This precious Maxine of his is nothing but a cheap tart! Carlos has thrown her out, of course. So I guess that's the last we'll be hearing of that one. Good riddance to bad rubbish, I say.'

She was waiting for a response. Juan opened his mouth to speak but couldn't find any words. His mind was racing.

'So, let that be a lesson to you, Juan. Sure, have your fun, sow those wild oats, but when the time comes to find yourself a wife, choose wisely, my boy. Find yourself a nice Catholic girl with high morals. That's where your father went wrong; he didn't know a good thing when he had it. If he'd stayed with me ...'

Esther was still talking but Juan wasn't listening. He was a million miles away.

'How do I look?' asked Lila, glancing up at Maxine nervously.

'A bit red but otherwise, fine,' replied Maxine. 'It'll take a few days, but you'll have the complexion of a ten-year-old after that. That's the beauty of a chemical peel. Can't believe you wouldn't have the Botox. Next time, I'll persuade you, I promise. But that peel will work wonders and the redness will have settled just in time for your party.'

'What party?' asked Lila. She didn't know about any party.

'The party I've organised for you at Cruise on Tuesday night,' replied Maxine innocently.

'Maxine, this is the first time I've left the house in weeks. I've only just got out of hospital. I can barely get dressed in the morning. I'm not ready to have a party,' insisted Lila. Her friend had gone mad.

'Nonsense. It's exactly what you need. And it's what Brett needs, too – to see you in the papers looking radiant, happy and gorgeous. You've got to show him what he's lost. It's the law. Maybe you should do a 'diss and tell' interview to go with the pics ...'

'But Maxi ...'

'No buts; it's all organised. The invitations were sent out this morning. Everyone who's anyone will be there and you are the guest of honour.'

Lila really wasn't sure she was ready for all this. It was touching that Maxi was taking such an interest in her recovery, especially seeing as she had problems of her own, but it was all moving a bit too fast. She felt safe only at her parents' villa. She wasn't sure she was ready to face the world yet. Just coming here to the beauty clinic had been a big step.

The women were waiting for their nail varnish to dry after their pedicures but otherwise they were done. Their bodies had been scrubbed, massaged and oiled, their faces injected or peeled and their nails filed and painted.

'Right, my nails are dry. Yours must be too. We'd better get a move on or we'll be late for the hairdresser,' announced Maxine.

'The hairdresser?' asked Lila. 'Are you having your hair cut?'

'No, Lila. You are.'

Lila's hand touched her shoulder-length hair automatically. She wasn't sure she wanted her hair cut.

'But I've had my hair like this for years,' she protested.

'Exactly. It's time for a change.'

Lila wasn't sure she could handle any more change. Christ, only a month ago she'd been a married woman of ten years' standing. Now she was single, chemically peeled and about to have her hair chopped off.

'There's a party on Sunday night at Cruise too, if you fancy it,' said Maxine as they got into the back of Lila's chauffeur-driven car. 'Jasmine's coming.'

'No, I think I'd better conserve my energy for Tuesday. So I take it Carlos is letting you keep the club?'

Lila had been worried that losing Carlos would mean that Maxi would lose Cruise. That would have been a tragedy; she'd made such a success of the place this summer.

'Yes, his lawyers called and said that he'd signed all the paperwork over to me. It's pretty amazing, really, considering what I've done to him. He paid for the place; he had every right to sell it from under me. He's a good man really,' said Maxine.

'Are you going to miss him?' asked Lila, watching her friend closely. Maxine was doing a great job of putting a brave face on things but Lila felt sure that she must be hurting pretty badly.

Maxine shrugged and turned away, staring out of the car window. 'We weren't right for each other. Otherwise I wouldn't have let this happen, would I?'

Lila watched as Maxine's hand fell to her stomach.

'And there's no hope of working things out with the baby's father?' asked Lila, gently.

She was longing to know who the father was but Maxine had made it quite clear that she didn't want to share that information. Maxi shook her head solemnly. They sat in silence for a while, each lost in their own thoughts, and then Maxine turned to Lila and smiled.

'So, I guess it's just like the old days again, isn't it?' she said. 'You and me, single young girls around town!'

Lila smiled. 'Yeah, I suppose so. But we're not so young this time. This time we've got wrinkles.'

'I haven't,' scoffed Maxine. 'I've just had them filled, remember?'

Chapter Forty-Five

Jasmine counted and recounted the money, glancing up at the bedroom door every now and then to check she wouldn't be disturbed. It was all there, all five hundred thousand euros of it. She collected the bundles of notes together and placed them neatly into a shoe box, then she locked the box in the safe she kept hidden behind her dresses in the walk-in wardrobe. She was ready for Monday. The blackmailer hadn't been in touch yet, but he would let her know what to do soon enough. She was sure of that.

The important thing was that she'd found a way of getting the money. Christ knows what Jimmy would do when he found out that she'd posed for *Playboy* but that was a problem for another day. She'd shot the campaign on a beach a hundred kilometres away and, for now anyway, Jimmy didn't have a clue. At that moment, she was just relieved to have the money in the safe. She felt sure that this would be the last she would hear from the blackmailer. Surely half a million would be enough to make him go away! And she'd promised herself she'd done her last glamour shoot, too. She'd taken her clothes off for *Playboy* but from now on she was going to concentrate on her real passion – singing. Yes, from now on everything would get better.

She found Jimmy in the living room staring wide-eyed at the TV screen.

'All right, babe?' she asked.

He didn't seem to hear her. He was transfixed. Jasmine looked at the screen. He was watching Sky Sports News. The commentator was saying there was speculation about a buyout at Jimmy's football club and they were showing a picture of the silver-haired Russian man Jasmine had seen Jimmy talking to at their wedding.

'Is that man buying the club?' asked Jasmine.

'I fucking hope not,' muttered Jimmy, pushing past her.

'Where are you going in such a hurry?'

'To make an important phone call,' shouted Jimmy. 'In private!'

The door slammed behind him. Christ! It was like living with an overgrown teenager.

Charlie couldn't sleep. He was like a cat on a hot tin roof. His heart pounded in his head, sweat trickled down his face and nightmare scenarios of torture and murder played like horror movies in his mind. Every leaf that rustled in the breeze made him jump. What the fuck had he done? He was supposed to be protecting Lila and instead he'd put her right in the firing line. And Jasmine, too. He had four days left to find Nadia and then it was game over.

What the hell had he been thinking when he'd reckoned he could leave his old world behind? He'd been born into a life of crime. He couldn't just jump on a plane and escape. Charlie 'The Char' Palmer, brilliant at cleaning up messes – now that was a flaming joke. He couldn't clean up his own mess, could he? He didn't even know where to start.

There was no point in lying here worrying. He had to *do* something. Charlie got out of bed and reached for the new phone he'd bought earlier that day. He called Gary.

'Tell me you've found Nadia,' he barked.

'I can't, boss.' Gary sounded defeated. 'She's disappeared into thin air.'

There was no point in getting back into bed just to stare at the ceiling in a cold sweat. Charlie picked up a torch, let himself quietly out of his apartment and into the garden. He checked the gates. They were firmly locked and most of the paps had slunk off back to their hotels. He shone the light out into the street beyond and noticed that even the die-hard all-nighters were asleep in their cars. He walked around the house. All the lights were off. He thought of Lila, sleeping peacefully in her bed upstairs and shuddered at the thought of the danger he'd put her in. Christ, if anything happened to that woman because of him ... the thought turned his blood to ice in his veins.

He wandered down towards the beach and stared into the darkness. The sea was choppy tonight and the waves crashed angrily on to the shore. He shone the torch across the beach from left to right. Out of the corner of his eye he sensed a movement coming from the direction of Jasmine's property. He thought he saw a shadow disappear quickly behind the fence that separated this private beach from the one next door. Charlie had always prided himself on having nerves of steel, but tonight he was feeling seriously jumpy. The visit from the Russian giant had scared the shit out of him. The truth was, he was bricking it.

It was impossible to hear anything over the sound of the crashing waves, but Charlie was convinced he wasn't alone. He switched off the torch and dropped down on to his stomach. There was definitely someone else there on the beach; he could sense it. Charlie crawled, commando style, through the sand towards the fence and listened intently. No, it was no good; the sea was too angry tonight. The sky was dark, stormy and the stars were hidden by heavy clouds. Charlie could barely see a couple of feet in front of his face. God, he wished he had his gun.

Now he'd reached the boundary and he'd pushed his face up against the fence. He squinted, trying to make sense of the blackness beyond. And then it happened: just the slightest hint of movement about five metres away on the other side of the fence. Holy shit; he was right. There was definitely somebody there. Charlie forgot his fears as adrenalin pumped through his veins. Fight or flight? Charlie was a fighter every time. There was no *good* reason for anyone to be here in the middle of the night. Who was in danger? Was it Jasmine? Or Lila? Whichever it was, Charlie had to protect them. He loved Jasmine as if she was his own daughter. He'd happily kill anyone who touched a hair on her head. And Lila? Well, the truth was he loved her too – but in a very different way.

The fence was too high to scale quietly but Charlie knew every inch of this property. He'd noticed a cracked plank in the fence when he was doing his rounds and had made a mental note to fix it. Now he was glad that he hadn't got around to it. He worked his way along, trying to find the cracked plank and when he came to it he stopped, took a deep breath, and then gave one hard shove with his shoulder. The wood split in two and Charlie was able to squeeze through the gap. He crawled on his stomach back down the beach, towards the intruder. Now he was grateful for the crashing waves. He could take the bastard by surprise. He could make out the shape of a man in front of him. He was sitting on the sand, staring out to sea. Waiting? For what? Charlie wondered. A partner? Was there more than one of them?

Charlie lay still for a minute, just watching his prey. And then, when he was sure the man was alone, he pounced from behind. With one arm he grabbed the man by the neck, and with the other he twisted his arm up behind his back.

'What the fuck do you want?' he hissed into the intruder's ear.

'Wh-wh-what the fu … fuck!' spluttered the man. 'Wh-what's happening?'

The man was slighter in build than Charlie had imagined he would be and he smelled of aftershave.

'Let me go!' the man squealed, struggling in Charlie's grip.

The intruder was not Russian, as Charlie had expected. No, this bloke had a distinct Scottish accent. Charlie felt the adrenalin drain from his body and he let the man go. It was Jimmy. Just Jimmy.

'Jimmy, what the fuck are you doing here at this time of night?' he spluttered. 'I thought you were a . .'

'A what, Charlie?' Jimmy demanded, rubbing his neck. 'What did you think I was?'

'I thought you were a burglar or something,' said Charlie, feeling relieved but a bit stupid to have overreacted.

'You're bloody paranoid, man,' said Jimmy angrily. 'You're not even supposed to be on my property. You work for Lila.'

'I'm just trying to keep everyone safe. What are you doing here anyway?'

'Thinking,' said Jimmy. 'At least I was until you half killed me, you fucker.'

'Sorry, mate,' said Charlie. 'You OK?'

Jimmy kept rubbing his neck. 'No, I'm not bloody OK. You're a nutter, Char. You nearly broke my neck. Christ! I was having a bad enough day before this.'

Charlie patted Jimmy on the back by way of an apology. He didn't particularly like the boy but he didn't wish him any harm.

'You got problems?' asked Charlie, wondering what Jimmy was up to, sitting on the beach in the darkness.

'Yeah, no, oh, I don't know . . .' Jimmy mumbled. He didn't seem in the mood to talk.

'Anything I can help with?' offered Charlie. He owed Jimmy one after what he'd just done and anyway, if Jimmy had problems that would mean Jasmine had problems too, and Charlie couldn't be doing with that.

'No,' said Jimmy quietly. 'It's my business.'

But he didn't sound sure. Charlie could sense that Jimmy had been seriously rattled by something.

Suddenly, a clap of thunder rumbled overhead. Jimmy nearly jumped out of his skin and he clutched Charlie's arm like a teenage girl watching a scary film.

'You are jumpy,' said Charlie. 'You'd better let me know what's going on. You're shit scared about something.'

Big, fat drops of rain started to fall on their heads and the thunder rumbled on. A flash of lightning lit up the sky and for the first time Charlie could clearly see Jimmy's face. The boy looked as if he'd been crying.

'It's nothing,' he muttered, almost to himself.

'Bullshit. Come on, spit it out.'

Jimmy sighed and dropped his head into his hands. The rain was heavy now and the men's clothes were starting to stick to their skins.

'I owe money,' said Jimmy eventually. 'A lot of money.'

'But how?' asked Charlie, confused. Jimmy was a premiership footballer. He earned more in a week than most people earned in a year.

'I got into gambling,' he said. 'We all did – me and the boys. It started as a laugh. We'd go to this casino in Mayfair after we won a game and just bet a few grand. But then it got serious. I started going on my own, even if we lost. I couldn't stop, Charlie. Now I'm fucked.'

'What do you owe? Thousands? Ten of thousands? Hundreds of thousands?'

'More like a million,' muttered Jimmy.

'Jesus! How the fuck did you get into a mess like that?'

'The more I owed the more I risked. I kept thinking my luck would change and I'd win it all back, maybe make a profit.'

'I always thought you were stupid, Jimmy, but this is mental. Everybody knows gambling's a mug's game. And you're still spending. Jasmine came back from the shops with a load of new gear the other day. She said you'd bought it for her. And that ring you gave her is the biggest bit of bling I've ever seen …'

'I know, I know,' wailed Jimmy. 'But I can't let Jasmine know there's anything wrong, can I? I've been putting it all on plastic.'

Charlie sighed. '*She's* not stupid, Jimmy. She *knows* there's something wrong. She keeps saying what a moody little bastard you've been.'

'Does she?' Jimmy asked. He sounded hurt.

'Well, not in so many words, but that's what she means.'

They sat in silence for a while, getting drenched, and then Jimmy said, quietly, under his breath, 'It gets worse.'

'What? The casino want you to cough up?' asked Charlie with a cynical laugh.

Jimmy nodded.

'Well, of course they do, you plonker. They're not a bleeding charity for mentally challenged footballers, are they?' How could Jimmy be so dense?

'The guy who owns the place is pretty heavy duty,' said Jimmy. 'He's been phoning me, demanding his money back. Even when I was on my honeymoon he wouldn't leave me alone and then Jasmine got pissed off with me and we had a fight and … Oh, Charlie, it's doing my head in.'

Charlie knew about casinos and about the men who ran them. They weren't the sort you messed with. Christ, he'd even killed for a couple of them in the past. He was quite aware of what they would do to get their money back.

'Who is it?' asked Charlie, thinking that maybe he'd be able to help – not for Jimmy's sake, of course, but for Jasmine's.

'Actually you know him,' admitted Jimmy nervously. 'It's Vladimir Dimitrov.'

Charlie closed his eyes and felt his heart sink into the sand. Of all the people in the world to piss off, Jimmy had chosen the one man who terrified Charlie. The rain lashed down on them, the thunder rumbled all around and every now and then lightning flashed across the bay.

'You fucking idiot,' said Charlie, coldly. 'You fucking, stupid, ignorant little idiot.'

'I know, I know,' said Jimmy. 'That guy could ruin my career. I saw it on TV earlier. He's buying my fucking football club. He'll have me transferred to the arse end of nowhere.'

Charlie shook his head. Jimmy was even more naive than he'd thought.

'Never mind your fucking career, Jimmy,' he warned darkly. 'He'll hurt you if you don't get that money back to him. Seriously hurt you. Or, worse, he'll hurt someone close to you – like Jasmine. That's how guys like Dimitrov work.'

Jimmy burst into tears. 'I didn't think he was serious,' he wailed. 'I thought stuff like this just happened in gangster films. I thought it was some sort of joke.'

'You thought *what* was a joke?'

'The letter,' whispered Jimmy.

'What letter?' Charlie grabbed hold of Jimmy's T-shirt and pulled the smaller man towards him. 'What fucking letter?'

'The letter I got today that said something bad would happen if I didn't pay up,' sniffed Jimmy pathetically.

Charlie let go of Jimmy's T-shirt and threw him down on the sand. The boy disgusted him. He'd had a warning from Dimitrov, and all he was worried about was his poxy career. Did he not understand what a letter like that meant? As if Charlie didn't have enough to worry about without Jimmy making matters worse. He felt as if life was closing in on him and he had no room to breathe. Every way he turned it seemed like Dimitrov was there, sneering at him, taunting him, threatening to turn everything he cared about to dust.

'Pay him back. I don't care how you get the money. Beg, steal or borrow it from your mates. But pay him back.'

'I don't want my mates to know I'm skint,' sniffed Jimmy. 'I'm ashamed.'

'This is no time to be proud!' yelled Charlie, standing up and towering over Jimmy. 'It's time to save your fucking skin, boy. Yours and Jasmine's!'

Chapter Forty-Six

Jimmy's world was falling apart. Or at least that's how it felt as he walked on to the boat for yet another of Maxine's parties. They were all going to be here tonight, the whole gang, but Jimmy was in no mood to party. His life had turned to shit. Not only did he have the Russian breathing down his neck, demanding money that he simply didn't have, but he'd had Charlie fucking Palmer threatening him too. Where the fuck was he going to get the money, anyway? Christ! He didn't have a clue. What Jimmy needed was a drink. Tonight was a night for a guy to drown his sorrows. Problems could be faced tomorrow. Or at least, some of them could. The thing was, Dimatrov wasn't the worst of Jimmy's problems. What was really eating him up was a niggling feeling that he was losing the one thing that mattered more than anything else – Jasmine.

Jimmy had always been good at games, so he knew when it was 'game over' too. He felt as though the final whistle was about to blow and he had nothing left in the tank to score that winning goal. Och, maybe it wasn't such a big deal. All she did was let go of his hand, but Jimmy felt the insult like a knife to his heart. Her fingers slipped out of his grip as she rushed ahead, leaving him behind. He felt like he was losing her for good. She looked like an angel tonight in her pretty white dress with her hair in ringlets bouncing down her back. He watched her drift further away, into Cruise. He had to strain his neck to keep sight of her. She was kissing all her friends hello, laughing at some in-joke that Jimmy wasn't a part of, smiling at whatever they were saying, clutching their arms ... The place lit up when Jasmine entered a room. Everybody wanted a piece of her, but Jimmy didn't like to share.

He necked a glass of champagne without taking his eyes off his wife. Then he necked another, and another. Oh Christ, now Louis was all over her again. The stupid Portuguese twat was always bothering her, telling her about history and culture and all that boring crap. She said she didn't mind, but surely she was bored shitless.

Jimmy ordered a beer and a whisky chaser from the bar. He sat on a bar stool, drank and observed. His wife was deep in conversation with Louis, their heads almost touching. Jimmy narrowed his eyes and glared at his team-mate. As he watched, a terrible thought crossed his mind. What if Louis wasn't gay? What if they'd all got it wrong? He'd never actually admitted he was a bender and there had never been any sign of a boyfriend. Jimmy began to panic. What if all this girlie, bag-carrying, intellectual crap was just a trick to get into girls' knickers? What if he was trying to get into Jasmine's knickers?

Jimmy emptied his glass and grabbed some more champagne from a passing waitress. Tonight he was going to get wrecked. His life was going tits up and he needed to get so fucking smashed that he'd forget about all the bullshit. He didn't have any money, he had some Russian lunatic on his back and Charlie Palmer was giving him a hard time. And now Jasmine didn't love him anymore. She'd let go of his hand. He noticed things like that. If he wasn't careful she'd be jumping into bed with that Portuguese wanker.

Jimmy slid off the barstool and swaggered towards his wife. Louis looked up and saw him coming and then the cowardly prick whispered something in Jasmine's ear and disappeared off into the crowds.

'Was Louis bothering you, sweetheart?' Jimmy asked, joining the gang.

'No, why would he be?' said Jasmine, all wide-eyed innocence. 'He's just gone to the bar to get me a mojito. Did you know he was getting married, by the way?'

Jimmy frowned. 'Who?'

'Louis, of course. He's marrying a girl he's known since he was thirteen. Sweet, isn't it?'

That threw him. Fuck, he didn't see that one coming.

'See,' giggled Jasmine. 'Told you he wasn't gay. I always knew he was straight. A girl can tell these things, if you know what I mean.'

Flirty little … Argh! So she did fancy him! How else would she have sussed that he was straight? Jimmy felt his nails dig into his palms. He was angry. Angry at everyone. They were all having *such* a good time – Calvin, Cookie, Crystal, Paul, Blaine and that Maxine bitch. She didn't like Jimmy, he could tell. Stupid cow had had the cheek to stay at their place all week, too. Well, she was nothing but a cheap slapper anyway, getting knocked up by some bloke who wasn't her old man. He didn't like Jazz hanging around with her. She was a bad influence. How was he supposed to keep Jasmine in line when her friends behaved like tarts?

Now they were all laughing and joking around. Blaine was telling his stories about all the celebrities he'd 'created' and banging on about what great mates he was with the A-list. He was so full of crap. He thought he was God, the way he lorded it around, but nobody actually liked him; didn't he realise that?

'And so I said to her, "Kylie, baby, if you need a man, look no further. A nice Aussie bloke to keep you warm at night!" She was tempted by the Blainester, I could tell ...'

The fat bastard had plonked himself right in the middle of the group and had his arms draped around Cookie and Crystal. He was wearing his loudest green Hawaiian shirt, which was straining to stay closed over his jelly belly. Ugh! Jimmy downed another glass of bubbly.

'But Kylie had better look out, eh Jazz?' Blaine was still holding court. 'When we launch your singing career no one else will get a look in.'

'Yeah, you were great the other day, Jazz,' said Cookie.

Jimmy had to admit that his missus could certainly sing. And anything was better than her getting her tits out for a living.

'So, you won't be modelling anymore?' asked Paul.

Jimmy glared at his mate. He sounded almost disappointed. Filthy scumbag. Just because his bird was up the duff didn't mean he could go leching at Jimmy's woman.

'Nah, but at least we got *Playboy* under our belts before you hung up the old g-string, eh Jazz?' Blaine was shouting over the music.

'Blaine! Shut up!' Jasmine yelped.

'Oh, oh, oh ... right ... yeah ... wasn't supposed to say anything, was I?' Blaine stammered, glancing up at Jimmy nervously.

Jimmy stared from Jasmine to Blaine in disbelief. Everyone had gone quiet. They could tell something was wrong. Blaine shrugged at him as if to say, 'No big deal' but it was a big deal. It was the biggest deal. Jasmine had lied to him. Defied him. Sneaked off behind his back. Jimmy felt the anger rise in his chest. He looked at his wife, willing her to say it wasn't true, but she wouldn't look him in the eye. Instead, she stood up and ran away from the table.

'Where is Jasmine going?' asked Louis, reappearing at the table. 'I have got her a cocktail.'

Jimmy felt himself explode.

'Nobody buys my wife drinks, except me!' he spat at Louis through gritted teeth. 'Do you understand, you wet fucking bastard?'

And then he grabbed the glass from Louis's hand, threw the contents over his head and ran off after Jasmine.

Jasmine ran towards the ladies' washrooms with her heart pounding in her chest. Time had frozen as the words had spilled from Blaine's big, fat, boastful mouth. She'd known, as he'd started the sentence that he was going to drop her in it, but there was nothing she could do to stop him. It was the feeling you got as the door slammed shut and you realised your keys were left inside. Too late. And then, all she could think was that Jimmy would kill her this time. And she'd fled. Now she barged into the toilets, locked herself in the furthest cubicle and tried to catch her breath. When she heard the door bang open she just knew it was Jimmy.

'Jasmine!' he shouted. His voice was all wrong. It sounded tense and so very, very angry. She was shaking with terror. 'Where are you?' he demanded icily.

She could hear him kicking open all the cubicle doors, getting closer and closer.

'You can't escape, Jazz. I know you're in here.'

She squeezed herself against the wall, shivering with fear, praying that he would go away. She was crying uncontrollably; her whole body shook. And then he tried to open her door.

'Unlock it!' he demanded. 'Let me see you, you lying little bitch!'

He kicked at the door. The wood splintered but it didn't break. Jasmine nearly jumped out of her skin. Then he kicked again, harder this time, and the lock burst open. For a moment they stared at each other, husband and wife.

'I'm sorry, Jimmy,' she sobbed.

But it was too late. He grabbed her hair and pulled her out of the cubicle. He smashed her head against the tiled wall, threw her to the ground, punched her in the stomach, the ribs, the back. Then he dragged her back up to her feet, again by her hair, and started pummelling into her face with his fists. His face was contorted with anger. She felt her cheekbone crack. Blood dripped down her forehead and into her eyes until she could barely make out his angry, ugly, hateful face.

She heard a woman's voice shouting, 'Jimmy, for Christ's sake, stop it!' It was Maxine.

And then all hell let loose. The ladies' washrooms were filled with people. Women were screaming, men were shouting, hands were trying to pull Jimmy off. But still he hit her, over and over again.

'Leave her alone, you animal!' she could hear Louis bellowing.

And then Jimmy was being dragged away from her by strong hands – Louis's hands. She saw Jimmy turn on Louis and start punching him instead. There was nothing Jasmine could do but flee.

She pushed past people in the club, spilling their drinks as she rushed by. She saw the looks of horror on their faces as they noticed her swollen face and blood-splattered clothes. She ran and ran, out of the club, past the paparazzi with their cameras flashing in her face and jumped into a waiting taxi. The Spanish driver stared at her quizzically but didn't ask any questions. As the taxi sped off she glanced behind her and saw Louis running after the car. For a split second she thought about asking the driver to stop and let Louis in but something prevented her. No, he didn't need to get involved with her mess. He was a good man and, besides, he was getting married. The last thing he needed was to get mixed up with Jasmine. No, Jasmine knew what she needed to do and she needed to do it alone.

When Jasmine got back to Casa Amoura she made her way hurriedly to the bedroom. She felt bruised and sick to the pit of her stomach. Her head ached and her cheek throbbed where Jimmy had broken the bone. But something kept her going. She knew now what she had to do.

There was something she had to collect, but she'd have to be quick; she couldn't risk Jimmy coming home and finding her there. She never wanted to see that animal again in her life. Desperately, she pulled designer clothes off their hangers, out of the wardrobe and flung them in crumpled piles on the floor until she found what she was looking for. Her hands were shaking so much that she struggled to unlock the safe. She placed the shoe box of money carefully in one of Jimmy's sports bags, then discarded her dainty white dress on the bed, kicked off her high heels and got dressed in jeans, an old T-shirt, and flip-flops instead. She went to the bathroom, pulled her hair into a ponytail and washed off the blood and smeared make-up, wincing at the sight of her swollen face in the mirror. Her nose looked broken but at least she still had all her teeth. Finally, she took off her wedding ring, engagement ring and eternity ring and placed them on the kitchen table where Jimmy could find them. They'd only been married for six weeks. But she didn't feel sorry. In fact, it felt almost liberating to be letting go.

Jasmine grabbed Jimmy's car keys, picked up the sports bag and her beloved Chanel bag (she would leave everything else but she wasn't going without *that*) and called to Annie to follow her. The puppy trotted happily beside her, out of the house, and jumped into the passenger seat of Jimmy's red car. As Jasmine raced down the drive and out of the gates she didn't bother to look back.

Chapter Forty-Seven

'Where is he?' roared Charlie Palmer.

He was standing in Lila's garden in his boxer shorts. He'd been in bed when Maxine had arrived to tell him what had happened at Cruise.

'He's next door,' explained Maxine. 'Blaine and Louis took him home to try to calm him down and sober him up and … God, I don't know. Louis looked as if he wanted to kill him.'

'And Jasmine? Where's Jasmine?'

Maxine shrugged sadly. She wasn't sure. She followed Charlie into his garden apartment and waited while he pulled on some trousers and a shirt.

'Was she badly hurt?' he asked, his face full of concern.

'Her face was a mess. Her eyes were all puffy and closed and her nose was bleeding and she had a huge lump on her cheek.'

Maxine winced at the memory. She felt sick to her stomach to have witnessed something so disgusting. Jimmy Jones was a monster. She saw a dark shadow cross Charlie's face.

'But she ran out of the club at quite a speed so she must have been OK,' added Maxi, trying to reassure Jasmine's godfather.

'What's going on?' asked Lila, appearing behind them in her dressing gown. 'I saw the lights on down here. Has something happened?'

'Jimmy beat Jasmine up at the club tonight,' explained Maxine, almost sheepishly. She felt ashamed that it had happened at Cruise – responsible even. Her security should have been able to stop something like that from happening but she'd ordered them to stay out front and watch the door. She needn't have worried about gatecrashers ruining the party; she'd invited that scum in herself.

Lila looked horrified. 'Is she OK? Is she here? Can I help?'

'We don't know where she is,' said Charlie darkly. 'The best thing you two can do is go back in to the house, lock the door and stay put. If the buzzer goes, ignore it.'

'Where are you going?' asked Lila. She looked seriously worried.

'To sort things out,' he replied.

'I wouldn't want to be in Jimmy's shoes right this minute,' said Maxine to Lila, as she watched Charlie stride purposefully towards the gate.

Grace's head was spinning as she pulled away from the hospital. She'd just spent several hours with Julie Watts and what the woman had told her was unbelievable – except she *had* to believe it, because it was true. It was all bloody well true. Julie had shown Grace old photographs that had backed up the story. Phew, fact could be so much stranger than fiction!

Now Grace was grateful for the long journey home because it gave her some time to digest what she had heard. Still, she kept shaking her head. The truth about Jasmine's parentage was utterly mindblowing.

'Why are you telling me this?' Grace had asked Julie in grateful disbelief. 'Why me? Why now?'

'I made a choice,' Julie had explained. 'A simple choice. After you left the other day, I was heavily sedated. I lay in bed for hours, drifting in and out of consciousness with all these thoughts and memories floating around my mind. I felt sure that if I'd wanted to let go and just die, there and then, I could have done it. It was as if I had the choice whether to live or die.'

'And you chose life?' Grace had asked gently.

Julie had nodded and smiled. 'I chose life on one condition. No more lies. No more secrets. I've wasted too many years running away from the past. It's time to lay a few ghosts to rest and then I'll be ready to face the future, whatever it holds.'

It was dark and late and the M25 was quiet. Grace got back to Highgate just before midnight. Was it too late to call Jasmine? Grace dialled her number but the line was dead. Strange, she thought. Oh well, she was tired. She'd go to bed, get some sleep and try Jasmine again in the morning.

Charlie strode purposefully past the photographers, pushing them out of his way like skittles, and buzzed the intercom on the gate next door. Blaine Edwards let him in.

'Where is he?' bellowed Charlie, half-running down the drive. 'Where is the little bastard?'

Blaine said nothing, just pointed towards the terrace.

Charlie hurried round the house until he could make out Jimmy's pathetic form, crouched in a ball, with his back against the wall. Louis Ricardo was pacing the terrace, wringing his hands and throwing filthy looks in Jimmy's direction. Charlie shook Louis's hand. He noticed the footballer had a black eye.

'He is scum,' said Louis, nodding towards Jimmy. 'What he did to Jasmine, it is disgusting.'

Charlie nodded, but said nothing. His instincts told him to break the boy's neck but his head told him to hold back. There was no point in being arrested for murder and spending the rest of his days in a Spanish jail. He'd be no use to Jasmine in prison.

When Jimmy saw Charlie approaching he raised his hands above his head and cowered against the wall.

'Don't hurt me,' he begged. 'I'm sorry. It was a moment of madness. It was the drink. It was—'

Charlie leaned down and grabbed Jimmy by the scruff of the neck. He lifted the smaller man off the ground until his eyes were level with Charlie's.

'Where is Jasmine?' he asked slowly.

'I d-d-d ... don't know,' stammered Jimmy. 'She's gone. She's left me.'

'Of course she's fucking well left you, you maggot,' Charlie spat, tightening his grip on Jimmy's shirt. 'What I want to know is where she's gone.'

'I sw-sw-swear, I d-d-don't know.'

Jimmy's breath stank of booze. Charlie felt the boy squirm in his grasp and thought how easy it would be to crush the life right out of him. He was sure he'd killed better men in his time. For a moment he was filled with a rage so furious that he could barely control it. His grip tightened further and Jimmy's face started to turn white and then blue. All the while Charlie stared straight into Jimmy's eyes. The boy was clearly terrified. Charlie could see that he thought he was going to die. He held him there, just long enough for the fear to really set in and then he let go and threw him down on the ground. Jimmy was flailing around, gasping for breath.

'I thought you would kill him,' said Louis to Charlie.

'He's not worth it.'

Louis shook his head. 'No, he is not.'

Charlie patted Louis on the shoulder. He was a good bloke. He obviously cared about Jasmine. Charlie could still see the shock in his eyes from what he had witnessed earlier.

'So Jasmine's been back to the house?' asked Charlie.

Louis nodded.

'Did she leave a note?'

Louis shook his head. 'But she changed her clothes, took the dog, left her wedding ring ...'

Charlie nodded thoughtfully. Jasmine had obviously been thinking clearly when she left. Still, it wasn't safe for her to be out there alone. Not today of all days. He glanced at his watch. It was after midnight. His deadline was up.

'And she also took Jimmy's car,' added Louis. A hint of a smile played on his lips.

'That's my girl,' said Charlie. 'He'll probably miss the car more than he'll miss his wife. Right, I'll go and look for Jasmine. You call the police. Get him done for wife beating. It's the least he deserves.'

Charlie collected his jeep from the drive next door and started cruising the streets of Puerto Banus. He barely knew where to start. Where would Jasmine go? She wasn't with Maxine, so maybe she'd gone to Crystal's place. He screeched up outside Crystal and Calvin's villa and banged on the door. Calvin opened the door. He could see Chrissie standing in the hall with her mobile phone lodged between her shoulder and her ear. She shrugged at Charlie and shook her head.

'She's been trying to call Jazz for an hour, but the line's dead,' explained Calvin.

Charlie just nodded and then jumped back in the jeep. This was no time for polite chit-chat. It was the same story at Cookie and Paul's hotel; they'd tried Jasmine's number but couldn't get through. Charlie drove for hours, crawling along endless empty streets, desperately searching for Jimmy's bright-red car, hoping to catch a glimpse of Jasmine's long, dark hair. It was a Sunday – well, Monday now – the early hours of the morning. The bars and clubs had already closed up. Other than the odd drunken straggler, staggering back to their hotel, the streets of Puerto Banus were deserted. Charlie checked every hotel in the area but Jasmine hadn't checked into any of them. Then he headed towards the centre of Marbella instead. He scoured the old town for signs of her, but she wasn't in any of the hotels there either; her favourite bars were all closed and she was nowhere to be seen.

By the time Charlie gave up his search it had been light for a couple of hours and the German tourists were already heading for the beach. Lila and Maxine were sitting at the kitchen table and Charlie could tell from their bloodshot eyes that they'd been up all night too.

'No sign?' asked Lila.

Her huge blue eyes were pleading him to say he'd found Jasmine, but Charlie couldn't put her mind at rest. He shook his head sadly and slumped down on a chair. Maxine made him a strong coffee and tried to force a smile.

'She'll be all right,' she said. 'Jasmine's made of strong stuff.'

Charlie pinched the bridge of his nose. His head was pounding. The thought of Jasmine being out there alone scared him shitless. He needed her safe. He needed her nearby, where he could watch her and protect her. Especially today.

'We phoned all the hospitals, in case she'd gone for treatment but ...' Lila shook her head to show that they'd had no luck there either.

'And Blaine's on the case with the press,' Maxi added. 'He's tipped them off that Jazz has gone AWOL, so they're all out there searching for her. I mean, they're doing it for selfish reasons, obviously, but if anyone can sniff out a missing celebrity it's those vultures. I never thought I'd see the day when we were asking them for help.'

'I thought it was quiet out there,' said Charlie. Only now did it register with him that the street had been almost empty of photographers.

'You should try to get some sleep,' suggested Lila gently. 'You look exhausted.' She stood up and started rubbing Charlie's tense shoulders. It was the first time she'd touched him and, despite the terrible circumstances, Charlie felt himself melt under her touch.

'I'm sure she's just gone off somewhere to get her head together,' Maxine added. 'She'll turn up when she's ready. I mean, it's Lila's party tomorrow night and there's no way Jasmine would miss that!'

Charlie almost laughed in her face. Oh, they meant well, he knew that. But Maxine and Lila had no idea what had been going on right under their noses, beneath the clear blue Spanish skies. How could they even begin to guess what Charlie was involved in? They didn't have a clue about his past, or Dimitrov's threats, or Jimmy's debts. They couldn't begin to understand the world that he and Jasmine had been born into. Oh, they probably knew that Jasmine had been poor, and he was sure they'd tried to imagine what her life had been like as a kid. But all they would see was what the rest of the world saw – a glossy, glamorous sex kitten, with endless designer dresses who'd cheated destiny and made it big. But Charlie knew that Jasmine couldn't escape her past that easily. Old ghosts had a habit of sneaking up behind you and pouncing when you least expected it. He knew that better than anybody. How could he explain to Maxine and Lila that what he'd done could put Jasmine in serious danger? In their world, revenge meant bitching over cocktails, or giving a stinging interview to the press, but in Charlie's world it meant that people got killed.

The fact was it was now Monday morning. Dimitrov's deadline had arrived and Charlie still didn't have a clue where Nadia was. Of all the days for Jasmine to run off, hurt, upset and totally alone, this was the worst. The Russian had promised 'a girl for a girl'. Lila was here; Charlie could protect her, but Jasmine? Wherever she was, Jasmine was a sitting duck. For a moment he considered calling Dimitrov but then thought better of it. That could be the worst thing to do. Jasmine was probably just off licking her wounds somewhere. Calling the Russian would let him know she was on her own and that was dangerous. No, there was nothing more Charlie could do. His hands were tied.

Chapter Forty-Eight

'I'm sorry, Maxi, but this doesn't feel right,' Lila was saying. 'Not without Jasmine.'

The stylist Maxine had called in was sifting through a rack of dresses and pulling out options for Lila to wear to her party tonight.

'Lighten up,' said Maxi, handing her friend a glass of bubbly. 'Jasmine will be back in time for the party. I'm sure of it.'

Lila didn't look convinced, and to be honest, neither was Maxine. The truth was she was worried sick about Jasmine but she couldn't cancel the party now. The guest list was full, the press had been tipped off and Lila's makeover was all but complete. Lila deserved this party. Jasmine knew it was important; surely she would make the effort to turn up, or at least to call and let them know she was all right.

'Do you think she's gone back to London?' Lila was asking.

'I don't think so,' said Maxine. 'Charlie checked with the family – she's not close to any of them so there's no reason for her to go back there.'

'There's an aunt she gets on well with, isn't there?' Lila asked hopefully.

'She's in hospital. Charlie's tried her too.'

'Oh …' Lila's voice trailed off. 'I wish we could do something. I mean, I'm sure you're right – Jasmine is probably fine – but poor Charlie is worried sick. He hasn't slept for two nights now.'

Maxine watched how Lila's face softened when she talked about Charlie Palmer.

'You like him, don't you?' she teased.

Lila frowned. 'The man saved my life; he looks after me; of course I *like* him,' she scoffed. 'But not in the way you mean. I've barely got my head around what's happened with Brett. I'm not about to fall into the arms of my bodyguard. Really, Maxine, you do have an overactive imagination. You read too many of those trashy romantic novels. Anyway, he's not my type at all.'

'Methinks the lady doth protest too much,' giggled Maxine, jumping out of the way of Lila, who tried to hit her with a hairbrush. 'Anyway,

Charlie's a big boy. I'm sure he can look after himself without you worrying about whether or not he's had enough sleep. Honestly, Lila, you've got to shake off the maternal role and wake up your inner sex siren. You look the part, so start acting it!'

It was true. Lila looked amazing. The work she'd had done was subtle. She still looked like Lila Rose, but she looked like the Lila Rose of five years ago, rather than the one who'd fallen to pieces a few weeks ago. Maxine was very proud of her makeover skills. Her friend was one hot mama and when the paparazzi saw her tonight they would go wild. Lila Rose was back – newly single and even more gorgeous than ever.

'I'm still not sure about my hair,' said Lila, fingering the sharp jaw-length bob uncertainly. 'This blunt fringe is a bit severe, don't you think?'

Maxine shook her head with certainty. 'No, you look fan-fucking-tastic, hun. Like Louise Brooks in the twenties. Oh, God, yes, that's inspired me. It's perfect!'

Maxine spun round and grabbed the stylist by the elbow. 'Did I see you with a flapper-style dress, Daisy?' she asked excitedly. 'Yes, yes, that's it. Perfect! Don't you think that will just look spectacular with her hair?'

Daisy held up an oyster-pink, delicately hand-beaded dress with a distinctly twenties vibe and nodded enthusiastically. It was Dior couture and worth a fortune. The dress was short. It had a dropped waist, a low back, a scooped neck and tiny, delicate, spaghetti straps. It sparkled like pink champagne in the late-afternoon sun.

'Twenty-thousand pink Swarovski crystal beads,' announced Daisy proudly.

'It's exquisite,' said Lila. 'But don't you think it's a bit revealing for a woman of my age?'

Maxine and Daisy shook their heads in unison. In fact, compared to what Maxi was planning to wear, Lila's dress was positively conservative.

Chapter Forty-Nine

Everything has come to a halt. Time seems to be suspended in space and the girl feels as if she's watching herself in a film. It's a death scene. For now she's still breathing; her chest is rising and falling so rapidly that she can hear herself panting like a dog. Is this how it ends? Is his rancid breath the last thing she'll smell? It doesn't seem right.

He's finished with her now and the gun is aimed at her head. She is staring death in the face. And what a repulsive face. The girl knows she has nothing left to lose. She wants to let him know that he hasn't broken her – that he never will. She spits in his face, right in those evil grey eyes.

The man wipes his face and grins. The gun makes a loud clicking noise and then he pushes the cold metal against her temple. He disgusts her. She's better than him. Somewhere deep in her soul, a fighting spirit is still alive and unbroken. She's not going to go quietly.

The girl is much smaller than her captor and weak from the beatings she's endured. She hasn't eaten for … well, she has no idea, but it's been a long time. She can't overpower him but she's alert and brighter than he is. He pauses for a moment, distracted by something in the distance. She watches him frown. He seems puzzled. The girl seizes her one chance. While he stares above her head, she somehow finds the strength to push the gun away from her head. She throws herself at the man and tries to knock the gun from his hand. Now, they're on the floor, struggling, flailing around like a couple of fighting dogs. His grey eyes bore into hers and she hates him like she's never hated anyone in her life and then suddenly, somehow, from nowhere, there's an almighty bang.

The girl gets to her feet shakily. The gun is trembling in her hand. She stares at it, uncomprehending, and then she stares at the body of the man. His eyes are still open, staring straight back at her, but the life has gone out of them, like a dead fish. There's a perfect round hole in his forehead. She watches the blood trickle along the furrows in his brow and then drip on to the floor in an ever-increasing puddle. And then a noise, from far away. A clanging sound, heavy footsteps getting closer and closer. She's frozen to the spot. The door opens slowly. The girl looks up. He's dead at her feet. The gun is in her hand. She's killed a man and now she's not alone.

Chapter Fifty

Charlie paced the hall like a caged tiger. He felt as if he was losing his mind. He wasn't used to feeling so powerless and he couldn't handle it. He couldn't handle it at all. The stretch limo Maxine had booked to take them to the party was waiting in the drive. Charlie was all dressed up in his best suit but he felt like a fraud. He didn't belong in this world of champagne and caviar and he was in no mood to party with the A-list.

Peter and Lila's parents were hovering expectantly by the door. Every now and then they would glance up the stairs to see if Lila and Maxine were ready yet. They were already half an hour late. But Charlie didn't care about getting to the party on time; all he cared about right now was the fact that Jasmine was still missing.

He'd called Gary yesterday and asked him to do some digging into Dimitrov's movements. Maybe if Charlie knew what Dimitrov was up to he could second-guess what was going to happen next. The boy had tracked the Russian down to his casino. Apparently Dimitrov had been in high spirits. Charlie hadn't known whether this was a good or a bad sign. He'd had no word from the Russian, even though the deadline for finding Nadia had passed. He'd been expecting a visit from a couple of Russian thugs at the very least.

And then, an hour ago, Gary had called and given him some terrible news: this afternoon Dimitrov had boarded his private jet and flown to Malaga airport. He was here, in Spain, and Charlie could only guess at his reasons for the trip. Did his heavies have Jasmine? Was Dimitrov flying in to finish the job in person? Or was Jasmine somewhere else entirely, safe like Maxine said, just licking her wounds? Maybe the Russian was coming for Charlie. Or worse, for Lila. Perhaps he'd heard about the party ...

Holy fuck, this was a waking nightmare! Charlie was stuck between a rock and a hard place. He was worried sick about Jasmine, but he couldn't go hunting for her because that would leave Lila unprotected. Now he was sweating in his stupid suit with a million terrible thoughts buzzing around his confused, sleep-deprived brain. He had a bad feeling about tonight. It didn't feel right. It didn't feel right at all.

Charlie heard a collective gasp from Peter, Eve and Brian. The noise made him jump and he almost tripped over as he readied himself for some unwelcome surprise. His hand reached automatically for his gun pocket but, of course, there was no gun there. He followed their shocked gazes to the top of the stairs and suddenly he was lulled. There stood Lila. Charlie felt his mouth drop open at the sight of her. The sun streamed in the window behind her, framing her face and casting a heavenly glow around her. Charlie had never seen anything as beautiful in his life. Lila was an angel in the midst of his living hell.

Charlie didn't have to act when he told Lila how lovely she looked tonight, but everything else was a sham. He went through the motions of enjoying the limo ride to Cruise, but as the others talked in excited voices about the party ahead, he stared out of the window, still hoping in vain for a glimpse of Jasmine.

When they arrived the limo forced its way through the hoards of photographers and pulled up at the entrance to the club. The minute Lila stepped out of the car the press went wild, screaming her name. Charlie stood at her shoulder, staring into the crowds, trying to spot anyone suspicious in the sea of faces. But the flashes of the cameras blinded him and he couldn't make out a thing. The photographers pushed forward, getting closer and closer to Lila, and still the flashes made it impossible for Charlie to see what was happening right in front of his nose. This wasn't safe. Lila wasn't safe. Charlie put himself between Lila and the paps and started pushing them back, giving her some space.

'Quick,' he ordered her. 'Get inside.'

He glared at them and then followed Lila indoors.

'That was all very macho,' Lila grinned. 'But you didn't have to be so heavy-handed, Charlie. They were just doing their job. It's all part of the game.'

'Sorry,' said Charlie. 'I was just trying to keep you safe.'

'I know.' She squeezed his arm. 'And I appreciate it. I really do.'

But how could she appreciate what Charlie was trying to do? He was playing a very different game from her.

Lila must have noticed the pained expression on his face. 'Jasmine will be OK,' she whispered in his ear. 'I'm sure of it.'

Charlie wished he could be so sure.

'She's been through a lot,' Lila continued. 'Maybe she just needs some space. I'm sure if you leave her to it, she'll come back when she's ready.'

He wanted to believe her, but what was it Dimitrov had threatened? A girl for a girl. Nadia for Jasmine. It was a straight swap.

The club was soon full of the beautiful people. Everywhere he looked girls in fancy frocks were dancing with the type of men who smelled of money. The champagne flowed and some trendy band whom Charlie had never heard of was playing a live set. He prowled the dance floor, the bars and the decks, looking for danger, but all he found were couples stealing illicit kisses in the moonlight. The crowd seemed to be enjoying the loud music, but the thumping base thundered through Charlie's head and added to his dark mood.

Every now and then he'd catch sight of Lila, glowing in her sparkly pink dress, as she spun around the dance floor with Peter and Maxine. Her cheeks were flushed and her eyes shone. She looked more alive than ever. Charlie prayed to any God that might be listening that he'd be able to keep her that way. Now she looked up and caught his eye. She smiled over at him, whispered something in Maxi's ear and then she was heading his way. Charlie couldn't take his eyes off her. The slinky dress clung to her figure, leaving nothing to the imagination. Her hips swung sexily from side to side, her breasts bounced like a couple of eager puppies and Christ! Charlie had to shake his head to clear the filthy thoughts that were going on there. This was no time to be getting steamed up about his boss.

She grabbed his arm and pulled him towards her. Charlie could feel her sweet breath on his cheek.

'Go!' she said into his ear. 'You're not happy here. If it'll make you feel better, go and look for Jasmine. That's what you want to be doing.'

'I can't,' said Charlie firmly. 'I need to stay here and look after you.'

Lila shook her head. 'No. Maxine's hired some more security. Nothing bad's going to happen to me here. I mean, I might fall over and twist my ankle in these ridiculous shoes but other than that I'm quite safe, I promise. You go and look for Jasmine. You're not going to relax until you find her.'

'Well, maybe,' said Charlie. 'I'll go outside and make some more phone calls. I can't get reception in here. She might have left a message, or somebody might have seen her by now. But I'll be back in a few minutes.'

Lila nodded and pushed him towards the door.

'I just want to see you smile again,' she called after him, and then she disappeared back into the throng of dancing bodies.

Charlie had a quiet word with the security guys on the door and then stepped out into the night. A black limo had just pulled up outside the club and a large, silver-haired man in a black suit was emerging from the back seat. His hair was swept back off his face and he wore dark sunglasses, even though it was ten o'clock at night. Charlie felt the air being sucked out of the night. His heart jumped into his mouth as he stood frozen with fear. Dimitrov was here. Charlie glanced around desperately. There was nowhere to escape. The entrance to the club was narrow, carpeted and roped off from the press. The only option was to go back inside, but then he would be trapped on board with the Russian. He could jump overboard and swim to shore, but that would leave Lila alone with a madman.

Anyway, it was too late. Dimitrov pushed his sunglasses on top of his head and levelled his steely eyes directly at Charlie. And then the weirdest thing happened. Dimitrov smiled. Not in a sinister, threatening way, but in a warm, welcoming manner, as if he were greeting a long lost son. Now he was striding towards Charlie with his arms outstretched, palms open and a huge friendly grin on his face.

Charlie didn't know where to look. What the fuck was going on? Dimitrov grabbed him in a bear hug and embraced him.

'Charlie! Charlie, my boy!' he boomed in heavily accented English. 'I feel I must apologise for my Nadia's behaviour.'

Over Dimitrov's shoulder a blonde head appeared and then a familiar cheeky smile. 'Hello Charlie,' giggled Nadia. 'Is so good to see you, baby. I miss you on my travels.'

Charlie stared uncomprehendingly from father to daughter. He felt as if the ground was moving underneath his feet. Nothing made sense. One thing was clear, though – Nadia was safe. She was here, standing right in front of him, as blonde and gorgeous as ever, and very definitely alive.

'I don't understand,' he said, shaking his head. 'You wanted to kill me.'

Dimitrov threw his head back and laughed heartily. 'Oh, is just my sense of humour, Charlie. You must not take Vladimir too seriously.'

'He think I am dead,' Nadia grinned mischievously. 'But I am sailing around Greek islands with Bulgarian friend. Actually, he's not so much my friend now ...'

'A baron's son!' boomed Dimitrov. 'A no-good druggie type with too much money and not enough sense.'

Nadia winked at Charlie and then ran into the club. Dimitrov rolled his eyes and shrugged his broad shoulders.

'Young girls, ha? Such trouble, Charlie.' And then he slapped Charlie so hard on the back that he nearly fell over. 'I am sorry I get angry with you. My boys play a little rough. I owe you favour now. You need help, you just ask Vladimir, ya?'

Charlie nodded, still in shock.

'Come, come, Charlie Palmer. I will buy you drink,' ordered Dimitrov, steering him back on board Cruise.

Charlie followed the Russian towards the bar. What was he doing? Was this OK? Did this mean Jasmine was safe? Slowly, he allowed his shoulders to relax. Dimitrov did not have Jasmine. No one had Jasmine!

He remembered what Lila had said. Perhaps she just needed space. God, he'd been paranoid! There was nothing to worry about. Jasmine would come back when she was ready.

'Where is Jimmy Jones?' demanded Dimitrov, downing his neat vodka and surveying the club through narrowed eyes.

'He's not here. Jimmy's not very popular at the moment.'

'Is shame,' muttered Dimitrov. 'Little prick owes me money. I need quiet chat with him.' And then he laughed heartily and said, 'No problem. I have just bought his football club; he will get no wages until he has paid me every penny. Anyway, is just small change.'

He didn't sound like a man who wanted to kill Jimmy's wife. What was a million pounds to Vladimir Dimitrov? And anyway, loath as Charlie was to admit it, Jimmy was a talented little footballer. The Russian would be mad not to keep the boy sweet. OK, so he had sent Jimmy a threatening letter. But that was just his way of doing business, wasn't it? No, the more he thought about it, the more certain he became that Jasmine had just run off to lick her wounds like Lila said. He laughed to himself. What a paranoid idiot he'd been.

Charlie felt the weight of worry begin to lift off his shoulders. Who else would want to harm her? Christ, Charlie had been so sure that the Russian had Jasmine that he hadn't really considered any other possibilities. Yeah, he'd called Cynthia, the stupid old bitch, not that she'd seemed too concerned about her daughter's safety. But Jasmine had lots of friends and Charlie hadn't tried them all. There were the girls she used to work with at Exotica; maybe she was with one of them. Maybe she even had a secret lover. Or maybe she was with Juju. He hadn't managed to speak to Jasmine's aunt. He had called the psychiatric hospital where Juju had been treated and they said she'd been discharged. She wasn't answering her phone at home, either. Maybe Jasmine and Juju were spending some time together recovering from their ordeals. Anything was possible. The sense of relief was intoxicating. What a night to celebrate! Jasmine was OK. Everything was going to be OK!

Nadia slunk up beside Charlie and snuggled into his chest.

'Is over now, with Bulgarian boy.' She smiled up at him. 'I am free as a bird if you still want me, baby.'

Charlie ruffled her hair affectionately. 'I think we should just be friends, sweetheart,' he told her.

God, he was happy to see her in one piece, but after the trouble she caused … no way! Nadia Dimitrova was the last woman on Earth he wanted to be involved with. Besides, Charlie's heart belonged elsewhere.

He peered over the top of Nadia's blonde head and watched Lila as she danced. No, he could never be interested in a girl like Nadia again. Not when there was a woman like Lila in the world.

Chapter Fifty-One

Maxine watched her club fill with glamorous people. They all kissed her cheeks, told her how gorgeous she looked and gazed round her club in awe, telling her what a success she'd made of the venture. She'd put on her best party-girl face and a suitably tiny mini-dress for the occasion. She was smiling and laughing with her guests on hostess autopilot but, beneath the surface, Maxi didn't feel like a success. The truth was she'd never felt so low in her life. The morning sickness was getting worse and seemed to have turned into afternoon and evening sickness too. Just the thought of champagne made her want to retch. She was holding a flute in her hand to keep up appearances but she hadn't managed one sip.

Maybe it was the hormones playing havoc with her emotions, but Maxi felt on the verge of tears. Her smile was frozen on her face. In two days' time she was booked into a private clinic in London to get rid of her little problem. But the appointment loomed heavy on her heart. She felt as though she was about to make the worst mistake of her life, but what was the alternative? She shuddered. How had she got herself into such a God awful mess?

She surveyed the club. It was all good. Lila looked spectacular and she was clearly having a ball. There she was dancing with Charlie and Peter, her two adoring employees. They seemed to be competing for her attention, taking turns to spin her round, each of them trying to impress her with their best moves. Charlie was surprisingly light on his feet for such a big man. Maxine managed a weak smile. There had been so much misery in her friend's life lately that she didn't begrudge Lila her happiness for a moment. And Charlie seemed more relaxed suddenly too. Maybe he'd heard from Jasmine.

But Maxi couldn't share her friends' high spirits. She felt wrung out, drained, exhausted. The fixed smile was slipping from her face and she knew she couldn't keep up the pretence anymore. She needed some air.

The deck was empty. She leaned against the railings and stared out across the bay. The lights of Marbella twinkled like the stars in the sky above her. It was a perfect, still night but somehow the beauty of the evening just made her pain more acute. How had it come to this? Why did her dreams always turn to dust?

Maxi let her mind drift back over the years – the poor little rich girl whose parents had ignored her, the teenage love affairs with inappropriate men, the weddings, the disappointments, the heartbreaks, the divorces. She'd always managed to bounce back, to put a brave face on things and keep going, believing with the blind optimism of youth that somehow, some day, things would get better; her time would come. But those years had slipped away, she was older now, and what had she learned? She was in more of a mess than ever. All she'd ever wanted from life was happiness but, despite her success, it was the one thing that evaded her.

So here she was, the wrong side of thirty, pregnant, alone and unloved, still unloved, just as she had been as a child. Maxi wasn't normally one for self-pity but now, as the tears streamed down her face, she couldn't help but feel sorry for that little girl, who'd dreamed of a better world and truly believed that she would find one.

'Maxine?'

The voice was familiar but for a moment Maxi couldn't place it. She blinked back her tears and wiped her face on the back of her hand. She couldn't let anyone see her in this state.

'Maxine? Are you OK?'

It was a deep, velvety voice with an American accent. Maxine's heart jumped into her mouth as she turned round. And then he was there, standing two feet in front of her face, like a vision appearing out of the shadows.

'Juan,' she said, her voice breaking with emotion. 'Wh … what are you doing here? How? Why?'

'I've come to make an honest woman of you,' he said with the same glint in his eye that had got her into this trouble in the first place.

The electricity sparked between their bodies and then she was in his strong arms and her lips were hungrily searching for his and she was lost in the smell of him and her dreams were alive again.

Charlie was drunk. He didn't usually let himself lose control but tonight had been so bloody mental that he couldn't help himself. Nadia was alive! Dimitrov was his friend! Jasmine was safe! What a night to celebrate! Those waitresses kept handing him glasses of champagne and he'd lost count of how much he'd had. Now, as the limo sped through the streets, pulling further and further ahead of the paparazzi who followed behind, his head was spinning and his heart was pounding because somehow, with the nerve of a drunk man, he'd managed to slip his arm around Lila's bare shoulders. He could feel his fingers brushing the side of her breast and the most fucking amazing thing was, she wasn't complaining. She hadn't pushed him off and when he smiled down at her, she smiled right back. His mind was racing. Did she like him too? In *that* way? Nah! Don't be a dick, Charlie. How could she? Why would she? But then again … maybe …

Charlie had never had any trouble with the ladies. He couldn't remember a girl he'd wanted who'd turned him down. But this wasn't some blonde dolly bird in an East End nightclub; this was Lila Rose, international sex symbol. Christ, he felt like a fifteen-year-old virgin again, sitting up the back row of the cinema in Canning Town, wondering whether or not Jackie Enfield, the girl sitting next to him, would mind if he slipped his tongue down her throat. Turned out Jackie hadn't minded at all and by the end of the night, Charlie had been a virgin no more. Charlie would always remember Jackie fondly, bless her; that girl had made a man of him, but she was hardly in Lila's league, was she? Just because Jackie Enfield had been willing, didn't mean Lila Rose would be too. Those women inhabited different worlds. In fact, last he'd heard of Jackie, she was a single mother of five who ran a launderette in Leytonstone.

Charlie had lost all sense of time and was surprised to notice that they were whizzing through the gates and pulling up in the drive. Lila slipped out from under his arm.

'Nightcap, anyone?' she asked.

Her eyes sparkled in a way Charlie hadn't seen before. It excited him to see her like that. He had the taste of anticipation in his mouth, all the more delicious because it was so rare. She half ran down the drive towards the house with her dress sparkling in the moonlight. Charlie began to follow her.

'Charlie!' a voice yelled behind him.

He hesitated.

'Come on!' called Lila.

'Charlie!' the voice sounded desperate.

Charlie sighed. What the fuck was it now? He turned round and saw Jimmy's pathetic face, squashed up against the gate. He was waving at Charlie frantically.

'Charlie! Come here! Please!' he shouted.

The paps had arrived and pulled up on the street. They piled out of their cars and started snapping Jimmy but it was as if he couldn't see them. He just kept shouting at Charlie to hurry up and come here.

Charlie hadn't seen Jimmy since the night he'd beaten up Jasmine. The truth was he'd hoped he'd never see the little shit again. But here he was, begging Charlie to help him. Jimmy was the last man on earth he wanted to help, but something in the tone of the boy's voice told him this was serious. He watched Lila disappear into the villa and felt his fantasies melt into the hot, dark night. Suddenly, he felt as sober as a judge.

Charlie let himself out of the gate. 'We'll talk once we're inside,' he snarled into Jimmy's ear.

He gave the boy a push, turned his head away from the cameras and followed him into Casa Amoura. In the harsh light of the living room Charlie could see just what a state Jimmy was in. He looked as if he hadn't slept in days. His face was ashen and he had black circles under his eyes. His hair, usually groomed to within an inch of its life, looked unwashed and unbrushed. His clothes were dirty and crumpled.

'You're fucking pathetic, Jimmy,' spat Charlie. 'You know Jasmine hasn't been seen since you used her as a human punch bag, don't you?'

Jimmy nodded solemnly. Charlie noticed that his hands were shaking.

'You've got a fucking nerve asking me for help. You're lucky I'm a reasonable man, or I'd be ripping your scrawny little head off right now.'

Jimmy didn't seem to be listening. He picked up a package and held it out to Charlie with his shaking hands.

'What's this?' demanded Charlie.

'Open it,' urged Jimmy. He looked weird. Haunted.

Charlie took the package from Jimmy and thrust his hand inside. His fingers touched something soft and silky. It felt like a wig. Confused, he pulled the contents out of the package and stared, uncomprehending, as two feet of glossy, dark brown hair fell out of his hands and tumbled on to the floor. He felt his mouth drop open in horror.

'What the hell?'

'I found it on the kitchen island,' said Jimmy, wide-eyed. 'They've been in the house! They got in to my fucking house, Charlie!'

A cold hand grabbed Charlie's heart and twisted it in his chest. He dropped to his knees and began desperately gathering up the hair. He buried his face in it and breathed in the smell of Jasmine's perfume. He could barely breathe, never mind find the words to ask Jimmy what the fuck was going on. All he could manage to say was, 'Jasmine,' weakly, under his breath, over and over again.

'There was something else in the package too,' said Jimmy, grimly. 'A DVD. I'll show you.'

Charlie watched Jimmy walk towards the home cinema equipment. Eventually, he found the power to speak.

'But I saw Dimitrov tonight. He was friendly. I don't understand.'

'I don't think this has anything to do with the Russian,' Jimmy replied. 'Watch.'

Charlie stared up at the huge plasma screen, still clutching Jasmine's hair in his hands. The footage was grainy and black and white, and there was no sound, but Charlie recognised Jasmine's image immediately. It was an old film. Jasmine was still a kid. She was dressed in a school uniform and there was a man tying up her hands, gagging her, binding her feet with rope. The poor girl looked terrified. At first Charlie couldn't make out the man's face but then he looked up and Charlie saw a ghost. Sean Hillman. Terry's brother. Jasmine's 'uncle'. The man had been dead for seven years. Charlie had known the bastard all his life, and he'd never liked him, but this made no sense at all. What was he doing to Jasmine?

Now Jasmine was lying on some sort of table, tied down, and Sean was climbing on top of her, pawing her young flesh with his filthy hands. On the huge screen, Charlie could clearly see the desperation in her eyes. Charlie felt the bile rise in his mouth. He couldn't look at the images anymore. He ran to the bathroom, retching. He'd never been so sick in his life. He was disgusted that he'd let such a horrific thing happen to her. How could he not have known about this? Why hadn't he stopped it?

Chapter Fifty-Two

The girl stands shaking with the gun in her hand, still staring at her uncle, who lies dead at her feet. She kicks the body tentatively with her toe but he doesn't move. Then she drops the gun, falls to her knees and begins to sob in huge gulps.

'What have you done, Jasmine?' comes a voice from the doorway. 'What the fuck have you done?'

Chapter Fifty-Three

'There's more,' said Jimmy grimly, when Charlie returned from the bathroom.

'I've seen enough,' said Charlie, gently gathering together the hair he had dropped.

'No. You've got to see what happens next. It's what this whole thing is about.'

'What whole thing?'

Charlie didn't understand any of this. Finally, tonight, he'd let himself believe Jasmine was OK, and now? Now he was holding her hair in his hands and he had no idea where she was or what sort of danger she was in.

'What the fuck is going on, Jimmy?' he shouted, desperately.

'Watch,' said Jimmy, in a shaky little voice. 'You'll see.'

He forwarded the DVD. Neither man could stomach the footage of Sean Hillman raping his niece. Then the film continued. Charlie watched, open mouthed, as Sean reappeared on screen holding a gun to Jasmine's head. It was difficult to make out exactly what was happening but suddenly Sean looked up and seemed to stare directly at the camera.

'Look, he's only just noticed he's being filmed,' said Jimmy.

Charlie watched as Jasmine grasped her one chance of survival. She pushed the gun away from her head while Sean was distracted and then the pair were struggling, falling to the ground. The teenage Jasmine was slightly built and tiny compared to Sean Hillman but she was fighting for her life like a wild animal. Arms flailed and legs kicked out and for a moment Charlie lost sight of the gun. Then suddenly, the two bodies were very still. Slowly, Jasmine stood up, holding the gun, staring down at the body on the floor. She kicked him gently with her foot but he didn't move. And then she dropped the gun and fell on to her knees. Charlie noticed that Jasmine's head turned towards an opening door and then the footage went fuzzy and finally stopped.

'She killed someone,' said Jimmy, as if he still couldn't believe what he'd seen. 'Jasmine killed a man.'

Charlie nodded, grimly. 'Sean Hillman,' he replied. 'Terry's brother. But that's not the problem. She had to fucking well kill him or he was going to kill her. No, the problem is that someone caught her. Someone taped the whole bloody thing. Did you see that door opening? There was someone else there.'

Jimmy nodded. 'Read the note,' he urged, handing Charlie a typed letter. 'I'm being blackmailed. I think Jasmine's been paying this guy for a while. I found a bank statement of hers. She's taken out about eight hundred thousand euros in the last few weeks.'

Charlie read the letter hurriedly. Whoever it was who had Jasmine, he was a greedy bastard. He wanted Jimmy to cough up a million euros for her release. And he wanted the money tonight or the footage of her shooting Sean Hillman would be posted online.

'You've got it, right?' Charlie asked Jimmy, willing the boy to say yes.

But Jimmy shook his head pathetically and started to cry. 'I told you, I haven't got any money left,' he sobbed. 'I gambled it all away.'

'But your mates ...' Charlie could hear the anger in his voice. 'You could get it from your mates, surely.'

Jimmy glanced at his watch. 'What? Now? At midnight? Do you think they have that sort of money just lying around? Do you think they need to be dragged into something like this?'

Charlie felt as if he was going to explode with rage. He grabbed Jimmy's shoulders and shook him violently. Part of him wanted to kill the little bastard for being so weak. He should have been able to help Jasmine but he'd thrown his money away. As if beating the poor girl senseless wasn't enough, now he was just going to let her be destroyed. But more than anything Charlie was angry with himself. Why hadn't he stopped Sean Hillman raping Jasmine? After Kenny died it had been his responsibility to look after the girl. But this had gone on under his very nose.

'Lila,' said Jimmy, suddenly. 'She can help.'

Charlie thought of Lila, of how she'd sparkled this evening, and shook his head. There was no need to bother her. Charlie had a much better idea. Somebody owed him a favour.

'Are you sure about this?' asked Jimmy nervously, as Charlie dialled the number. 'He's the man to help?'

Charlie nodded his head confidently. He'd never been so sure of anything in his life.

Chapter Fifty-Four

Dimitrov swept into Casa Amoura with the air of a man who could solve any problem. He'd arrived on the beach by speedboat so as to avoid the press. He'd left two heavies standing guard at each door. His very presence made Charlie breathe easier. Dimitrov ignored Jimmy but patted Charlie firmly on the back.

'We find her, Charlie,' he barked. He snapped his finger at Jimmy. 'You have video footage of parcel being delivered, boy?'

Jimmy nodded. 'In the security room, above the garage,' he said.

The three men stared at the computer screen in the security room, watching the footage from earlier that night. Casa Amoura's security cameras covered the entire property, inside and out. At ten p.m., while Jimmy had been watching TV alone, a tall blonde woman in a white bikini had swum ashore on the Jones's private beach. She was carrying a sealed plastic package. Charlie, Jimmy and Dimitrov watched the woman walk gracefully up the steps towards the villa, calmly step inside the open patio doors and place the package casually on the kitchen island. She took a peach from the fruit bowl, then she turned around and sauntered back down towards the beach, enjoying her snack. She tossed the peach stone on to the beach, ran her fingers through her damp hair and then dived back into the waves and out of view.

'I recognise that girl from somewhere,' said Charlie, scratching his head. Where had he seen her before?

Dimitrov nodded. 'Yah, Is Yana!' he declared.

'Yana?' asked Charlie, knowing the name was familiar.

'Yana! Frankie's whore! I know her too well. She used to work for me. Is Angelis who has your Jasmine, Charlie.'

Jasmine perched on the edge of the plush velvet sofa with Annie on her lap and glared at the crazy old man sitting opposite her.

'Drink your tea, sweetheart,' he urged. 'Have one of those lovely little fairy cakes Ekaterina made for you. Or a cucumber sandwich.'

Jasmine shook her head. This whole situation would be funny if it wasn't so sinister. Frankie Angelis was a pathetic, perverted old man, sitting here in his stupid mansion, wearing that ridiculous silk dressing gown, surrounded by Eastern European prostitutes who he'd convinced himself were in love with him.

Angelis was treating her like a visiting relative. He enjoyed playing his role as the benevolent uncle. He always had done, since she was a young girl. He had this way of pretending to care about her, as if he had her best interests at heart. As if! She was sleeping in a four-poster bed in the best guest room and being cooked roast beef and Yorkshire puddings for dinner. One of the girls, who Frankie explained used to be a nurse in Slovenia, had dressed Jasmine's wounds from Jimmy's beating and given her painkillers. Even the dog was being treated well and being fed steak for dinner. But it was a sham. Frankie had a tighter grip on her than ever before. She knew she wasn't free to leave. All the doors were locked and Frankie's girls followed her around the house, watching her every move. She wasn't even allowed out to the pool.

Now she'd been woken up and ordered to have tea with Frankie in the drawing room. It was madness. It was the middle of the bloody night and the last thing Jasmine felt like was fairy cakes and cucumber sandwiches, even if they did have the crusts cut off. Frankie smiled at her.

'You look cute with short hair,' he said. 'Like a naughty little pixie. But then we know what a naughty little minx you can be, Jasmine, don't we?'

She ignored him. It was Yana – Frankie's favourite and the girl Jasmine had seen at the aquarium and the museum – who had taken great pleasure in hacking off Jasmine's crowning glory with blunt kitchen scissors. Jasmine still wasn't used to the naked feeling on the nape of her neck. She felt exposed. She was used to having her hair for comfort. Her fingers touched the blunt ends of her short hair. It felt alien, as if it didn't belong to her. Still, it was only hair. It didn't matter. Not in the grand scheme of things.

'How long are you going to keep me here?' she asked Frankie.

'Until Jimmy turns up with the money,' replied Frankie, still smiling, still keeping up the pretence of a polite tea.

'He won't come,' replied Jasmine with certainty. 'He doesn't have the money.'

'Don't be silly, Jasmine. Of course he has the money. He might tell *you* he doesn't have the money because he doesn't want you spending it all on pretty frocks, but he's a footballer; he has money.'

Jasmine shrugged. She couldn't make Frankie believe her, but what about her bruises? Her bruises he could see for himself.

'He doesn't love me,' she told him, pointing at her battered face. 'He beats me up.'

Frankie nodded. 'Jimmy made quite a mess of his princess, didn't he? But that means he really loves you. A man has to adore a woman to get that angry at her.'

'You're mad,' said Jasmine, flatly. 'He doesn't love me and he won't come. This is a waste of time.'

'He'll come. Here, have an iced bun.'

She'd driven straight to Frankie's place after Jimmy had beaten her up, to hand over the five hundred grand. She'd thought it would get the old creep out of her life for good. There would be no more skulking about with bags full of money. She would end the nonsense face to face. Jimmy had beaten her to a pulp but the shock had knocked some sort of sense into her. Suddenly she'd felt brave. The worst had happened. What was there left to be frightened of now? Jimmy had blown it and her marriage was over. All she'd wanted was to regain some control. But things hadn't gone quite to plan.

She'd known Frankie had been the one blackmailing her from the start – who else could it have been? He was the only one who'd known what had happened with Sean Hillman. He'd walked in and seen her with the body and, one way or another, he'd been holding her to ransom ever since.

'What have you done, Jasmine?' His words still rang in her ears. 'You've killed him.'

She'd tried to convince Frankie that the gun had gone off by accident, that she hadn't meant to kill Sean, but he would never listen.

'No, Jasmine, you killed him, it's as simple as that, and now it's down to me to clear up your mess.'

And after a while she'd started to believe him, that maybe she had shot Sean in cold blood. She was young and scared and impressionable. The fear of being found out had turned her into Frankie's puppet over the years. She'd even thanked him for his help. He always said she would be able to repay him one day. Boy, was she paying now!

Sean and Terry Hillman had worked for Frank. Christ, everyone Jasmine knew as a kid seemed to work for the guy. He was Mr Big in their world. Everybody was terrified of him. When Sean had abducted her he'd taken her to one of Frankie's buildings – an old meat factory where Angelis stored his dirty money and 'dealt' with his enemies in peace. Sean can't have known about the security camera Frank had installed – he'd never have raped his niece there if he'd known. Jasmine certainly hadn't been aware of the camera. But then she hadn't known much at all back then. She'd just turned seventeen.

Frankie had sorted it all out for her. He'd cleaned her up and dropped her home before anybody had even noticed she was missing. It wasn't as if her mum kept tabs on her. Maybe Charlie would have noticed something was wrong if he'd been around, but Sean had been smart. He'd pounced while Charlie was away on business. By the time Charlie got back the whole mess had been cleaned up and Jasmine felt too ashamed to tell her beloved godfather what had happened.

Sean's body turned up in Epping Forest a few days later and no one suspected a thing. He was a gangster with a single gunshot wound to the head. Everybody assumed he'd just got what was coming to him – a bullet from a professional hit man. Even the police seemed relieved to have him off the streets and they didn't make much effort to investigate his death. Frankie had known it would be that way. Only Terry Hillman had been upset. Jasmine remembered cowering in the bedroom while Terry ranted and raved to her mother about what he would do to the bastard who killed his brother if he ever got hold of them.

But of course Frankie hadn't helped Jasmine out of the goodness of his heart. From the start, he'd made it quite clear that she owed him big time. He told her that if she ever stepped out of line he would tell her stepfather the truth about what had happened to his brother. So, when Terry came home one night saying that Frankie Angelis wanted her to start stripping in one of his clubs, she'd had no choice but to agree. She'd have liked to have stayed on at school and gone to college but ... well, girls like Jasmine didn't have choices. Especially not with the likes of Frankie Angelis pulling their strings.

In a way, Frankie had kick-started Jasmine's career. Now she was rich and famous he wanted his dues. In his mind he owned her, just like he owned the poor bitches locked up here in his mansion, and he was entitled to a cut of her earnings. But the *Playboy* money hadn't been enough. Frankie was a greedy man and he always wanted more. Much more. And so he'd sent the package to Jimmy.

Christ, what would Jimmy make of the tape? Jasmine shuddered at the thought. He wasn't a strong man. He'd probably gone to pieces. She wondered what he was doing now. Would he have gone to the police? She felt sure he wouldn't come here. He was too much of a coward for that.

And so here she was, still Frankie Angelis's prisoner after all these years. Jasmine sipped her tea and waited. For what? She didn't know. And yet she felt everything was different now. She was older and stronger and had nothing left to lose. Recently the nightmares had been clearer and as she slept she would relive those terrible events. Jasmine remembered what had happened as if it had all been yesterday. She did not shoot Sean intentionally. The gun went off while she struggled to save herself. She knew the truth now, and whatever Frankie said, Jasmine would never take the blame. He might have her imprisoned in his house, but her mind was free of him now. He had lost his hold over her. She no longer believed what the old man said. Somehow, in the middle of the chaos, Jasmine had found the strength to know her own mind.

Yana entered the room and whispered something in Frankie's ear. Jasmine watched a broad grin spread across the old man's face.

'Jimmy's here,' he told Jasmine, cheerfully. 'You see, you should have more faith in your husband.'

Jasmine didn't understand. Why would Jimmy come?

'And he's brought a friend with him, to hold his hand. How touching.'

'A friend?' Jasmine was confused. She couldn't imagine Paul or Calvin coming to a place like this.

'Yes,' said Frankie. 'Charlie Palmer. What fun!'

Chapter Fifty-Five

Charlie knew the plan. They'd discussed it in the car on the way here and, as long as Jimmy didn't bottle it, they'd be all right. The adrenalin was pumping through his veins and he felt almost superhuman. If anyone could rescue Jasmine it was him. Well, with a bit of help from his KGB-trained friend, of course. Dimitrov crouched behind Charlie and Jimmy as the gates buzzed open and then darted behind a bush out of sight. He was a powerful man, a large man, but he was stealthy, like a Siberian tiger. The Russian would make his own way into the house. Angelis wouldn't have a clue he was here.

Charlie was the one carrying the bag full of rolled up newspaper. Jimmy didn't have to do a thing. Still, the boy was bricking it. He'd been pale all night but now he looked ghostly white to Charlie.

'You've got to keep it together,' Charlie warned him. 'Stay strong.'

'Will he have a gun?'

'Of course he'll have a fucking gun, you numpty. He's not a bleeding scout leader; he's a gangster. A bit long in the tooth, but still a dangerous man.'

Their feet crunched up the gravel drive until they reached the steps to the grand entrance.

'I don't think I can do this,' whispered Jimmy, stopping suddenly.

Charlie pushed his knuckles firmly into Jimmy's back and said, 'If you don't do this I'll fucking kill you, and that's a promise.'

Jimmy continued reluctantly up the steps to where a young blonde girl stood at the front door waiting for them. She scowled at Charlie and Jimmy and pushed them hurriedly into the grand hall.

'In there,' she grunted, pointing to the door which Charlie remembered led to some sort of lounge.

Charlie braced himself. He hadn't seen Jasmine since Jimmy beat her up, or since Frankie had cut off her beautiful hair. He didn't want her to see him looking shocked. He just wanted to make her feel safe. He pushed the door open slowly and entered the enormous room. His eyes darted around. Frankie Angelis stood in front of his grand fireplace, in his poncy red dressing gown, puffing on a cigar with his chest puffed up and grinning proudly. Charlie almost smiled. Dimitrov would soon wipe that grin off his face. The old timer had no idea what was coming to him, but it was no more than he deserved.

At first Charlie couldn't see Jasmine in the vast room, but then he spotted her, perched timidly on an antique wooden chair in the corner. He noticed that the little stray dog Jasmine had adopted was cowering under the chair, terrified, but loyal to the end. Jasmine's hair looked as if it had been cut by a chimpanzee with a knife and fork. Great clumps had been hacked off; some bits had been missed and were still long, and there were patches of bare scalp showing in places. Her face was swollen, bruised and puffy. Charlie couldn't believe the damage Jimmy had done. He shot the little shit a menacing look, just to let him know he hadn't forgotten, but Jimmy turned away. Fucking coward – too ashamed to look at Jasmine or Charlie, too scared to look at Frankie Angelis. Jimmy cowered behind Charlie and stared at his feet instead.

Charlie winked at Jasmine to show her that everything would be all right. She was bruised and battered but her eyes shone out at him and he could tell that her spirit hadn't been broken by any of the bastards who'd used and abused her. Sean Hillman hadn't managed it, Jimmy hadn't either, and now Frankie Angelis had failed too. She was some girl.

'Good evening, gentlemen,' said Frankie, still grinning. 'I believe you have something for me.' His eyes fell greedily to the bag Charlie was holding.

Charlie stepped forward. 'Let Jasmine go first,' he said firmly.

Angelis laughed. 'No, I don't think so, Charlie my boy. First things first. We need to destroy all evidence. Did you bring your copy of the film?'

Charlie threw the DVD on to the Oriental rug. Frankie threw an old video down beside it.

'Burn them,' he ordered Ekaterina. The young blonde picked them up and hurried out of the room. 'Now. You give me what I want and I'll give you what you want.'

'No deal,' said Charlie. 'Untie her, you senile old bastard. Or you won't get a penny.'

'There's no need to be rude, Char. I'm sure your old man raised you better than that.'

Charlie flinched. How dare Angelis drag his dad into this. He thought of the years his old man had spent in prison for Frankie and his venom grew. He took a deep breath. Now wasn't the time to go ballistic. He had to channel his anger and use it wisely. He had to stay calm and play for time until Dimitrov turned up. He had no money and no weapon. He was surviving on his wits alone – and so was Jasmine.

'Let her go and I'll throw over the bag,' said Charlie.

Frankie shrugged. 'OK, that seems fair.'

Charlie knew Frankie was a greedy old git; all he was thinking about was the money he believed to be in that bag. He was not going to be a happy man when he realised he'd been done. The moment Yana untied Jasmine, she threw herself across the room into Charlie's arms. He hugged her tightly and stroked her short hair.

'I'm here. Everything's going to be all right now, baby,' he whispered in her ear.

He remembered saying the same thing when her dad died. Fat lot of good that had done her. He'd let her down. But not this time. This time Charlie would be as good as his word.

'Very touching, I'm sure,' said Frankie. 'Now give me the money.'

Charlie threw the bag at Frankie's feet and started to back away towards the door, still holding Jasmine. He nodded his head at Jimmy, letting him know to do the same. Charlie's eyes darted from the door to Frankie. It was as if the whole thing was happening in slow motion. The old man picked up the bag and his finger was on the zip. Charlie reached the door and his hand was grasping for the handle. Now Frankie had opened the zip and he was frowning, pulling rolled up pieces of newspaper out of the bag and throwing them on the floor. Charlie was turning the handle, opening the door, inch by inch. The bag was empty now and Frankie's face had turned purple.

'Where's the fucking money, Charlie?' he shouted.

And then Frankie's hand was reaching into his pocket and Charlie knew what was going to happen next. He just had time to throw open the door and shout, 'Run, Jasmine!' before Angelis pulled the gun. Jasmine managed to take a couple of steps towards the door, away from Charlie, but she didn't have time to escape. She was frozen in the doorway with Frankie's gun pointing at her head.

'One step, and I'll shoot her,' he warned. Then he turned to Jimmy. 'Run along and fetch me my money, Jimmy. Or I'll shoot your pretty little wife dead.'

Charlie watched Jimmy closely. The boy couldn't speak, let alone move. His jeans had turned dark blue around the groin and a puddle of urine was collecting at his feet.

'He doesn't have any money, Frankie,' said Charlie. 'He's a waste of space.'

'So what do we do now?' asked Frankie, his eyes flashing with anger. 'We were quite comfortable with one house guest, weren't we, Yana?'

Yana nodded in agreement.

'But I don't think we need three of you.'

He stepped closer to Jasmine.

'You see, even a house this big feels claustrophobic with too many guests. So perhaps I'll have to get rid of you,' he threatened. 'One. By. One.'

Frankie unlocked the safety catch with a loud click. Charlie saw how Jasmine jumped; he noticed the fear in her eyes and he couldn't stand it anymore. The girl had been through enough and it was time somebody stopped this torture. With one leap he threw himself between Jasmine and the gun. It was risky, but Charlie had always lived by his instincts and he reckoned his reactions were faster than the old man's.

'OK, OK, you can die first if you insist, Charlie,' said Frankie, grinning again now. 'But I'm still going to shoot your precious little Jasmine. She'll just have to watch you die first.'

Frankie couldn't see the French doors opening behind his back, or the burly Russian in the expensive suit sneaking into his drawing room, but Charlie could. He noticed that Yana had spotted Dimitrov too. She recognised him and she looked terrified. Charlie noted, with interest, that she didn't warn her boss about the armed intruder. He was just in time. Frankie's finger was twitching on the trigger as Dimitrov walked silently up behind him and held his own gun against the old man's head.

'Zdravstvuj, Frankie,' said Dimitrov in a voice so deep that it filled the room. 'It has been long time, no?'

Charlie watched the grin freeze on Frankie's lips and the colour drain from his cheeks. Now it was Charlie's turn to smile.

'I think you should drop your gun, Frankie, no?' suggested Dimitrov.

The gun fell to the floor with a thud. Charlie kicked it out of the way.

'You go,' boomed Dimitrov to Charlie. 'Mr Angelis and me, we have private business to discuss.'

'Are you sure, mate?' Charlie asked.

'Quite sure,' he replied. 'And Jasmine, she get her money on way out. I am sure Yana knows where it is.'

Yana nodded at Dimitrov subserviently.

'Bye Frankie,' called Charlie over his shoulder. 'I'd say it's been nice knowing you but we both know that would be a lie.'

He threw his arm protectively over Jasmine's shoulder and led her down the hall. He felt sure Frankie Angelis wouldn't be bothering them again.

'You haven't got rid of me that easily, Charlie Palmer,' yelled Frankie after them. 'I already sent that tape to Terry Hillman. Not all of it, mind. Just the bit where Jasmine shoots his brother. Call it my insurance policy. He won't see the rape and he'll never believe Sean was a pervert. You'll get what's coming to you, both of you!'

'Evil bastard,' muttered Charlie. 'What did he have to go and do that for? Don't worry, darling, I'll sort Terry out for you.'

But Jasmine shook her head.

'Don't bother,' she said. 'I want to go to the police.'

Charlie was shocked. 'You want to do what?'

Jasmine nodded. 'You heard. I'm going to the police. I'm telling them everything. I've got the whole film on my computer. Frankie emailed it to me. And there's a copy hidden in the apartment in London. It was self-defence. I've got all the evidence I need.'

The firm set of her chin told Charlie that her mind was made up.

'I didn't do anything wrong,' she said. 'I was just a kid. Anyway, I want it out in the open. No more secrets.'

Yana appeared with Charlie's bag. The zip was open and she showed them the contents. 'Eight hundred thousand euros cash,' she said. 'Is yours.'

She handed the bag to Jasmine.

'And I am sorry,' she called after them as Charlie opened the door. 'For cutting your lovely hair.'

It was getting light outside. The sun was rising above the mountains, casting an orange glow over the sleeping town.

'What do we do now?' asked Jimmy quietly.

Charlie spun round and stared at him. 'Are you having a laugh?' he said, and then he turned to Jasmine, shaking his head.

Jasmine glared at her husband in amazement. 'Jimmy,' she said, calmly but firmly. 'There is no "we" anymore. You can do whatever the hell you like but you're not coming with us.'

'Jasmine, baby, don't walk out on me,' Jimmy begged. He looked pathetic and bedraggled in his urine-soaked jeans.

Charlie helped Jasmine climb into the jeep, called to the dog to follow her, and then jumped in himself. As he drove off he glanced in the wing mirror and saw Jimmy. He was on his knees on the pavement, crying like a baby, looking totally out of place on this smart residential boulevard in his dirty clothes and tangled hair. Stripped of the trimmings of wealth, Jimmy Jones was nothing. Just a boy with a troubled past and a bad temper who wanted to vent his anger on the world. There was nothing special about him. Boys like that were ten a penny back home. For a moment Charlie almost felt sorry for the bloke. But it was a fleeting thought. Jimmy Jones was where he belonged – in the gutter.

Chapter Fifty-Six

When Lila woke up Charlie was nowhere to be found. The garden apartment was immaculate, the bed was made and all his clothes and possessions had gone. It was as if he'd never been there at all. Last night she'd been giddy with champagne and excitement. She'd felt happy – yes, really, truly happy – for the first time in, God, what was it? Weeks? Months? Years? And for a brief moment in the limousine on the way home, when Charlie had put his arm around her shoulder, she'd felt something stir deep down inside. Was it just the touch of bare skin on skin? Had it been lust? Desire? A yearning to be held and wanted? Oh, Lila didn't know. In the harsh light of day it seemed like a crazy, mixed-up dream.

Charlie had disappeared. One minute he was there behind her in the drive and the next he'd vanished into thin air. She'd poured him a whiskey and waited. And waited. And waited. But he'd never reappeared. Now all trace of him was gone. She wandered around the apartment, searching for some sort of sign or explanation. And then she saw it: an envelope on the window ledge with her name on it. She sat on the edge of the bed and read the neatly handwritten letter she found inside. And then she read it again, and again, and again …

Dear Lila,

I apologise for running out on you like this. I can't explain what is going on but, in time, I think it will become clear. The good news is that Jasmine is safe. She is with me and we have gone back to the UK. The police might be looking for me. Don't be alarmed. None of this has anything to do with you and you are not in any danger. You might hear some things about me that will shock you, but please don't think too badly of me. The Charlie you know is the man I really am.

I might not get the chance to speak to you again so I wanted you to know that I think you are the most amazing woman I have ever met. You are beautiful, intelligent, compassionate and brave. There, I've said it. I know a woman like you could never have feelings for a man like me, but I had to get that off my chest in case I never get the chance again. Please don't laugh!

Protecting you has been a privilege and an honour. Please look after yourself. I'll miss you.
Charlie

Lila's head was spinning. It didn't matter how many times she read the letter, none of it made much sense. What did he mean by 'things that will shock you'? Why had he and Jasmine taken off back to the UK in the middle of the night? Why would the police be involved? And why could she never have feelings for a man like Charlie? It was too late for that. She suspected she already did.

'Lila!' She heard Peter calling for her outside. 'Lila, the police are here! They're asking questions about Charlie.'

Lila folded the letter into a neat little bundle and stuffed it inside her bra. She knew already that she wouldn't show it to the police. She had no idea what Charlie was involved in but she was sure of one thing: Charlie Palmer was a good man.

When she made her way, blinking, into the bright morning sunshine, she found Peter surrounded by swarthy Spanish policemen. He looked both scared and excited – probably because he was surrounded by handsome young men in uniform. They were not the friendly Policia Locale who wandered the streets of Marbella helping tourists find their hotels, or the green-uniformed Guardia Civil she had passed on the roads; these guys were the Policia Nacional – the big guns. Whatever Charlie was involved in must be heavy enough for the cavalry to be called in.

An older man in plain clothes seemed to be in charge. He was talking to Peter in an urgent, almost bullying tone.

'What's he saying?' asked Lila, whose Spanish was nowhere near as good as Peter's.

'They're looking for Charlie,' Peter explained. 'They want to talk to him about the suspicious death of some English bloke called Frank Angelis.'

'I've never heard of Frank Angelis,' said Lila to the policeman. 'And Charlie Palmer is a good man. A kind man. You must have got this wrong.'

'You know where he is?' demanded the policeman in heavily accented English.

Lila shook her head firmly. 'I have absolutely no idea,' she lied.

This was like a scene out of one of Brett's action movies. Two police cars were parked in her parents' drive. Jimmy Jones was sitting, head bent forward, in the back of one of the cars. It looked as if he'd been arrested. At the gates, the paparazzi were even more agitated than usual. There were hundreds of them, cameras held above their heads, each clamouring to get to the front. Lila felt sure if it wasn't for the police holding them back they'd have broken the gates down.

The policeman was getting agitated too. He was firing questions at Peter.

'He wants to know if Charlie left anything behind. A note or something?'

Lila shrugged innocently and shook her head. The policeman watched her reaction closely and then smiled politely, nodded and walked away. It was the best piece of acting Lila had done in years.

Inspector Joaquin Garcia was having a bad day. Was it not bad enough that the British insisted on letting their ageing gangsters relocate to his beautiful town? Now, their overpaid, ill-educated footballers were contaminating the place too. And they were causing trouble. Garcia had realised quickly that Jimmy Jones was a moron. Even with a translator, he had been able to make little sense of what the boy had to say. And he was not such a great striker either, in Garcia's opinion.

These were the facts: Jasmine Jones (missing) had been kidnapped by Frank Angelis and held to ransom. Charlie Palmer (also missing) and Jimmy Jones (currently crying in his cell) had rescued her in the early hours of the morning although it remained unclear exactly how they had managed to do this. According to Jimmy, Mr Angelis had been alive and well when they left. He also claimed that Angelis kept a harem of blonde sex slaves at his mansion. It was ridiculous.

At six a.m. this morning, an anonymous call had come into the police station, saying that Mr Angelis was dead. The caller did not leave her name but apparently had an Eastern European accent. When the police arrived at Mr Angelis's home, he was indeed dead but he was alone on the premises and no women, sex slaves or otherwise, could be found. There was no sign of trauma to the body.

Joaquin Garcia could have done without this today. These people should not be his problem. His phone rang. It was the coroner with the results of the Angelis autopsy.

'Are you sure?' asked Garcia, perplexed.

But the coroner was convinced – Frank Angelis had died of natural causes. Heart failure, to be exact. He had been a heavy smoker all his life and his heart was badly diseased, the valves weak and the arteries blocked. The coroner had also found cancerous tumours in his lungs. Frank Angelis had been a walking corpse. Nobody had killed him. Over time, he had done that to himself.

Garcia placed his paperwork in a neat pile and handed it to his secretary to file. He told the duty officer to let Jimmy Jones out of his cell. The moron was free to go. Of course, Garcia was not a stupid man, and he knew there was more to this case than an old man with heart disease. Why had Jasmine Jones been kidnapped in the first place? Where was Charlie Palmer now? And how had a harem of pretty blonde girls disappeared without a trace? Garcia sighed. There was no point in worrying himself about these people anymore. There were so many other cases to solve with victims who deserved his full attention. He had no time for these incomers. Marbella was a better place without Frank Angelis around. He was just one fewer British gangster Garcia had to worry about from now on.

Vladimir Dimitrov sat back in the comfortable leather seat on his private jet and smiled contentedly to himself. Life was good. He had his Nadia back safe and sound. He'd bought a new club in London called Exotica and the football club would be his this week too. His lawyers were just finalising the contracts. Even better, that bastard Angelis was out of his life for good. The police would think the old man had had a heart attack. Ha! Idiots! Dimitrov had ways of getting rid of problems that even the FBI couldn't imagine.

Although Vladimir had not managed to retrieve the money Angelis owed him, he had repossessed some valuable stolen goods. The girls were in high spirits, giggling and gossiping behind him on the plane. Only Yana was miserable. Hah! Maybe the silly girl had actually believed Angelis was her ticket to freedom. But they must have been bored senseless locked up in that house. At least with him they would be free to dance at his new club. Well, not free exactly …

Dimitrov was not concerned about the police. No one would dare speak his name. Charlie Palmer would never talk – he was a smart man. And, although Jimmy Jones was stupid, he would be too terrified to say anything. He had noticed the look on the boy's face when he'd spotted the gun last night. And anyway, he still owed so much money. Ha ha! What fun he would have at the football club terrorising that boy!

Charlie was pleased to see that McGregor was being gentle with Jasmine. The detective had met them from the plane this morning. He was there, on the runway, in the driving rain, with a golf umbrella to shield them as they ran to the waiting unmarked police car. He'd arrested Jasmine immediately in the back of the car. He'd explained gently to her that he had no choice – Terry Hillman had already given the tape of the shooting to a journalist, who had immediately informed the police. But McGregor didn't cuff her and he didn't treat her like a criminal either.

They'd driven straight to the station. Now Jasmine was in an interrogation room with McGregor, a more junior detective, and a rather glamorous lady lawyer in her mid-fifties. The lawyer had arrived at the police station in an Armani skirt suit and a cloud of Chanel No. 5 only minutes after Jasmine and Charlie. At first Charlie had been confused. Who was she? How did she know about all this? And why was she so keen to represent Jasmine? She'd introduced herself in a clipped accent as Judith Smythe-Williams of Williams, Wardour and White, which meant nothing to Charlie. McGregor obviously knew who she was because he'd practically bowed at her feet when she walked through the door. But then Ms Smythe-Williams had whispered, 'Vladimir sends his regards,' into Charlie's ear and everything had fallen into place. If Dimitrov had sent her, she would be the best. And Jasmine deserved the best.

Now the poor girl was being questioned about the murder of Sean Hillman seven years ago. Charlie felt confident it would be a clear case of self-defence. Surely the CPS wouldn't even let it go to court, not with the video evidence of the rape. And McGregor wouldn't want to piss Charlie off, would he? Not with what Charlie had done for him over the years. But still, it would be tough for Jazz to relive those terrible events after keeping it all bottled up inside for so many years.

Police stations were not Charlie's natural habitat. In fact, as he waited in reception under the watchful eye of the desk sergeant, he couldn't have felt more uncomfortable if he'd been dumped in a tank of piranhas. They'd been there for three hours by the time Ms Smythe-Williams reappeared.

'Let's go for a coffee,' she ordered as she disappeared through the revolving doors.

Charlie jumped to his feet and followed her, chasing her up the street as she clip-clipped in her high-heeled court shoes with her shiny black briefcase swinging by her side.

'But, Ms Smythe-Williams, what about Jasmine?' he said breathlessly, as he caught her up.

'She's fine,' she replied firmly. 'And please, call me Judith.'

Judith entered the nearest coffee shop and ordered a skinny latte.

'You?' she asked Charlie impatiently.

'Tea, please.'

She barked the order at the poor young guy behind the counter and told him to 'hurry up about it, for crying out loud,' as he tried to froth up her milk. The woman was frightening. Charlie imagined being up against her in court and understood immediately why Dimitrov rated her.

He followed her to a table in the corner. She took a sip of her coffee and shuddered.

'Ugh! This is foul,' she said.

'Have they finished questioning Jasmine?' asked Charlie.

Judith shook her head and glanced at her watch. 'No. It's just a short break. They've given her something to eat and a coffee which probably tastes better than this one.' She pushed her coffee cup to one side and levelled her eyes at Charlie. 'They're going to take this one to trial,' she explained.

Charlie spluttered on his tea. 'What? But it was self-defence. I've seen the tape. He kidnapped her, raped her and then tried to kill her. Jasmine says she didn't even mean to shoot him. The gun just went off in her hand.'

Judith nodded. 'Yes,' she said. 'Jasmine told me what happened and I believe her, but the fact is that we don't have a copy of the whole tape. All we have is what Terry Hillman gave to the press, which shows her shooting Sean Hillman.'

'But Jasmine had the whole thing on her computer and another copy in her flat . . ' Charlie said, but Judith held up her hand to silence him.

'They've gone. There are no emails from Frank Angelis on the laptop and the DVD is not where Jasmine left it in the apartment.'

'But ... I don't understand. Someone must have hacked into her computer, broken into the flat. Yana! I bet it was Yana.'

Judith shrugged. 'The fact is we have no evidence of any rape. All we have is Jasmine's word against the video evidence. And, to be honest, it doesn't look good. Jasmine did not report the incident to the police. Nor did she try to call an ambulance or help the victim at the scene.'

'Sean Hillman was *not* a victim,' said Charlie, angrily. What was wrong with this woman? She was supposed to be on their side!

Judith Smythe-Williams ignored him. 'The death was covered up and the body dumped in Epping Forest. Jasmine says she had help from this man, Frank Angelis, but he's dead so he can't corroborate the story.'

'Angelis is dead?' Charlie scratched his head. 'But I saw him last night.'

'He had a heart attack. McGregor got a call from the Spanish police this morning.'

A heart attack? Charlie didn't believe it for a minute. What had Dimitrov done after they'd left? Still, it was good to know that Angelis wouldn't be bothering him again.

'So, they'll go after her for murder, withholding evidence, perverting the course of justice, disposing of a body and so on and so forth ...' Judith continued as Charlie's mind raced, trying to keep up with the unfolding events.

'But all she did was save herself from a monster. It was Angelis who did the rest,' he protested.

'They're trying to get us to make a deal. If Jasmine puts her hands up to it, they'll drop the charge to manslaughter,' said Judith. 'She'll get six years at the most.'

'But she did nothing wrong!' Charlie shouted.

'Calm down, Mr Palmer,' said Judith. 'I agree with you. That's why we'll let them go to trial. No jury in the land will find Jasmine guilty. She's obviously telling the truth. Her family are lowlife. Her uncle was a known criminal. She was just a girl. She'll walk free. I guarantee it.'

'So, why are the police even bothering to pursue this?'

'Sean Hillman's murder is a high-profile unsolved crime. Jasmine Jones is a celebrity. They don't want to be seen to be lenient on her just because she's in the public eye. Besides, it's good for their league tables to get a result.'

'But poor Jasmine ...' Charlie shook his head in despair. 'This is the last thing she needs.'

'Jasmine seems to be prepared to take it to court. She knows she has nothing to hide. In fact, when I put it to her, her exact words were, "bring it on", said Judith briskly. 'She won't be held on remand; she'll get bail and I will insist that she's given full police protection and a safe place to stay while we wait for the trial. I will also insist that the trial takes place ASAP. Right, let's get back.'

She stood up and hurried out of the coffee shop with Charlie struggling to keep up. He'd only had one sip of his tea.

Later, he waited for McGregor at the back of the police station. The minute the bastard stepped out of the door Charlie had him by the scruff of the neck.

'How can you take this to trial?' he demanded. 'She doesn't deserve it.'

'Get off me, Charlie,' warned McGregor calmly. 'There's a video camera right above your head and one of my officers will be out here arresting you if you don't let me go *now*!'

Charlie pushed McGregor away. The last thing he needed was to be arrested himself. But this was crap. It was first-class gold-plated crap.

'You owe me, McGregor,' he seethed. 'I know stuff about you—'

'Don't threaten me. Remember, I know stuff about you too. Now, listen to me. There will be a trial. My hands are tied on this one. I pushed for the case to be dropped but orders are coming from above my head. The commissioner wants a trial and what the commissioner wants he gets, OK?'

'But it was self-defence,' Charlie insisted. 'And she was a kid.'

'She was seventeen,' said McGregor. 'That's old enough to be tried as an adult.'

McGregor lit a cigarette and leaned against the wall. He sighed and shook his head.

'I'm tired of all this, you know, Charlie,' he said. 'Do you think I want Jasmine to be put on trial and have her private life plastered across the front pages? I want to be putting real criminals away, not making the headlines.'

'Is that what this is all about?' asked Charlie. 'Is it because Jasmine's famous?'

McGregor nodded. 'The big boys are salivating at the thought of the headlines they're going to get when this one goes to trial. They think they might get their pictures in the papers. Honestly, I can see it now. My boss queuing up after a day in court to get Luke Parks's autograph for his boy.'

McGregor laughed and shook his head.

'I've had enough of this game,' he said. 'I'm thinking of retiring. I quite fancy Spain. We could go into business together. You and me. An unstoppable team. What do you say, Char?'

Charlie watched McGregor stub out his cigarette against the wall. 'I think you've finally lost it, McGregor,' he said. 'But I'm flattered.' He patted the copper on the back and started to walk away.

'Charlie,' McGregor called after him. 'You know your name will come up in this trial?'

Charlie nodded but he didn't look back.

'I'll keep the worst out of it. And that's a promise.'

Charlie raised his hand and waved goodbye. What was McGregor's promise worth? Well, Charlie guessed, he was about to find out.

Chapter Fifty-Seven

Jasmine had learned to love this place, with its craggy mountains and rugged coastline. She could walk for miles along the beach and hers would be the only footsteps in the perfect white sand. Annie was out of quarantine now and she loved to play in the surf as it fizzed around her paws. Summer here had been cool and breezy but Jasmine hadn't missed the heat of Spain. She had needed to get away. The isolation of this place had given her time to heal.

The bruises and cuts from Jimmy's beating had long since disappeared and, other than the slight bump on the bridge of her nose, there was no sign that he'd ever laid a hand on her. Her hair had started to grow back and after a trip to a salon in Inverness, Jasmine was quite pleased with her short, choppy crop. Her heart was mending too. Marrying Jimmy had been a mistake; she could see that now, with this huge distance between them. She wasn't even sure she had ever loved him. She'd been more in love with the idea of being Mrs Jimmy Jones than with the man himself. She'd seen their marriage as a way of escaping from her past. But she'd done a lot of thinking these past few months and now she realised that she could never escape what went before. Good memories, bad memories, mistakes and successes, they were all just a part of who she was and they would stay with her for ever.

It was October now and winter had come early to the Highlands. They would still be sunbathing on the beaches of Marbella but here, in the Murray Firth, Jasmine was happy to feel the cold wind on her face. It made her feel alive. Anyway, she was well protected from the elements in Charlie's old puffa jacket and she'd long since traded her stilettos for a pair of green wellies.

This place was her hideaway from the 'real' world. But the longer she stayed here, the more the Highlands felt real and the rest faded into insignificance. What could be more real than mountains and rivers, waterfalls and wild deer? And what was so real about her old world, anyway? The truth was Jasmine felt liberated – no paps, no photo shoots, no parties, no pressure – and now, with the trial looming, just days away, she dreaded the thought of leaving this beautiful landscape. In her old life, silly little things had seemed so important – what dress she wore to a party, or which celebrity she stood next to in a photo opportunity. Now, she could stand beneath a mountain and feel as tiny and insignificant as an ant. It was a great feeling to know that nothing she did really mattered at all.

It was beginning to get dark. Charlie would start to worry if she didn't get back to the cottage soon. She called to Annie and started back towards home, across the beach, over the dunes, and back along the sandy path that led to their isolated fisherman's cottage. Jasmine spotted an unfamiliar car parked beside Charlie's Range Rover. The bright red mini looked totally out of place here in the wilds. It was too sporty, too urban, too clean!

She paused a hundred feet from the door. McGregor visited sometimes in his dark-blue Saab and Judith Smythe-Williams had been here last week in her black Audi R8 to discuss the trial. But mostly she and Charlie were left alone in peace. Charlie would venture into Inverness once a week to do the shopping but Jasmine had only been into town a couple of times. They had a TV and the internet, of course, and inevitably the outside world intruded sometimes. Jasmine knew that the press had worked themselves up into a lather about the upcoming trial. She had braced herself for next week, but she wanted to enjoy these last few days of solitude alone. Just Jasmine, Charlie and Annie. So, who was this intruding now?

She took a deep breath before opening the front door and then took her time removing her wellies and rubbing the dog dry with a towel. She could hear voices in the front room. Charlie was laughing. Whoever it was must be an ally, she supposed. Jasmine pushed the door open slowly and poked her head round the corner. She spotted Grace Melrose first, immaculately dressed, perched on the edge of the sofa with a cup of tea in her hand. And then she noticed Aunt Juju sitting next to her.

'Aunt Juju!' she squealed, rushing into the room and hugging her. 'It's so good to see you. Are you better? Are you out of hospital for good?'

'Much better thanks, darling,' said Julie. 'And even better for seeing you looking so well.'

Jasmine grinned at her aunt. God, she loved this woman. The rest of the family wrote her off as crazy but Julie Watts had been the only woman who had loved Jasmine unconditionally as a child and she would never listen to a bad word anybody said about her. She hadn't seen her since the wedding and she'd missed her desperately. How lovely of Grace to bring her here. Then Jasmine paused. Why *had* Grace brought her here? It was a strange alliance. Did this have something to do with her birth parents? So much had happened since Jasmine had asked Grace to do some digging into her background that she'd pushed the subject to the back of her mind.

'Hi Grace,' said Jasmine, bending down to kiss Grace on the cheek. 'What a lovely surprise.'

Grace smiled, but she looked a bit nervous. 'You look really healthy. The fresh air must suit you,' she said, but she couldn't look Jasmine in the eye.

'What's going on?' asked Jasmine. 'Has something happened?'

She watched as Grace and Julie glanced at each other nervously. The two women were holding hands like old friends. How did they even know each other?

'Jasmine,' Grace started tentatively. 'You asked me to look into your background.'

Jasmine nodded.

'And the truth is, I now know who your real parents are.'

Jasmine felt her mouth drop open.

'Fucking hell,' said Charlie. 'This is a turn up for the books.'

'Let me explain,' said Grace. 'I found out who your mother was some time ago, but Julie wanted to tell you about it herself so we've waited until she felt strong enough.'

'You knew?' asked Jasmine, staring at her aunt in disbelief. 'You knew who my mum was all this time and you didn't tell me?'

Jasmine could feel herself shaking now. She'd waited for this news all her life but now that the time was here she wasn't sure she was ready. She thought her legs were going to buckle beneath her.

'Sit down, babe,' said Charlie. 'Let them explain.'

'I wanted to tell you so many times but I couldn't,' said Julie, her voice breaking. 'I just couldn't.'

She was crying now and the sight of her tears made Jasmine cry too.

'Who is she? Is it someone I know?'

Julie nodded, but she was sobbing so loudly now that she could barely speak. 'It's me,' she whispered eventually. 'Jasmine, it's me. I'm your mum.'

Jasmine felt the world stop spinning for a moment as the words seeped into her brain. She blinked at the woman who she'd always thought was her aunt and tried to make sense of what she'd just heard.

'You're my mum?' she repeated.

Julie nodded. Grace nodded. Charlie shook his head.

'This is mental,' he said. 'Juju, how can you be Jasmine's mum?'

'I was very young,' she said. 'Unmarried. I was scared. Kenny wanted a baby and he couldn't have one, so I gave him mine.'

'You gave me to Cynthia!' said Jasmine, her head still reeling with unanswered questions. None of this felt real. It was like watching a scene from a soap opera.

'No, I gave you to Kenny,' cried Julie. 'He loved you as much as I did. I knew you'd be safe.'

Jasmine felt hot tears pour down her cheeks as her childhood flashed in front of her eyes.

'But I wasn't safe, Juju,' she sobbed. 'Cynthia used to beat me. Kenny was sick. And then he died and I had no one.'

'Except Charlie,' said Julie quietly. 'And me. You always had me.'

'So why didn't you tell me? Why didn't you take me back?' asked Jasmine, desperately. 'Do you know how I used to wish that I had a mum like you instead of Cynthia?'

'Jasmine, sweetheart, I wanted you. I wanted you so much that it drove me insane. I watched how Cynthia treated you – *my* baby, my precious baby – and it tore my heart in two!' Julie stood up and walked towards her. She dropped down on to her knees and held Jasmine's hands in hers.

'There was nothing I could do. After Kenny died, I went to Cynthia and told her I was going to tell you the truth,' explained Julie, desperately. 'You've got to believe me, Jasmine. But Terry and Sean Hillman threatened me. They said that they would kill you rather than let you find out the truth and I couldn't take that risk. You know what those men were capable of. I couldn't let them hurt one hair on your head.'

'But they hurt me anyway!' shouted Jasmine. 'You should have kept me. You should never have given me up in the first place!'

Julie nodded and clutched Jasmine's hand harder. 'I know that now, sweetheart. But I was just a girl. I had nothing. No job. No money. No home of my own. I thought Kenny would be able to give you a better life than I would. He was a good man. He loved you like his own.'

Jasmine chewed her lip and tried to sniff back her tears. What a mess. What a bloody, God awful mess. All those wasted years of feeling unloved and unwanted and her own mother had been right under her nose the whole time.

'We would have been OK,' said Jasmine, still unable to look her aunt, or her mother, or whoever this woman was, in the eye. 'If you'd kept me, we'd have muddled through because we'd have loved each other and that would have been all that mattered.'

Julie nodded again. 'You're right. Of course you're right. And I see that now and, in fact, I've known that for a long time, but you can't undo a mistake, can you? You can't turn back the clock and do it all over again except better this time. I wish I could, Jasmine. With all my heart I wish I could have my time over again, but I can't, darling. I can't. All I can do is beg you to forgive me for making such a dreadful mistake.'

The words soaked into Jasmine's brain and tugged at her heart. Who was she to judge? Had she never made a mistake? What would she have done if she'd found herself in Julie's position? She let her eyes meet Julie's for the first time. Those pale-blue eyes were so full of love and sorrow and pain that Jasmine felt her heart melt and she fell into Julie's arms.

'It's OK,' she whispered into her mother's ear. 'I understand.'

They knelt there on the floor, entwined for the longest time.

'I can't believe this,' said Jasmine eventually, breaking the silence. 'Did you know, Charlie?'

Charlie shook his head. Jasmine could see that even he had been crying.

Grace made room on the sofa and Jasmine and Julie sat down, side by side. Every few seconds, Jasmine found herself glancing at Julie, trying to let the truth sink in. Aunt Juju was her mum!

'So, who was my dad?' she asked eventually, feeling brave.

Jasmine didn't look much like Julie. Her aunt, or should she say her mum, was blonde, fair-skinned and blue-eyed. Jasmine was dark, brown-eyed and tanned, even in winter.

She noticed that Julie looked to Grace for reassurance and that Grace gave her a nod as if to say, 'It's OK.'

Julie reached into her bag and brought out an old red photo album. She opened it flat on her knee and pointed at the first photograph.

'I was a dancer,' she said. 'Quite a good dancer, really. At sixteen I started dancing professionally.'

Jasmine looked at the photograph of Julie – a complete eighties babe in a pale-blue Lycra catsuit with a peroxide-blonde perm. She was on stage with several other glamorous young women. Julie flicked the page.

'I got jobs dancing on tour with some big stars,' she explained.

Another photo, this time of Julie in a red and white cheerleader's outfit with pom poms.

'I danced at Wembley Stadium and the Royal Albert Hall and in America ...' She hesitated.

'Was my dad another dancer?'

'No, darling. He was a singer.'

'Aha! That's why I love singing,' said Jasmine, starting to feel excited. 'Was he any good?'

'Jasmine, he was a star,' explained Julie, still clutching the photo album.

'What? Like, famous?'

Julie nodded and then slowly turned the page. The next photo was very faded. It showed a handsome young guy in flares and an unbuttoned shirt, with bouffant hair and a gold medallion. Behind him, dancing in a pink chiffon gown, was Julie.

343

'Is that him?' asked Jasmine, squinting at the photo. She couldn't really make him out. 'I don't recognise him.'

'He was one of the biggest stars of his day,' said Julie. She sounded almost proud. 'He was huge. A megastar.'

'What? Don't talk nonsense!'

Jasmine's world spun on its axis. Her dad could not be an international superstar. Juju was an unemployed forty-something from Dagenham who'd spent most of her adult life in psychiatric care. She wondered, for a moment, if Julie was at all well. Whether any of this was actually true, or whether Julie was having one of her infamous 'funny turns'. But Grace was here, an investigative journalist, and she was nodding furiously at what Julie said.

'It's true. I was a dancer on his European tour in nineteen eighty-three. He was quite a ladies' man and he took a real shine to me. I don't know why. I wasn't the best-looking dancer, or the flirtiest girl; I was really quite shy and I'd never even had a proper boyfriend before. But, anyway, he always came looking for me after the show and he would buy me drinks and pay me compliments. I knew he was married, but he said things weren't going well at home and that his wife didn't understand him and ... Oh, I was very, very young. Just seventeen. He told me I was beautiful. I thought he was falling in love with me.'

Jasmine rolled her eyes. 'Christ, you were naive, weren't you!'

'Yes, I was very naive. He asked if I was on the pill and I said yes because I thought it made me sound grown-up and sophisticated, but the truth was I was a virgin, so what did I need with the pill?' Julie's eyes were very wide now, as if the truth shocked her as much as it did everybody else.

'And this guy, this famous man, is definitely my father?' asked Jasmine, just to make sure she'd got this right.

Julie nodded. 'Sweetheart,' she said. 'He's the only man I've ever slept with. Your father can't possibly be anyone else.'

Jasmine swallowed hard. What a tragedy. Julie had almost escaped. She'd been a good dancer, got a great job, travelled and then in one night her world had been turned upside down. She'd got pregnant, given away her baby and then gone mad watching her child being brought up by a woman like Cynthia Watts.

'So, who is he?' asked Jasmine. 'Would I know him?'

'Just wait, sweetheart. Let me explain it all and then I'll tell you.'

'Did he know? About me?'

Julie shook her head. 'I never even told him I was pregnant. After we, well, you know, after that one night he never really spoke to me again and a few days later I heard him telling everyone that his wife had just given birth to their first child. I realised he'd been lying to me. Then, of course, I found out that I was pregnant too and I didn't know what to do. So I just went home.'

'Oh, Juju, you should have told him,' said Jasmine, sadly. 'It was his responsibility too.'

Julie shook her head. 'No, he thought I was on the pill. I tricked him. If I'd told him he would have thought that I'd trapped him on purpose.'

'So you never saw him again?'

'Not until recently,' said Julie. 'At your wedding, in fact.'

Jasmine felt the air leave the room. She gasped. What would this man be doing at her wedding?

'That's why I flipped. I saw him sitting there at the next table and I nearly died of fright. I didn't know what to do so I just ran away. Charlie had to pay for a taxi to take me all the way home to Essex. It was such a shock.

'Juju, who is my father?' demanded Jasmine desperately. It made no sense. How could her real dad have been a guest at her wedding?

Julie turned the page of the photo album and let it lie open on her lap. Jasmine stared at the photograph for a very long time. This one was a close-up and her father was very clear indeed.

Suddenly, so many pieces of Jasmine's broken jigsaw slotted into place. Julie's fragile mental state. Cynthia's resentment towards her. Kenny's unconditional love. Christ, even her brown eyes and her love of singing made sense now. She'd inherited them from her father.

'I want to tell him,' said Jasmine firmly. 'After the trial. I want him to know that he's my father.'

Julie nodded. 'I understand,' she said.

'God, there's been so much wasted time!' cried Jasmine, hitting her knee with her clenched fist. 'This could all have been so different!'

'I'm sorry I've let you down so badly. I promise I'll never let you down again. I'll be strong, I swear, and I'll come to your trial every day and I will never, ever, let you down again, darling.'

Julie stroked Jasmine's short hair, then her soft hands brushed away her daughter's tears. 'I need you to know that I could never have loved you more. I did everything I could to make you happy and to keep you safe. I know it wasn't enough, but you were always my baby. It was me who named you Jasmine. I carried you inside me for nine months. I gave birth to you. I watched you grow up into this beautiful, kind, talented girl and I thought I would burst with pride. But I couldn't tell anyone. I had to keep it all inside. '

Jasmine wrapped her arms around Julie's frail frame and buried her face in her hair. She realised now how lucky she was. She had a mother who loved her. Who had always loved her. And that love would keep her strong. It would get her through the trial and out the other side. Then she would start putting things right – for herself and for Julie, her mum. And as for her father? He could wait. For now.

Chapter Fifty-Eight

Peter had begged her to stay away from the trial and for three weeks she'd done as he'd asked, but Lila couldn't miss this, the last day. She wanted to be there for her friend when the verdict was returned. Jasmine's trial for murder at the Old Bailey had been the most scandalous, shocking, celebrity-packed event that the country had ever seen. It was as if all other news had ceased. The tabloids were filled with pictures and stories from the trial and even World War III would have been relegated to the back pages if it had broken out this week. Lila couldn't switch on her television without seeing a picture of Jasmine's beautiful, determined face as she stood in the dock. Even the fashion pages were filled with what the accused and the witnesses were wearing and Jasmine's new short haircut (the 'Jop' – or Jasmine crop – as the press were calling it) was now the most-requested hairstyle in salons across the country.

Until now, Lila hadn't been there in person; she'd been in LA, auditioning for a new film role, but she had followed every detail from a distance. This was the most star-studded trial in history, with footballers, models, journalists and gangsters all being called as witnesses. The public gallery had been filled every day with the A-list and television crews had been fighting for space on the steps outside. Of course, all sorts of ugly truths had come out. At first it had looked bad for Jasmine. It had been her word against the hard proof of video evidence that showed her shooting her uncle.

Lila had shuddered when she'd read Jasmine's testimony about Sean Hillman's sick sexual obsession with his teenage niece and she'd cried and cried over the details of the rape. Of course, she'd believed every word Jasmine had said and she'd hoped and prayed that the jury would too. But there had been no proof. At least, not until a Russian prostitute called Yana Urovski had come forward and saved the day. At the end of last week, she'd handed in the full tape to Jasmine's lawyer and then everybody had seen what had really happened all those years ago. Lila had stopped short of watching Jasmine's 'rape tape' on the internet but Peter said it was the most disgusting thing he'd ever seen. Still, now everyone knew it had been self-defence.

And Lila knew who Frank Angelis was now, too. He was a lowlife sex trafficker who'd caught Jasmine with the gun in her hand and blackmailed her ever since. He was dead, of course. It had been natural causes. Nothing to do with Charlie at all.

Jimmy Jones had been publicly humiliated by Jasmine's lawyer. Lila wished she'd been in court that day to watch the little twerp being unveiled as the filthy wife-beating bastard he truly was. But the most difficult part of the trial for Lila to swallow had been the revelations about Charlie Palmer. It turned out that her hero – the man who'd saved her life - was in fact some sort of gangland mobster who had worked for Frank Angelis. He'd admitted to being violent, to owning guns and to being involved in protection rackets in Soho and the East End. Lila found it almost impossible to imagine Charlie – her lovely, kind Charlie – doing all the things they said he'd done. But he'd admitted it, on the stand, under oath, so she guessed it must be true. Now all she had to do was figure out exactly how she felt about these revelations.

Peter helped Lila push her way past the baying mob outside the Old Bailey. Even with her darkest sunglasses on the flashes of the cameras hurt her eyes.

'Lila!' they shouted. 'Lila!'

She pretended to be deaf and kept going, fighting her way through the crowds.

'Lila, do you think Jasmine Jones should be found innocent?' called one journalist.

'Will you visit her in prison if she's found guilty?' asked another one.

'What do you think of her hair?' cried another.

Lila kept her head down and joined the queue for the public gallery. In front of her were Luke and Madeleine Parks; behind her was Juan Russo.

'Juan,' she smiled, happy to see a friendly face. 'How's Maxine?'

'Getting big,' grinned Juan, using his hand to indicate Maxine's growing bump. 'And hungry. Man, that girl can eat! She had an entire tub of Ben and Jerry's to herself last night as a midnight snack.' He shook his head but it was clear from the smile on his face that just talking about Maxine and their baby made him proud.

'She's got high blood pressure, so the doctor said she shouldn't come here today,' he explained. 'She sent me to support Jasmine in her place.'

Lila smiled. He was young, but he seemed committed to Maxine. Maybe this time her friend would get the 'happy ever after' she deserved.

'Are things any better with your dad?' asked Lila. 'Maxine said he'd disowned you.'

Juan shrugged, 'He's hurt, but he'll calm down. I know my old man.

He's a pussy cat, really. He won't hold a grudge for long. My mom, on the other hand, well, there's another story. She was never exactly Maxine's biggest fan and now we've gone and made her a grandmother before she was ready, so you can imagine how well *that* relationship is going.'

Lila winced. 'Ouch,' she said.

The line started surging forward and Lila found herself pushed inside. Peter grabbed for her hand and pulled her up the stairs behind him. They jostled their way through supermodels and footballers, elbowed soap stars out of the way, and Lila even stood on a reality TV star's toes (accidentally on purpose) until they'd secured themselves seats on the front row of the balcony.

'This is wicked! It's better than that time I got a backstage pass for a Justin Timberlake gig,' Lila heard one well-known girl-band member whisper to another behind her. 'Shhh, look, here she comes.'

And then the courtroom fell silent as all eyes turned to watch Jasmine Jones enter the room and sit with her lawyer. Looking down on her friend from her seat in the gallery, Lila thought Jasmine looked terribly small and vulnerable. She was dressed soberly in a neat little navy shift dress and matching ballet pumps. Her cropped hair gave her face an elfin quality that Lila hadn't noticed before. Jasmine looked as beautiful as ever, but something had changed. Gone was the carefree girl who had taken Marbella by storm with her dark curls and killer curves. In her place sat a rather serious young woman with the weight of the world on her shoulders. The sight made Lila want to leap from her seat, scoop Jasmine up and put her back in the sunshine where she belonged.

As the lawyers summed up their arguments, Lila let her eyes wander the courtroom. She could see Louis Ricardo at the end of an aisle, near the front. His crutches were propped up against the end of his seat. Lila had read how he'd had his leg broken in a football match a few weeks before and that his career was rumoured to be over. His love life was in turmoil, too. He'd cancelled his wedding to his childhood sweetheart just weeks before the big day and the papers had branded him a love rat. Lila wasn't convinced by that. Louis struck her as a kind and sensitive man and she was sure he must have had good reasons to call off his wedding. Yes, Louis definitely had problems of his own. But still he'd been here every day, supporting Jasmine through the trial. Lila had seen him in the papers and on the news wearing his best suit and a serious expression. Today, he was clutching a bunch of sunflowers.

Jimmy Jones was conspicuous only by his absence. But Blaine Edwards was here. In fact he was hard to miss with his bright-blue Mohican, leaning back in his seat, chewing gum and gazing at the ceiling. He looked bored beyond belief. At one point he looked up behind him, caught Lila's eye and winked. Ugh! What a repulsive Antipodean toad! A few seats along from him, Madeleine Parks fidgeted in her seat in her too-tight black dress. That one was even worse. She was dressed more appropriately for a cocktail party than for court and she'd decided to keep her sunglasses firmly in place. Lila watched as Madeleine kept whispering into her husband's ear and giggling at inappropriate times. It made Lila's blood boil to see what little respect these people had for Jasmine. There was a young woman's life hanging in the balance today and they treated the event as some kind of publicity stunt.

Lila eyed the rows hungrily, desperate to catch a glimpse of one particular face. And then she saw him – Charlie, *her* Charlie – sitting on the front row to the far right of the courtroom wearing a seriously sharp suit. He was even more handsome than she remembered. She was surprised to see how different he looked now his hair had grown. Without the skinhead he looked softer, less aggressive, more of a teddy bear. His hair was darker than she'd expected it would be – almost black. He sat a foot taller than the women who flanked him on either side. His shoulders were as impossibly broad and strong as ever, but they were hunched forward slightly now as the prosecution lawyer argued his case that Jasmine should be found guilty. Lila watched Charlie's profile carefully. She noticed how his strong jaw was set, and that his brow creased into a frown above his intense blue eyes. He was listening intently to every word the lawyer was saying and every now and then he would mouth, 'No!' or drag his fingers through his hair in a gesture of desperation.

To his right sat a tiny middle-aged woman with greying blonde hair. She clutched Charlie's forearm like a timid child and Lila guessed this was Jasmine's beloved Julie. To his left sat Grace Melrose. At first she thought this was just a coincidence, but then, during breaks in the summing up, Lila noticed that Charlie would bend down and whisper in her ear and then nod thoughtfully as he listened to her response. Lila wondered what their connection was. Grace was a very attractive woman. And smart, too. Was something going on between them? They would make a good-looking couple, that was for sure. But the thought of Charlie being in love with Grace made Lila want to cry.

It's funny how the threat of another woman can make confused feelings suddenly crystal clear. As Lila watched Charlie with Grace, all doubts about him disappeared. She realised that whatever he'd done in the past didn't matter. It was irrelevant. Lila wanted Charlie. She yearned for him. She only hoped that she wasn't too late.

Once the summing up had finished the judge sent the jury off to deliberate on a verdict. The crowds poured out of the courtroom and filled up the corridors and lobbies, chatting excitedly and speculating on what would happen next. Lila heard Madeleine Parks shout, 'I'm off to do some shopping; text me when the jury comes back in!' over her shoulder to Luke as she disappeared towards the exit, flanked by two burly security guards.

'Shallow bitch,' sneered Peter. 'Right, what now?'

'Wait here,' Lila told him. 'I'll be back in a minute.'

Peter opened his mouth to argue but Lila squeezed through the throng and escaped before he could stop her. It took a while for the crowds to thin out and at first she thought she had missed him. But then, just as she was about to give up and go back to Peter, she spotted Charlie. He was standing with his arm around Julie's shoulders, deep in conversation with Grace. Lila stood stock still, just staring at him for a while, summoning up the courage to approach him. He hadn't seen her and if she'd turned on her heel at that moment she might never have seen him again. It was a risk she wasn't willing to take.

She walked towards him on shaking legs until she was only two feet away and tapped him gently on the arm. 'Hello stranger,' she said nervously.

He turned towards her touch and she watched his mouth gape open in surprise. 'Lila!' He looked shocked to see her. 'I ... I ... I wasn't expecting to see you here.'

Charlie let his hand drop from Julie's waist and took a step towards Lila as if he was going to embrace her. Then he seemed to think better of it and stepped back again, thrusting his hands into his trouser pockets instead. He fidgeted nervously from foot to foot.

Grace seemed to sense Charlie's discomfort. 'Hello Lila,' she said politely.

'Hello,' said Lila.

'I'm just going to take Julie to the ladies,' said Grace, leading the older woman away. 'We'll be back in a minute.'

And then Lila and Charlie were alone with their awkward silence.

'About what happened in Spain,' mumbled Charlie, staring at his feet. 'Running out like that. I'm sorry. It was very unprofessional.'

Lila nodded. 'Yes, well, you're definitely fired,' she said.

Charlie was clearly embarrassed and didn't know where to look. He avoided Lila's gaze and watched Grace's and Julie's retreating backs instead.

'I didn't know you knew Grace Melrose,' said Lila, trying to sound casual and keep the jealousy out of her voice.

'Oh, I don't really,' he answered, a little too quickly. 'I mean, not well, anyway. She's been helping Jasmine with some ... stuff.'

'So, you two aren't ... erm, you know ... you're not an item, or anything?' Lila asked.

Charlie blushed and shook his head. 'No, no, nothing like that. I'm not involved with anyone right now. I mean, I'm totally single and available and ...' he rambled, now staring at a spot above Lila's head.

'Good,' said Lila.

'Yes, it's good,' agreed Charlie.

Silence again. More foot-staring. More awkward silence.

'And that letter,' Charlie spoke quickly. 'I shouldn't have said that stuff about you. It was stupid and I know I must have made a fool of myself and I'm sorry if it embarrassed you.'

'What? This letter?' asked Lila, rummaging in her handbag and producing the neatly folded note. 'This letter that I've carried around with me every day since?'

At last Charlie met her gaze. Lila felt her stomach lurch as his piercing blue eyes bored into hers.

'You kept it,' he said in disbelief.

Lila nodded and smiled. 'Of course I kept it.'

'You didn't give it to the police?' he was obviously amazed.

'Of course not. You're not the only one with a dodgy criminal past.' She grinned at him.

'Oh God, I've made a dishonest woman of you,' he replied, grinning back.

'So, what are you going to do about it?' she asked.

'I don't know,' he said. 'Apologise?'

Lila shook her head.

'Grovel?'

Lila shook her head more firmly this time.

'Well, what?'

Lila pointed to her lips with her index finger.

'Kiss you?' Charlie's eyes were almost popping out of his head. 'You want me to kiss you? What, here? Now?'

Lila nodded firmly.

'And that's my punishment?' he asked, his eyes twinkling.

'Oh yes,' confirmed Lila.

'Some punishment,' mumbled Charlie, pulling her behind a stone pillar out of sight.

And then his lips were on hers and his strong arms were around her waist and he'd lifted her clean off her feet. Charlie was a huge, strong man but this was the sweetest, most tender kiss imaginable. As she closed her eyes and lost herself in the smell and the feel and the taste of him, Lila knew that finally she'd found her home. And as she tore her lips reluctantly from his, and stared straight into those sparkling blue eyes, she realised suddenly where she'd recognised him from. Charlie Palmer was the one she'd been waiting for. A memory flashed before her eyes of strong arms pulling her from beneath the waves and that handsome face gazing down at her. She'd known it then, at the moment she'd chosen to live, that Charlie was hers, but somehow the memory had been lost until now. Lila had struck gold – she'd found the man of her dreams.

He placed her gently back on the floor and kissed the top of her head. 'You have no idea how long I've been waiting for that,' he whispered.

She smiled up at him and rubbed his broad chest with her hands. 'Well, you won't have to wait so long for the next time,' she promised. 'Tonight, we'll take Jasmine out to celebrate her freedom and then you're coming home with me, big boy.'

'I am?' asked Charlie, grinning.

'You are. Because I have a new job for you.'

'You do?'

'I do. A new position, if you like,' Lila teased.

'A new position. Well, that certainly sounds interesting.'

'It would be a permanent arrangement, if you're comfortable with that,' she continued.

'I'm definitely comfortable with that.'

Grace and Julie reappeared at exactly the same time as Peter came searching for Lila. The couple stumbled out from behind the pillar and sprang apart. Grace and Julie were chatting to each other and seemed oblivious, but Peter eyed them suspiciously.

'Hello Charlie,' he said, narrowing his eyes. 'Have you two enjoyed catching up?'

'Yes thanks, Peter,' said Charlie politely. 'Right, we'd better go and get Julie a cup of tea. It was nice to see you again, Lila. Peter.'

Lila nodded and tried to stop smiling. 'I'll give you a call later about that position I mentioned,' she called after him.

'You do that,' replied Charlie, winking at her over his shoulder. 'It sounded like a very interesting proposition. I can't wait to start.'

Lila watched him go and sighed. She couldn't wait to kiss him again, to feel his touch on her naked skin, to explore every inch of that Adonis body, to … Jesus, she would have to stop thinking about that right now. This was not the right place.

'Lila, have you been snogging a known criminal in the Old Bailey?' demanded Peter, hands on hips.

Lila just grinned.

'Christ, you have, haven't you? I'm sure that must be against the law. You'll be held in contempt of court or something,' he pouted. 'And anyway, Charlie's my crush and you just stole him.'

'Sorry,' said Lila breezily.

'That's OK. I forgive you. He bats for your team, anyway. But what about poor Jasmine? Do you really think that's appropriate behaviour when that poor girl's fate is hanging in the balance? Well, do you?' Peter scolded.

'Jasmine will be OK.'

'How do you know?'

'I've just got a feeling,' Lila said. 'Today is a good day.'

Jasmine had never felt so nervous. Ms Smythe-Williams had promised that she would be found not guilty from the start and since Yana had come forward with the full video she'd started to believe it herself, but now, as she stood here, waiting for the verdict, anything seemed possible. Her head buzzed with 'what if's. What if the jury found her guilty? What if she ended up in prison? What if she couldn't handle it? What if she'd inherited Julie's genes? What if she had a breakdown? What if she was locked up for the rest of her life?

The trial had been worse than she could ever have imagined. She hadn't been prepared for the way the prosecution lawyer went in for the kill. He'd painted her as some sort of teenage temptress who'd manipulated all the men in her life. Even after the full tape was shown in court, he'd insinuated that she'd led Sean Hillman on, suggested that they'd been having an affair and that the rape was just some sort of sex game that had gone wrong. He said she'd killed him in cold blood and then persuaded Frank Angelis to help her to dispose of the body.

During the first week, Cynthia and Terry had been in the public gallery. Terry had shouted obscenities at her, called her a murdering little bitch and yelled that he was going to kill her when she got out, for what she did to his brother. He'd been removed from court, kicking and swearing, with Cynthia in tow screaming, 'You're no daughter of mine!'. This from the woman who had been the only mother she'd known for nearly twenty-five years. They were a pathetic excuse for a family. But they'd been the only family she'd known and being rejected by them so publicly still hurt.

And then there was Jimmy. Or, at least, there was *no* Jimmy. Because, apart from the day that he had to give evidence himself, the cowardly little bastard didn't turn up at all. Oh, what had she expected? Support? Ha!

354

That was a joke. They were still married on paper, but in her heart Jimmy Jones was as dead to her as Sean Hillman. He could rot in hell for all she cared.

Now she stood in the dock and stared out at the sea of faces swimming in front of her eyes. Most she recognised, but there were only a few she really knew. Some she wished had stayed at home; others she was pleased to see. But three faces leapt out at her from the front row – Julie, Charlie and Louis Ricardo. They were the ones who'd been here every single day for three weeks. They'd smiled at her when she was feeling unsure and cried for her as she'd relived what had happened all those years ago. But more than anything they'd just been here for *her*. Not for the cameras or the scandal, or to see or be seen, but just because they cared. Those three people had given her more strength than they could ever know. She'd expected loyalty from Julie – she was her mum, for Christ's sake! And Charlie? Well, Charlie had never let her down before and he was hardly likely to do it now. But Louis had surprised her. Yes, he was a friend, but they hadn't known each other *that* long and they didn't know each other *that* well. She was beginning to think that maybe he liked her as more than just a friend, and the funny thing was, she kind of liked the idea.

He was catching her eye now from behind his glasses, nodding at her in his serious but reassuring manner, trying to tell her that everything would be OK, that this nightmare was finally going to be over. The judge was asking the foreman of the jury if they'd reached a verdict upon which they'd all agreed. He answered that they had. Jasmine's legs felt as if they were going to buckle beneath her. Bang, bang, bang. Her heart was beating so loudly that she felt sure the whole courtroom must be hearing it too. The judge asked for the verdict. The room began to spin. Jasmine locked her eyes on to Louis's and refused to let go. She could get through this with him. He made her feel strong.

'Not guilty,' said the foreman of the jury.

Jasmine felt like someone had pressed a pause button. Not guilty. The words took the longest time to seep into her brain and for a moment it seemed as though the whole courtroom was frozen in time. And then suddenly there was a whoop of joy coming from somewhere in the gallery, and then another, and another and people were standing up, punching the air. A surge of excitement filled the room but Jasmine kept her eyes firmly locked on Louis. She watched as he got up on his feet and began to clap. He was holding a bunch of sunflowers and yellow petals were showering the courtroom like confetti. Charlie stood up and joined his applause. Then Lila and Peter were doing the same up in the balcony, and Cookie and Crystal too. Before long, everybody was giving her a standing ovation.

Jasmine watched in amazement. Tears of joy and relief poured down her face.

'Order! Order!' shouted the judge, but no one was listening.

Finally, Jasmine's team of lawyers whisked her away.

'What happens now?' she asked Ms Smythe-Williams.

'Now you collect your things and go home,' said the lawyer.

Home? It was a nice idea. But where was home, exactly? Jasmine really wasn't sure.

The sun had set while they were making love and now all that lit the bedroom was the light from the street outside. Charlie couldn't take his eyes off Lila as she lay there beside him, naked in the half-light. He was scared that if he looked away, she'd be gone, still just a fantasy, just a dream. He stroked her cheek. It was hot, still flushed from lovemaking.

'You're perfect,' he told her.

She shook her head. 'I'm not perfect,' she said. 'Look, stretchmarks.'

'Well, perfect for me,' he replied, stroking the tiny white lines on her thighs.

'Maybe,' she mused. 'I hope so.'

She snuggled into his chest and they lay there in comfortable silence for a while. Her hand stroked his back gently. Somewhere, in another room in the house, a radio was playing an old jazz funk tune. Eventually Lila spoke.

'Charlie, have you ever killed a man?' she asked.

Charlie closed his eyes and cursed the life he'd led. What did he do now? Did he lie, like Brett had lied to her, and start their relationship off under false pretences? Or did he tell her the truth and risk having to watch her walk away? Did she really need to know *everything* about him? Did a relationship have to be one hundred per cent honest to be real? Charlie guessed it did. He needed to know that Lila could love him, flawed as he was. It was a test. The ultimate test.

'Yes,' he said, simply. 'Yes, I've killed a man.'

'I thought so,' said Lila. 'I mean, they didn't say so at the trial; at least not in so many words. But it was kind of hinted at.'

She was silent again for a while and then she asked, 'Have you ever killed a *good* man?'

Charlie pictured Donohue's face the moment before he'd died – twisted and contorted with a mixture of hatred, bitterness and fear.

'No,' he said with certainty. 'I've never killed a good man.'

'I'm glad,' she replied. 'I just needed to know.'

She didn't seem fazed, or even surprised. She didn't stand up and walk away. She just hugged him as she'd done before. Charlie felt a weight lift off his shoulders and fly out of the open window, over the rooftops of London and into the dark sky beyond. The truth had always been his greatest enemy. It had stalked him, lurked in the shadows and threatened to jump out and ruin everything that was good in his life. But now there were no more secrets and the truth couldn't hurt him anymore. The ghosts had gone. All that stretched before Charlie was a clean white page. The future was yet to be written. It was perfect. Unblemished. Pure.

Epilogue

The following summer ...

There was no doubt the bride looked beautiful. The frothy white flamenco dress wouldn't have been Grace's first choice of wedding attire, but on Maxine de la Fallaise it looked, well, *right*, she supposed. Only a woman with killer curves, legs up to her armpits and a mega-watt smile could have carried off so many flounces. Maxine would never top *Vogue*'s best-dressed list, but as Grace watched her sashay down the aisle, she thought she had never seen such a radiant bride.

Juan Russo grinned back at his wife-to-be. He wore a white tuxedo and black shirt, no tie. On his feet was a pair of pristine Converse All Stars. He pushed his gold Aviator shades up on to his head and let out a loud wolf whistle as Maxi did a twirl for the crowd. Nothing about this wedding was conventional. The couple's adorable baby daughter, Inez, was wearing her own tiny red flamenco dress and gurgled happily in her aunt Jasmine's arms in the front row. The bride's father – an ex-racing driver and infamous womaniser who still dyed his hair peroxide blonde – winked at all the pretty girls in the congregation as he passed by. Instead of walking down the aisle to the 'Wedding March', the bride had chosen an R&B band who sang TLC's 'Crazysexycool' while she half-danced towards the altar. Even the priest was a funky young dude – Grace had never seen such a blinging crucifix before.

The Spanish sun had delivered a blazing hot day for the nuptials and the exquisite gardens of the Alhambra Palace in Granada were the perfect backdrop for such a glamorous event. All the big names were there: Jasmine Watts, of course, cuddling her niece and snuggling up to her gorgeous boyfriend, Louis Ricardo, Lila Brown (she'd reverted to her maiden name since her divorce from Brett came through) and her new husband Charlie Palmer too. They were so loved up that it was almost embarrassing to be in their company. Grace noted that Lila looked more gorgeous than ever. She seemed to be born again – happy, healthy and successful, having just landed a role in the new Bond movie. Juan's mother was the only guest who managed to look miserable, but then it was no secret that she and Maxine had got off to a rather shaky start.

Juan's father, Carlos Russo (whom Grace had had the *biggest* crush on since she was seven) had eventually been persuaded to attend by Jasmine, despite the fact his son was marrying his ex-girlfriend. No, nothing about this wedding was conventional. Nothing at all. But it was all good inspiration for the novel Grace was working on, now she'd finished writing Jasmine's official biography. The truth was certainly stranger than any fiction she could have dreamed up. Still, despite the unconventional wedding party, this was one of the most joyful days Grace had ever known and as the couple were pronounced husband and wife, and the bride snogged the face off her groom, even cynical old Grace had to brush a stray tear from her cheek.

That evening a lavish reception was held along the coast at Charlie's Bar, the Costa del Sol's coolest new beach hangout. It was owned by Charlie Palmer and his partner, a fat, middle-aged ex-policeman called McGregor. A strange partnership – the ex-cop and the ex-con – but, still, it seemed to work. Even the bar manager, Gary, a lanky red-headed Essex boy was proving popular with the ladies.

Now Grace watched in awe as Juan serenaded his new wife with his latest Latino love song.

'I wrote this one for you, baby,' he told her from the stage, and then he launched into the most sexy, sincere declaration of love that Grace had ever heard.

What a lucky lady Maxine Russo was. Grace could only imagine how it must feel to have a man so desperately, crazily in love with her. As usual, she was at this wedding alone. Now Carlos Russo had taken the stage and was singing a selection of his biggest hits from the eighties. Grace was desperate to get up and dance, but she seemed to be the only single girl there and there were no available men to dance with.

When Carlos finished his set, he made an announcement. 'Now I introduce my beautiful daughter, Jasmine Russo, to the stage. She's gonna be huge star! Bigger than her brother!'

'Thanks for the support, Dad!' shouted Juan from the dance floor. But he was laughing, obviously proud of the new sister he'd discovered.

Carlos shrugged. 'Is true!' he insisted.

And now Jasmine had taken the mike and her powerful, velvety smooth voice was caressing their ears as she sang the bride's favourite song – 'Somewhere Over the Rainbow'. Grace watched as couples poured on to the dance floor and their bodies merged together, swaying beneath the stars. Fairy lights twinkled all around. Grace sighed. It was all so romantic. Where was her partner?

'Somewhere over the rainbow,
'Skies are blue,
'And the dreams that you dare to dream
'Really do come true,' sang Jasmine.

Grace watched Carlos Russo slide through the crowds of dancing cou-ples. Now *there* was one seriously handsome man. What she couldn't do with a man like that ... He seemed to sense her eyes on him. He stopped, looked up and caught Grace's eye. He smiled, swept his peppery black hair out of his chocolate-brown eyes and started walking purposefully towards Grace's table. She felt her stomach lurch. God, that man was exactly her type – rich, powerful, older, *married* ...

'If happy little bluebirds fly
'Beyond the rainbow
'Why, oh why can't I?' sang Jasmine.

'May I have the honour of this dance?' asked Carlos Russo. His eyes twinkled as he offered his hand to Grace.

'It would be a pleasure,' smiled Grace, taking his hand and letting him lead her on to the dance floor.

The music played late into the night. Grace felt her body melt into her partner's. Her cheeks glowed with joy and her heart pounded with the sweet anticipation of a new love affair. The air seemed filled with love and laughter. Sisters, brothers, husbands, lovers, wives and girlfriends swayed together under the stars in the balmy Spanish sky. And for this moment at least, everything was right in the world.